Defector

DAVID GLEDHILL

To Jill,

Love & kisses

Dave

Copyright © 2015 David Gledhill

Published by DeeGee Media Ltd

All rights reserved.

ISBN-13: 978-1493567591

DEDICATION

This book is dedicated to

the aircrew and groundcrew

of the Royal Air Force Phantom Force,

both living and deceased.

ACKNOWLEDGMENTS

The events and characters in this book are fictional. The views and opinions expressed are those of the author and should not be taken to represent those of HMG, the MOD, the RAF or any Government agency.

CONTENTS

	Preface.	1
	Prologue.	5
1	RAF Wildenrath, West Germany, 1980.	11
2	Decisions.	27
3	Partytime.	61
4	The Trap.	77
5	Battle Flight Scramble.	81
6	Allstedt, East Germany.	93
7	Compromise.	107
8	Defection.	111
9	Challenge.	121
10	Engagement.	125
11	Plans.	191
12	Inbound.	217
13	Snatch.	221
14	Insertion.	237
15	Admissions.	255
16	Feint.	261
17	Deception.	265

18	Infiltration.	275
19	Firefight.	285
20	Escape.	309
	Glossary.	327
	About the Author.	333
	Other Books by the Author.	335

PREFACE

RAF Wildenrath, the setting for the novel, is no longer an active airbase testimony to the end of the Cold War. Victim of the defence cuts of the 1990s, the runway is closed and the hardened complex disused. The domestic accommodation was used for some years as a satellite for the nearby RAF station at Brüggen, also now closed, but the only part of the station still used for its original function is the Golf Course. The German company, Siemens, has taken over the land as a test track for trains and the locals use the area for walking and cycling. The hardened buildings have been demolished, with the exception of the 92 Squadron Battle Flight hardened aircraft shelter, and the dispersals are covered in soil and returned to nature. Anyone looking at the airfield would be hard pressed to recognise its former use.

In its heyday the station was a key link in the NATO air defence chain being the only UK contribution to air defence in West Germany. Of the four Royal Air Force Stations, the so called "Clutch Airfields, it was particularly relevant because the post-war four power arrangement charged Britain, France, The United States and The Soviet Union with the duty of policing German Airspace. RAF Wildenrath was the means by which that duty was discharged.

The fall of the Berlin Wall in 1989 was remarkable in its unpredictability.

Peace campaigners believed that vigils outside airbases such as Greenham Common in the UK were the cause of its demise. The truth is that it was testimony to a robust defence posture. The Soviet Union had assembled the most formidable war machine in history and had concentrated its efforts in the communist state of East Germany with the prime aim of rolling through Western Europe and reaching the Channel Ports in four days. There was little doubt in military minds that it was achievable; the only doubt being the cost that the Soviet Union was prepared to pay to achieve the aim. Ultimately, programmes such as The Strategic Defence Initiative (Star Wars) and the deployment of cruise missiles in Europe proved either too expensive or too risky to match. The rest is history but, undoubtedly, clear proof of deterrence as a concept.

During the Cold War thousands of dedicated people gave their all to the pursuit of deterrence. Some gave their lives. The glamour of aviation depicted in subsequent Hollywood blockbusters such as "Top Gun" is offset in the real world by years of training, unquestioning loyalty and, for some, the ultimate sacrifice, albeit freely given. It was their contribution to peace. We who remain look to the politicians to build on the progress but, at times, world events question whether it was a hollow victory.

The characters and events in this book are entirely fictional. The settings, however, are real as are the descriptions of the weapons systems. The Phantom was a true man's aeroplane. Originally designed for carrier operations, it was able to take anything which was thrown at it. Deployed to the West German theatre of operations it was the most capable fighter in service in its day, only later surpassed by American and Soviet air superiority fighters. Its ability to engage targets flying at very low level using Sparrow missiles which were able to engage targets beyond visual range, made its contribution unique. For the pilots it was a difficult aircraft to fly in pure handling terms and, for the navigators, the weapons system was complex requiring skill and intuition to achieve the best results. Above all it was a challenge, and there are few aircrew who flew the aeroplane who would deny a feeling of sadness at seeing pictures of the "Phantom Graveyard" at RAF Wattisham in the early '90s. Entire squadrons of RAF Phantoms were consigned to the scrapheap when the aircraft retired. They lay abused in a corner of the airfield, easily visible to satellites overhead. The early demise was the visible demonstration of the Cold War windfall.

An epitaph appeared on a sticker commissioned by the last Phantom aircrew:

The Phantom - A Legend in its own Lifetime."

PROLOGUE

A FORWARD AIRFIELD EAST OF BERLIN, 1945.

Dawn was breaking on the eastern horizon as the two pilots walked across the grass airfield towards the squat Yak 9 fighters. Dispersed around the perimeter under the cover of trees ringing the temporary airfield, they were hidden from the air. The camouflage covers which were intended to protect the aircraft from marauding German fighter sweeps, had been pulled back and bundled under the trees. At this stage of the war these precautions seemed unnecessary as there was little chance of an air attack. The Russians dominated the skies. The confident swagger of the fighter pilot was still evident but the reality was that the pilots were tired. Even at this early hour, the noise of the Soviet artillery could be heard in the distance shattering the calm. The battle was almost won. The struggle had started back in Mother Russia where the apparently invincible German invaders had been checked then, slowly but surely, forced back from the outskirts of Leningrad. It had been a long campaign pushing the German forces inexorably towards the capital but Berlin was, finally, within striking distance. They were now within a few kilometres of Hitler's bunker and victory was within grasp.

The pilots separated with a slap on the shoulder and headed for their individual aircraft. The young Igor Sokolovskiy pulled on his leather flying helmet and cast his eyes over the small propeller driven fighter as he approached it. The Soviet fighter had been in service since 1942 and had seen combat during the Battle for Stalingrad. Its flexibility saw it used against tanks, as a light bomber and in the escort role. At low altitude it was faster and more manoeuvrable than the Messerschmitt Bf 109 but, like the British Spitfire, it lacked punch as it was less well-armed with only a single cannon. By now this was almost irrelevant because, with the chronic lack of aviation fuel, the Russian pilots had not seen a German opponent in days. With the lack of any serious challenge, the fighters had been co-opted to supplement the Illyushin IL2 Sturmovichs in support of the ground forces. Carrying four 50Kg bombs under the wings the ground attack missions went against the grain for the fighter pilots who flew them. Sokolovskiy dropped into the familiar routine. As his mechanic was finishing the preparations and giving the windscreen a final polish with a rag, he pulled himself up on to the wing and climbed into the cockpit. They exchanged a few words of greeting and he began his pre flight checks. In the calm before he fired up the engine, Sokolovskiy allowed himself a brief moment of reflection. Could it be that both he and his brother, who was about to fire up his own engine in the other Yak, might yet survive this war? Maybe the unthinkable could actually become reality. He cycled the throttle, pushed the mixture lever to rich and hit the start button.

Safely airborne, he unconsciously monitored the steady drone of the engine as he dropped a wing to watch his leader. As usual the skies were quiet and they switched their attention to the target, a heavily defended bridge to the east of the city. There was no intent to damage the structure only to winkle out the stubborn defenders to allow the Soviet ground troops to take the bridge. The first pass was ineffectual and bombs from each of the three aircraft in the section landed harmlessly in the mud alongside the road. The Yak was a rugged fighter but he was well aware that the small 50 Kg bombs were woefully inadequate for serious interdiction against the troops who were well dug in. He was no coward but Sokolovskiy was, nevertheless, questioning the point of this attack as he pulled hard on the stick lagging the turn outside his leader, Kazenko. They positioned for a second and final pass with their remaining bombs. Time to go home he urged subconsciously as he watched the rising mayhem, which once again erupted from the flak pits embedded in the concrete structure of the bridge. The gentle bursts of flak ahead of the fighters gave a false impression of the lethal reality. It was well past time to call in the professionals from the bomber squadron who were better equipped and trained for the task, carried more bombs and were only a few kilometres to the rear.

Tracer from the easterly emplacement arched lazily upwards as the small aircraft settled into its dive. Initially wide of the mark, he watched the deadly rounds from the anti-aircraft artillery march inexorably towards the Yak. Small pockets of dark smoke bloomed ahead of the aircraft as the bombs lurched off the wings and it rotated into its recovery manoeuvre. Almost inevitably, rounds thudded into the engine cowling heralding a release of thick, oily, black smoke in the damaged fighter's wake. It faltered momentarily, veered crazily before slowly recovering limping away from the target trailing smoke. Sokolovskiy's frustration boiled over. Now was not the time to die in a futile gesture. It was time to hit the secondary target and save the heroics for another day. Too many brave men had already been lost. He listened to the clipped message from Kazenko, his leader, reporting in on the radio. The rough note of the engine was apparent in the background and he immediately offered to shepherd the crippled fighter back to base. Hoping for common sense but anticipating the inevitable he waited. Sure enough, the hastily retreating section leader ordered the remaining aircraft to press their attack on the target. The flak around the bridge resumed its crescendo as the fighters wheeled around to begin their follow up attack. It did not take a genius to spot that the guns had refined their range to the attackers who were now much more vulnerable. Equally evident was the wisdom of the old fighter pilot's adage, so recently demonstrated, that the risk of being shot down increased exponentially on the second pass. A third pass was suicidal. By now, far heavier than anticipated, the determined response from the ground was a final gesture of defiance from the defending troops. It was also apparent from his lofty perch that the retreat was already underway. The German convoys, which snaked along the road below, had retired safely across the bridge and were already running for the apparent safety of the city. The bombs had done little to influence the tactical situation and the sight of his leader's crippled Yak, which had already beaten a smoky retreat, was in danger of tipping the psychological balance in favour of the defenders. Far from helping, if they remained much longer, it could spur the defenders to greater efforts and might prove terminal. What he could not know was how prophetic his thoughts would prove to be. He struggled to control his emotions as he listened to the clipped radio calls from his brother setting up for his pass. Did he detect an air of fatalism in the radio call? If he did it made no difference as, in true military fashion, his brother complied unquestioningly with the orders. Sokolovskiy held his Yak in loose formation until, with an impressive flash of a planform, the fighter on his wing peeled away and dropped into a 30 degree dive.

Again the tracer winked and began to advance slowly towards the recklessly persistent aggressor. The similarity between this pass and the previous futile effort from his section leader was all too apparent. He could not prevent the image of a wasp and a fly swat forming in his mind. After what seemed like a lifetime, the small bombs dropped away towards the bridge and the Yak, suddenly relieved of its load, pulled into a hard turn across the top of the turrets jinking frantically amid the blinking tracer. It passed within feet of the concrete buttresses in an attempt to spoil the gunner's aim and dropped to a few scant feet above the flowing water. Inevitably, but seemingly in slow-motion, it drifted relentlessly into the path of the crossfire from a flak pit on the far bank. Struck from both sides as the first gunner re-established his tracking solution, the hapless Yak shuddered under the impact of the cannon shots. It rotated gracefully before giving up the fight. Suddenly deprived of lift from the right-hand wing which had detached from the small aircraft it shook as shells continued to pepper the airframe. The outcome was predictable as the fighter flicked and plunged into the surging torrent below. A massive wall of water was quickly spent and enveloped the plane rapidly quenching the flames leaving just a few pieces of steaming flotsam on the surface. A few ripples were swiftly covered by the fast-moving current masking the most recent casualty of the long war. He could stomach no more. Stunned, he set a course back to the airfield. He had given his best to drive back the invaders from the Rodina but he was no fool. He recognised poor leadership and the example he had just witnessed ranked with the worst. His brother was dead.

Letting down to low level, threading his way past the detritus of war as he headed back to the airfield, his thoughts turned to retribution. He lined up his gunsight on the road that had become an apparent sanctuary for hundreds of retreating German troops who streamed back towards the city, ostensibly to safety. Dropping his sight onto a lumbering tank, he released his final bombs unwilling to return to the airfield still carrying the weapon but not really caring whether it struck the target or not. Suddenly incensed, rather than pull off into his escape manoeuvre, he held his sights on the dregs of the battered Army. His finger tightened around the trigger, locking, almost as if rigor mortise was setting in. The cannon shells kicked up dust as they ripped into the luckless troops below while, with gritted teeth, he made no attempt to stem the tears which streamed down his face under his mask. A vivid image was burned into his consciousness as he relived the moment when his brother's aircraft had smashed into the fast-flowing river. His futile response was retribution of a sort but was he any better than Kazenko? It was a balm but it was not the retribution he had in mind.

He pulled back into the dispersal, closed down the engine which shuddered to a stop and silence descended. As he dropped to the ground he pulled his leather flying helmet from his head and threw it angrily at the squat wheel of the fighter. Watching the unfolding scene, his emotion was suddenly replaced by an eerie calm. Kazenko was being lifted from the cockpit of the shattered Yak and lowered to the waiting medical orderlies below. Down the flank of the machine, the scars from the shells had picked a vivid weal emphasising the energy and ferocity of the recent battle. But the apparent badges of courage did not tell the true tale. The airman should have felt pity at the sight of his wounded comrade who was clearly suffering, but his thoughts had turned to revenge. It may take time, he thought but eventually Kazenko would feel a suffering to match his crime. The sun had barely risen but the day was over. Sokolovskiy drifted away to begin his grieving. Vodka would help.

1 RAF WILDENRATH, WEST GERMANY, 1980.

The doors of the Hardened Aircraft Shelter swung outwards beneath the protective concrete canopy, the clang echoing around the revetment walls as the massive clamshells shuddered to a halt. On the apron, the groundcrew moved with a purpose assembling the equipment that they would need for the see-in, the noise of the approaching aircraft emphasising the urgency of their task. Across the dispersal, the nose of the Phantom fighter appeared around the bend in the loop taxiway as it emerged from the trees which ringed the site, making its way purposefully towards HAS 54. Out of its element it looked ungainly, yet its functional, to some, ugly profile imparted an air of menace. With its pronounced cheek air intakes, upturned wingtips and matt green gun pod slung beneath the fuselage, it was described as the triumph of thrust over aerodynamics. The crews who flew the Phantom had a love-hate relationship with the machine. By now, the appearance of the modern American F-15A fighter threatened to negate the invincibility they had once enjoyed. They had become used to being the only fighter in Europe equipped with the long range Sparrow air-to-air missile and a look-down shoot down air intercept radar. Losing their preeminence did not sit well with some. Even so, detractors could criticise the machine but no one could ignore it.

Another Station Exercise, Exercise Wildman, was in full swing. It was a monthly event to keep the crews of the airbase, a key link in the NATO Air

Defence Chain, in shape. It had already been going for three days and, by now, tempers were fraying and energy was rapidly ebbing away. Stamina rather than enthusiasm had taken over. The crew chief sprinted out into the neck of the hardened aircraft shelter, or HAS, and held his hands above his head to attract the attention of the pilot of "Mike Lima 66." The immediate flash of the taxi light embedded in the nosewheel door of the aircraft was his acknowledgement that the pilot had seen him. Unbidden, another airman moved out in the lee of the revetment walls ready to check the clearance on the wing tips as the Phantom entered the confined area of the HAS neck. Large concrete walls protected by the heavy earth overburden ringed the enclosed dispersal. A scraped wingtip would be costly, not to say embarrassing to aircrew and groundcrew alike. No one could afford for the aircraft to be out of action for the days it would take to fix a mistake.

As the aircraft pulled to a halt, nodding forward briefly on its oleos, a piercing wail split the air barely audible above the noise of the jet engines.

"Attack, Attack, Attack. Air Attack. Wear respirators, take cover. Air Raid Warning Red!"

The moaning siren emphasised the depressing message but achieved the desired response as the actions around the HAS took on an added urgency. The immediate priority was to shelter the aircraft quickly before the air raid struck. The HAS site would be a prime target for the incoming bombers already approaching the airfield boundary at high speed on their attack run. Working furiously, the Crew Chief attached the towing arm to the nose undercarriage leg ready for the push-back while, ten feet above in the cockpit, the pilot pushed his mask back to his face and slid his clear visor down, protecting himself from what he feared would be a chemical weapons attack.

"Just our bloody luck. All I wanted was a coffee and a stretch," he said to his navigator in the rear cockpit.

"What d'you bet that it'll be a quick turn and another scramble without even ten minutes off?"

"Think positive," came the voice from the back seat, "the low flying system closes at Five so we've only time for one more sortie and that should be Endex. I reckon the bar will be humming tonight once this is over and that new WRAF Air Trafficker will be in............"

"You concentrate on the nav kit and leave me to sort out the women," retorted the pilot. "Anyway, there's a war on!"

The quiet banter in the cockpit was in total contrast to the frenzied activity below. Having experienced total concentration for the last hour flying at low level over the North German countryside, the relief in the cockpit was apparent. On the ground it was a different matter. The pressure was now switching to the groundcrew to move the jet to safety and rearm for the next task. Seeing a figure reappear from underneath the aircraft, the pilot opened his clenched fists above his head, the hand signal indicating to the crew chief that the brakes had been released. Almost simultaneously, the tractor which had been hitched to the tow bar which was in turn attached firmly to the nose wheel of the Phantom, revved slowly inducing an immediate judder through the airframe as it began to ease the massive aircraft slowly back into the shelter. In the cockpit, the crew craned their necks re-checking the wingtips of the slowly moving fighter as the shadow of the HAS encroached on the rear fuselage. Meanwhile, the flight line mechanic at the wingtip, his hands held apart, reassured them that the wing was safely clear of the doors. The Phantom eased slowly into the safety of the shelter, engines still spooling noisily and with another gentle jolt came to a halt, the rearward motion arrested by large chocks which had been carefully pre-positioned in its path. After another frantic flurry, the groundcrew released the towing arm which was pulled swiftly away by the tractor. Still without a word spoken, another curt gesture to the Crew Chief from the pilot, a suggestive plugging motion of his hands, prompted the connection of the external power supply and the telephone briefing facility known as the telebrief into the housings in the main undercarriage bay. Until the power was restored the pilot could not shut down the engines allowing the groundcrew to close the clam-shell HAS doors providing shelter from the incoming raid. HASs were not a perfect way to protect the aircraft and crews from precision guided munitions but against the free-fall bombs that the Soviet bombers carried, they would be more than up to the task. Shielded by the thick concrete walls of the HAS, contact was restored with the Wing Operations Centre and the crew reported in.

"Seagull, Mike Lima 66, HAS 54 on turnround."

Seagull was the unlikely callsign for the Wing Operations Centre. Jim Gordon, not surprisingly "Flash" to his mates on the Squadron, passed his message in a monotone over the telebrief from the rear cockpit of the fighter. It was vital that the ops staff were kept informed of the status of the aircraft during the refuelling and rearmament phase between missions. With so few fighters available, time on the ground was critical and air battles were won or lost by aircraft being in the wrong place at the wrong time or serviceable aircraft being overlooked.

"Roger 66, this is Seagull, call turnround complete and come up to Readiness 10. Expedite your turnround. Intelligence reports raids building to the east," came the disembodied voice of the Duty Controller from the Combined Operations Centre on the North side of the airfield. The crew were wanted back on alert as soon as possible.

"66," the Navigator replied in acknowledgement. He switched his attention back to his avionics gear.

"The INAS is back in align, confirm the external power's connected and you're clear to shut down," he announced as the Rolls Royce Spey jet engines rapidly died, the pilot silently acknowledging the command by closing the throttles. The scream of the engines was quickly replaced by the whine of the Houchin auxiliary power unit in the HAS next to the aircraft as the small unit immediately took over the task of providing power for the aircraft systems.

Abruptly, a deafening scream overhead followed by the rush of departing jet engines drowned all conversation as the simulated air raid flew directly over the HAS.

"Guess that one was for us." remarked Flash, as another rush from an entirely different direction announced the second pass of the attacking formation.

"I wonder who they were?"

"Probably Jaguars from Brüggen," his pilot replied distractedly. "Those guys are on exercise this week as well."

"Come to think of it, they're coming over to Happy Hour tonight," Flash replied changing the subject and moving the conversation skilfully on to his favourite pastime. A grunt from the front implied that his pilot was still busy finishing his shut-down checks so he returned to his own tasks, oblivious of the apparent snub.

"That is if we've all had enough fun by then," he added.

As the groundcrew busied themselves around the aircraft checking the vital systems and replenishing oils and hydraulics in preparation for the next flight, a shrill ringing from the HAS phone announced the arrival of the fuel bowser which had been trapped in the open during the air attack. Whether it would have survived for real was debatable but for this exercise, simulation could only go so far. The crew chief looked up questioningly at the pilot as the HAS doors should have stayed firmly closed during an air attack. Keen to be airborne as soon as possible, the pilot nodded, endorsing the illicit shortcut. Daylight flooded in once again as a single massive clamshell door swung open to allow the truck inside. A brief unearthly halo effect from the intense sunlight ringed the bulky vehicle before it slotted into the gap alongside the fuselage the noise of its massive diesel engine reverberating around the HAS. As soon as it pulled to a stop the driver dropped from the cab and began to unwind the heavy hoses ready for the refuelling.

In the cockpit the crew were still strapped in as the turn-round began, although both had eased off their ejection seat straps giving a temporary respite from the bite of the coarse harness which chafed ruthlessly during the sortie. Any attempts at comfort were impossible in the cramped confines of the cockpit because the clumsy survival equipment restricted even the simplest movement. Even so it was a necessary evil. The seat held a survival pack with an inflatable dinghy, emergency flares and other survival gear not to mention the parachute which would be their lifeline in the event of an ejection. Crews had been grateful to be attached to it by the flimsy lanyard on many occasions.

Overhead, the strip lights embedded in the roof along the length of the HAS barely lit the space. Down below in the Phantom cockpit the instruments hummed, bathed in the red glow of the cockpit lights, a sea of light in the darkened HAS. Flash, his face etched eerily by the red light, drew out his respirator from the rear of the cockpit console, dragged the mask from its protective case and stared tiredly at the rubber contraption. It was a constant companion to the crews faced with the permanent threat of attack by chemical weapons from the eastern bloc forces. Universally reviled in peacetime it would, undoubtedly, be the most important piece of personal equipment in wartime. He was still winding down after the last sortie, the adrenaline slowly subsiding but there were things to do. Closing his eyes he held his breath and flipped up the visor on his helmet, untoggled the chin strap and rolled the "bonedome" forward onto his lap. The heavy helmet was quickly replaced by the respirator closely followed by the protective cowl of his Nuclear, Biological and Chemical hood. The rubber of the mask felt uncomfortable against his face, sticky after the hectic sortie and it was the last thing he needed. He would have preferred to rid himself of the bulky equipment but accepted the need to play out the bizarre charade as the simulated air raid ran its course. Outside the protective cocoon of the HAS, others would be checking the airfield for evidence of chemical contamination.

Climbing tentatively from the cockpit, clutching his "Noddy Guide" which contained all his vital tactical data he had collected during the sortie, he paused to put his helmet onto the top box of the ejection seat. Moving to the top of the aircraft ladder already clipped in place by the groundcrew across the broad engine intake of the Phantom, he began to let himself down. There would be all hell to pay if he was late putting in his ADMISREP - the post mission air defence mission report. There were strict rules about getting it to the Sector Operations Centre within minutes of landing. Feeling for the steps with his foot, he began to descend, the activity around him almost surreal through the tunnel of the gas mask eyepieces. He unconsciously acknowledged the effort needed to keep these functional machines airborne as the groundcrew around him worked away at their servicing tasks. Swiftly covering the short distance to the HAS management cabin, he pushed in through the door making his way directly to the phone on the far wall. Let's hope the "all clear" is sounded soon so that I can ditch this damned gas mask, he thought to himself. As if prompted by his thoughts, the tannoy rang out again.

"Hostiles Clear, Hostiles Clear, Hostiles Clear. Air Raid Warning White, Air Raid Warning White, Air Raid Warning White. NBC State White. Shelter Marshals carry out further gas checks and report."

The message rang out again, repeated to make sure that harried troops digested its important information, their senses dulled by the restrictive chemical gear. The words echoed around the busy HAS signifying that the air raid had passed through, the fighter bombers already egressing at high speed back to their own bases leaving Wildenrath to recover from the consequences of the simulated attack. Around the airbase, the drone of the public address system was accompanied by the wail of the all-clear siren spreading the message station-wide. Flash gratefully slipped off his respirator and threw it onto the dirty counter.

The stocky, dark haired navigator, his face sporting the archetypal Air Force moustache, had spent his younger days watching the Lightning fighters flying from RAF Wattisham near Ipswich and those early impressions had steered him towards a career in the Air Force. Despite the strains of the latest exercise, he was happy with his lot but the noise and glamour of airshow stunts he had watched as a boy had long ago been replaced by a healthy dose of reality. A Cold War exercise was a far cry from the escapism of an airshow. Leaning against the grimy bench he began the routine post flight litany. Gripping the sticky handset he struggled with the plastic pages of the "noddy guide" which held the coded details of his mission which when collated would allow the intelligence experts to assess the effectiveness of Wildenrath's response to the NATO Air Defence exercise.

Frustratingly, the telephone handset was picking up the hubbub of activity in the HAS which repeated itself causing a distracting ringing in his ear. He raised his voice to compete.

"Intercept, two F104 Starfighters, position 5150 degrees north, 0700 degrees east, heading 210 degrees at 250 feet at 450 knots. Engaged with 2 Sidewinders. No evasion seen......."

He droned on. Each piece of information pinpointed precisely the details of the engagements he and his pilot had made during the previous sortie for the benefit of the statisticians and intelligence experts in the Sector Operations Centre. The bland statistics could never reflect the effort and adrenaline which had been spent achieving the kills. The chaos in the shelter was transparent to the young WRAF at the far end of the telephone who copied the data carefully.

"Affirmative, that was for callsign Mike Lima 66, landed at 1502," he finished.

"Thanks Sir" she trilled as the line went dead.

Flash stretched with evident relief and exchanged a few brief words with the "liney" filling in details in the Form 700. The accumulated stress was rapidly catching up. In a couple of hours he could relax for the weekend but, in the meantime, he had one last sortie to finish. The planners normally made a big effort for the final event of an exercise because everyone loved a finale and, to a man, wanted to be in on the last one. He would need to tap his energy resources just one last time this week but he would fix the important things first. He filled 2 plastic mugs with a foul smelling brew from a flask on the counter and took a short sip; Nectar! Anything would taste good after a sortie! Walking back to the jet he hauled himself up the front ladder and passed the second cup to Mark Keene, "Razor" his pilot, still strapped in the cockpit.

"Thanks Flash, do I need that."

"Not so fast, you may change your mind when you taste it," he replied. "It's a NAAFI special brew!"

As he sipped at the steaming cup, suddenly the pilot's brow furrowed and not from the bite of the caffeine but from something unheard by the others in the HAS. He slipped the mask back to his face. A Londoner, he epitomised the stereotypical fighter pilot; young, handsome and eligible. His major flaw was the parlous state of his bank balance but, by his reckoning, life's fun quotient was not reconcilable with his financial resources. What self respecting bachelor could live without a sports car and skis? Luckily, he didn't allow the fact that his Bank Manager had banked successfully with him for many years to inhibit his enjoyment of life. He and his navigator, both bachelors, lived life to the full despite the mundane financial constraints of daily life. He listened intently to the message, keying the microphone on the front of his oxygen mask in response.

"That was Wing Ops," he said dropping his mask. "They want us airborne as soon as the turnround's complete. Apparently Intelligence reckons that the Red Hoards are massing along the IGB ready for the big one! I guess we'd better stop them!" "How long until the turnround's finished Chief?" he called to the harried senior NCO below.

"About 5 minutes, Sir. The bowser driver's just pumping the last of the fuel now. The rest is done."

The unwieldy fuelling coupler had already been plugged in to the receptacle underneath the jet and 13,000 lbs of fuel were being forced into the Phantom's tanks. Despite the hassle from Wing Ops, Razor unstrapped, stood up on his ejection seat and stretched, grateful for the opportunity for the brief respite.

"I need a leak and then I guess we'd better get this show back on the road."

*

Yuri Andrenev looked down at his wife. She lay propped up in bed supported by large pillows, her eyes closed. He leaned forward and gently stroked a lock of hair from her eyes, his look one of sympathy not animosity. She sighed, moving imperceptibly before dropping back into a deep slumber. Reaching into his pocket, he took out a small pill bottle and pressed it into her cold hand. He leaned forward and kissed her tenderly on the forehead before edging quietly towards the door careful not to disturb her. Leaving the flat, he strode along the corridor to the small room where the building attendant could be found. She smiled as he entered fussing ineffectually with a dusting cloth as he handed her the door key.

"See the nurse does her job properly today," he chided. "She's been cutting corners recently and I don't care for it. My wife is a very sick woman and needs constant attention. If the lazy bitch doesn't arrive on the dot at 10 o'clock, I want you to let me know; you know my number."

She nodded deferentially. The Colonel was a generous tenant and she had no wish to alienate him. Although military salaries were pitiful by western standards, he did not begrudge the small tip every week which supplemented the old woman's meagre income. She in turn rationalised that, having a sick wife, he had enough to worry about particularly with a job as dangerous as his. Anyhow, where else would she get hold of the paraffin that the Colonel brought in every week for her small lamp? She would keep him sweet. As Yuri pulled the large main entrance door to the apartment complex closed he paused, glancing around the drab suburb. His eyes were glazed and maybe even slightly moist and a debilitating indecision gnawed away within. He had provided the means but did his wife have the will?

*

Flash moved slowly up the rear ladder and, as he reached the top, he donned his helmet before climbing back into the cockpit. Waiting for the thumbs-up from the Crew Chief signifying that the Phantom was turned and ready to go, Razor watched Flash drop back onto his ejection seat.

"I'll check in while you sign the 700," Flash called to Razor who was resting against the front windscreen arch of the jet, his feet on the canvas seat of the ejection seat. The pilot looked vacant, tired.

The Form 700 was the aircraft's log book which the pilot inspected and signed before every sortie. Among other things it detailed the aircraft's fuel and armament state and it was the crew's way of finding out every minute detail of the aircraft's history. Who had last flown it, what rectification the aircraft had undergone and any defects it was carrying were all carefully logged. Ultimately, it was the pilot's responsibility to ensure that all was as it should be before he accepted the jet for a flight. A minor snag which may be acceptable to the engineers may not be so minor to the aircrew. Equally, crews pushing for another sortie might be frustrated when their precious jet was declared unserviceable with a snag which they would have been happy to carry until the end of the flying day. Flash ran quickly round the gauges in his own cockpit as he settled back into "the office." He checked the status of the systems, confirmed that the INAS was realigning and would be ready for the next sortie and flicked a few switches back into the correct positions. As he watched, the crew chief passed the bulky document to the pilot who signed on the dotted line for the jet. They were ready to go. Flash hit the transmit button.

"Wing Ops, Mike Lima 66, turnround complete in HAS 54."

"Roger 66, standby for scramble instructions!"

Surprised that Wing Ops had stuck to their plan, Flash banged the side of the jet frantically.

"Scramble Message," he yelled inducing the familiar panic around him.

"Rats," groaned Razor, "lunch out of the window again."

The telebrief buzzed heralding a connection to the Sector Operations Centre.

"Wildenrath, alert 2 phantoms!"

"Mike Lima 66 and Mike Lima 72."

"66 and 72 scramble for low level radar CAP. Join Alpha Lima 07 Flight, two F-16s for mixed fighter operations. Vector 030 for low level transit to

Radar CAP 2. Join 07 Flight on CAP, contact "Crabtree" on TAD 079, scramble, scramble, scramble, acknowledge."

The unintelligible string of instructions was crystal clear to the navigator.

"66 scrambling," called Flash as Razor, breathless from the exertion of strapping in checked in on intercom.

"72 scrambling," they heard from the other Phantom in an adjacent HAS. Mike Lima 72 was another 92 Squadron Phantom.

"I got the scramble message. We're tasked for a mixed CAP with a pair of Beauvechain F-16s in low fly 2; we've got Nozzles and Killer as Number 2. It'll be a Low Level North Departure. The INAS is in nav - go for it!"

Razor wound the Speys into life after signalling urgently to the Chief with a spinning motion of his right hand, his index finger raised. To the front and rear of the HAS, the heavy doors were opening as the noise built to a crescendo. Pilots had been known to be over-enthusiastic on start and beat the groundcrew to the start. Rotating engines and closed HAS doors had proved to be a flawed combination as engines thirsty for air were slowly strangled. No such problem as the see-off crew were on top form. Razor ran through his pre taxy checks as he prompted the groundcrew to button up the external servicing panels and make the jet ready. With a thumbs up from his crew chief and a nudge of the throttles, he coaxed the heavy jet from the chocks and it surged forward, emerging from the fluorescent gloom of the HAS into the bright sunlight. The noise fell away as the concrete receded and Razor cut the power as he emerged into the tree-lined dispersal. Engaging the nose wheel steering with the bright red button on the stick followed by a quick waggle of the rudder bars prompted a shimmy from the jet confirming that the nose wheel steering was working as he rolled towards the adjacent taxiway. He looked across to the nearby HAS as callsign 72 appeared and entered the loop taxiway to his right. His wingman was already in place. Spot on! Easing the rudder bars left, the Phantom responded with a sharp turn and the nose swung round to follow the curve of the taxiway. To his right, the PBF or Pilots Briefing Facility, a dull squat bunker which housed the Squadron's briefing rooms and domestic area, was picked out in sharp relief in the afternoon sunlight as the crew began their preparations. His mind drifted briefly to his missed lunch as his stomach growled before he switched back to matters in hand. Up ahead, one of the sector guards, grateful for the diversion, pulled the barbed wire security fence back from the taxiway alerted by the noise of the approaching aircraft allowing free passage for the formation racing towards the runway threshold.

"Stud 2's up," offered Flash from the back as he switched the radio across to Tower frequency.

"Tower, Mike Lima 66 and 72 scrambling from Delta Dispersal."

"66 and 72 are cleared for scramble take off from Runway 09 for a low-level North departure. Surface wind is easterly at 10 knots. After takeoff, switch to tactical pre-brief."

Razor keyed the transmit switch.

"Clear for takeoff, 66, 72."

They had been cleared as briefed in the scramble message which meant that the ground controllers were talking to each other. So far, so good. The pair of Phantoms emerged from the trees around Delta Dispersal while in the cockpit Flash ran rapidly through the checks, monitoring his pilot's responses. The taxy distance from the dispersal to the runway was short and time was at a premium:

"Steps."............"Up."

"Oxygen."............"On, contents checked, connected, winking and blinking."

"Engine Anti-ice.".."Normal."

"Bleed control."...."Normal."

The checks rolled on, each one vital to ensure that the myriad of systems were functioning correctly before takeoff; mistakes were more difficult to rectify once airborne. In his mirrors, Razor could see Nozzles and Killer in the Number 2 Phantom easing up closer behind them, ready to turn onto their own side of the runway as they prepared to line up as a pair.

"Runway checks," the pilot called. Already anticipating the call, Flash had the checklist open at the page although the string of checks was burned into his memory.

"Pitot heat."......"On."

"Wings."............"Spread and Locked."

A glance in the external mirror confirmed the fact. A few years earlier inattention to this vital check had resulted in a Phantom launching with the vital locking pins unlocked. As the wings loaded up, the crude attempt at a handclap proved inadequate to lift the aircraft into the air and the crew ejected!

"Flaps."............"Half."

"Stab augs."......."Engaged."

"Anti skid."......."On, caption out."

"Engine checks."

Razor had already eased both throttles to maximum military power, max mil, having given the wind-up signal to his wingman. The challenge and response checks were a well practised ritual. Returning his gaze to the instrument panel he noticed that the TGT, the Turbine Gas Temperature or internal working temperature of the engine, was fluctuating around 640 degrees Centigrade, the limiting value.

"We may have a snag here," he said to his back-seater almost casually, "the right's looking a bit hot."

Neither of the crew wanted to abort at this stage as the exhilaration of the sortie beckoned. The pilot's eyes were glued to the gauge willing it to respond and gratefully, he watched it slowly creep down to a more normal reading.

"No, it looks OK. Engine checks are good."

"Warning lights."

"All out."

"Ramps are retracted," confirmed Flash glancing at the position of the intake ramps. This was another vital check because left in the wrong position, supersonic airflow would pass through the engines or, alternatively, the engines could be starved of air at low speed, neither of which were particularly attractive options. He looked back over to his wingman who was still head down completing his own checks.

"Come on, come on," he murmured.

Nozzles finally returned his stare giving a thumbs up in his front windscreen, his white leather flying glove in stark contrast to the black cockpit coaming, sun glinting momentarily from his dark visor as his head moved. Razor tapped the front of his helmet, the signal for his wingman to follow him for a formation take off, the fastest way to get both aircraft airborne as a fighting element. His head rocked aft in an exaggerated gesture and after a brief pause, nodded firmly forward, at the same time as he rocked the throttles outboard and advanced smoothly through to full afterburner. He watched the engines stabilise before backing off leaving just enough power in hand for his wingman to stay in formation. The Phantom reacted slowly at first but, within seconds, the burners bit and the aircraft surged forward, the Speys roaring behind, only a dull reminder, almost inaudible to the crew, of the immense power forcing them into the air. Flash, checking that Nozzles had stayed in position during the take off roll, gave a reassuring call as both aircraft sped down the runway.

"2's in position. Speed's reading. 100 knots.. 120.. 140.. Go!"

At "Go" speed they were committed to the take off. The cadence underlined the rate at which the jets gathered speed, bizarre conjoined twins locked together in a mad dash. As the nose wheels lifted in stereo, the jets lumbered into the air, already too fast to stop even with the assistance of the Rotary Hydraulic Arrestor Gear or RHAG, the cable arresting system which stretched across their path towards the far end of the runway.

"180.. 200," advised Flash.

"Gear and Flaps travelling," retorted the pilot, the jet gathering ever more momentum as he allowed himself a tentative glance over his shoulder, immediately reassured by the sight of his wingman rigid in formation, his gear cycling upwards into the wheel wells and locking home. The other pilot's head remained fixed on the lead aircraft's cockpit as he jockeyed for position, playing the stick and throttles.

"250.. 300.. 350." A mere 20 seconds since brakes release and the two aircraft were airborne as a fighting unit. Nozzles, eyes now glued to the formation references of the other Phantom only yards from him, smoothly maintained formation but in an instant, all his efforts to maintain the perfect formation position were negated by a simple hand signal, a "kiss off" from his leader. The two aircraft racked on 90 degrees of bank, belly to belly, pulled hard away from each other before returning to level flight in close battle formation, line abreast one mile apart. A close formation take off put them in the air quickly but tactics took over once airborne and a formation pair, whilst pretty, was particularly vulnerable. None of the aircrew had time to admire the scenery. Seconds later, a mere 5 miles east of the airfield and unbidden, Nozzles cranked on 90 degrees of bank towards his leader to head north for the low level departure as his leader followed the turn holding precise tactical formation at 500 feet altitude, still one mile apart. Soon, the communications tower of the Headquarters of the 2nd Allied Tactical Air Force, or 2ATAF at RAF Rheindahlen passed to the left of the formation. They were established on track and threading their way carefully through the crowded airspace around the clutch airfields of Brüggen and Laarbruch avoiding the civil zone around Düsseldorf.

"Mike Lima 66 and 72 clear of the Zone switching to tactical," Razor called to Wildenrath Tower. "TAD079, TAD 079, go!"

2 DECISIONS

Yuri drove along the rutted road avoiding the worst of the potholes and, as he rounded the bend, the trees gave way to a wire security fence giving a much better view of the airfield. His mind was elsewhere. Ahead, an enormous Tu-142 bomber, known in the West as a Bear Golf, lumbered over the fence only metres above the ground, its undercarriage retracting almost out of necessity to allow it to clear the obstructions at the end of the runway. He recognised the aircraft from its bulbous nose which contained the targeting radar for the long range missiles. He knew that it was near to completing its operational test programme at Ramenskoye Test Centre and, when operational, would carry the new class of longer range stand-off missiles. These would give a much improved capability against the American carrier battle groups and static targets in the United Kingdom and beyond. It was a capability that was much needed by the Soviet Long Range Air Force to counter the threat posed by the huge aircraft carrier which represented the land mass of the United Kingdom. As they did in World War 2, it was here that the Americans would marshal their reinforcements during any future conflict and the Soviet Union could not allow them to do it with impunity. The constant tit-for-tat spawned ever-increasing numbers of weapons systems. In the West, it fed the lucrative arms industry providing jobs and prosperity for thousands. In the East, arms were produced in similar vast quantities but at the expense of the living standards of the population, fuelled by the paranoia of politicians countering a non-existent threat of attack by NATO. His reverie disturbed,

Yuri saw the entrance to the Test Centre looming ahead and he turned into the access track. His progress was immediately slowed at the control point, the red and white barrier barring the way.

"Good Morning Comrade Colonel Andrenev," called the guard who stood alert at the piquet post.

"Good Morning," he replied casually, his tone reinforcing his status.

"Your identity pass please."

Yuri felt in his pocket for the familiar document but could not immediately put his hand to it. Strange he thought distractedly, it had been there earlier. His movements became more rapid as he fumbled in his attempts to find the elusive pass but without success. His poise was temporarily shaken.

"Look, I'm sorry but I appear to have mislaid the damned thing; must have left it at home. Give me a temporary one."

The guard hesitated.

"You recognise me!"

"Maybe, but it's against the regulations Comrade Colonel, I'm afraid. I shall have to contact your section and ask for someone to vouch for you. They will have to have someone come down to escort you."

"But you know me – this is bullshit!" he fumed.

"The regulations, Comrade. The Guard Commander would have me on restrictions if I broke the rules."

Yuri watched him closely looking for just the smallest hint of insubordination but the guard was not yet finished. He had not yet had his full vengeance.

"You realise that I will be forced to report the incident. It's an offence not to carry your identity card."

Finally, a suppressed smirk gave away his evident pleasure at Yuri's misfortune. Yuri let it pass with a sigh. It was not worth the heartbeats.

"Yes, yes, just contact the Test Centre and let me get on with some work," he snapped. "Here, ring this number."

Pulling over to allow the stream of traffic which had begun to build up behind him to pass, he began the undoubtedly long wait for the promised "escort." Bloody mindless, he fumed as his engine died in a splutter and a bang prompting another curse.

*

The Phantoms headed North at low level. Razor left a short pause to allow the Number 2 to follow the frequency change.

"72 check."

"72," responded Nozzles perfunctorily.

The pair was airborne and safely established on their operating frequency.

"Fuel contents are good, external tanks feeding, system pressures are good," he called completing his first round of housekeeping checks. There were a host of complex systems which kept the fighter airborne and between the crew, they would monitor them relentlessly throughout the sortie, checking and cross checking. Unlike a family saloon, if a major fault developed it wasn't possible to draw into a lay by to fix it. Pre-empting difficulty was undoubtedly the best course and forewarned was forearmed. The small fuel gauge showed him precisely the location of the precious fuel and how much of it remained. The size of the gauge was in total contrast to its importance. He would keep a constant eye on the contents and make sure that it remained in the correct tanks and available for use throughout the sortie. His navigator, who did not have the luxury of a fuel gauge, would pester him endlessly to ensure that he did. Fuel was life. They had not yet crossed the River Rhine or entered the low flying area but this was an exercise and any "hostile" aircraft passing the formation would collect a missile shot.

"Master Arm is live, coolant on, tone set, CW is on, interlocks out, Sparrow selected, LCOSS uncaged," he called, rapidly running through his complex sequence of weapons checks. Once these checks were complete the Phantom was turned from a functional but ugly airshow machine into a lethal weapon. The nitrogen coolant cooled the seeker heads of the AIM-9G Sidewinder missiles ensuring that they could pick out minute amounts of reflected infra-red energy from a potential target against the background environment. In other words, it allowed the seeker head to pick out the infra-red equivalent of the proverbial needle in a haystack. The Sidewinder tone, a grating electronic rattle relayed from the missile to the crew's headsets, or the "growl" as it was colloquially known, alerted the crew when the missile had acquired a response from its victim and was able to track. The insistent electronic chatter, whilst functional, psychologically inspired the necessary aggression in the minds of the crew as they engaged in their potentially lethal task. CW, or the continuous wave radar, was a separate radar tracking beam directed by the main AWG 12 air intercept radar which guided the Sparrow semi-active missiles. "Locking on" the main radar directed the beam of CW onto the target and provided the missile with a radar beam for guidance which its seeker head would follow relentlessly until it passed within lethal distance of its quarry. At that stage, the fusing system in the missile would sense the proximity of the target and would discharge its deadly warhead. The linked metal rods packed tightly in the fuselage of the missile would expand as a continuous ring until, stretched to their limit, they would break into shards of lethal shrapnel and finish the task by tearing into the victim airframe. The final element of the weapons system, the Lead Computing Optical Sighting System, or LCOSS, when released from its mechanical caging system which protected the sight on the ground, made the gunsight live. This gyroscopic device instantaneously computed the dynamics of the three-dimensional air battle and provided a sighting solution to the pilot by projecting a reticule on the sight glass in the windscreen of the Phantom. To maintain the guns tracking solution so vital in air-to-air combat, the small computer, constantly updated complex dynamic geometric calculations. If the pilot aimed directly at the target, the bullets from the Suu-23 cannon would pass harmlessly behind. With the lead computing sight came the incredible rate of fire of 6,000 rounds per minute from the Suu-23 gun. The pilot would pull "lead" so that the bullets were aimed ahead of the victim. By the time they arrived at their target, the victim had arrived at the predicted impact point. Whilst a hit on the target was not assured, hits from only two or three armour piercing rounds were needed to disable most modern fighters. Despite this, one lesson that Phantom crews through the years had learned and relearned was that it was folly to stay and turn with an agile opponent such as the Mig-21 Soviet fighter. Better to disengage and exploit the superior long-range strengths of the Phantom's missiles.

"Fights on!" called Razor to his formation as he finished his checks, content that his own jet was ready for action and prompting his wingman to arm up. The call should have been redundant as the other crew would already have prepared their jet for action without prompting. In this aerial battlefield, no one flew with switches safe for longer than absolutely necessary. The pair turned northeast abeam the Nike missile site near Kempen. The shimmering of the Wesel was already visible in the distance, an unusual phenomenon at this time of the year. Northern Germany was renowned for murky visibility and it was much more common for the Wildenrath Phantoms to be the only aircraft low flying. The murk was colloquially known as "Brit Visual Flight Rules" to other locally based NATO aircrews! VFR set the separation criteria for avoiding clouds and allowing aircraft to operate without reference to instruments. Too hazy on the average day for most of NATO to be low flying, the RAF crews would fly and fight in the murk, training for the worst. The nightmare scenario was undoubtedly a mass attack from the Eastern Bloc forces precede by massive air attack. It would be too late to try to acquire the skills as a panic measure at the last minute prior to an attack. They had to be carefully nurtured over months if not years of practise. Operating at low level would keep them out of the weapons envelopes of a large proportion of the likely threat systems. Their efforts in the difficult conditions would give them the vital edge on day 1 of the conflict everyone hoped would never come. In the meantime, they trained. Clearing the Wesel river, the pair let down to 250 feet in the low flying area, easing out into wider battle formation and the heads in the cockpits began to move as if on gimbals, alert for other aircraft operating in the low flying area who would be grateful for the chance of a quick kill on the formation, if given the opportunity. Flash finished his own checks of his AWG 12 radar selecting his primary radar mode, pulse Doppler or "PD" before glancing briefly at the secondary pulse mode which glowed bright with returns from the ground. "Ground clutter" hid returns from an airborne target except at the shortest ranges or over the flattest terrain. In this environment, at low level overland, pulse mode was virtually useless. It was PD which differentiated a moving target from the background noise and made the Phantom such a formidable fighter giving it the ability to track targets at low level. It was still one of the few aircraft able to do so.

"Scope's clear," he reassured his pilot, the radar display devoid of radar contacts. "No trade right now but plenty of time yet," he bantered.

*

The articulated lorry thundered along the E73, its progress around Düsseldorf slow but steady. The TIR plate above the Polish number plates and the gaudy vegetable insignia across the side of the truck hid the true reason for its journey. True, the cargo it carried really was Polish root vegetables destined for market in The Netherlands but, in reality, the driver was a Russian tank commander from the 2nd Guards Tank Army stationed in East Germany. The whole purpose of his visit was to reconnoitre the terrain to the west of Düsseldorf to allow him to formulate precise battle plans for his section. There was little point in studying endless grainy satellite pictures when he could drive unhindered through the very countryside which interested him. Equally, his co-driver alongside him was a Spetznaz captain who was also taking the opportunity to visit Amsterdam Docks. His role in the glorious liberation, when it finally came, would be to cripple the resupply operation from the United States by targeting key installations for neutralisation and by mining the sea approaches to the deep water harbours. He and his team would be inserted by submarine and would operate deep behind enemy lines waiting for the armoured thrust from the east which would link up in less than five days. He would enjoy his brief sojourn and the wad of hard currency he had in his pocket would be spent on things other than hotel rooms. A subdued groan cut through the monotonous drone of the tyres on concrete and the curtain across the sleeping space behind the two men stirred and drew back slowly. A pair of legs emerged followed in short order by their owner who suddenly propelled himself forward dropping stiffly onto the seat between the men. Viktor Kamov stretched and yawned.

"How are we doing?"

"Just passing Düsseldorf," replied the driver. "We should be at the border in about an hour."

"Do you still want to be dropped in Elmpt?" queried the passenger?"

"Yes, that will do just fine," he replied. "I have a little business at the Clutch airfields before going on to Bonn."

"You never did tell us what you were up to," the driver said, fishing for facts.

"Oh, just checking out a new installation on the airfield at Brüggen," he replied evasively. "The Brits have been putting up some new buildings and we think it may be associated with a new anti-radiation missile they are about to deploy. If I can get a close enough look, perhaps I can confirm it."

His response was far from the truth. Kamov was a member of a secretive division of the KGB and his main role was to recruit western personnel to provide real-time intelligence. It was a task for which he was particularly suited. His gregarious personality and flawless English accent had trapped many unwary soldiers and airman in bars around NATO installations in West Germany. His was a subtle technique. He would watch for the regulars, ideally the quieter ones and make his introductions posing as a businessman. A few glasses of beer during the first contacts, on "expenses" naturally, would oil the wheels of friendship. Initially, he would show casual interest in his new-found friends and his apparent interest in snippets of information about the military hardware would be completely innocent; facts which could do no one any harm and could be found in Flight International or at any airshow. He came across as an interested enthusiast. He would, however, make absolutely sure that the discussion was documented; carefully filmed and taped. That would be the start but it was rare to find a target even at that stage, who would have the guts to talk to the security authorities. He would quickly weave such a web of complicity that the hapless victim could never free himself.

As the truck sped on, Kamov settled down. He would be away soon and was anxious to get on with his task. His thoughts drifted idly to the woman with whom he would spend the night. A local whore, she was grateful for his generous contribution to her domestic expenses and he was always careful not to interfere with her business activity. It was an arrangement which suited them both as it offered him a guaranteed bed for the night whenever it was needed and it kept the Madam sweet. Who was to say, perhaps one of these days he would hit pay dirt and find one of her clients ripe for picking. A signpost for Mönchen Gladbach flashed past. Not long now.

*

The radar warning receiver, better known as the RWR, bleeped noisily from the left instrument console in the rear cockpit, there to warn of any radar-equipped systems showing undue interest in the formation. At the moment, its lethargy interested only Flash. The 360 degree display flashed with darting green vectors showing potential threats around the aircraft, each unique to the type of radar being detected.

"72 We'll take an F-16 each," he instructed, keen to complete the domestic trivia before arriving on CAP.

"72" responded his wingman slotting into the familiar routine. One more call to make and they were ready to fight.

"All stations, Mike Lima 66 Flight, 2 F4s, 20 miles south of RCAP 2. On station in 3 minutes, both serviceable awaiting Alpha Lima 07 flight."

"Crabtree copies," came the response from the Control and Reporting Centre at Eudem who had been monitoring the frequency, silent until now. At this height the CRC would not be able to see the Phantom formation on their huge ground based radars. For that matter it was pretty unlikely they would see the incoming threats either due to the patchy radar coverage in the rear areas. The fighters would be more effective operating autonomously, relying on their own radars to detect any incoming tracks. The fighter controllers would act as asset managers making sure each CAP area was manned and provide a link with the command network relaying vital tactical data to base and carrying out the key battle management tasks. Razor had deliberately kept radio calls to a minimum as the formation were practising wartime "min comms", or minimum communications procedures. There was little point in allowing the Soviet monitoring systems who listened constantly, the chance to gain more intelligence information than was absolutely necessary and it was a good way of avoiding the attention of unwanted communications jammers who may be monitoring their frequency. Razor hoped that the CRC would not chatter unnecessarily for the time being and negate their efforts! The lack of response to his radio call suggested that the F-16s had not yet arrived so Razor vectored his formation on towards the combat air patrol area. Suddenly, Nozzles in the other Phantom rocked his wings violently, the sign that Killer, his back-seater, had detected a target on radar. The wingman immediately turned away through 30 degrees taking up his attack vector, his turn initiating the attack. Both Phantoms eased even lower to their minimum height aiming to set the approaching targets, which as yet remained invisible to Razor and Flash, against the skyline to try to gain the quickest visual sighting. Switches were already armed, although on exercise, live missiles were replaced by electronic simulations to give the indications of the real thing but without the consequences.

"I'm coming head-in," said Flash as he switched his whole attention to the radar, letting his pilot know that he was no longer clearing his designated visual search area. Automatically, Razor's visual scan expanded to cover the area previously covered by his navigator who began to think about his tactical plan. Not the best weather today, he reflected. With the smoke that the engines push out, the Bogeys will pick up a "Tally" at long range. Maybe with the flat terrain in this area we should be thinking of approaching from above; give ourselves the height advantage and stay out of their visual cone. He tweaked the gain setting on his radar and rolled the antenna thumb wheel gently to position the radar scanner accurately to where he expected the target to appear. He was working hard to gain contact but obviously, Killer had a better radar set than him today. His radar remained stubbornly barren. Suddenly there was a fleeting contact. The other Phantom doggedly held its heading vectoring towards the unseen target.

"Got it on the scope Razor," he announced. "Looks like a singleton doing about 450 knots. Taking a snatch lock for ranging." In PD mode, without locking his radar, he could see the target but would not get vital range information. He knew the target was there but how far away? He needed that range.

"Got any height on it?" said Razor.

"Yeah, it's on the deck with us," replied Flash checking the position of the scanner.

"20 degrees right, range 25 miles. Breaking lock."

He looked immediately for signs of evasion which would signify that he had been detected on the target's radar warning receiver. Nothing.

"We're just North of the Reken Mast," said Razor, conscious that his navigator would now have his head buried in the cockpit concentrating hard on the radar scope trying to work out the geometry needed to convert the fleeting contact into a good intercept. He would no longer be able to keep tabs on the aircraft's position.

"It's starting to climb and the speed's dropping off," Flash called almost immediately. Had he been detected? "It looks like it's on recovery," he said relating the target's manoeuvre to its position. It was approaching the recovery datum for the Clutch airfields.

"Skip it," he called over the radio to Killer terminating the intercept and allowing the contact to continue unmolested. Leader's prerogative! The single Jaguar passed abeam the formation already pulling up to recovery altitude and contacting Clutch Radar to begin his approach into Laarbruch its climb totally innocent. The pilot was probably unaware of his recent escape.

"It's a 2 Squadron recce bird," said Razor recognising the markings on the fin of the small fighter-bomber. "They're on our side today."

The small jet was almost certainly taking back important pictures to its base at Laarbruch showing the effects of an earlier NATO attack on the simulated enemy forces. The Phantom aircrew had their own interpretation of events.

"I guess he's already on his way to the Bar," said Flash, an element of jealousy in the front of his mind, savouring the thought of his first beer for a week. This contact had been friendly but by now the "Red Hordes" would be massing in the exercise area and the Phantoms had a task to complete. The formation pressed on towards their CAP datum.

*

Finally unburdened by the trivia which had dogged his morning Andrenev walked across the short stretch of tarmac to the prototype Su-27. A formidable fighter aeroplane it represented a massive step forward in operational capability and had been designed to match the combat capability of the American F-15 Eagle. The basic configuration was similar with twin vertical fins and a low wing loading to give it the edge in air combat. The broad forward fuselage leading to the massive radome would house the new air-to-air radar once deliveries began. Blended leading edge root extensions and a very thin rear fuselage all showed its air superiority credentials. Once fully developed, 2 R27 missiles known as AA-10 Alamo to NATO would be fitted to launchers under the centre fuselage with another 2 on pylons under the engine intakes. Even more missiles could be carried on pylons under the wings and a new infra-red guided air-to-air missile, the R73 known as the AA-11 Archer, had been designed to equip the new fighter in the short range fight. If the specifications were to believed it would have a truly stunning ability particularly when coupled with the helmet mounted sight which was also under development. The Su-27 still sported a 30mm GSh-301 gun with 150 rounds of ammunition because, unlike the Americans, Soviet pilots still recognized the need for the, supposedly, obsolete weapon in so many operational scenarios. For the first time a comprehensive avionics suite had been specified including a pulse Doppler radar, the Phazotron N001 Zhuk known to NATO as Slot Back 2 which would give a rudimentary track-while-scan capability.

Although the information would be shown on a traditional radar scope it would also be repeated in the head up display allowing the pilot to keep his eyes on the world outside the cockpit instead of staring at a display buried somewhere around his knees. It also had a new onboard jamming system the L0005 known as Sorbtsiya which could, not only act as a self defence jammer but could talk to other members of the formation and choreograph complex jamming sequences to confuse western radars. The chaff and flare dispensers and an updated SPO-15 radar warning receiver completed the suite. Yet another step change was the impressive OLS-27 infra-red search and track system mounted in a blister on the top of the radome just in front of his cockpit which also incorporated a laser range finder. With this he could see an infra-red image of his opponent miles away from the merge in combat. This would mean that once his radar had cued this sensor, he would be able to go electronically silent and even the best radar warning receiver would be unable to see his approach. He could make the final attack entirely passively until he fired his radar missiles. The laser ranger would give him a range to his target without using radar so he could go straight into an R73 shot. Unfortunately, the dreaded data link was even more capable in the new jet meaning he would still be controlled in his every move by ground controllers. With this complex suite he could select the best sensor to suit the tactical scenario giving him a massive advantage over his opponents. Whilst his prototype didn't yet have all the goodies fitted, he had seen the mock ups in the development rig and couldn't wait to begin the weapons testing phase.

He selected full afterburner and the prototype accelerated rapidly down the runway at Ramenskoye Test Centre. This was to be the final sortie of the development programme before moving into the tactical evaluation phase. NATO had already spotted the prototype with their reconnaissance satellites and had first designated the twin-finned air superiority aircraft as the RAM K but now it had a full nickname, the "Flanker." Modelled on the American F-15, the jet had all the classic hallmarks of a true fighter with its sleek lines, aerodynamic fairings, bubble canopy and massive engines. He pulled up sharply from the runway into a 60 degree climb which was way less than the fighter could achieve. The Lyulka turbojets were pushing out in excess of 123kN of raw thrust each which more than matched the weight of the unarmed prototype. He could have taken it into the vertical and with the thrust to weight ratio of the jet he would have been at 3000 metres in a blink of an eye. He could maintain this climb to something approaching the service ceiling of the aircraft way up in the upper airspace. He screwed his head around looking back at the outline of the runway behind him between the twin fins of the Sukhoi. It was an impressive picture postcard tableau. Air Traffic Control had already given him precise vectors to position the aircraft in the correct area for his fuel consumption evaluation which was the purpose of today's test flight. He reluctantly complied, despite a feeling of irritation, knowing that the western pilots about whom he had read so much, were not constrained in such a fashion by their ground controllers. He felt suppressed by the system and hankered for some freedom of action.

The aircraft entered a smooth climbing left hand turn and steadied on a westerly heading. The test profile required a short period of manoeuvring to explore the aircraft's limits before establishing a long steady racetrack at 15,000 metres. The manoeuvring would be fun but the fuel monitoring runs would be deadly boring. If he was honest, he was not relishing the event. He gazed down at the stark analogue instruments reflecting on the accounts in the GRU intelligence reports describing the new glass cockpits in the latest western fighters such as the American F-15 and the European Tornado. He was conscious of the outstanding aerodynamic performance of his own machine yet could not rationalise the fact that a system which was capable of producing such a fine airframe, with equally impressive engines, could be so deficient in the production of high quality avionics. Down to his right, the one digital screen was for the data link system which was only designed to allow his controller to exercise even more control over his actions. Yet another example of the attitude of the Party machine he thought. Politics over capability every time! British fighter pilots seemed to be encouraged to interpret the tactical scenario; Russian fighter pilots are not even provided with the tools to do the basic job and are fed every piece of data from the ground controllers. Still, he mused, the new radar was a major improvement over the old pulse equipment in the Mig-21 and Mig-23. Perhaps he should be grateful for small mercies? He levelled off at 7000 metres and carried out his checks before he began his first serial. The radar scanned the airspace aimlessly, the time base on the scope moving back and forth rhythmically. A quick glance confirmed what he already suspected that the area was clear of other traffic. There was no possibility of another aircraft within 100 kilometres of his still secret charge; the good old ground control would take care of that. He craned his neck, looking past the right hand air intake at the surrounding countryside, the fields and fences etched in sharp relief around him. He still felt a deep loyalty for the Motherland but an increasing frustration at the dogma which was slowly but surely squeezing the life from his country. It was ironic but, even as an officer in the Armed Forces where the vast majority of the Nations resources were directed, he could see how uselessly those riches were being squandered. He of all people should be grateful but wasn't. Corruption was rife to such an extent that, even in war, the military machine could never function effectively because small but vital elements, the glue which held the machine together, had been systematically stripped and plundered. There were no millionaires in the Soviet Union, only a disparate mass of peasants who eked out their existence by methodical fraud.

A harsh command in his ear snapped him back to the present as he heard his callsign over the radio.

"Ramrod this is Ramenskoye Centre, you are entering your operating area and clear to manoeuvre between 5,000 and 10,000 metres for 10 minutes. Call me complete."

"Roger Ramenskoye," he replied, automaton-like, simultaneously acknowledging the command on his data link equipment. He had briefed and practised this profile for 5 days now so how could that idiot on the ground think that he knew better? He stifled his frustration knowing that the cockpit of a high performance aeroplane was no place for distractions. Plugging in the afterburners, he immediately rolled into a 90 degree maximum performance turn. Entering the turn at 0.5 Mach, slow for the altitude, he watched the speed build, acknowledging the outstanding performance of his charge. Most aircraft would have been pressed to even maintain the high performance turn but his Su-27 was accelerating through it like a thoroughbred! He felt the pressure of the G-suit build around his legs at the rapid onset of the G forces, He grunted, straining hard to increase his tolerance as he registered 8G, the forces pressing down on his body. His right arm maintained the firm back pressure on the stick but rather too firmly as he felt the first effects of the accumulated forces take their toll and the world began to "grey out" bringing the onset of tunnel vision as the blood drained from his brain. The great pressure of his magnified body weight pressed down through his buttocks onto the hard canvas cover of the ejection seat and his head felt heavy. His neck was immediately strained by his flying helmet which suddenly exerted a pressure 8 times its former weight. A little too enthusiastic, he decided as he eased off to 4G allowing his vision to return to normal. Looking through his head up display he watched the numerals, projected ahead of him, rotating manically and as the heading approached west. He recorded yet another fuel check on his kneeboard for the statisticians. Easing the nose down, he allowed the speed to build again to 550 kph and levelled off setting up for his next manoeuvre which would be a cold power loop without the aid of afterburner. Pulling up, swiftly checking the wingtips against the horizon, he passed the vertical noticing the rounded form of the wingtips of the prototype against the skyline. Beautifully aerodynamic, he mused but each could carry an additional weapon station. He would suggest that to the designers when he got back. He coaxed the aircraft's nose smoothly through the vertical and, looking directly behind, waited for the horizon to reappear. Sensing a momentary loss of spatial awareness, he watched the ground pass through the apex of the loop but above him rather than below. The nose dropped, allowing reality and gravity to reassert itself as he adjusted the back pressure on the stick finessing his recovery levelling off precisely at his check height of 7,000 metres. Effortless. The profile progressed and, at each stage, Yuri noted the fuel figures which the scientists required, each statistic annotated meticulously on his kneepad in tight Cyrillic script. The final manoeuvre was one of which he was particularly proud. He called it the "Cobra." Overriding the spin prevention system, which would otherwise compete against him and prevent him from completing the manoeuvre, he adjusted his speed. It was important that he entered the manoeuvre at the correct speed; too fast and he would not be able to kill the forward momentum, too slow and he would not have sufficient control to lift the nose past the vertical. He hauled the stick rearwards simultaneously closing the throttles. The nose of the aircraft reared upwards, 30 degrees nose high, 60 degrees, 90 degrees, the artificial horizon rotated crazily in its mounting gimbals. The nose reached 120 degrees, well past the vertical and all forward speed died and, from outside the cockpit, the aircraft took on the startling resemblance of a Cobra poised for the strike, the image emphasised by the leading edge root extensions which resembled the hood of the deadly reptile. Yuri marvelled at the nose authority; the ability to control the nose of his fighter at such slow speed even though all aerodynamic assistance from the airflow had ceased at this unnatural angle. It was this feature of the Sukhoi which would soon make it so potent in combat. He checked ahead as the speed fell to zero bringing the nose sharply back to the horizon and, simultaneously, he applied full power to recover to level flight. That should break the lock of even the best western radar he thought with satisfaction. I must let Pugachev into that little secret he reflected. As he builds his confidence he should be able to slot that into his aerobatic routine.

"Ramrod this is Ramenskoye Centre, I see you completing your serial. Set heading 160 degrees for your next event."

"Roger Ramenskoye," he snapped, unable to control his frustration at the continued intrusion of the ground controller. Now for the really exciting part he thought.

*

Back in the low flying area, the Phantoms eased back up to 1500 feet ready to join their combat air patrol. Their defensive battle formation, 1 mile apart, chosen to offer mutual support if threatened by a hostile fighter, became even more important as they left the relative sanctuary of low level and suddenly the focus of attention for any roving fighter. Flash prompted a quick check of the fuel state while things were still quiet receiving reassuring noises from his pilot who had already turned his attention to formulating a plan for controlling the F-16s when they arrived.

"Think we'll go for a split CAP today Flash," said Razor looking for encouragement from his back seater yet confident that he would agree. "We'll take an F-16 each and set up a coordinated CAP."

He intended to put an F-16 onto the wing of each Phantom with each element positioning at opposing ends of a racetrack. This plan would favour the strengths of each jet in the formation, utilising the longer range radar of the 2 seat Phantom with its ability to engage targets beyond visual range yet retaining the high performance of the F-16 dogfighter once pulled into an engagement. Unlike the single pilot in the F-16, the navigator in the Phantom had time to spare for handling the avionics suite allowing the pilot to concentrate on flying the aircraft at extreme low level only 250 feet above the ground. Although only equipped with a stern-aspect Sidewinder, unlike the all-aspect Sparrow of the Phantom, the tactic that Razor had chosen gave the F-16 pilot the luxury of having another aircraft lead him into the fight where he could use the legendary turning performance of his machine to best effect. Arriving over the CAP datum, a large mast at Osterwick just to the south of the German towns of Hopsten and Munster, the Phantoms turned onto their patrol heading. The red and white markings of the tall radio mast bright in the afternoon sunlight would offer a distinct landmark which was visible for miles and would make the task of rendezvousing with the formation much easier if they became separated. On their easterly heading they would detect targets leaving the Army exercise area some 50 miles away to the east in the Bielefeld area. With luck, the big push would be imminent.

"Alpha Lima 07 flight, check in." The F-16s had arrived!

"Bravo"

"Mike Lima flight, Alpha Lima flight on frequency, 30 miles southwest at 5000 feet descending, both serviceable.

"Alpha Lima Flight loud and clear, how me?"

"Loud and clear also."

"We'll set up a coordinated CAP at 1500 feet. On CAP."

In an instant, he had relayed the plan to the F-16s, his snappy commands building an instant air picture. Once on CAP they would adopt tactical callsigns. Razor and Flash would become Red 1 and 2 and the other formation Blue 1 and 2. In the heat of an engagement it would be easier to work out the tactical picture. With luck it would all slot into place as professionalism and training took over.

"Got them on radar", called Flash as the Phantoms turned through southwest on their inbound CAP leg, momentarily pointing at the inbound fighters.

"Buddies, 240 degrees at 20 miles at 3000 feet descending," he called to his wingman. A few minutes elapsed.

"Visual, range 8 miles." Unfortunately, the first sight was by the F-16 pilot.

It came as no surprise to the Phantom crews that the first visual call was from the F-16s. An F-16 head-on was virtually invisible with its tiny cross section and low smoke signature. Quite often, it would manoeuvre unsighted into a killing position before making its presence felt. The Phantom by comparison was large and smoky and only succeeded by virtue of its superior weapons system and longer range missiles. Together, however, they were a perfect combination.

"Lead on the left" he called to orientate the F-16 flight leader, receiving two blips of the transmit button on the radio, the universal acknowledgement signal of fighter pilots the world over. The F-16s hove into view as they selected their allocated Phantom and joined purposefully on the left side of each. A true fighter pilot's aeroplane, sleek and aerodynamic with its chin air intake and bubble canopy, the F-16 could turn up its own backside. As the small fighter slotted into place, Razor looked across the drill Sidewinder missile mounted on the wing tip and felt a brief moment of envy. Despite his love of the Phantom, he hankered after the performance of the tiny fighter. His thoughts were fleeting as he turned back to matters in hand.

"Turning outbound," he called, "Blue rotate at CAP and call me Hot."

"Hot" and "Cold" were terms which denoted which direction the formation's radars were pointing. "Hot" would tell him that the other element was flying towards the threat whereas "Cold" meant it was flying away. His aim was to achieve spacing between the two formations to ensure that at any time at least someone's radar was pointing towards the threat. They were now scanning the airspace for the incoming raids. The package was in shape and ready for all comers.

*

The massive Polish truck ground to a halt on the outskirts of Elmpt village, its brakes shuddering and hissing. The door opened and both Kamov and the passenger jumped down, briefly shaking hands before Kamov slipped away into the back streets and the truck resumed its journey. He reappeared moments later glancing around furtively his appearance transformed into the guise of a western businessman. Making his way along the street he stopped at the car hire office; just another traveller needing transport.

*

"Bogeys," called Flash from the back of the lead Phantom, indicating that he had a radar contact which he intended to engage. "080 degrees."

The formation eased onto the heading, the F-16 already at very low level, "in the weeds" where it had been since they turned outbound. The pilot scanned the surrounding countryside for "trade," fighter pilot parlance for targets. The Phantom was higher and more vulnerable at 1500 feet but had to be there to give the radar a better chance of detecting the inbound targets. His wingman in the weeds would, hopefully, not be as visible and would provide cover for him should they be "tapped" as they flew around the holding pattern.

"Multiples, heading west."

His call raised the tension amongst the formation.

"Blue turn Hot."

He would turn all 4 fighters towards the radar contacts and take all the aircraft into the engagement with him to employ the maximum firepower of the combined formations. As he watched in his mirrors, he could see the other jets a few miles behind pulling around to follow. Flash glanced briefly at the radar warning receiver which fortunately remained silent so he pressed the attack confident in the knowledge that whatever was showing as a blip on the radar screen was not yet aware of their presence. There were targets out there to engage. Razor had pushed it up to 450 knots. Good so far.

*

Halfway through the third boring racetrack, with nothing to stimulate his interest and well into the boring fuel calibration runs, Yuri's thoughts wandered. His wife had seen the Doctor again yesterday and it was unequivocal. The cancer was terminal; a rare form of leukaemia he had said. Even the best of medical care available to someone of his seniority and status could not cure the relentless destruction of the disease. Perhaps the drugs could ease the pain. The treatment may even extend her life by weeks if not months but the disease was so far advanced that the kindest course of action would be to allow her to die in peace as quickly as possible. He wondered if she would have the courage to use the pills that she had pleaded with him to obtain. What do I really have to look forward to, he considered morosely. The Party will never change and how valuable is an ageing test pilot? Maybe prospects would be better elsewhere? This nagging thought would not go away.

"Ramrod, Ramenskoye Centre, you have drifted off track adjust your heading." The superfluous command grated but had served a purpose. He had an aircraft to fly but the constant irritation had set a trigger and a plan began to form in his mind.

*

"We're clean," Flash prompted rechecking his radar warning receiver. There was still no response from the hostile formation and the RWR remained blissfully quiet, the small instrument blank as the formations drove towards each other at the combined speeds of 1,000 miles per hour. Hopefully, he had detected a bomber formation without embedded fighter escort and could notch up some easy kills. As the formation vectored eastwards, the elements were in perfect tactical formation with his Phantom and its F-16 in the lead and the other pair in trail formation just a few miles behind. After their initial identification the trail pair could enter the fight with missiles in the air.

"5 miles astern," prompted Killer from the other Phantom, "contact the bogeys."

"Roger, bracket north."

Flash relaxed. Killer in the back of the other Phantom also had the blips on his scope and would now start to ease the other formation to the north to attempt to out-pincer the incoming hostiles. Flash would ease his pair to the south bringing the two formations into the merge from opposite sides in a classic pincer attack. As leader, it was his choice whether to lock his radar onto his chosen target and launch a Sparrow missile on entry. If he did he would have the luxury of following a smoking missile into the fight, guaranteed to put any potential enemy on the defensive. His wingman would take his prompt. The downside was that to do that he would need to be sure they were "hostiles" and not returning "friendlies." Engaging beyond visual range would advertise his presence well before his pilot was visual and able to press the advantage in air-to-air combat but the psychological impact of entering a fight watching an approaching air-to-air missile was massive and simply could not be ignored. He stared at the scope deciding when to lock on. At the minute he knew the formation was there but not how far away it was. He badly needed that important range but knew from experience, that if he locked too early, the formation would react and he would never see them again. The standard reaction to a lock was to turn away through 90 degrees making the attackers invisible on a pulse Doppler radar. He compromised, deciding that he would lock when he began to break out the individual aircraft in the formation. He hoped that would be about 15 miles. He made a few reassuring noises to his pilot.

"OK, Razor we'll take a snatch lock shortly. If the Bogeys break we'll follow the evasion. If not, we'll get a Fox 1 in the air."

His commands were short, sharp, to the point.

"Bogeys on the nose, estimate range 20," he called for the benefit of his wingman in the F-16 who had eased even lower, acting as sentinel for the Phantom. The Belgian pilot was, for the moment, relegated to the role of guardian but his time would come soon. In the other cockpit the pilots head was on gimbals rotating constantly through almost 360 degrees. The irony was that, with his new track-while-scan radar, the F-16 pilot might have more information than the Phantom navigator at this stage of the intercept. Flash returned yet again to the RWR; still silent, the circular instrument winking quietly with the electronic clutter from the mass of radar emitters which littered the North German Plain. None of them paid any attention to the Phantom.

"Ease it down Razor, I'm starting to break out the formation. Looks like two battle pairs with a two mile frontage. Could be more in there."

He was looking at a typical bomber formation with four hostile aircraft at the four corners of a square known as "card formation." The radar was breaking out a solid mass of targets and he would dearly love to engage the lead element before the mêlée which would ensue. If he was to make best use of the assembled firepower he must also watch out for the trail element of the attacking formation who would be following their leader hoping for an unwary fighter to drop into their formation and roll out ahead of them within their missile envelope. The first Phantom and F-16 into the fight would not be able to turn on the leaders but he also knew that the opposition would not deliberately engage in air-to-air combat if they had not yet dropped their bombs. They would have a time on target to meet. Shots on fighters were a bonus but their main aim was to destroy their nominated target on the ground. If they were post target all bets were off. In this instance their target was the Dutch airbase at Gilze Rijen some miles to the west of the simulated Fighter Engagement Zone but Flash was not to know that critical fact. If they had been Soviet fighters their mission could have been to hit any of hundreds of military targets. He called the F-16 to cross to the southern side of the formation anxious to give him as much turning room as possible and give him the best tactical position on entry. His plan was to extend through the formation along with his F-16 shooting the back markers leaving the trailing section to mop up the front pair. He knew that the F-16 would be looking to turn in no matter what. He just had to persuade him not to commit too soon

"Locking up." He hit his IFF interrogator, the electronic device which would check for a friendly electronic code and gave him a final check that he was not targeting a NATO aircraft. This was the critical moment. Soon the task would fall to his pilot as the fight progressed from the radar arena into the visual combat phase.

"Good lock," he shouted.

As the radar shuddered to a halt and pointed at the bogies, Flash began to talk rapidly trying to talk his pilot into a visual pick up.

"Got 'em, hostiles, Fox 1." There was no fanfare just short sharp words as the pilot squeezed the trigger holding the wings level for a couple of seconds to allow the simulated missile to leave the aircraft. Anticipating the point at which the missile would have launched, he drove the Phantom down towards the ground to the relative safety of low level, the F-16 still in battle formation on his starboard side and twitching for his opportunity to engage.

"Trailers," called Flash, "Extending."

The call prevented the F-16 from turning in behind; with trailers, he was duty bound to stay with the Phantom to engage the trailing element which, until the Sparrow missile had timed out, Flash could no longer see on the radar. Despite the logic of the tactical situation, the Phantom crew could almost feel the pent-up frustration from the Belgian's cockpit as the missile flight time ticked down to the point at which it would have struck home. They could sense him chafing at the bit, desperate to register a kill of his own.

"Red, Lead bogey on the nose 2 miles, right to left," he called to his formation, "still heading west."

He tried to reassure his leashed wingman that his chance was imminent. His simulated missile was nearly at its target but it was vital to keep the other players in the picture until they had visual contact. So far the opposition were playing to his tune and walking onto his Sparrow missile. He willed the F-16 pilot to stay with him just for a while longer.

"Red 1, splash, southerly bogey, extending," he announced, the first blood taken.

The radar broke lock and he switched his attention to the trail formation locking to the nearest aircraft.

"Trailers at 3 miles."

Too close for a further Sparrow shot. The radar was not properly locked and if it broke lock as another missile was committed the Sparrow would lose guidance and miss its prey.

"Trailers on the nose, 3 miles," he called to the F-16 the pace of the engagement quickening. He felt the familiar slug of adrenaline course through his veins.

"Tally Ho!" Without further prompting, now seeing the opponent, the F-16 pilot pulled a spine-shattering 9G turn towards the hostile aircraft.

"Ginos," he heard as the Phantom passed directly overhead the trail formation which had begun to turn hard. The F-16 careered through the slipstream and he could see a visible jolt as the airframe passed through the turbulent air converting rapidly into the stern sector of the hapless German Fiat G91 fighter bomber acting today as a simulated Soviet Mig.

"Fox 1 on the northerly man of the lead element," Killer almost shouted from the other formation, announcing his own entry into the mêlée. "Heads Up."

The atmosphere heightened. It was the most important call in beyond visual range air combat and everyone in both formations immediately checked his own RWR. If targeted, it would mean that he was receiving the unwanted attention of his own wingman. It would be the only opportunity to haul off within the next 10 seconds to avoid collecting a friendly missile. In this instance it was the F-16 tucked in astern the hostiles who was the one at risk. His turn had taken him directly into the path of the incoming Phantom and in the heat of the engagement Killer could just as easily lock to the F-16 as a G91. No one wanted a "blue on blue" engagement and his reaction must be positive and rapid if targeted. The engagement whilst aggressive, was perhaps ill-advised with Sparrow missiles still being launched from the other attacking formation; aggression over sanity.

"Red 2, Fox 2," called the F-16 pilot simulating a Sidewinder launch and racking his aircraft into a climbing turn away from the incoming Phantom. With his own kill in the bag he was looking to rejoin his leader who was already extending easterly at low level. Pushing the throttles to the firewall, he quickly slotted back into tactical formation a short distance behind the rapidly receding Phantom bringing the lead element together again.

"Blue 1, kill on the northerly," came the almost casual call from the other formation announcing that the lead element of the attacking formation was history. With the kill from the F-16, 3 out of 4 of the attackers had been destroyed. Self-satisfaction proved to be short-lived.

"Blue, heads up. Escort fighters entering from the north."

A new danger.

*

"Yuri, the Director wishes to see you in his office," shouted Kazenko his fellow test pilot from across the room. Yuri pulled himself resignedly from his chair and made his way slowly along the dingy corridor towards the Director's door knocking briefly before entering. He could see the Su-27 through the window at the end of the corridor, parked imposingly on the flight line where he had left it as he finished the earlier sortie. He wished he was airborne. Things were easier in the air.

"Andrenev, come in and be seated," muttered the Director. "The test results from the fuel evaluation sortie have been collated and are much as expected. It would appear that our predictions were accurate and the Su-27 has a combat range of approximately 4000 Kilometres which includes the allowance for a five minute air combat engagement."

Yuri marvelled at the pompous man's ability to accentuate the trivial. He could win a prize for stating the obvious.

"I have to say, however, that some of your readings were wildly in error and the evaluation staff has been busy extrapolating the results to compensate. You must pay more attention in the air Andrenev, even if the profile is boring and you consider it to be below your dignity. The data gathering events are no less important you know! Such inaccuracies will not be tolerated."

Yuri blanched at the criticism. Pay attention in the air, he fumed inwardly. How would he know, he's a scientist. He wouldn't recognise a Cobra unless it bit him on the arse! In any case he was wrong and Yuri would now have to spend time with the analysts to work through the numbers and find out why they thought there was an error. It would be obvious when he took a look. The Director droned on, his monologue emphasising points of esoteric scientific interest and Yuri was struggling to stop his attention from wandering. Suddenly, something registered as a subconscious trigger clicked.

"You will take the second prototype to Allstedt in the DDR next week. As you are aware, it is equipped with the full combat avionics suite and we need to begin to assess the supportability and deployment capability in rough field operations. There is a highway strip near to the base at Allstedt which will suit our purposes perfectly. Unfortunately, the chase aircraft is on lay-up for installation of test instrumentation and you must, therefore, undertake the trip alone. Be off now and make your preparations. Do you have any questions?"

"No," he snapped, hardly able to believe his luck and not wishing to show any emotions. He excused himself, rose and turned to leave wishing that he could appear more reluctant but inwardly he was singing. A plan was crystallising and the fuel figures which he had just collected slowly ran through his mind. With 2,000 Kilometres radius of action the fuel was more than sufficient for his plan. What ties me to this place any more he thought? His decision came abruptly with a clarity of thought which had evaded him for too long.

Defection. He would defect!

*

With his F-16 wingman firmly back in position Razor shifted his head to look around the heavy ironwork of the Phantom windscreen. He could see the tell-tale smoke trails above the wispy cloud line from a formation of German Phantoms tasked as escort fighters out to avenge the loss of the hapless G91s. The F4F doesn't have a pulse Doppler radar he thought so they will be blind coming in from above. They would have to break out his own formation visually against the backdrop of the fields. It could mean more kills for the tote.

"Blue what's your position?" he asked.

*

Horst Klingmann in the lead F4F listened to the high pitched chatter from the G91s on the tactical frequency frustrated at being late on task. Had his wingman not had a problem on start they would have rendezvoused with the Ginos before they penetrated the CAP box. They could have diverted attention away from the bombers and made it a more even fight.

"F-16 turning in, 9 o'clock two miles, counter left."

He listened to their ineffectual manoeuvring. The G91 was no agile fighter and woefully mismatched against an F-16 or even a Phantom. Too late, thought Kingman. Without RWRs, they would not have seen the attack coming until the last few miles. Some of the G91's were already history. They wouldn't even have had warning of the Sparrow missiles from the Phantoms before they struck home.

"Reverse right, he's hauling off, head 270 degrees."

Hauling off, mused Klingmann! The F-16 had almost certainly taken his shot and was by now rejoining in formation, a fleeting snapshot all that was needed for the agile fighter to achieve a kill. "Mud-movers" had little idea when it came to air-to-air combat! Another pang of frustration hit him as they were still too far away from the Ginos he was supposed to be protecting. They were already decimated and he was about to engage a mixed formation of Brit Phantoms, equipped with pulse Doppler radars which could look-down and shoot-down at low level, and F-16s, which could turn in half the radius of his own F4F. His own jet still had an old pulse radar and stern only Sidewinders and the planned upgrades were years away. His back seater was disturbingly quiet in "the pit" but at this level had little chance of breaking out the opponents with his obsolete radar. Good odds!

"Daimler," his own formation callsign, "Tally, 2 o'clock, five miles, low level. Taking it down."

Was that really his own voice prompting the engagement? The RWR on the cockpit coaming suddenly came alive as the Phantoms showed renewed interest directing their radars unerringly in his direction. Conscious of the smoke from his J79 engines he nudged the throttles forward into min burner. The smoke trail from a J79 was its biggest problem and announced the entry of an F4F into a fight well before the aircraft was visible. He had to get down into the weeds as soon as possible and he initiated a defensive, descending break to confuse the attackers. He faced up to the threat once again with a great deal of trepidation.

*

Nozzles in Blue 1 looked up at the tell-tale smoke trail which announced the entry of the F4Fs. Further north he was closer to the new threat than his leader.

"Blue engaging" he called to his leader receiving a brief acknowledgement as he eased the nose round onto north, He plugged in the afterburners watching the speed build back up to 420 knots. Within seconds he had reached his best cornering velocity. The F-16 had drifted back slightly but was still in battle formation on his left and holding it low. He pulled back firmly on the stick and the Phantom responded entering a gentle climb pointing at the nearest F4F which was descending slowly. He wanted a minimum separation pass which would leave his opponent with no turning room. Head-to-head at a combined closing speed of 900 knots, he would pass within feet of the other aircraft. If he could hold him off, he knew that he was safe from the obsolete Sidewinders which the F4F carried and meanwhile his F-16 wingman would use his superior turning ability to take the missile shot.

"Lead man's on your nose. Further bogey smoking at 2 o'clock high" called Killer from the back. Nozzles could see both.

"The F-16's low and on the left," Killer intoned. "Padlocked on the bogey on the right," meaning that he would monitor the other F4F and only call instructions if it started to threaten their aircraft. This left Nozzles free to devote his whole attention to the bogey which he was now engaging. He drove hard at the incoming Phantom still a dirty speck, positioning it directly in his gunsight. If he held this heading, the two aircraft would collide, showering wreckage over the countryside but there was no danger of that. All the aircrew in both formations were professionals and knew their trade intimately. At what he estimated was 2 miles, he pulled hard away and broke the collision positioning the incoming threat in his 2 o'clock.

"No lock," called Killer from the back, the frustration evident in his tone. The lock attempt had failed; he had been unsuccessful in his attempts to set up a head-on Sparrow shot and they were now committed to closing on the threat and entering an air combat engagement.

"The F-16's staying low," he called, "He's going to convert in the vertical!"

Nozzles knew that if he could attract the F4F pilot's attention he would force him into a predictable flight path which would leave him as an easy target for the F-16 allowing the Belgian to turn in behind and claim his kill. He eased the nose back towards the threat now wary of placing the gunsight directly onto the rapidly closing aircraft thereby generating that fatal collision. He knew that peacetime rules would only allow him to pass within 500 feet of his opponent; the safety bubble. Today he would play by the rules; in wartime, the pass would be as close as he dared make it.

"It'll be a right-to-right pass," he advised Killer, allowing his back seater to ready himself to keep sight of all the players after the merge. If the other

Phantom turned towards him as he expected it would make him even more predictable for his wingman.

"Tally," called Killer. "Other bogey still at 2 o'clock, one mile, 20 degrees high."

The back seater was already well aware of the tactical situation. The F4F whistled down the right hand side, scant yards away. Nozzles cranked the stick hard to the right but switched his attention to the other F4F to the east which was maintaining its downward vector. The F4F pilot seemed not to see him and had left far too much turning room which Nozzles knew he could exploit.

"He's only seen the F-16," shouted the back-seater. "He doesn't have us."

Both knew that this particular Phantom driver had made a fatal error.

*

Klingmann watched the light grey Brit Phantom pass close down his right hand side. He had caught sight of the F-16 below them but the geometry of the engagement made it impossible for his back seater to keep his eyes on it. The small fighter was buried somewhere deep beneath his belly. Klingmann had been forced to honour the approaching Phantom as it drove directly at him demanding his whole attention. He knew that in doing so he had left himself wide open to the F-16 pilot who must have seen his entry to the fight and would know he was predictable. The Phantom passed close aboard still climbing steeply and he racked on maximum G towards his opponent, his manoeuvre slats on the leading edge dropping into the airflow to help his turn. By now the hairs on his neck were rising. Where was that F-16 now? He screwed his neck around tucking his helmet into the headbox of the ejection seat to ease the strain looking over his shoulder into his six o'clock.

*

Captain Alain Boudain in the F-16 pulled hard towards his leader in the Phantom, although with his side stick control column in the F-16, little physical effort was needed. As he watched the two larger aircraft pass each other, he saw the F4F pull hard towards the other Phantom. He had hoped that by staying low, the crew in the other F4F would not see him leaving him the opportunity for a quick kill. He brought his nose up onto the bogey and, as he had hoped, the F4F kept the hard turn going, belly up to him as it desperately tried to bring its own nose around to threaten the other Phantom. His gunsight covered the target and he released the Sidewinder missile head into auto track listening to the change in tone as it acquired.

"Fox 2 on the F4F turning right through west," he called.

Click, Click, on the radio was his only reward as his leader acknowledged his success without fanfare. He craned his neck switching attention to the wingman that was pulling around and starting to become a threat. He cranked hard towards, negating any danger and saw his leader pulling hard around the circle in a descending flight path already threatening the wingman. He passed head-on close to the F4F in a classic "dust off", pulling up at the pass, checking the reaction of the bogey to his move. Nothing; he followed his leader. It would be some time before the Phantom could bring its nose back on.

*

Nozzles drew his gunsight onto his quarry and waited for the tone from the Sidewinder signifying that the missile had acquired its target. Nothing! His left hand dropped to the missile control panel and clicked the Sidewinder reject switch to reselect the acquisition missile knowing that at any moment the F4F crew might spot him. Dropping his head into the cockpit meant he couldn't keep the pull and his turn rate was suffering allowing the Phantom to generate angles. He cursed the lack of a weapons selector on the stick and the artificiality of only having the single training missile on the LAU missile pylon. He was expecting at any moment to lose the shot opportunity but what was the German back-seater doing, playing scrabble? He still hadn't seen him! Maybe the F-16 was more inviting? A strident tone assailed his eardrums as the missile came up. He had a steady growl from the Sidewinder.

"Fox 2 on the F4F descending on south passing 1500 feet." The relief in his tone was evident as he simultaneously pulled the trigger.

The call came out of the blue.

"Blue 2 break starboard," Killer almost shouted to the F-16 pilot. He had been watching the F-16 move back into tactical formation behind them but all was not well. "Bogey in your 6 o'clock at one mile, missile break!"

*

In following his leader, Boudain had unwittingly left his own 6 o'clock open to the trailing F4F formation who had yet to enter the fight. Jürgen Helle in one of the trailing F4Fs felt grateful for small mercies. The F-16 pulled a majestic wing over, belly up through his windscreen and rolled out perfectly in his gunsight. A swift squeeze of the trigger and......one in the bag! His gunsight camera whirred. Not many gunsight films from F4Fs tracking F-16s he thought. This would be on the wall of the Squadron tonight he thought.

Boudain realised too late that he had blown it. The F4F had him cold.

*

"Blue disengaging and hauling off east," called Nozzles resignedly bringing his formation round and putting his wingman back into battle formation, his casual manner belying the annoyance that they all felt at the simulated loss of the F-16. They drove for the sanctuary of low level realising that, if this had been for real, the F-16 would have been a smoking hole in the North German Plain. Still engaged, Flash looked at the mass of blips on his radar unable to break out the hostiles from the friendlies. He knew that Blue section was already disengaging and that they had already taken out the leading section of the hostile formation. Red's task was now to mop up the trailers. He could see Blue moving slowly from left to right across his radar display followed by a pair of contacts which he assumed must be the leading F4Fs. Looks like they're trying to take some cheap shots to save a little face he thought to himself.

"Blue 1 from Red 1, you have two Bogeys following you out," he called.

"Affirmative, already splashed" responded Nozzles aware of the terriers snapping at his heels. Flash switched his attention to the other F4Fs. Reselecting pulse Doppler mode he moved his acquisition markers around the nearest contact on his display and squeezed the trigger. The radar stopped its scan and directed its energy at the selected target as the full track display popped up.

"Good lock" he called to Razor "Fox 1," he called prompting his pilot to pull the trigger as another simulated Sparrow was launched. Immediately, the closing velocity fell away rapidly as the F4Fs turned away from their tormentors dropping chaff as they did so, alerted by the sudden intrusion of the RWR. A Sparrow would be following them as they hauled off but whether it would reach is prey after the turn away was debateable. They were aborting their attack and leaving the fight and might live to fight another day.

"Missile trashed. Bogeys disengaging. Red hauling off and returning to CAP." called Razor, more than content with the kills which they had already claimed.

"See you back at CAP datum, Blue."

The fight had lasted less than 5 minutes. On this occasion the shots had been simulated but the practice would keep the front-line crews at peak efficiency. Had it been for real, five hostile aircraft and one F-16 would have been destroyed. Good odds for NATO on this occasion but not always so one-sided.

3 PARTYTIME

Mark Keene and Jim Gordon walked back across the dispersal towards the Operations complex. The exercise was over and all around the dispersal there was frantic activity to return equipment which had been in constant use for the last three days. Razor, his bonedome in one hand and his respirator haversack in the other chatted animatedly with Flash as they crossed the taxiway.

"Couldn't handle the fighters eh!" rang out a pointed jibe from across the dispersal. "Had to leave those to the experts, huh?"

Killer and his pilot had shut down their own jet and were following them back towards the operations complex.

"Just do your sums mate. Let's see who gets the biggest score when the QWIs have assessed the films!"

The four aircrew walked into the locker room depositing flying helmets onto the felt-covered table by the door. The over-worked safety equipper was working away trying to clear the rapidly growing pile of flying gear. It would be some hours before he completed the after flights and stowed the kit back in the aircrew lockers. For some, a beer was farther away than for others. Flash forced his way over to his own locker past the knot of bodies which had formed inside the doorway and began to strip off the layers of kit that he wore on every sortie. Undoing the breast plate of the life-saving jacket which would keep him afloat if he landed in the water, he stepped out of the complicated arrangement of straps and webbing which made up the torso harness, part of the equipment which would suspend him in his parachute if he was ever forced to eject. Next he unzipped his G-suit, a green corset which fitted snugly around the legs to prevent blood from draining to the legs and away from his brain during high G manoeuvres. "Greying out" as it was known, was the phenomenon whereby vision gradually disappeared leading ultimately to loss of consciousness if left unchecked. This had caused the loss of many an aircraft in the early days of high performance flight. His pilot had often told him not to bother wearing it as it was quieter in the cockpit when the blood drained away. Well, until he came round at least! Free of the expensive kit which was unceremoniously dumped in the pile on the counter he renegotiated the minor traffic jam through the milling bodies. Returning from a sortie followed a standard ritual and the next port of call was the line hut to sign the aircraft back in.

"Afternoon Chief," called Razor to the Line Controller as he walked into the busy room. "It's a real hive of activity in here this afternoon."

"Amazing that is Sir," replied the Controller with a wry grin. "Looks like the lads want to get away for the afternoon. It's not like them to be quite so keen is it? Rumour is there's a party on tonight!"

"No surprises there," replied Razor.

The end of an exercise was the one time when aircraft were put to bed carrying snags. Everyone had given 100% effort during the exercise and small problems would be fixed another day; even if SENGO would need a little creative accountancy to meet the aircraft generation targets.

"Whiskey is serviceable so that shouldn't hold you up," Razor continued. "The right engine was a bit hot during the engine checks but we'll keep an eye on that. I'll put in a flight requirement for the next pilot to keep an eye on it. Just gas it up and lock the doors. I think Papa has a minor snag but we can probably lim it."

A lim, or flight limitation, was a minor snag which had no operational impact and could be rectified next time the aircraft was unserviceable.

"Flight Lieutenant Norris is just on his way in now, he'll give you the story."

Nozzles, Flash and Killer pushed up to the counter to complete their own paperwork. Both Navigators filled in the avionics diaries which allowed the aircrew to monitor the performance of each aircraft's weapons system. A quick look in the log would tell whether the sortie had a chance of getting by with a working radar. He passed the radar films to the Line Chief for processing. Nozzles called for an avionics tradesman to debrief his own snag. The avionics specialist ambled over.

"The radio is hopeless on Papa, Serge. Reception breaks up every time you put on any G and it makes it a bit tricky in combat," he explained. "We could probably live with it for another sortie but it's getting worse. If you've got any spares it would be best to change it."

The Phantom's radios were bad at the best of times, particularly at the higher end of the frequency range but any degradation from the already poor standard made the crew's lives even more difficult. Even as he said it, Nozzles could see the grin spreading across the sergeant's face.

"I think we'll probably have to leave it until Monday Sir," he replied. "I think stores will probably have packed up by now. Getting spares might be tricky."

Norris smiled in return. "I think that might be the best bet Sarge, under the circumstances. How about a flight check next sortie?"

"Good plan Sir!"

At the end of an exercise, the highest priority was to pack up and get to the pub as quickly as possible. Everyone worked flat out and some would have no escape even though the exercise had finished. The lights would burn around the dispersal until a lot later. Even so, the strenuous efforts of the previous days were easily relieved with a swift alcoholic inject and suddenly became tolerable. The reaction was entirely predictable. Finishing their paperwork, the aircrew drifted through the maze of corridors into the unhardened annex attached to the main ops complex. Normally, there would be a comprehensive debrief covering each and every aspect of the sortie, dissecting it into its constituent parts and extracting lessons from every manoeuvre. Each event would be analysed in turn to attempt to learn where different moves may have made an impact on the outcome; where altered tactics may have made the execution more effective. Today they would be spared the ordeal. On exercise, the effectiveness of the sortie stood or fell by the radar film. No film, no kill was the adage. Results from the precious celluloid would be published the following week after the weapons instructors, the QWIs, had analysed each film in detail and assessed all the relevant aspects. Was the tracking time for the semi-active Sparrow sufficient? Was the trigger press marker caught on film. Was the target inside weapons parameters? All these items would be checked and double checked and each claim categorised. The accolade would be to top the list of confirmed claims; more than five conferring "Ace" standard, even if only simulated. The most heinous crime was to make a claim which could subsequently not be ratified. If in doubt it was wise to be reticent. Record the shot but don't claim the kill. In the crewroom, the remainder of the squadron crews gathered around the coffee bar each holding the obligatory post-flight cup of coffee engaging in the equally obligatory dissection of the exercise. Hands moved in simulated combat describing the thrills and spills of the engagements and their successes or otherwise. These discussions would go on long into the evening. "Slats", Phil Ranger, was describing one of his intercepts.

"We were half way to RCAP 1, just past Smokey Joe's in Area 2 and we picked up a slow mover. JB set up a stern approach; we figured it was a helicopter so we decided to identify it first. As we tipped in, I could see it was a CH53, one of the big heavy-lift jobs, but it had something hanging beneath it. We pulled alongside and, bugger me, it was carrying an under slung load! It was the VAK 191, the old kraut Harrier - in a sling!" Hoots of derision erupted from the other side of the crewroom.

"Bet you claimed two kills on that, you old goat." shouted "Tom", Andy Sawyer amid protests of innocence from the bantering pilot. Razor moved behind the coffee bar and poured two cups of coffee handing the other to Flash.

"Just time for a quick shower, into our party suits and over to the Bar for a few sharpeners, or three!"

"Yeah, you need to change that flying suit, Old Son," offered Flash, "otherwise it's going to the party on its own!"

The cockpit environment of the Phantom was not renowned for comfortable living. It was either so cold that it spat ice cubes through the conditioning vents, or so hot that the sweat would pour freely. There was no happy medium.

"Time to hit the Pub. The Jaguar guys from Brüggen are coming to Happy Hour tonight and they're arriving by train!" called out a strident voice from the far side of the room. Brüggen was only 5 miles from Wildenrath as the crow flies, but served by a rail link for shipment of heavy munitions and for resupply. Tonight it would be used for an alternative purpose.

Razor and Flash ambled across the quiet dispersal. The HAS doors were now firmly closed, the brooding Phantoms dormant behind the dark green clamshells. The angular concrete shelters were sprayed with a dark brown tone-down paint to make them more difficult to see from the air and, therefore, harder to target. They took on a more sinister appearance in the fading light but the effect was lost on the aircrew who just thought of Delta Dispersal as a place of work. Razor unlocked his car, a black MGB roadster, and leaned over to open the door for Flash. He fired the engine into life and manoeuvred the car slowly past the bollards and barbed wire traps which peppered the dispersal before easing the car out onto the perimeter road. It picked up speed as it slipped past the HASs set deep in their revetments, surrounded by fir trees and protected by grassy banks. The barbed wire which ringed the dispersal appeared menacing in the gathering dusk, there to dissuade any would be intruder that Delta Dispersal was no easy option. Following the road which curved gently right and crossed the end of Runway 09, the thrum of the car engine was strangely settling after the roaring whistle of the Phantom cockpit. The approach lights which edged the runway still glowed brightly as Razor looked down the strip. As he crossed the threshold, registering the familiar sight, albeit from a slightly different angle, the lights blinked out and the runway faded into the darkening horizon. Endex really did mean Endex and there would be no practice diversions to Wildenrath tonight. The car continued past the vast hangars, unused by aircraft since the commissioning of the hardened sites. The Army parked their bulldozers which were used for battle damage repair in the hangar nowadays. It crossed over the main drag and into the domestic area where the Officers' Mess and its associated buildings nestled in the pine trees which covered RAF Wildenrath.

The lights shone a welcome as Razor allowed the MGB to coast into one of the parking slots at the front of the low, single storey building. Even the domestic accommodation was protected by trees and painted green to reduce its visibility from the air. Inside the Mess, Happy Hour was already in full flow. "The Dolphins", 19 Squadron, otherwise known as "The Cod Squad" because of their squadron crest which depicted a dolphin, had been at it for some time already. Debbie Harrie blared out from the jukebox next to the dance floor in the Bar Annex but thoughts were far from dancing. For this short period during the week, women, other than WRAF officers, were not overly welcome. Some aspects of life on a fighter squadron were still utterly chauvinistic. The time was for drinking. Clusters of green suits interspersed with others wearing "cabbage kit" jostled to attract the attention of Frederick the German Barman. Razor and Flash waited impatiently but finally caught his eye and Razor ordered two large Dortmunders.

"The first of the night," said Razor. "Cheers!"

As the amber liquid slipped down, the partition between the Bar and the Ante Room suddenly burst open and the roar of "Fighter Sweep!" erupted as the pilots of the Brüggen Jaguar Wing burst across the Bar in a solid line of green, flying-suit clad bodies. The Phantom crews, caught temporarily unawares, stayed back against the Bar knowing that it would be impossible at this stage to break the momentum of a properly organised "Fighter Sweep". The line of bodies swept across the room catching one unwary Air Traffic Control Officer, his beer cascading in a violent spray all over the carpet. The sweep finally spent itself against the far wall of the Bar and a heap of cackling Jaguar pilots demanded beer. Happy Hour had begun. Within minutes, beer in hand, friends and acquaintances from the two Wings were deep in serious conversation but at this stage the topic was exclusively flying.

*

Flight Lieutenant Keith James, the Station Intelligence Officer eased his Golf GTi into the parking spot. The village of Wassenberg was quiet, the streets dully lit by the lamps along the main road. Should I be doing this he thought to himself? I've only been here 3 weeks and already I'm on the razzle. No time for cold feet now he decided, Helen will be arriving next week and I won't be able to pop out to the club when she arrives will I? He quickly locked the car and, turning the collar of his coat up around his ears, set off across the road where the lights of the Bar Femina glowed. The glaring red neon light at the top of the window showed the true nature of the business which went on in this particular club. Still can't believe that this is legal in Germany he thought to himself. Couldn't happen in downtown Stoke could it? He walked quickly across the street and knocked on the discreet side entrance to the brothel. After a short delay, the door opened slightly, the tug of a security chain restraining further movement of the door.

"Ja, was möchten Sie?" came a sharp feminine voice.

"Guten Abend," Keith responded.

"Come in Liebling," replied the Madam, her face relaxing visibly. "You are English Ja?"

"Yes."

So much for the discreet approach he thought, I guess it stands out like a dog's balls!

"Come in, come in. Let me take your coat and I will introduce you to some of my fräuleins," she said, happier now that she had a customer. I have some of the prettiest girls in West Germany and they have been waiting just for you."

She led him across to the Bar where another man whispered quietly, his head close to the ear of a slightly bored looking girl. As the slightly inebriated punter turned to look at her, her face was transformed and she smiled seductively, suddenly apparently enraptured by his overtures. Keith spotted the change and realised that love was not high on the agenda here. There were, however, other offsets. She was very pretty. As he eased onto the barstool, another girl appeared from behind a curtain and slid onto the stool beside him.

"Hello Schatze!" she purred. Keith turned towards her and was immediately taken aback. She was absolutely stunning; he felt instantly shy. Her sultry brown eyes gazed from beneath long dark hair. This was not at all what he had expected; more a worn, tawdry prostitute yet he gazed at a beautiful woman.

"Would you like to buy me a drink?" she asked. "I only drink champagne but then, I know you Englishmen always buy a lady the best, do you not?"

"Err, of course," he stuttered, totally oblivious to the cliché but quickly recovering his composure, before realising that a drink had already appeared in front of her.

"A Pils for me."

"Are you from the airbase," she asked, knowing the answer perfectly well. "Are you a flyer?" Her eyes appeared to brighten at the prospect.

"No," he responded, "I'm the Intelligence officer on the Wing Operations staff," he replied realising that within seconds, he had broken the prime rule. Here he was in a foreign "Club" discussing his role at the base with a total stranger. Suckered in by a cheap compliment but what a stranger!

"I knew it. You look intelligent, Schatze."

Behind the Bar, the Madam smiled, turned and walked slowly through the door into the back room where a man lounged on a sofa, arms behind his head apparently sleeping.

"We have one," she whispered in German. "Quite young, very nervous and very married. What is more, he says he is the Station Intelligence Officer. I think he should suit your purposes very nicely."

Viktor Kamov smiled. The Madam had responded well to his financial proposal and apparently success was swift. Climbing the stairs quietly, he let himself into a room and double checked the layout. All was in place. The mirror to his left had been carefully cleared of obstructions and gave an uninterrupted view of the large bed which was covered in red-trimmed black sheets. An ideal contrast he thought irreverently, adjusting the spotlight trained on the bed before closing the door and letting himself into the adjacent room. Two cameras were directed at the two-way mirror, one a large video camera, the other, a single lens reflex camera sporting a long lens. He sat down to wait.

Downstairs, Keith James was deep in discussion with the girl who had moved closer. He could smell a musky perfume and realised that he wanted her badly.

"How much......"

"Schhh," she whispered, placing a long elegant finger to his lips, the long red finger nail stroking him provocatively.

"I like you so much that I am going to ask my friend to join us. She knows things that will bring you to the heights of....."

The suggestion hung tantalisingly in the air.

"Only 500 Marks for both of us, Schatze. Think of the experience."

With that she coaxed him, unresisting from the bar stool and led him gently upstairs. He let his hand drop around her waist as they climbed the stairs and, as the door to the room on the landing opened, he felt himself propelled gently forwards. Another stunning blonde girl lay on the bed highlighted by a spotlight. I'm in heaven he thought! The blond rose, her lace negligee flowing behind her. Keith was aware of her generous breasts restrained by tight black lingerie emphasising a deep cleavage. She moved slowly towards him, her slight waist moving seductively, and draped her arms around his shoulders kissing him slowly and sensuously. Her hair fell around his shoulders as she enveloped him. Behind, Keith felt the firm pressure of voluminous breasts against his back as hands forced their way between him and the gently moving blonde and began, slowly, to unbutton his shirt. The dark haired girl behind him moved suggestively against him and he caught the heady air of mingling perfumes as the blonde turned her attention to his Levis. Naked, he was forced back onto the bed. Mixed sensations assailed his mind and he could feel one girl working him slowly and expertly, while the other massaged strong oil into his chest. It made his mind swim as he tried to identify the elixir. What was it? Who cares, he decided. The blonde straddled him and eased herself slowly onto his erection, writhing and groaning as she did so. He arched his back in pleasure.

"Keith, Keith," the blond groaned as the dark haired girl ran her fingers over his chest kissing him. His heightened senses briefly questioned the fact that he had not told her his name. How could she..........? She cut short the question as her tongue probed areas which he had never before even considered. He groaned in total delight and pleasure. Next door, the cameras clicked and whirred.

The dark haired girl sat at the dressing table staring vacantly at her reflection as her hand moved to her throat and unfastened a black choker. She began slowly and deliberately to remove her makeup. Satisfied with the transformation, her hand moved to her forehead and peeled back the long wig and unceremoniously deposited it on the floor.

*

The level of noise had steadily built in direct proportion to the amount of beer consumed. In the corner of the Bar, a pyramid of bodies was forming, green flying suit interspersed with blue uniforms. A Jaguar pilot was orchestrating the growing structure with gusto as a Phantom pilot, now divested of his flying suit, was prepared with boot polish. The aim of the exercise was clear; to imprint a "cheek" mark on the Bar ceiling. The pyramid was ready and the not unwilling volunteer climbed gingerly to the apex. A ceremonial dropping of the boxer shorts and the deed was done. A bum print on the roof! The pyramid collapsed amid a cacophony of mirth as chuckling aircrew returned to the serious business in hand. More beer. Meanwhile, the erstwhile willing victim began to consider the problems associated with the temporary embellishments. As the evening progressed, discussions became more and more intense and the world was, increasingly, put to rights. Conversation turned to more important topics such as where the first million was coming from and how to trap more women; complex in a bar full of males. Attention was suddenly drawn to the main door as Burner and Tom, a 92 Squadron crew, dragged in a piano which the squadron had been saving for the occasion.

"Is it a player?" shouted JB.

"No it's a burner," responded Killer setting the seeds in the minds of the assembled crowd. Slats drew up a chair and launched into his repertoire of bar songs as the small gathering around the piano rapidly grew and more joined in. The strident tones of "The Flag" and other squadron favourites rang out through the Mess but it was already apparent that, despite valiant efforts, the piano was long past its best and beyond salvation. The notes became increasingly flat.

"Burn it," shouted a voice from the far side of the Bar.

"It's 'orrible," called another. The suggestion grew in popularity and eventually, the piano was dragged bodily, a determined Slats still attempting to complete his portfolio as it passed through the doorway. The well-oiled team somehow managed to negotiate a highly polished table in the Mess foyer and manhandled the piano inexorably towards the car park. En route, a sledgehammer appeared from nowhere along with a toilet seat from the Mess annex. The prime rule in piano burning was that all pieces of the piano should be small enough to pass through the latter having been rearranged by the former. The piano was ceremoniously placed at the centre of attention in the car park. As efforts intensified, the sledgehammer swung majestically to the accompaniment of more bar songs, although by now without the assistance of the piano. The instrument was rapidly reduced to matchsticks and a funeral pyre began to form. As the incipient fire was stoked, flames began to lick around the base and larger items were added, including remnants of the keyboard. Bodies linked arms and the strains of "I'm a Lumberjack" rent the night air with the gathering taking on the appearance of a tribal ritual. Suddenly, the roaring of a powerful engine drowned the proceedings as one of the Station fire engines hove into view, its blue light flashing urgently.

"All right Gentlemen," said the Crew Chief, "party's over," as the fire crew set about dousing the inferno. There were groans and jeers as the aircrew watched the remnants of the piano hissing while the flames slowly died. Prospects dampened; they drifted slowly back into the Bar.

In the Bar Annex, Flash had moved across to talk with Julie Kingston, the new WRAF air traffic control officer. She had watched the increasing mayhem with just a little concern as it was a far cry from the more ordered existence she had become accustomed to during her recent training at RAF Shawbury. Although taken aback by the antics; she had only been at Wildenrath for three weeks, she had already made a great impact on the bachelors of both squadrons. Her long blond hair normally tucked neatly in a tight bun at the nape of her neck and her strikingly pretty features, turned heads in any company. In the largely male confines of the Officers' Mess, she was noticed by everyone without exception. Flash opened the conversation carefully, aware of the dangers of Dortmunder and its ability to kill the most promising of relationships before it had even developed. He restricted himself to the safe topics at first.

"How did your first exercise go?"

"Oh fine," she replied "I haven't been categorised yet and I guess I only saw the easy side of it. Some of the guys were working 12 hours on and 12 hours off for three days."

"Did you spend your whole time in the Tower?"

"No, SATCO thought I should get around a bit so after a couple of shifts, he sent me on walkabout with the evaluation staff."

"Did you get over to Delta?"

"Yes but you were all airborne. I got to chat to the Boss on the operations desk for an hour."

"Lucky old Boss," said Flash grinning and he meant it. Behind them in the Main Bar, there was more hooting and roaring as the piano team returned, frustrated by their lack of success when confronted by the fire engine. Glasses were immediately recharged and more war stories were offered up to anyone who would listen. Flash and Julie became more and more engrossed in their conversation as the dull roar continued unabated next door. Shortly, a barked command announced the departure of the return transport for Brüggen and the indisputably drunken pilots of the Jaguar Wing were poured onto the large coach for the short trip home. There was much back slapping and happy camaraderie as the stragglers were rounded up by the more sober spokesmen, although by this stage, sobriety was a relative term. As the diehards drifted out, Flash and Julie were still deep in conversation and he had switched his efforts to attempts to convince her of his prowess on the ski slopes which he would happily prove, given the opportunity in the near future. Razor sidled over, considering the ethics of making a play for the girl but his navigator had invested a great deal of effort under extremely demanding circumstances considering the rabble which had just been deposited on the coach. He grudgingly accepted that crew loyalty might be more important than personal gratification; but only on this one occasion.

"Tom's cracking a few bottles open in his room when you're finished Flash," he suggested. "How about you Julie?" he offered with a suggestive wink. She smiled at the offer but returned her attentions to Flash. Razor moved off back to the juke box where a huddle of aircrew from the other squadron were deep in meaningful conversation and, never one to tread lightly, barged his way into the conversation. Flash looked around. The shutters had been drawn over the Bar which had rapidly emptied. Apart from a few stalwarts who had yet to solve the problems of the universe, he, Julie and the group by the juke box were the only ones who remained.

"Do you fancy a nightcap in Tom Sawyer's Cabin?" he asked not sure if it was a good or a bad idea.

"I think I'd rather have a quiet nightcap in your room." She smiled engagingly. Flash needed no further prompting as he helped Julie down from the bar stool and directed her discretely to the door lest the juke box crowd should notice and spoil all his efforts.

They left the Mess aiming towards the group of single storey buildings which housed the single officers' quarters. The noise of the party which continued in Tom's room rang out through the still night air. The first chill of autumn cut the air and Julie shivered slightly as they crossed the road. Flash moved closer and draped his flying jacket around her shoulders. She turned and smiled, passing her arm around his waist as he drew the jacket closer around her. He could smell her perfume as she let her head fall onto his shoulder and the slightly irreverent thought crossed his mind that he would have problems explaining that perfumed smell on his flying kit on Monday morning. They arrived at the door of his room and he pushed his way in. It was compact and functional, fitted out with standard RAF issue furniture with a small sink in the corner. Opposite his bed, the items essential for any bachelor were crammed next to the wardrobe - golf clubs, skis, squash and tennis racquets. Large German beer steins lined every shelf around the room. The functional appearance of the furniture was in total contrast to the rack of expensive hi-fi equipment which sprang into life as he selected a tape from a large carousel nearby. The strains of Barbara Streisand's "Woman in Love" melted from the large speakers as he turned, smiling, hoping that the lyrics would strike a chord with Julie. He poured two large Asbach brandies from a decanter and sidled over, taking a small sip from his own before offering her the other large glass. She took both glasses from him and placed them down carefully, drew him towards her by the lapels of his flying suit and kissed him sensuously on the lips. Flash responded moving his hands around her back and dropped them to her firm, pert rear and pulled her gently towards him. At that moment the door burst open and, amid hoots and roars of delight, Razor and the 19 Squadron aircrew tumbled into the room.

"Party time in Uncle Tom's Cabin," they announced dragging Flash bodily from the room. Razor stepped forward and offered his arm politely to Julie. She smiled as he escorted her smugly through the door.

Much later, and the crews lay in a wide circle on the floor of Tom Sawyer's room the last of the energetic banter having died. The hi-fi still pushed out the strains of haunting love songs, entirely optimistic in the largely male environment but eyes were drooping. Others lay back appreciating the mood, eyes all but closed. Some gave in to the alcohol-induced stupor and, gradually, the numbers dwindled. JB stumbled out waving his arm and muttering subdued goodbyes looking decidedly green. Flash and Julie were closeted in the corner, Julie with her head resting gently in the crook of his shoulder, whispering quietly in his ear. They rose slowly and eased past the dormant bodies; this time maybe.............

"G' night Dude," whispered Razor as the door closed quietly.

4 THE TRAP

Keith James sauntered into the Officers' Mess through the large glass double doors and exchanged a few words with the young receptionist. Walking over to the small alcove which contained the mail racks, he noticed an airmail letter in his personal slot. Unusual he thought, most mail normally comes through the BFPO system. How come this one is air mail? He opened the letter and immediately recognised the address of his old friend, John Kitching who said he would be passing through Wildenrath on his way to a convention in Düsseldorf and could stop for lunch. How about the Haus Sell in Arsbeck where they had eaten last time? Why not hit the Company expense account? John obviously has one of those new word processors thought Keith. Nice typing; he smiled and pocketed the letter. Had he been more observant he would have spotted the London postmark, many miles distant from his old friend's home in Stoke. As it was, he looked forward to seeing him again. It had been too long. He rifled through the other packages beneath the rack collecting one which he had been waiting for and returned through the foyer to his car which he had left, engine running, outside the main entrance.

*

In a small village 10 km from Ramenskoye, Yuri Andrenev drew up alongside the small public phone booth outside the Post Office and killed the engine of his jeep. He sat for a few moments watching the random movements of a few locals around the front of the village store. Satisfied that no one was showing any particular interest, he climbed from the car and opened the door of the empty booth. Picking up the handset, he dialled a Moscow number, involuntarily tapping his fingers nervously as he waited for a response.

"British Embassy Moscow. May I help you?"

"I would like to speak to the Duty Officer and please make it quick. I have very little time."

"Can I say who's calling?" replied the pleasant female voice.

"Not at the moment," responded Yuri tetchily, "please make it quick."

He listened intently for the warning click on the line which would signify that his call was being intercepted but could hear nothing. Perhaps he should have left the jeep around the corner away from the phone booth, he suddenly realised. If they managed to tie the call to this particular booth he could be in trouble. He thought about ringing off and moving the car as a precaution just as a voice came on the line.

"Duty Officer, can I help?"

"Listen carefully because I can't be too specific. You have no need to know my name at present but I have a proposal to put to you which I feel certain you will be interested in. Can you arrange for us to meet somewhere in the Ramenskoye area?"

"Perhaps....."

He cut in, deliberately dropping the carrot. Using the name of the secret test centre, he was certain the British operative would recognise the value of the contact.

"It would be difficult for me to arrange for travel papers at the moment," he teased.

"I'm sure that would be possible but you realise that we operate under fairly strict travel restrictions ourselves and I would have to be fairly sure that the effort was going to be worthwhile."

The man was slow. If only you knew, thought Yuri.

"I know you will not be disappointed but you will have to take my offer on trust," he replied. "I have already taken a great risk just in contacting you. Please arrange to meet me by the park benches at the Lakeside at 1030 on Sunday. Come alone because I shall want to make sure that no one is watching us. That is most important or the deal is off."

Yuri replaced the receiver hoping that he had not spent too long on the phone but not really knowing how he could have avoided it. He could have tried the direct approach to the Embassy but it would have been equally fraught with danger. As he made his way from the booth, he glanced around rechecking that no one was taking an overt interest in his activities. You're being paranoid he told himself.

*

The young KGB operative lolled against the desk his hand holding the earphones in place on his head, listening to the turgid conversation between an engineer from the Test Centre and a specialist from the Tupolev Design Bureau in Moscow. Unable to understand the majority of their discussion, he listened for any of the key words which his brief suggested he should watch for, words that could highlight any particularly sensitive conversations which may interest his superiors. A light flashed on an adjacent console showing that a public phone box in the village close to Ramenskoye had been connected to the national network automatically triggering the recording equipment which was always rigged. It was Party policy; all calls to Moscow were automatically recorded and analyzed for the good of the citizens. As the ancient reel-to-reel device began turning, the tape immediately fouled on the recording heads and began to deposit itself uselessly in a pile on the floor beside the machine. The young conscript, intent in his task, failed to notice the growing heap and continued to listen to the rambling conversation. Perhaps he would try the telephone circuits to the officers' married quarters next. This stuff was all well and good but there had been a particularly interesting conversation between an Officers' wife and the manager of the local store last week. It was amazing the lengths to which some people would go in order to supplement the weekly ration. He hoped the meat had been tasty! Across the room, the tape recorder ground to a halt as the heads became hopelessly tangled by metres of unravelled tape. Meanwhile, the operative flicked his selector to the military network hoping for something more interesting. The indicator light on the console flashed off as the connection was broken.

5 BATTLE FLIGHT SCRAMBLE

The 92 Squadron Battle Flight hardened aircraft shelter sat in the middle of the sister squadron's dispersal at Wildenrath. Battle Flight at Wildenrath was the Quick Reaction Alert Facility or QRA. As with all of the installations on the base it nestled in the midst of the pine forest sheltered from prying eyes. Few knew the things that passed between the controllers in their bunkers well to the east and the aircrew who sat on alert in the rear area ready to scramble at any time. Their target could be a light aircraft straying into the Air Defence Interception Zone or, just as likely, a Soviet Mig-21 Fishbed straying over the Inner German Border. Either way, if the hooter sounded, the Phantoms would scramble and had to be airborne within 5 minutes of that call.

"Mike Lima 74, this is Loneship you are loud and clear on hand over, how do you read?" came the distinctive tones of the German Fighter Controller.

"Loneship, 74, loud and clear also," responded Razor.

"Request snap vector," called Flash, anxious to intercept their target as soon as possible. Any delay could mean the contact might cross the border.

"Slow mover bears 090 range 35 at 5,000 feet, interrogate and report."

"Roger Loneship, Judy," called Flash, the codeword signalling that he had radar contact on the target and had taken control of the intercept. The target was difficult to track being so slow and Flash had his work cut out to maintain contact. They had been launched to investigate a slow moving contact in the ADIZ, the Air Defence Interception Zone, and had been tasked to visually identify the unknown contact approaching the border between east and west; the "Iron Curtain." They were now within 45 miles of the Inner German Border and suddenly, navigation was very important as in 7 short minutes they could be in East German airspace. Any cock-ups now and they could be in as much trouble as the pilot of the aircraft which Flash was tracking and about to lock up. The odds suggested it would be a light aircraft pilot who had become a disorientated.

"Come starboard 20 degrees Razor, I've got the guy on the scope but he's hard to track. It must be a puddle jumper," said Flash.

"20 degrees it is, rolling out 110 degrees, "Delta H shows he's 10,000 feet below. Taking the height down to 3000 feet."

"Best make it 4,000 feet Razor, there are some big hills around here and the safety altitude is 3400 feet in this area. I'll set up an 8 mile displaced stern approach," he called. "We don't want to get too tight on him. If he's a light aircraft he may be difficult to track in pulse as we come round the corner. We may need to go radar to visual."

Flash knew he would have difficulty keeping contact on the target and that his pilot may have to complete the intercept visually. There were just some things the radar couldn't do and light aircraft stretched it to its limits. In the meantime he had to get his pilot's eyes onto their quarry.

"Got it, I'll keep my eyes peeled."

"Come back port onto east. He's on a 90 intercept displaced on the left and he's range 20 miles. The final turn will be to port."

"Loneship Mike Lima 74, range 20, switches safe," called Razor. This safety check was important because Battle Flight aircraft flew fully armed at all times, ready for Armageddon. The last thing the crew wanted to do was shoot down this light aircraft when their task was to prevent it straying into hostile foreign airspace. Underneath the aircraft, 4 Sparrows, 4 Sidewinders and a fully loaded Suu-23 Gatling gun hummed quietly, one switch selection separated the target from oblivion.

"74 switches safe," acknowledged the controller.

"Range 12," called Flash watching the blip on the scope, all the time calculating the geometry to make sure that his approach would roll him out at the correct range. He was cross-checking key ranges and azimuths on his radar display; if the target met these gates he would roll out two miles behind.

"Start your final turn now. On the nose range 4 miles, 1,000 feet high," Flash intoned, the cadence alerting Razor that they were approaching the critical phase of the intercept. It was here where mistakes could be made. "Contact on the nose at 2 miles. He's only doing 200 knots Razor. It's going to be a passing visident so bring your speed back to 250 knots."

250 knots was the minimum comfortable manoeuvring speed for the Phantom. Razor immediately dropped ½ flap to give him more control over the large and now lumbering aircraft. The Phantom was cumbersome at slow speed and exhibited some particularly vicious handling characteristics. If the pilot used aileron to control the turn, as he would in a traditional aircraft, it would respond in exactly the opposite sense and enter an uncontrollable spin in the opposite direction. At 4,000 feet or below it would be the end of an expensive airframe and the spin would be irrecoverable.

"Tally Ho," he called, telling Flash that he could see their quarry, still a dot in the distance. "Keep talking."

Flash set up the identification profile. He would close in 1,000 feet below the target directly below the belly before starting a slow climb holding the target dead ahead. At 1000 yards he would throw in an offset manoeuvre pushing the target away from the nose and attempt to identify the light aircraft as the fighter passed close by. The procedure assumed that it was dark and that the target would not be visible until very close range. Today much of the pressure was off as Razor could already see their quarry in the bright sunlight. Despite this, the crew stuck to the familiar procedures to ensure success. It was very easy to overcook a visual join on a slow target and flash past too quickly. If they failed on the first pass it may be too late for this unwary private pilot who may well stray over the border in his enthusiasm.

"On the nose, 8 degrees high, 2,000 yards, 50 knots overtake." pattered Flash. He would keep this commentary going for as long as his pilot needed the information. "On the nose.....", the litany continued.

"Loneship, 74, tally one light twin, heading 080 degrees at 5,000 feet. Closing for identification," called Razor to the ground controller.

Back in the cockpit, they readied for the pass which would be fleeting.

"I'm happy with the profile Flash, get ready for the pictures."

"Roger 74, Loneship, instruct him to recover to Gutersloh. He has some explaining to do!" answered the controller, the frustration clear in his tone.

Flash dragged a camera from the housing on his cockpit console and prepared to document the misdemeanour. This particular pilot would be answering for his navigational error in court. Indeed, it may cost him his pilot's licence as the intercept had occurred only 15 miles from the border; a further 15 miles could have cost him his liberty. As a minimum, an invoice for an aircraft load of aviation fuel for a Phantom would be coming his way and that was not cheap. Razor manoeuvred the Phantom slowly down the left hand side of the Beech Baron and waggled his wings, the international signal that the offender had been intercepted and should follow. The motor drive on Flash's QRA camera whirred rapidly at the pass documenting the disbelief in the German pilot's eyes. As he flew by, unable to match the slow speed of the small Beech Baron, Razor commenced a lazy left hand turn and both he and Flash craned their necks to ensure that the light aircraft followed. Razor had jotted down the registration of the offender.

"Give me 121.5 Flash," he snapped. He needed the international distress frequency which he knew the German pilot would be monitoring and he needed it fast. It was just a few miles from the border and the pilot was still heading doggedly eastwards.

"Delta Alpha Bravo Oscar Mike" he called using the callsign which he had just scribbled down, "this is Mike Lima 74 on 121.5, come up this frequency."

He continued the lazy turn watching the Baron commence a left hand turn back towards a westerly heading. A long pause.

"Mike Lima 74, this is "Delta Alpha Bravo Oscar Mike" on 121.5 go ahead," came a tremulous, heavily accented and obviously German voice.

"Delta Oscar Mike you have violated the ADIZ. You are to land immediately at Gutersloh. Gutersloh bears 240 range 37 miles. Contact Loneship on 132.65 for recovery vectors." Short, sharp and to the point.

"Roger, turning left onto 240" came the response from a very worried private pilot whose aviation aspirations had just evaporated.

"You got enough pictures Flash?" asked Razor receiving a positive response from his back-seater as he rolled out a mile behind the Baron and pushed open the throttles picking up speed. The Phantom began to feel more like a fighter again. He passed the Baron leaving a comfortable margin pulling up into the vertical and rolling away from the light aircraft as he passed signifying that he was clear to proceed as ordered. The ground controller would monitor the progress and vector him back in if needed.

"Mike Lima 74 this is Loneship. Continue for Border Patrol stand by for vectors," came the instructions from the controller. Being so close to the border, this was one occasion when radar vectors from a ground agency were mandatory and very few crews would quibble with the chance to do a run down the Inner German Border. Task completed, the aircrew gazed down at the countryside below them as they waited for instructions. The ribbon of the fence cut a swath through the pine forests below, a scar dividing the former German State. This was a fence to keep the population of Eastern Germany in, not to keep the West Germans out, thought Razor in a more reflective moment. On the radar warning receiver a number of emitters had sprung into life. An Sa-6 Gainful, a Soviet low level surface-to-air missile system much feared by bomber crews was tracking the Phantom from its site just the other side of the border. To the northeast, the onboard sensor detected the radar signal of a Mig-23 Flogger interceptor. Soviet QRA had been launched to monitor the activity of the hapless Beech Baron in the ADIZ and the arrival of the Phantom had raised the stakes. The game of tit-for-tat was relentless but his senses were heightened.

*

"Thank you for arranging to meet me," said Yuri as the rain-coated figure eased onto the seat beside him. I'm sure that you can appreciate that it was impossible to talk on the phone. All the circuits in the Ramenskoye area are monitored and it would only have been a question of time before we had been detected. Once that happens they have little difficulty tying an individual to a call with fairly predictable results."

"You suggested that you had something that may interest us," said the operative tentatively.

"In more ways than one," replied Yuri easily. "It is my intention to leave Russia. I believe that I have the ideal opportunity and I have something of value to offer you in the process."

"I'm sure that you would have some interesting things to tell us my friend," he responded, perhaps failing to appreciate the importance of the opening gambit "but do you not think, perhaps, you are being a little hasty? Such things take time to set up and in the meantime, perhaps we should keep in contact to build up an element of mutual trust. A little information in advance would build a rapport."

"I hear that," replied Yuri "but you misunderstand me. I don't need your assistance to leave as I have already made the arrangements myself." He paused allowing the facts to sink in. "You do know that I am the principal test pilot for the Sukhoi Su-27 fighter programme or the Flanker as you refer to it in NATO."

There was a pregnant pause.

"Yes, we took the precaution of checking out your background and as you say........."

"Look let's not waste time. My part of the bargain will be to deliver the avionics prototype of the Su-27, or RAM K as you call it across the border and, what is more, I already have the opportunity to do it. Your side of the contract is to convince me that the risks are worth taking."

He turned to look at the British agent sitting alongside wondering if he had any idea of what was really on offer. The erstwhile stony facade wavered slightly as the enormity of the situation registered. This was no hardened field operative thought Yuri and he would have to be very wary in how he played his hand otherwise his inexperience would prove fatal.

"I understand your offer Colonel Andrenev but obviously in view of the importance, I will have to return to the Embassy to make some further arrangements. At least he was smart enough to have worked out who he was working with. The nature of the deal had finally sunk in and the operative was hastily backtracking.

"In the meantime, as you say, it is vitally important that we don't attract attention to ourselves. Let me brief you on the communications arrangements that you should adopt. Please, there must be no deviations if this is to work. To set things going I will need a few details such as where and when you intend to cross the border. I'll need to consult with our military experts but I feel sure that we can come up with a very attractive package for you if you come across. Again, the details will have to be worked out."

Yuri began to outline his plan.

*

"Wildenrath, Mike Lima 74 on recovery, 10 miles east for visual rejoin, switches safe."

"74 you are clear to join, Runway 27. The wind is 270 at 10 knots and the circuit is clear."

Perfect thought Razor, a light wind straight down the strip. He eased the Phantom lower to 400 feet which was just a little below the authorised break height. He would position the aircraft overhead and then turn aggressively downwind to complete a circuit of the airfield to land. A visual run in and break was the traditional recovery method for a fighter and started in the days when it was vital to retain fighting speed for as long as possible during the approach to land. In those days it had proved fatal to many a recovering aircraft, short of fuel, when bounced by an enemy fighter as the pilot configured for landing dropping the gear and flaps. These days, with the advent of surface-to-air missiles, it was less advisable to approach an airfield at 400 knots looking aggressive; friends could easily be mistaken for enemies despite electronic identification systems. For day to day training, however, it was still an efficient means of recovery.

"74, on the break to land."

The Battle Flight Phantom nosed into the neck of the Battle Flight HAS and the normal flurry of activity began. It was vital to service and replenish the aircraft as soon as possible to get it back on state and ready for any further tasking. There was no back up during the turnround. Until the Phantom was back on state the other Phantom on QRA was holding alert. It was the constant story; crews ready to be launched wherever they were needed, at an instant. Battle Flight, located on Bravo Dispersal at the opposite end of the airfield to Delta Dispersal contained the two HASs of the alert facility, directly adjacent to each other. Each HAS housed a Phantom and its associated air and groundcrew on 24 hour shifts, 365 days per year, ready at all times for the unthinkable. It was the West's "Armageddon Insurance." There were no excuses for failure, other than, perhaps, the exception of an unserviceable aircraft. To fail to provide an aircraft at readiness for Battle Flight would be the last mistake a Squadron Commander would ever make. Equally, for the aircrew to fail to be airborne within 5 minutes, which was the stipulated alert state, would result in a "hats-on interview" for everyone even loosely involved in the debacle. The HAS was equipped with every item of support equipment imaginable to ensure that tasks were completed efficiently. It was, after all, the primary task of the Station in peacetime. The small accommodation complex was just large enough to house the 5 man team and contained an operations room connected to the Wing Operations Centre by phone and telebrief. For 24 hours, the crews would eat, sleep and live Battle Fight. Such a tight readiness alert took its toll and crews, aware of their responsibility, would wear the majority of their flying equipment, including their survival equipment and G-suits, throughout the day and in some cases the night to ensure minimum delay in the event of a scramble. The staccato blare of the alert hooter was loud enough to wake the dead and the resulting shot of adrenaline was enough to launch aircrew even without the aid of their jet!

Razor and Flash returned to the small lounge which doubled as the operations room and slumped into their chairs, tired after the sortie. The adrenaline buzz had faded and fatigue had begun to set in. The phone rang and Razor dragged the handset from its cradle. It was the Duty Controller to tell him that an intelligence officer from Rheindahlen, the Headquarters of The 2nd Allied Tactical Air Force would be arriving shortly to brief the Battle Flight crews. The Station Commander and the two Squadron Commanders would also be along in a few minutes.

"Heavy stuff, Flash," he muttered returning the phone.

"The Station "Wheels" are about to arrive with a briefing from 2ATAF. They want the other Battle Flight Crew over here as well. It must be serious if it won't wait until we're back on the Squadron. Best get this jet back on state before they arrive."

The Station Commander, Group Captain Alastair Lennox, a cheerful Scot pushed open the door to Battle Flight and the aircrew jumped to their feet. He was a popular commander and the aircrew held him in the highest esteem.

"Hello chaps, let me introduce Squadron Leader John Silversmith who's come down from Rheindahlen. He's already briefed us but he has some very important news that you need to hear. Pay very close attention."

"Thanks Sir," said Silversmith easing to the front of the group as the remainder of the bodies attempted to shuffle in any available space in the cramped confines of the Battle Flight bedroom which had been commandeered for the impromptu briefing. The crews stayed closest to the doors just in case the hooter should sound again.

"What I have to say is protected at the highest classification so please treat this briefing as strictly "Need to Know." We've had some fairly dramatic developments over the last two days and I've spent a good deal of time on the secure net to the Embassy in Moscow. I won't beat around the bush gentlemen. I believe we are about to take delivery of the latest Russian fighter the Flanker. A Soviet test pilot has indicated that he wishes to defect and has come up with a plan to bring his jet with him. I need to emphasise again the sensitivity of this information. The reason that you are being briefed now is that there is every possibility that we may have to react at very short notice if and when we hear that the Flanker is airborne. Battle Flight will obviously be our quickest reaction if a pre-planned operation is not possible. Obviously we'll brief a couple of crews as the primary option but you, Gentlemen, before tomorrow you may be escorting a Russian aircraft to your own base!"

There were looks of absolute incredulity around the room. Flash caught Razor's eye and smiled, the thought holding everyone's undivided attention. His concentration drifted momentarily.

"...............so if you are called to cockpit readiness, those are the procedures we will adopt," said Silversmith. "Any questions?"

Heads shook. As the Station Commander dismissed the group and the cluster of bodies drifted away there were some serious faces.

"Mark, Jim, I'd like a word." said the Station Commander. "Are you perfectly happy with the brief because if this starts on your watch there will be no time for questions. You'll have to think on your feet and some of the decisions will have serious implications."

"No I think we got the drift Sir," said Razor. "Just confirm we are clear to engage any aircraft in hot pursuit of the defector."

"Yes, but only in NATO airspace. I don't want any border crossings or smoking holes in East German territory. Undoubtedly the Sovs will make a big thing of losing their prize possession but I don't intend to hand them any free propaganda which they can peddle. I'll make sure that you get written confirmation of the Rules of Engagement within the hour. Just remember, despite everything which has been said today, you always have the right of self defence under International Law and I'll back you to the hilt if it comes to it. Even so, we do this by the book. If there is one," he muttered ominously.

The room had cleared and as the Station Commander climbed back into his car they were suddenly alone again with their thoughts. Razor had heard rumours that the Americans operated a squadron of Migs from a secret desert base in Nevada. He also knew that there was a hangar at an American base in Germany full of fighters, fighter bombers and surface-to-air missiles that the Soviets operated in East Germany and Russia. One of the 19 Squadron crews had been lucky enough to see the stuff and crawl all over it. That was exciting enough but the thought that they might actually have one of the latest Soviet fighters land here at Wildenrath was the stuff of dreams. It couldn't happen could it? It was deathly quiet interrupted only by the incessant metronome from the telebrief.

6 ALLSTEDT, EAST GERMANY

Andrenev moved his hand to the lever and selected the gear down subconsciously registering the vibration as the undercarriage cycled. He looked down and confirmed that he had three positive indicators. His gear was down and locked. As the speed dropped through 335 Kph, he lowered the flaps to increase the lift over the wing and the aircraft became noticeably more ponderous and lethargic as it settled into its landing configuration.

"Ramrod, you are left of heading, come port onto 215 degrees to recover the centreline."

Yuri adjusted the heading minutely only small corrections required at this stage. He looked ahead through the hazy atmosphere, shifting his head to peer around the head up display which might be obscuring his view but he could see nothing but trees around him as he descended through 300 metres. There should be a runway here somewhere, he thought, if this Bozo in the radar room is giving me good information. Suddenly the runways lights snapped on and the runway was instantly etched indelibly in the forest as he popped below the cloud. He could now see the motorway feeding in from his left hand side. This was to be his refuge for a while. A short highway strip tucked amongst the East German forests.

"Turn starboard onto 220 degrees, your final approach heading. You are four Kilometres from touchdown call me visual the lights."

"Ramrod is visual"

"Roger Ramrod look ahead and take over visually. You are cleared to land, wind is from two o'clock at 15 Kph."

Yuri felt a brief twinge of apprehension at the narrow aspect of the runway which was enclosed on all sides with huge pine trees. He was about to land on a section of the East German National highway system and hoped that the Army had got their act together and closed it to traffic or he may be playing footsie with a Trabant. The runway stood out clearly now and, as he let down towards the ground, he sensed the trees growing larger in his peripheral vision and felt gingerly for the runway with his long undercarriage. The brief kiss of the main gear finding concrete prompted that superfluous feeling of elation which, despite the accumulated skill of years of flying, always followed a safe landing. He held the nose off the "runway" demonstrating the outstanding controllability of the Sukhoi to the troops who he knew would be ranged around the site witnessing this extremely important event. Waiting for the speed to decay, he lowered the nose slowly to the runway dabbing the brakes as the nosewheel bit, slowing the aircraft to a walking pace. The Flanker was slowly cocooned by the gently waving pine trees.

"Ramrod, taxy to the end of the strip to the dispersal on the left. Park next to the Mig-21," came the voice of the Air Traffic Controller from his tactical control vehicle parked at the end of the impromptu airfield.

"Ramrod parking on the left." he repeated as he manoeuvred his large fighter into the enclosed dispersal area, more often used by holiday trippers for picnics rather than military units for an exercise. He was aware of a knot of spectators who had formed nearby, all clearly overawed by the sight of the spectacular fighter which dwarfed the smaller Mig. Yuri could see two ZRK, Zentniy Raketniy Komplex, missile systems parked at the entrance to the highway strip. These mobile surface-to-air missiles with the NATO designation Sa-8 were mounted on six-wheeled vehicles and the quadruple Gecko missiles mounted on the top of the armoured chassis on launchers fitted on either side of a rotating plinth, guided by the Land Roll monopulse radar. Perversely, the system which had for so long protected him during his flying task might suddenly play a part in his demise. It underlined the enormity of his task as he realised that many more equally capable weapons systems would be deployed between him and the border and would try to prevent his departure as his plan unfolded. The highway strip was served by a railway line and a small branch line terminated alongside the parking area. Nestled amongst the trees was a freight train containing fuel trucks, support vehicles and flatbeds for the military equipment. A camouflaged command post had already been unloaded and manoeuvred into a screened revetment in the trees. As the Lyulka engines died, he unstrapped and stood on his ejection seat placing his flying helmet carefully on the topbox. He stowed his life-saving jacket in the cockpit and climbed over the side using the trusty pitot probe alongside his canopy as a handy stepping off point as he felt carefully for the steps which had been wheeled into place. The solidity of the aircraft's construction comforted him; he would need it over the coming days. As he jumped from the bottom step he turned to face the Detachment Commander who offered a hearty welcome.

"It is a pleasure to have you with us Comrade. Our facilities are spartan but rest assured that we know how to look after ourselves and our guests when we are in the field. I can guarantee that you will enjoy your brief stay with us."

"Thank you Colonel," Yuri responded hoping, desperately, that he was correct and that his stay would be a pleasant diversion on the way to better things. If he was wrong, he knew that the same deployed troops were capable of inflicting misery on those who proved untrustworthy.

"I have nominated Senior Lieutenant Saruvin to be your liaison officer," continued the Colonel. "If you have any needs, any whatsoever, you need only ask and I can promise you that they will be satisfied."

Yuri turned to the rather young looking officer to his right and nodded.

"Oh no Comrade, this is Lieutenant Saruvin" said the Colonel gesturing behind Yuri who turned and stared into the deep blue eyes of a beautiful woman. There was an immediate bond; an electric spark. The Colonel noticed the reaction and smiled.

"First Comrade, I must ask you to come to the command post. I must give you a briefing on the operational procedures in this region. Saruvin will rejoin you later." Yuri looked back at the woman and smiled. Perhaps the delay at Allstedt, which he had assumed would be a distraction, would be a more comfortable distraction than he had thought. She matched his look hinting of things to come... maybe.

Yuri relaxed in front of a large screen and realised that if he was to be successful, the next hour would be critical. He must memorise as much of the detail from the briefing as was humanly possible. The key to breaking through the complex cordon between east and west was contained within the vast array of material which was about to be presented.

"We are an element of the Group of Soviet Forces in Germany or GSFG," intoned the Colonel, "which in turn make up the Western Strategic Direction. We are a unique organisation with two Tank Armies at our disposal, the 2nd Guards and the 20th Guards. Additionally, the 3rd Shock Army would provide the majority of our heavy armour. The 16th Tactical Air Army from its existing forward bases would support the ground forces. This demonstrates the importance our commanders attach to this region as they have assembled the mightiest army on this planet. Our operational plan in wartime would be to attack simultaneously on three fronts. The front that is most successful would be strengthened by the addition of a second front from Poland that would have the task of smashing through the enemy's defences. Afterwards, the Group of Tank Armies would widen the breach with a massive, crushing blow breaching the thin, although presumably, reinforced NATO front line. Should our thrust into France be successful, a further Group of Tank Armies would be moved forward from the Kiev Military District to reinforce the effort."

The Colonel continued his comprehensive lecture outlining the entire strategy of the Western Front. Yuri had heard the facts before but presented in this tactical headquarters by the staff who would implement them suddenly made them seem real. The stuffy air of the staff college briefing where he had last heard these details was absent as he listened intently.

"Missile cover is provided by an embedded Brigade with 10 to 12 battalions. Each battalion has six to eight launchers depending on the type of missile with which it is equipped plus several 5mm and 23 mm anti-aircraft guns which would repel low flying enemy aircraft. Air support is provided by the 16th Tactical Air Army as I have said, equipped with Mig-21s and Mig-23s of various marks. These aircraft provide both air-to-air and air-to-ground capability."

Yuri noted each and every fact, slowly revitalising his mental picture of the cordon which he would have to penetrate. A number of questions began to form in his mind.

Briefing complete, Yuri was driven to the Officers quarters in a small farmhouse some miles distant. As the orderly showed him to his room he could hear the strains of a traditional Russian love song coming from the room on the landing opposite. Let it please be Saruvin he reflected. As his overnight bag bounced onto the large bed the telephone rang.

"Andrenev."

"We shall assemble at Seven o'clock Comrade, in the Dining Room. Please be prompt, I have a number of officers who are extremely anxious to meet you."

"Seven o'clock Colonel. I shall look forward to it," he replied recognising the voice of his host. He was certainly being handled extremely carefully. The Su-27 must be seen as a prestigious project, he thought. Let's hope it's nothing more sinister but I'm just being paranoid. A light tap, the door opened slowly and Saruvin slipped into the room.

"I trust you're comfortable Comrade Andrenev. As the Colonel suggested, your every wish.........."

"Will you be joining us for Dinner?" he asked, sidestepping the question and avoiding the innuendo. Without a word, she moved over towards the bedside light, turned and looked directly at him fingering the light switch. His eyes followed her fingers as she played mischievously. Breaking the spell, she smiled before swirling around and returning to the door where she looked back directly into his eyes.

"Oh yes Comrade, I would not miss it for the world."

The door closed and only now he sensed her scent.

He pushed open the door to the large room feeling the instantaneous heat from the fire which glowed in the grate and scanned the officers grouped around it. Disappointed to see that Saruvin was not amongst them, he moved towards the small knot of bodies. Surely her earlier display had not been for show?

"Comrade Andrenev, let me introduce you to the other officers of the Regiment," offered the Colonel taking him around the small but select group. He tried to take in all the names but failed but he made absolutely sure of the details of two key men. Introductions over, they broke into smaller groups and, luckily, he found himself questioned by a slightly obese Ukrainian who commanded the Sa-8 detachment, one of his selected targets. To make sure that the exchange would not be totally one-sided, he began to quiz him on his methods of operation knowing that the Sa-8 was a fundamental element of the defensive line along the border. He would undoubtedly have need for some of the facts in the very near future.

"How does the system engage its targets" he asked openly, listening intently as the officer spoke dabbing away at his glistening forehead. The intricacies of the command and control procedures linking the missile batteries with the operational control centre were lost on him but he perked up instantly as the man moved onto the operational engagement sequence.

"The operators sit side by side in the tracked vehicle. The target acquisition radar picks up the nominated target and the operator places his cursor onto the radar contact. This designates the enemy to the target tracking radar operator. TAR hands over to TA he continued dropping into the acronyms and abbreviation loved by military operators the world over. He can track automatically using the inbuilt functions but when the enemy pilots use electronic countermeasures, he is often forced to use manual modes to counteract their efforts. Once he has a good track he launches two missiles which are guided by separate guidance beams which come from the missile guidance circuits on the vehicle. The missiles fly out at over twice the speed of sound along these radar beams and strike the target within seconds. My system is so effective that it can track targets at very low level in extreme clutter."

"What would it take to defeat the missiles?" Yuri asked trying to appear innocent and unwilling to interrupt the monologue. He paused, worried that the SAM officer would see through his feigned disinterest but his dinner companion pressed on undaunted.

"Without some fairly sophisticated jamming to tackle my monopulse tracking radar, my suggestion would be to fly at 10 metres" he chuckled. The exchange actually proved stimulating and he found himself providing a good deal of information on his new aircraft despite the fact that he would have preferred to keep it to himself at this stage. He could have quoted security protocol but he needed a dialogue and his silence might provoke a similar response. Even so, he kept back some key facts.

Despite his professional curiosity, his eyes scanned the room unconsciously trying to spot Saruvin. When she finally arrived, there could have been no danger that he might have missed her entrance. The door opened and, to a man, heads turned and watched her enter, the conversation dropping to a quiet hush. The simple black dress she wore fell just below her knee, edged with a silky material and set off by a flowing sash. The simplicity was stunning. Her hair hung loose framing her pretty face and the absence of makeup merely enhanced her flawless complexion. Yuri tried to appear indifferent but could not prevent his eyes taking in her every detail. She caught his eye and smiled knowingly before returning her attention to the Colonel who had walked across to greet her. Yuri, flushed at the secret exchange feeling like a schoolboy who had just been caught in the act and realised that he had missed a question which the effusive Ukrainian had just posed. He returned reluctantly to the conversation.

Most of the other diners were already seated around the large dining table but as Yuri took his seat, he had a slightly disconcerting feeling that he was invading a rather exclusive dining club. He noticed that life on the extremities of the Rodina were somewhat more palatable than life in the Moscow suburbs. Away from the fire, however, the room took on a distinct chill heralding the onset of winter. Winter gave major problems for flying as snow, ice and fog restricted operations significantly. He wondered with a hint of sadness that if his plan succeeded whether he would actually be flying at all this winter. Returning his thoughts to his dinner companions, he took in the faces around the table which were a mix of ethnic origins and, although he had spoken so far with white Russians, he was aware of the more oriental features of a Kazakhstani and a Chechen across the way. He found himself sitting, much to his discomfort, next to the Political officer and wondered whether this was by design or by accident. This man had been the other key guest. Saruvin, however, had positioned herself directly opposite and he hoped that her presence would divert the conversation away from Party matters. Ironic, he thought to himself; having made the momentous decision to flee, he would spend his last few hours playing political footsie with the Party man. From here on, caution would be the order of the evening and he would look for other opportunities to gather the background intelligence he needed. The meal was simple, a local schnitzel with boiled potatoes and sauerkraut but as the Colonel had promised, beautifully prepared and strongly influenced by local tastes. This unit seemed to be screened from the shortages which beset the military operating from their home bases.

"Tell me about Ramenskoye, Comrade Colonel. It is Ramenskoye where you are based is it not?"

Yuri turned to look at the bland face of the Political Officer next to him.

"Comrade, do you have a need to know?" he responded gently, his face breaking into a disarming smile. Whilst he wished to keep the Party man at arm's length, he had no wish to alienate him and he hoped the exchange would remain light-hearted.

"I'm teasing," he continued unsure of the reaction he would provoke. "I have spent quite some time in that area. After completing Test Pilot's School, I started my career on the upgrade programmes for the Mig-21 and the Mig-23. I flew the Mig-23M operationally, so it was a natural progression to become involved with the upgrade of the weapons system to the Mig-23P standard."

"How did you manage to make the move onto the new fighter programme?" the Political Officer responded showing his first interest in Yuri. Was the attention casual or was his line of questioning more menacing? Yuri continued without a pause deciding that hesitation could be fatal at this stage, determined to keep his cool despite the probing.

"It was more luck than skill, I'm afraid," he admitted. "The pilot who ran the Test Pilot's Course became one of the senior men on the Mig-23 programme and was later selected as Director for the Su-27 development. He asked me to join the team. Sadly, I rose through the ranks in dead men's shoes. Shortly after I arrived he was killed in a road accident of all things; ran off the road on his way home one evening. It was suggested that the brakes on his official car failed, although we all know that it's impossible to prove these things do we not Comrade?"

He turned to gauge the reaction but a stony face stared back, devoid of emotion. He pressed on.

"Then a matter of three weeks later, the Senior Pilot was killed evaluating a new radar in a Mig-21. Someone filled the aircraft with contaminated fuel and failed to do the proper checks. He suffered an engine failure only seconds after takeoff at about 50 metres. That's probably the most difficult phase in a Mig-21 as it is fitted with an old ejection seat with no capability until you climb above 100 metres. He tried to eject but it was outside the seat limits and he was still strapped in the seat when it hit the ground. The parachute didn't have time to deploy and he was killed instantly. A sad loss; he was a fine fighter pilot. Unfortunately, the replacement Director is a scientist not a pilot and has more radical views of what a fighter aircraft should do......."

He stopped short, careful not to adopt a tone that could be interpreted as dissent. Turning again to the politico, he saw the same emotionless facade. A cold fish.

"Comrade, what do you think of your temporary quarters," came the soft feminine tones from across the table."

Grateful for the diversion, Yuri switched his attention to his "mentor" opposite, feeling a slight brush against his leg in the same instant. Had he imagined it? He was suddenly alive again.

"You certainly know how to live here in the Western District," he responded lightly.

"At Ramenskoye we are fed once a week whether we are hungry or not!"

She laughed, despite the weakness of his quip and skilfully moved the conversation away from flying and on to lighter topics. He found himself responding and, no, he was not imagining things. At regular intervals the gentle brush became increasingly insistent as she held his gaze. The Ukrainian Battery Commander, whom he had pumped for information earlier, had been slowly increasing his intake of wine and vodka and was becoming increasingly worse for wear. He, undoubtedly, had sunk too much to offer any more tactical titbits and it was going to be touch and go whether he remained coherent or passed out. Drawing himself away from Saruvin's tantalising attentions, he attempted to draw the man back into conversation, aware that the Political officer on his other side was still paying an unhealthy attention to his conversation.

"Tell me more about the Sa-8," Yuri prompted, listening intently as the inebriated officer delved into the less technical merits of his system in slightly slurred tones. Yuri had heard most of this information before but a refresher may yet prove invaluable. A radar guided SAM, the officer explained, self- contained on a six wheeler chassis and sealed against the ravages of war. The crew, able to batten down the hatches were protected against chemical attack and its boat like hull would allow it to cross rivers unaided and it was thus able to advance with the infantry in their BMP armoured fighting vehicles; ideal for the river-cut battlefield of Western Europe. The weapon system elements sat atop the vehicle. The four Gecko missiles with the Land Roll tracking dish and two smaller command guidance dishes for missile guidance were resistant to electronic jamming. Should the electronic countermeasures of an attacking NATO jet prove effective, the missile could be manually directed by the gunner with an optical tracker which sat directly under the guidance radars. What Yuri desperately needed to know was more about how they used the system and he probed to elicit information before his fellow diner slipped under the table. Were there any weaknesses he could exploit? He caught the eye of the Political Officer and realised that his line of questioning was becoming too just a little too obvious so he backed off. He would take his chances rather than seem inappropriately interested but then his interest was tweaked yet again.

"..but the most obvious rule we always apply Comrade, is that we never mix aircraft and missiles. We always designate clear areas of operation for each weapon and that way we know that anything moving in our engagement zone must be hostile. It prevents friendly engagement."

There it was; that was it! The key fact he had been looking for. If he could break the tactical problem into smaller defined packets he had a better chance of succeeding. If he was threading through a SAM belt he should be relatively safe from attack from a fighter and vice versa. He stored the information away but little did he know at this stage the significance of the conversation.

"Comrade, you show great interest in the way our colleagues in the air defence regiments operate. Unusual in a fighter pilot. I thought you aircrew types were dismissive of ground based missiles."

"But of course," laughed Yuri, not feeling as confident as the mask he was trying to project. "Sa-8s can't reposition at 700 kph!"

He had pressed a little hard.

"Tell me about your wife Comrade."

The bald yet unexpected statement caught Yuri on the hop. He was immediately suspicious.

"What do you wish to know?" he answered, "You're obviously well briefed."

"We try to take an interest in our visitors in the forward area, particularly as your trip was so hastily arranged."

He couldn't possibly know anything, Yuri reassured himself. He's fishing; turn it to your advantage.

"She is a very sick woman I'm afraid," he continued. "I have tried all the best medical advice in the Ramenskoye area and even gone as far as consulting the Air Force experts in Moscow. Sadly they see no solution to the problem and I suspect it is only a question of time. It could be just months now but then again, it could be years." He wondered how well briefed the Political officer really was.

"It must be an enormous worry to you." A trap?

"Yes of course. My spare time is completely devoted to her care and I worry that occasionally I neglect my duties. Is that the reason for your interest Comrade? Has the Director asked you to keep an eye on me?" his smiles attempting to divert the line of questioning. "Am I failing in my duties?" He smiled again.

"Of course, I would hate to think that you were unable to give the task tomorrow your full attention. Please, if you have any problems which I can assist you with, just let me know." His voice dripped with insincerity. Yuri turned back to Saruvin wondering how to keep the man happy. He expected her to back off given the turn of the conversation but she showed little sign of having taken any notice. Maybe just a hint of a reaction? Was he being paranoid? The meal over, they moved over to the fire and finished with a traditional vodka binge. Yuri noticed that Saruvin appeared to be excused the vodka tradition and tried to keep his own intake down. He could plead for forgiveness with the need to be sharp for his flying task tomorrow. Around him, the conversations grew noisier and the toasts more aggressive until it became easier for him to dump his own share discretely in a plant holder next to him. What a waste of good vodka. Eventually, Saruvin detached herself from the attentions of another would-be suitor, who had clearly not taken the same precautions as Yuri, and was rapidly drifting into incoherence. She moved towards him.

"I had a problem with a light switch earlier," she murmured, "If I had another go at it now, do you think you could help me?"

"I'll be five minutes behind. Be careful with that switch."

He opened the door, slowly, and walked in. As the door closed gently behind him he felt the touch of soft hands on his shoulders. Stopping, he allowed himself to be turned slowly and the hands closed gently around the back of his neck drawing him closer. Saruvin dropped back against the door forcing it closed with a jolt and dragged him with her as she moved backwards. Almost losing his balance, involuntarily, his right hand braced against the wall and he trapped her firmly against the wall. She squirmed as if to escape but the motion heightened the sensuality of the contact and he could not resist as he bent his head to kiss her. Hands still wrapped around him, she responded fiercely and he concentrated on the feel of her soft lips that moved exquisitely but excitedly across his cheek. Her hands pulled back from his neck and, as she pushed to break his hold, her arched back thrust her breasts even further into his chest. The pressure further inflamed his passion and they sank to the floor, the embrace becoming more ferocious and passionate. Yuri slowed, looking into her eyes and, standing quickly, drew her up into his arms. He kissed her neck hungrily, his lips drawn to her cleavage, working as he did to release the fastener at the nape of her neck. Easing the now loose garment from her shoulder, he followed the line of her breast to her erect nipple and gently teased, before allowing his mouth to encircle the tip. His tongue worked furiously. She arched her back thrusting her pelvis into him and writhed in pleasure. Stimulated by the heady perfume, he drew the black dress downwards, dropping it at her feet and as she stood, clad only in the flimsiest of black silk, her leg coyly bent at the knee, a sultry look spread across her face. He gazed longingly at her full breasts, realising how long it had been since he had enjoyed the company of a woman and allowed his eyes to move slowly and hungrily down her body. Moving closer, he touched her gently, letting his hands drift slowly over the smooth skin of her flat abdomen before giving in to his desire. Stepping back, he slowly and deliberately removed his own clothes staring into her eyes all the while, before forcing her urgently onto the bed, falling after her. He straddled her, gently tugging at her remaining modesty before resuming his voracious efforts. They moved again, slowly at first but as the heat of passion built, his hand moved between her legs and she pulled him tighter, even more urgently. Feeling her wetness, he succumbed to the pleasure. There was just a nagging doubt that this was not a good idea. Should he take this risk with his plans so close to execution?

7 COMPROMISE

Keith James opened the door of the restaurant and scanned the room. There had been no sign of a British registered car in the car park but he was not sure what type of car John drove these days so he was not overly concerned. Probably some large company limousine he thought idly. The waitress approached him.

"Guten Tag Mein Herr, möchten Sie essen?"

"Ja bitte. Hat Herr Kitching angekommen?"

"Nein Mein Herr, aber bitte hinsetzen. Vielleicht wird er bald kommen? Nur einen Augenblick."

Keith struggled with the language as he recalled his pigeon German from Grammar School days deciding to order a beer as he waited for his arrival. As he gazed through the window the door opened and a man paused to remove his coat depositing it on the large ornate wrought iron coat rack in the corner before making a beeline for his table. The stranger glanced around unnecessarily as he approached as the restaurant was still quiet and the other tables were empty. He dropped himself heavily into the seat opposite fixing Keith with a piercing stare and placed a large envelope pointedly on the table in broad view.

"I'm afraid that seat is taken. I'm expecting a friend," he said to the newcomer who continued to scrutinise him disconcertingly.

"There's no mistake" replied Kamov, "I'm afraid Mr Kitching will not be joining us for lunch, he has been unavoidably detained. Oh and by the way, I already took the liberty of ordering Schweinehaxe for both of us. We wouldn't wish to attract attention by not taking lunch now would we Flight Lieutenant James?"

"How do you know my name?" asked Keith nervously, thrown by the unexpected challenge. It was increasingly apparent that a harmless encounter with a former schoolmate was inexorably turning into something for which he was ill-equipped.

"I've been doing a little research since we last met my friend." said the mysterious stranger "and I feel I know you intimately."

The hairs on the back of Keith's neck began to rise and the feeling of impending ill fortune heightened.

"I can't imagine what you mean" he replied indignantly, noticing for the first time just a hint of an accent which was most certainly not German. "We've never met."

"Oh but we have, we have. Take a little look at the contents of the envelope."

The waitress arrived with two plates of steaming Schweinehaxe and placed them on the table causing both men to sit back momentarily which broke the tension. She dithered, wiping away a drop of spilt gravy prompting Keith to clutch the envelope closer to his chest unsure of his next move. As he waited he looked closely into the eyes of his inquisitor knowing that if his fears about what was in the envelope were realised, his options would be limited. He tried in vain to think on his feet. The waitress made to move away proffering apologies.

"Noch etwas Mein Herr?"

"Nein Danke, gnädige Fräulein," responded Kamov anxious to press his advantage. He had already given her a generous tip to ensure that they were undisturbed and her attentions were less than welcome. As she withdrew and, alone once again, Keith opened the envelope and withdrew a large photograph. The image left nothing to the imagination showing him highlighted against the black sheets which he remembered so clearly. Was it really so recent? He was stark naked, astride the large breasted blond, obviously enjoying the experience. He blanched inwardly at the rapturous look on his face but more was to come. Pulling out a second photograph, waves of panic assailed him. Upright, again astride the blond, his head back in unmistakable pleasure, the camera had caught him coupled in frantic lovemaking while behind him the dark haired girl, her arms wrapped around his torso, fondled his chest. As his eyes registered the distressing implication of the erotic scene, he only now recalled her androgynous figure in more detail than he had noticed on that night. He had realised that she was different but, with horror, the difference became startlingly apparent as his eyes focused on the erect member threatening him from behind. Sickened, he thrust the picture back into the envelope staring wide-eyed at Kamov.

"How?" he stuttered incoherently.

"I should have thought that was manifestly plain," came the cruel response, "or are you in the habit of doing this type of thing regularly?"

"There has been some mistake" he said more in hope than certainty.

"Oh no, I think not. There's no mistake. The video was particularly explicit," said Kamov monitoring his every move and nuance. "Even more so than the photographs. I thought perhaps your wife may be interested............"

The threat hung in the air. A resigned look crossed his face as he realised that he was trapped. His career, reputation and dignity was in tatters if this came out.

"What do you want" he asked deflated, unconsciously conceding to the Russian.

"Nothing my friend. Worry not. We may have need to contact you in the future but at the moment, it is just reassuring to know that you understand our arrangement. But, let us not get our relationship off to a bad start. I am sure we can be of use to each other and as a gesture of good faith I have something else for you."

He handed Keith a smaller envelope from his inside pocket and naively, Keith dug inside and withdrew a bulky wad of Deutsch Marks which he stared at vacantly. Across the street another camera clicked.

8 DEFECTION

"Colonel, as you know, we have deployed the Su-27 forward for two main reasons. Firstly, we would like to assess the aircraft's capability in short-field and highway strip operations. Secondly, and more importantly, it is our first opportunity to evaluate the Su-27's weapons system in something more akin to combat conditions. The aircraft I am flying is the first avionics prototype and is fitted with a Zhuk radar."

"Of course Comrade Andrenev, if you could perhaps indicate the sortie profiles which you have planned, I will have an intelligence officer brief you on the local tactical situation. As you know, in this area we take life particularly seriously and I would hate to see any mishaps with your new aircraft. It would do neither of us any good at all."

At that moment, the door was thrust open and the intelligence officer entered. Yuri's heart sank as he recognised the political officer and it was clear from his gait that he was also the local KGB official. A significant aspect of the Soviet military system was that the appointment which an individual held was more important than his actual rank. Hence the Lieutenant's lowly rank belied his standing in the local hierarchy. More importantly, it was readily apparent that the Detachment Commander resented this fact greatly and his frown said it all. As the intelligence officer draped himself casually across a chair at the rear of the briefing room the tension was tangible.

"The sortie will involve a performance take-off from the highway strip," began Yuri returning to his brief. As the available take off distance is only 2000 metres and the aircraft is carrying a full weapons load, that in itself will give us some important data. After takeoff, I'll go straight into the air combat engagement with the Mig-21. You have specially selected the pilot and briefed him what we need. We normally limit our manoeuvring to opening moves but, in this instance, we will progress to free tactics. I hear he is a sniper pilot who has many years of experience in his Regiment and should be more than capable of achieving the aims. On completion, I shall be evaluating the air-to-air refuelling characteristics from one of the latest Illyushin IL-78 tanker aircraft. This is also a prototype and will be a significant exercise for both of us and tell us a lot about both types. Then I shall descend to low level and I thought it would be useful to make a run at the border to keep the western air defences on their toes.

"I'm sorry Comrade," cut in the political officer from behind. "We could not permit low level operations in the forward frontal areas for two reasons. Firstly, there are significant numbers of operational SAM units at extremely high readiness states who would not take kindly to high speed tracks intruding into their airspace. Furthermore, I am sure you would not wish to compromise your secret weapons platform. There are listening posts all along the border which would make capital of recording your radar emissions. You would not wish to give them the opportunity Comrade, would you?"

Yuri felt his cheeks burn and, despite his inward calm, he was aware of the intense gaze of the young Lieutenant. He would bide his time.

"No naturally Comrade, you are absolutely right," he answered casually, although he knew that once his fuel tanks were full he had to commit himself to his dash for the border without delay. At that point he would telegraph his plan given this unexpected turn of events. This was a setback which he would need to work around and his mind worked swiftly.

"My evaluation demands an element of low level work. Perhaps I could use the training areas to the east of Allstedt for the purpose?"

"That would be an acceptable compromise," replied the Political Officer, "but of course it is the Colonel's responsibility to control the airspace in his forward area and I would naturally have to defer to his decision."

The smile diverted any responsibility for mishaps to his superior and the ambitious young charger could not now be held to book for any problems which may befall the secret prototype. Yuri was only too aware that his plan had a serious flaw. He would now be forced to run at the border at considerable risk through one of the most heavily defended pieces of airspace in the world. The scenario which was unfolding did not give him a warm feeling.

"The outer ring of Sa-3 sites for the main base at Allstedt are located here," said the Lieutenant moving forward to a briefing board, describing a circle to the west of the airfield outside the wooded area. There are a number of Army level Sa-4 assets to the east but they have been briefed of your mission and will be "weapons tight" throughout the period. You may see some activity on your sensors from their tracking radars but rest assured they will cause you no harm. In the forward areas there are two battalions of Sa-6s with their Straight Flush radars, located behind a layer of Sa-8s with co-located ZSU 23-4 AAA systems. Each of these units has gunners with Sa-7 Grail man portable shoulder launched missiles. As an additional exercise, we have deployed a new system for your benefit. Like your aircraft it is still secret and your task will be to identify its type and report back.

"But Comrade," Yuri responded sarcastically, railing at the arrogant tone adopted by the Party man, "my RWR is one of the latest software driven devices. It will not be programmed to display an unknown radar."

"We are way ahead of you Comrade," replied the KGB man calmly. "I have spoken already to your Director at the Test Centre who has had our little surprise loaded into your equipment especially for our trial. I look forward to your analysis, as does your superior." Why the subterfuge? Why had he not been brought in on this unexpected addition to the test plan? Was this an insurance policy to protect someone else?

Briefing complete, Yuri walked from the room convinced that his plan could never work. The task was formidable. Even so he had come this far; too far to fail. Walking out to his aircraft, he passed the Command Post and saw Saruvin leaning against the entrance. She smiled shyly.

"Perhaps I shall see you later?" she inquired. He returned her smile avoiding the question but paused briefly and touched her cheek remembering the passionate embrace only hours before; the hectic lovemaking. The muttered platitudes seemed lame. I hope not, thought Yuri ruefully, returning his thoughts to the task in hand.

*

As he moved away towards the waiting fighter he glanced back towards the operations complex and caught sight of the Political Officer who stood partially concealed by a parked jeep staring at him intently. Realising that his brief display of affection towards Saruvin could have done him no harm; in fact could have positively helped things, he turned back to the Su-27. If he returned it might pose questions but why would an officer of his standing risk all if he planned anything sinister? Suddenly, escaping to the West taking the huge jet which sat in front of him seemed anything but simple. The Su-27, as yet dormant on the dispersal, was a classic fighter pilot's aeroplane from its twin fins to its bubble canopy, its sleek lines reminiscent of a big cat poised for the kill. Its lines hinted at latent aggression and its performance loaded with the latest Soviet advanced air-to-air weaponry was up with the best. In the recessed tunnel under the fuselage between the engines, were two Vympel R27 long range semi-active missiles, known as the Alamo to NATO. A further two were fitted to pylons on the wing stations next to a further two Vympel R73 Archer short range infra-red guided combat missiles. These sat on separate rails on the wing pylons. Later versions would carry extra missiles on wing tip stations and Yuri knew for a fact that there was even more scope for increasing the weapon load. Hauling himself into the cockpit having completed his pre flight walk round, he settled in. The light green shading of the instrument panel and the consoles was supposedly restful according to the Russian designers but he considered that it was more likely to be an anti air sickness device. If pilots could avoid a feeling of nausea as they strapped in, they would be immune for the remainder of the sortie. Cinched tight in the seat, he initiated the start sequence after he had aligned the inertial navigation system marvelling at the simplicity of the process. All he had to do was select all the systems to on and throw the start switch and the engines roared into life. Simplicity shone through complexity.

Across the tarmac, the Mig-21 pilot was climbing the ladder to his aircraft. The older jet, in comparison to the Su-27, looked slightly ungainly with its forward hinged canopy and its dated styling but Yuri knew it would be formidable opposition. Despite its age, the small fighter was agile and, more importantly, very difficult to keep sight of in air combat. He had arranged to get airborne before the Mig as he had significantly more fuel aboard than his opponent. What the Mig pilot did not know was that Yuri would need as much of that fuel load available to him as he could possibly hang onto if his plan was to come together. A successful engagement against the Mig would be a critical precursor to that plan. After a final glance around the cockpit, checking and cross checking the dials and gauges, he gestured to the marshaller and advanced the throttles, easing the heavy jet forward off the chocks. He taxied from the tree lined dispersal and as he passed through the Mig gunsight he saluted his opponent, a gesture which would prove to be prophetic before the day was over. The ground control frequency remained quiet; the absence of radio calls reflecting silent procedures. As he approached the temporary highway airstrip he noticed the runway threshold markings which had been painted onto the motorway to give the necessary visual references for aircraft operations. He had totally missed them during the landing roll as he had arrived. Allowing the Su-27 to roll onto the "piano keys", he brought the jet round with a push on the rudder bars, dabbed the brakes and lined up with the runway centre line. The jet rocked fore and aft on its oleos as it came to a halt and, suddenly, he was more aware of the proximity of the trees ranged along the periphery of the impromptu airfield. This prompted the familiar rush of anticipation which washed over him heightened on this occasion by the monumental task which faced him. He could see the additional markers half way down the motorway strip denoting the point at which a simulated bomb had cratered the surface. He was to practice a minimum operating strip take off using the maximum performance available to him each and every small item adding to the already enormous strain. He would complete that particular serial because, despite wasting precious fuel, he could top up on the tanker and replenish the vital commodity. Completing his pre take off checks, he wound the engines up to max dry. All the instruments were stable, the engines were within limits and the central warning panel to the right of the main instrument panel showed that his systems were fully serviceable. He was ready. He rocked the throttles into afterburner and immediately felt the aircraft judder forward as the thrust overrode the ability of the brakes to hold the aircraft stationary. Immediately releasing the brakes, he allowed the Su-27 to leap forward holding the aircraft in line using the rudder pedals, quickly feeling the aerodynamic effect of the airflow over the control surfaces as the aircraft picked up speed. Already at 150 kph and he could see the markers rapidly approaching; 200 and the nose came off the runway, the aircraft willingly becoming airborne; 230 gear up, systems still good, the feel of the jet in his hands; 260, 280, 310 and the flaps travelled. He held the nose down watching the bend in the motorway approach. At 480 kph he yanked the stick aft watching the climb bars in his head up display increase to a crazy angle the familiar sight of the trees and runway ahead disappearing underneath as the nose came up. He waited for 60 degrees nose high and checked forward holding the climb angle watching the world disappear from his peripheral vision as he rocketed skywards.

At altitude, he brought the Su-27 round on the Combat Air Patrol and rehearsed his plan yet again. This was something he had done regularly in his mind for a number of days and he was back on familiar territory. After the combat split with the Mig-21 he would top off his tanks from the tanker. Two engagements should leave him the majority of his fuel still available so the tanking should be relatively brief and he would then feint eastward as if he was entering the pre-briefed training area before reversing back westwards for his run to the border. He had repeated the route carefully in his mind's eye up to the point at which he crossed the border. After that he would have to play it by ear. His route would take him from the range near Naumberg, south of Mühlhausen to cross the border at Wanfried. He planned to fly through the gap between Fritzlar and Kassel hoping to lose himself in the high ground to the southern end of the NATO low flying area 3 assuming that, by then, he would have been intercepted by Battle Fight who would escort him back to one of the RAF airfields on the Dutch-German border. That was if he could trust his British Embassy contact who had made the arrangements. He knew that he would have to negotiate the NATO SAM belt which comprised a layer of Nike missiles covering the forward airspace. This large surface-to-air missile protected the high level airspace launched from sites well to the rear of the NATO airspace. Below this high level missile engagement zone sat the Hawk batteries which provided low level coverage plugging the gap. In peacetime, there was less chance of being engaged by these systems than by those operated by his own Soviet countrymen as NATO was somewhat less paranoid about the integrity of its airspace and was more likely to question before shooting. He had been reassured that they would be expecting his arrival. Further to the rear, there were three bases which held Quick Reaction Alert, the fighter reaction forces. The Americans at Soesterberg covered the northern flank, the Americans at Bitburg near Frankfurt, the southern flank and the British at Wildenrath completing the picture covering the central airspace. In all, the various elements produced a complex jigsaw providing a layered defence but his route had been carefully selected to ensure that his risks were minimised. He intended to enter the British area of responsibility and knew that it would be important to make contact with the Battle Flight fighters on the Guard frequency at the earliest opportunity to make his intentions known. He had little confidence in the clown at the British Embassy in Moscow or his assurances that he had communicated the plan to the NATO aircrew. His hollow promises still rang in Yuri's ears. First, however, he had to run the gauntlet of the Soviet defences to the west of Allstedt. The radio interrupted his thoughts.

"Arrow this is Ramrod on frequency and ready to play." Arrow was the callsign of his controller; Rifle that of his Mig opponent.

"Ramrod vector 090 degrees, maintain 15,000 metres and set speed Mach .95. For head-on engagement, your target bears 270 degrees range 60 at 12,000 metres."

Yuri listened intently to the close control from his ground controller giving him precise instructions to achieve his intercept on the Mig. Each turn moved him closer to the point at which he would activate his radar to launch his R27s but up to that point his radar would remain silent. Close control was efficient in these conditions when the target remained at high level in good radar coverage but not all targets were quite so cooperative. If the target reacted cleverly dragging him down to low level perhaps things would be more unpredictable.

"Ramrod activate. Target bears 100 degrees range 38 at 12,000 metres." The prompt from GCI to turn on his radar set.

"Ramrod contact" called Yuri instantly as he flicked his radar transmitter on, illuminating the target instantly in his scanning radar beam. A small smudge appeared in his head up display at the expected azimuth. He played with his radar controls on the throttles and highlighted the target. A squeeze on the lock button and the radar began to track the distant Mig-21. The data link panel to his right confirmed the commands from the ground controller.

"Simulated missile away."

The distinction was still important as he signalled his actions to his controller, although he may yet use his weapons in anger before the day was through. He watched the target march down the scope as his opponent moved inexorably closer, the target designator box hanging tantalisingly in his HUD, the tiny Mig still invisible. His weapons computer showed that his missile had timed out - had been given enough tracking time to have impacted its target - and he called the "kill" but instructed that the engagement should continue. He wanted to be sure that the Mig was out of fuel by the end of the engagement as he knew that it was not equipped to make use of the tanker which orbited to the east. It had no air-to-air refuelling probe and was woefully short of fuel at the best of times. Selecting his R73 missile he listened for an acquisition on the heat source from the still distant Mig. Faint but clear he could discern the warbling tone which meant the missile was starting to break out the tiny Mig from the background well before he could see it visually. As the tone grew stronger and more insistent, the tiny shape of the Fishbed enlarged in the TD box and he simulated a follow-on shot but this time uncalled to his controller. He was all the while forcing the issue, confident of his skills, dragging the small fighter into his carefully choreographed plot. The Mig suddenly grew rapidly in his windscreen catching him momentarily unawares and shocking his system into action with a rapid adrenaline shot. It flashed down the right hand side pulling into a flat turning manoeuvre typical of the limited Soviet air combat tactics. He matched it with a vicious climbing right hand oblique loop knowing that already the Mig was bleeding off its precious energy. He reckoned his opponent had entered the fight with about 600 kph, a good fighting speed which he had, stupidly, already squandered by pulling too hard. The Mig-21 could never hope to match the Su-27 in a vertical turning fight; so the only hope would have been to attempt to keep the fight flat and tight as he had done. Over his shoulder as he reached the apex of the loop he saw the Mig in its predictable turn. Although Yuri was slow he had height advantage which could be converted to speed........ and a kill. He held back waiting for the right moment. Well above and probably difficult to see in the bright cloudless sky he chose the perfect moment and buried his nose. His opponent was manoeuvrable but no match for him and he anticipated the move as he saw the Mig's nose come down trying to point directly at him. No danger yet. The Mig was not equipped with head on missiles and had already made an error by staying too predictable. He pulled hard back on the stick arresting the rapid descent and the nose slewed crazily around. The other pilot had generated an impossibly high angle off the tail which he countered, pulling the Mig directly down his canopy centreline with a spine shattering 8G pull. Even so he drifted into the blind spot below the Mig's belly. The Mig passed very close aboard, just above him, the nose dropping showing that he had bled off all his energy and with the nose now firmly buried it dropped earthwards with its speed building. Yuri held the pull realising that the pilot had lost sight. Easing the descending Mig into his gunsight he checked that the R73 which was still selected and waited for a tone; nothing! Momentarily taken aback, he realised that by now the Mig had seen him and had snapped back in another hard defensive break. Yuri pulled his nose ahead of the wriggling Mig closing down the range and realised that a gun shot was a possibility. Flicking the weapons selector on the stick, he saw the guns display appear in the HUD, bobbing and shimmying green in front of him calculating precisely the fall of shot from his 23mm cannon. The planform of the Mig grew as the pilot tried unsuccessfully to evade the kill, the delta wing shape distinctive as the range hit the cue. His hand flinched with momentary hesitation before moving slowly to the armament safety lock. Still hesitating, Yuri watched as the Mig tried desperately to carry out a last ditch manoeuvre. He flicked the switch arming the circuits and..... squeezed the trigger! He watched awestruck as the Mig in his sights erupted in flames as the cannon shells tore into the right wing. He could hardly believe his actions.

"Rifle this is Ramrod, you're on fire; eject!" he called simultaneously, the calmness in his voice hiding the turmoil beneath. The Mig pilot felt an instantaneous thump from the starboard side and saw flames emerge accompanied by a Christmas tree of lights on his central warning panel as the aircraft's systems reacted to the disintegration. Not realising the implications but knowing his aircraft was crippled, he took the advice and ejected. Yuri watched in fascination as the events unfolded in slow motion in front of him. The right hand wing folded and fell from the Mig as the crippled aircraft started a rapidly increasing roll to the right. After one complete rotation, the ejection seat separated from the inferno in a cloud of debris as the jet spiralled earthwards.

"Arrow this is Ramrod, Rifle 1 has ejected in this position. I am descending to low level to support. I'll call you back."

He knew that the time for action had come and descending rapidly, he aimed for the pall of smoke where the Mig had impacted aware of the pilot drifting slowly down in his parachute.

"Ramrod going dark," he advised the ground controller as the Su-27 disappeared from his radar display. This suited Yuri's purposes perfectly. "Roger Arrow, I'll call you when I climb back out," he called knowing that he had no intention of ever complying. He checked the fuel. It would have to do and he would forgo the tanking. He was heartened by the fact that the Mig pilot had survived and knew that the live search and rescue mission would give some additional breathing time. He had no desire to waste life unnecessarily and he was pleased that the seat had separated cleanly. Approaching 200 meters he flew past the crash site again, turning onto west, knowing he was inescapably committed. There was no turning back now.

9 CHALLENGE

"Thunder formation closing, switches safe."

Major Kalienko approached the prototype Illyushin IL-78 Midas tanker gingerly in his Mig-23 Flogger, cross checking the radar response which glowed brightly at 1km range and decreasing. He could see that the refuelling drogues were already deployed ready to refuel his thirsty formation. The remaining three aircraft in his element tucked into tighter formation as he eased his fighter slowly closer. Concentration emanated from the cockpit of each and he could sense the total fixation of each pilot in their attempts to maintain formation position. The hastily bolted on refuelling probe sat on the nose of his Mig-23 and he had been asked to evaluate its performance. One of the other jets also carried the new device but the youngsters in 2 and 4 were not to be trusted. Eventually, he advised the tanker captain that his flight were in position on the left hand side as he looked admiringly at the rounded curves of the airborne filling station. The new Midas tanker was a conversion from the Candid transport aircraft and, as with all Soviet aircraft, it was an almost direct copy of the American equivalent, the C141 Starlifter. The extensive modifications to enable air-to-air refuelling with two huge underwing refuelling pods would plug a significant capability gap in the Soviet Tactical Air Armies. It was a large aircraft with a hump-back appearance exaggerated by the high mounted wings and the bulbous undercarriage housings directly beneath the fuselage. The high T tail sported large bullet fairings fore and aft which housed electronic surveillance equipment to warn the crew of impending attack and carried twin radar-laid 23mm cannon which protruded ominously from the rear fuselage. The housings which contained the refuelling equipment were located under the wings outboard of the podded engines with a further pair protruding from blisters under the rear fuselage. Long hoses emerged from the rear, drogues trailing to allow airborne connection between the fast moving aircraft.

"Thunder Leader, you are clear astern the right hose, Thunder 3, clear astern the left." came the staccato instructions from the tanker captain.

"Thunder Leader clear astern the right."

"Thunder 3, clear astern the left," they acknowledged in sequence.

The Floggers moved slowly and deliberately into position, both pilots conscious that this was the time when accidents were possible. A few casual radio calls as they slotted into position made sure each was aware of the others movements, the aircraft hanging ominously behind the baskets, the refuelling probes ready for contact. Once the command lights on the refuelling pods changed it would allow them to close in. Kalienko glanced at his element leader and relaxed seeing him solidly in position, the R23 known to NATO as the AA-7 Apex and the R60 AA-8 Aphid air-to-air missiles gleaming white on the underwing pylons of the adjacent jet. Returning his gaze to the bulk of the tanker ahead, the red warning lights switched to amber and Kalienko tensed, ready for his joust with the lively refuelling basket. He had tried this exercise before when he had trained as a test pilot but it was a long time ago. His aim, as always, was to jockey his Mig from a position six metres astern the receptacle and to manoeuvre the probe into the centre of the bucking basket. That done, he had to maintain position until the fuel had transferred, all whilst flying along at 500 kph at 8,000 metres. A cinch.....maybe! He edged the throttles forward applying 2% additional power and stared fixedly at his references under the wing of the tanker. He tried desperately not to watch the basket otherwise he knew that he would over-control and set up an oscillation that would guarantee failure and derision from the younger pilots who watched. The probe eased gently towards its target which began to swing wildly in the disturbed airflow ahead of the fighter's nose. Kalienko avoided the urge to chase the oscillations and maintained a slow predictable approach trusting that the gyrations would damp down before he reached the basket. He was also aware that the remainder of his formation would be fixed on his performance, expecting him to make contact first time but willing him to miss. That way the pressure would be off when the 2nd jet took his turn. The basket rose crazily as he reached a point just 10 cm short, before sinking, slowly but surely, contacting the probe which checked the movement. The probe slid perfectly into the receptacle, a solid thump announcing his success. One swift glance at the basket to check that the contact was solid and he switched his attention back to the formation references. The lights on the pod flashed green as the fuel began transferring. Number 3 in the other Mig, after his third attempt, finally made contact his tailplane a blur of motion as he drastically over-corrected. The aircraft vaulted briefly before settling down into a steady position, the relief from the cockpit palpable.

"Thunder this is Arrow on frequency, stand by for re-tasking," came the intrusive directive over the radio. Who the hell is Arrow thought Kalienko.

10 ENGAGEMENT

Yuri orbited the crash site, the thick, black pall of smoke already obscuring the wreckage. They could not possibly be onto him yet but if he delayed his move any longer, the odds would shorten and the defenders would have more time for preparation. Avoiding further debate he picked up a course for his nominated waypoint and freedom. Only time would tell.

Just a few miles away, the Battery Commander of the Sa-6 site picked the handset from its cradle and dialled a number frantically.

"Control this is Mühlhausen 3, request permission to engage. I have just seen a fast-jet aircraft splash a Mig-21 in the area of Dingelstadt....... Negative, I have no identification but it looked like an American F-15; bubble canopy, twin fins.......What is strange is that I'm receiving a positive response from the IFF system........ Affirmative, the aircraft is squawking friendly......... Affirmative, he used guns; I could clearly hear the sound of the cannon fire......... Comrade, I am 100% certain and after the engagement the aircraft descended to low level and headed off west...... Standing by!

He slammed the telephone, frustratedly, back onto the cradle.

The Su-27, buffeted by the low level turbulence, settled on its westerly heading, the trees around offering some limited protection from the probing air defence radars. Yuri began to assess the tactical situation. There were two Sa-6 sites both to the north and the south of his present position but the signals on his SPO-15 radar warning receiver from the Straight Flush target tracking radars showed that they were already drifting back into his 7 o'clock and no longer a threat if he stayed low. He assumed, therefore, that he was safely through the first defensive zone and that he could disregard the Sa-4s and Sa-6s but he was only too aware that he still had to negotiate the most menacing threats, the Sa-8s, ZSU23-4s and Sa-7s. He was not carrying offensive air to ground weaponry and would have to rely solely on tactics to defeat them. As if to placate his concerns, he rechecked his jammer obsessively making sure that it was on. Whether the new program designed to counter the Soviet systems would work was untested. He selected the chaff and flare programmes to automatic. Those older systems were tried and proven in combat and he was confident that they would be effective. These defensive electronic warfare systems may be the key to his survival. His aircraft was well equipped with a comprehensive self protection suite and the software controlled system would automatically sense any threat and respond with an electronic countermeasure from its library of programmed responses. With luck, the response would target specific weaknesses of the electronic signal and disrupt the tracking, causing the missile to lose guidance. He also had numerous chaff dispensers located around the rear of the aircraft containing chaff cartridges, modern adaptations of the wartime "window", small packets of chopped aluminium foil which when ejected would simulate false targets on the hostile radar adding confusion to an already confused picture. His chaff was targeted at the radar guided missiles such as the Sa-8Gecko which lay in wait ahead of him. Also fitted in dispensers on the upper fuselage were flare dispensers which would fire pyrotechnic infra-red flare upwards and away from the aircraft to decoy incoming infra-red guided missiles. Once fired, the flares would burn brightly like a large firework offering a more attractive target to the incoming missile. Unconsciously, with these thoughts of survival in his mind he eased the Su-27 lower, his left thumb creeping along the line which he had drawn on his map which lay tucked into his kneeboard. The navigation equipment was still rudimentary and it would be important to follow the pencilled track precisely as his route had been planned to avoid the principal rear echelon threats.

As he approached the border, he knew that the engagement zones of adjacent batteries would start to overlap and it would become impossible to avoid them. He would be forced to route through the engagement zones as he made his final bid for freedom. Suddenly his radar warning receiver rattled. A threat in the 2 o'clock! The indicator warning light flashed in the front right quadrant indicating a SAM tracker its rapid blinking ominous. The amplitude indicator across the top of the gauge showed a full deflection signal. It was a strong response. He looked in the direction of the warning not wishing to take unnecessary avoiding action but realising that his intentions would by now be suspicious and that any reaction was possible from his erstwhile comrades. He simultaneously confirmed that his IFF was still sending friendly signals to the Soviet air defence system. There was a brief flash and, immediately, his radar warner erupted with the strident tone of a missile guidance signal from an Sa-8 Land Roll tracker. His blood froze. They had launched at him! How could they possibly have known so quickly? He snapped on 90 degrees of bank away from the missile putting it onto the beam and dispensing chaff. The classic tactics to defeat the radar guided missile which his warner had now identified came flooding through the adrenaline haze. Lower, he urged himself as the trees rose to meet him. Lower still! The instrument continued to telegraph its chilling warning showing that his evasive manoeuvre had not yet been effective and that the missile was still tracking despite his efforts. His jammers were useless on the beam, the threat radar at this aspect outside the coverage of the antennas mounted on the rear fuselage. He hit the chaff dispense button on the throttles yet again watching the indicators on the control panel counting down. His move was redundant as the system was already automatically pumping out chaff bundles in response to the persistent threat. Suddenly the warner fell silent but he continued with his evasive manoeuvre, trying desperately to increase his distance from the hostile SAM site, keeping it at arm's length. Looking over his shoulder he could see the writhing plume of smoke which marked the flight path of the incoming Gecko missile. Glancing forward, he realised that he had allowed the height to drop to 50 metres and that the trees were looking frighteningly large around him. They would be as unforgiving as a missile if he got too low so he eased the jet upwards away from the swaying treetops.

Back at a safe height, he screwed his head around staring over his shoulder and attempted to reacquire the missile. Chilled, he realised that the smoke had stopped and the missile had reached the end of its boost phase. All he could do was pray for the first time in years. A final, hopeful check of the radar warning receiver and he tensed. There was a brief explosion as the missile impacted well short of his aircraft. He sighed audibly in the noisy cockpit, his situation suddenly improved immeasurably. The short 10 second flight time had seemed like minutes. Allowing himself to relax, he eased the jet back around towards his planned track giving the SAM site a respectably wide berth precluding another launch. Attempting to calm his nerves, he checked the range and bearing on his inertial navigation system for the next waypoint trying to relate the jumbled numbers on the instrument into a position on the ground. As the adrenaline subsided he needed to be back on track. Happy again with his position and with his heart returning to a more regular beat, he adjusted once more to the gentle jarring of the airframe as it rode the turbulence. The features around him began to look less familiar still as he flew on into the restricted airspace closer to the border.

*

"Thunder this is Arrow, vector west and descend to 1000 metres. I have a target for you heading west range 20 km, at low level. This is a live intercept. Repeat this is a live intercept. You are clear to engage, I repeat you are clear to engage, check switches live."

The Controller completed the message with an authenticated codeword which Kalienko knew to be valid. Serious business, he thought, a descent to low level meant that it could not be a stray airliner or a snooper aircraft. The target was heading west and at low level which suggested a combat aircraft and he was already clear to engage!

"Thunder, check target speed," he requested trying to supplement the limited data which the controller had passed.

"He's at 550" came back the response, "Accelerate transonic."

Kalienko plugged in the reheat knowing that his formation hearing the same instructions would respond. His fuel tanks were full after tanking and the target already had a 20km head start on him. He eased the stick forward watching the altimeter unwind checking that his formation were in position.

A 20km rundown; it would be tight this close to the border.

"Thunder, high speed," he called as he watched the needle on the airspeed indicator pass Mach 1 and waved his formation off with a flick of the hand. The acceleration had already stretched the element but he didn't want anyone in close formation at supersonic speeds. They eased out into fighting wing.

*

Razor and Flash languished in the easy chairs in the Battle Flight crewroom dressed in their bulky flying kit relaxed after the thought provoking briefing. The TV blared out; another movie whiling away the hours of tedium as, in the background, the confidence tone on the telebrief system, a regular metronome ticking away, set the monotonous cadence.

"That was some briefing from the 2ATAF Int. Officer," muttered Razor. "It makes you wonder why the guys on the other side will go to such lengths to escape their own system. Thank goodness for western democracy is all I can say."

"I wonder if he will really go through with it. It's a long way from East Germany to Wildenrath and the system has some nasty surprises over there," answered his navigator thinking back to his briefings on the latest Soviet surface-to-air missiles. The telebrief clicked ominously interrupting their discussion and Razor immediately killed the volume on the TV as Flash moved nearer the telebrief box. He pressed his ear close, both aircrew diverting their whole attention to the small radio box listening intently; instantly alert.

"Wildenrath this is Crabtree. Alert Battle Flight!"

"Bloody Hell!"

They looked at each other almost in disbelief, as Flash erupted into action and thumped the alert klaxon causing instant chaos. The harsh wail of the klaxon rang out across the dispersal as they fell over each other pushing through the door in their race for the jet, the HAS doors already opening automatically in response to the hooter. The groundcrew burst from their own crewroom in hot pursuit as Flash struggled to close the breastplate of his life saving jacket as he sprinted up the rear ladder and dropped onto his ejection seat. He connected his personal equipment connector anxious to resume contact with Wing Ops.

"Wing Ops, Mike Lima 72, cockpit ready," he wheezed already suffering from his exertions.

"Mike Lima 61 cockpit ready," called the other Battle Flight crew from the 19 Squadron shed, just a fraction of a second behind him. Beat them to the check in he thought irreverently. Razor immediately fired up the right hand engine as the groundcrew struggled with the straps assisting the crew to strap in.

"72 and 61 this is Crabtree, vector 080 climb to Flight Level 70,Gate, contact Loneship on TAD037. You are cleared high speed, repeat cleared high speed, scramble, scramble, scramble, acknowledge."

"72 scrambling."

"61 scrambling."

Cleared supersonic at 7,000 feet overland thought Flash. It could mean only one thing. Bloody Hell!

*

Kalienko flicked on his radar and gazed at the jumbled mass of responses from his simple pulse radar system. He knew that there was no likelihood of achieving detection on the target so far ahead of him, particularly as it was flying at low level but felt duty bound to try. Disgustedly, he snapped the transmitter off. There was no point in advertising his presence before it was necessary. He would be relying totally on the fighter controller for information, assuming of course that he could see the target in this area and was able to maintain contact at low level. That was by no means a certainty. Kalienko swept the wings back to mid sweep on his swing wing fighter as he felt a brief shudder from the airframe as it protested against the rapidly increasing speed. Mustn't overstress the wings; still have a lot of work to do, he decided. The Mig-23 had many flaws and was a pig once it manoeuvred but it could fly very fast in a straight line. He eased the throttles up towards the firewall.

*

Razor waved the chocks away and pushed the throttles forward using a good deal more power than normal. If he was to believe the recent intelligence briefing, this was for real. Crabtree had ordered a double scramble which meant that the tactical situation warranted more firepower. Singleton launches were more the norm for violations of the Air Defence Interception Zone. As the Phantom nosed out of the HAS, he looked across to the other Battle Flight shed where the 19 Squadron jet was just emerging. He knew that being the nominated Q1, the primary Battle Flight aircraft, he would lead the mission.

"Mike Lima 72, 61 to Tower," he advised Wing Ops, "Stud 2, Stud 2 go!"

"61."

"72, loud and clear."

Both aircraft checked in ignoring the normal etiquette of air traffic control procedures, inappropriate for Battle Flight scrambles. No one delayed a live launch without an extremely good reason. The aircraft would take off unless vetoed by an agreed codeword.

"Tower 72, 61 scrambling."

"72, 61 clear take off, wind 270 at 12 knots. After takeoff contact Loneship direct on prebrief," called the Duty Air Traffic Controller.

Razor and Flash had already been running through the checks as they had taxied, even now making the final switches and struggling with the leg restraint lanyards on the ejection seat. Normally these procedures took 30 minutes to complete but today they had been achieved in a mere 5 mins from the telebrief's vociferous interruption. Checks complete, Razor rolled onto the runway, the jet having never come to a standstill since leaving the chocks. Afterburners engaged, a brief final check of the systems and the Phantom rolled in a shimmering haze and an immense roar. As the lead

Phantom left the runway, its gear and flaps already travelling, the wingman was also plugging in his burners, streaming off only seconds behind.

"61 airborne."

"72, 61 tactical, go!"

*

"Thunder this is Arrow, your target is dark to me. I estimate his position is 260 degrees range 10 reported height less than 200 metres. Stand by for Stargazer on this frequency."

Kalienko gritted his teeth and selected full afterburner. He assumed that Stargazer was an airborne early warning aircraft which should help the tactical picture. He might even get some decent control. Hang in there number 2, he grimaced as the junior pilot, loosely spread on his right wing, overcorrected inducing an immediate oscillation causing his aircraft to porpoise badly. He may be going home early unless he sorts his life out, thought Kalienko grimly.

*

Back at Wildenrath the phone rang on Delta Dispersal.

"Wing Ops here. We've just had a no-notice Battle Flight scramble. 72 and 61 will be airborne in a couple of minutes and Crabtree have asked for Q3 and Q4 to be brought up on state as soon as possible. Can you get things started."

"Roger......"

"Oh, by the way, have you been briefed on the background to all this because it'll be important to the crews."

Killer, on the 92 Squadron operations desk gestured frantically to the NCO on the adjacent engineering control desk as he listened to the Operations Officer.

"Yes, the Boss briefed us all when he got back from the Int briefing. As it happens, we were already planning an aircraft change on Battle Flight and we've got Mike Lima 77 loaded and prepared. I'll get a crew out there right now and we can have it on state in about 15 minutes."

He dragged the PA handset from its cradle.

"Burner and Tom to the Ops Desk, Urgent, repeat Burner and Tom to the Ops Desk."

He returned to the Ops Officer.

"I'll get the crew to check in on Stud 10 when they're ready."

"Thanks Cobra, call you back."

He turned to the ops assistant.

"Get the Boss NOW!"

The Eng Controller waited patiently in front of the desk.

"Chief, I want to walk a crew for Oscar in HAS 60 in two minutes. It'll be Hollett and Sawyer; can you get the paperwork out to the HAS. This is a possible Battle Flight scramble so make sure the lads on the see-off team are briefed and know that it might have to be airborne ASAP. No messing around!"

The Eng Controller moved off as Killer grabbed the PA handset again.

"Attention 92, this is not an exercise, repeat this is not an exercise. Battle Flight scramble from HAS60, aircraft Oscar. I repeat....."

"Chief, I want to bring up "November" to Readiness 5 right now, I'll get a crew."

The message droned out across the dispersal alerting the key players. Hopefully he had conveyed the urgency but it was now up to others to respond. He would see. Burner and Tom, unaware of the drama, had ambled into the Ops Room but quickly latched onto the fact that something was afoot. About to speak, they were interrupted again by the phone. Killer covered the mouthpiece whispering to Tom for him to draw a noddy guide from the safe as he waited.

"92 Ops."

"Wing Ops again. Instructions from Crabtree. 77 will be for a tactical towline in company with Mike Lima 57. After takeoff, vector 200 degrees and join with Ascot 9612, a Victor from Marham, at Flight Level 200. Tell them to fill to full and await further instructions."

"Holy cow, that'll keep them on their toes. It's not often we get tankers around here. I'll tell 'em."

He turned back to the crew. Burner had caught the drift and had already entered a Battle Flight mission into the flight authorisation sheets as Tom returned holding his guide.

"How long since you guys last tanked?" he asked.

"About 2 years ago at Coningsby," replied Burner, "Why?"

"You're going to love this," he said as the crew looked increasingly apprehensive.

"You've got a scramble message; a live mission against this defector who right now is attempting to fight his way through the IGB! Razor and Flash have already launched; a double Battle Flight scramble and have been vectored into the ADIZ. You're to launch with 57 and join a Victor tanker, Ascot 9612 on a tactical towline. Tom here's the detail," he said handing him a hurriedly scribbled piece of paper. "One you're airborne, contact Crabtree on the initial contact frequency and standby for further instructions. Are you signed out?"

"Yeah."

"Are you happy with the Rules of Engagement that the Boss briefed? They're in the noddy guide."

"Happy."

"Go for it and make it quick!"

Outside the PBF, the air was split by the roar of four reheated Rolls Royce Speys as the pair of Battle Flight aircraft began their take off roll. The crew rushed from the ops room, hastily collecting their flying kit as they passed through the flying clothing room. It was only a short distance across the taxiway to HAS 60 but the exertions of donning the heavy safety equipment meant that they were already breathless and sweating by the time they arrived at the jet. The see-off crew had already opened both front and rear doors of the HAS and the auxiliary power unit was plugged in and operating noisily. Tom had to remind himself that, despite the haste, he was about to climb into an armed aircraft and mistakes could be fatal. As he dropped into the front cockpit to complete the power-on checks, his pilot was already well into his walk round, checking the external condition of the aircraft and, more importantly, the status of the missiles.

"Ready for power?" he shouted above the loud drone of the power set. Making no attempt to compete with the mayhem, Burner merely responded with a raised thumb knowing what had been requested without needing to hear. Tom flicked on the generator switches connecting power to the brooding jet which immediately sprang to life with telelight and warning captions glowing red and amber around the cockpit. At the wingtips, the navigation lights sprang into life as Tom, complete in the front cockpit, raised himself, manoeuvring carefully along the canopy sill between the two cockpits and dropped onto his own ejection seat where he began preparing the avionics for flight. The crew flashed through their pre-flight checks taking short cuts where possible, conscious that some miles to the east, an unlikely scenario was already unfolding. They taxied a mere 5 minutes later still completing the last housekeeping checks as they rolled. Emerging from the HAS, the 19 Squadron aircraft was checking in on frequency almost simultaneously.

"That's pretty impressive," said Tom. "They must have had one loaded as well."

"Wing Ops, Mike Lima 77 scrambling from HAS 60," Burner called as they emerged from the neck of the Dispersal, the runway only a short distance ahead.

"Roger 77, ready to copy your scramble instructions?"

"Go!"

The scramble message reiterated the instructions which Killer had passed hastily at the Ops Desk.

"………await instructions from Crabtree on tactical, scramble, scramble, scramble, acknowledge."

"77 scrambling," Burner acknowledged cursorily.

"57's on frequency, acknowledged the scramble instructions, we're gun armed only," came the breathless response from the other scrambling aircraft.

"Oh great," breathed Tom. "A gun and no missiles. He's going to be a liability!"

"77, 57 to tower, stud 2, stud 2, go!"

Burner interrupted the back seater's tirade even though he shared his concerns. The implications of a partially armed Phantom going into what could be a live engagement did not fill him with confidence. Potent when armed with Sparrows, with only a gun, the Phantom could be a liability in a turning fight.

"57."

"You're loud and clear. Tower, 77 and 57 on frequency for scramble departure. Requesting opposition take offs; 77 from Runway 09 and 57 from Runway 27, 57 to roll first. Looking for an easterly vector and a max performance climb to Flight Level 190."

Thinking ahead, Burner was trying to get his formation airborne as expeditiously as possible. Each jet was leaving its dispersal at opposite ends of the airfield and if Air Traffic Control would approve the plan it would avoid a wasted 5 minute taxy to the opposite end of the airfield for 77. Those 5 minutes could yet prove significant.

"57, clear for takeoff Runway 27, wind 270 at 15 knots. After takeoff, immediate left turn onto scramble vector. Break, break, 77 line up and hold Runway 09." ATC were playing the game. For Battle Flight anything was possible.

"57, taking Runway 27."

"77 line up and hold Runway 09, thanks John," Burner replied to the Local Controller whose voice he had recognised, his momentary lapse in R/T discipline emphasising his gratitude. It went without saying that such unorthodox requests caused major ripples, particularly with the local German civilian air traffic control network and he appreciated the controller's flexibility even if he would have some sweet talking to do later. Nevertheless, the small concession would make a significant difference in getting the formation airborne as quickly as possible. As he lined up on the runway, the stark white dotted lines of the centreline markings which divided the runway, stretched out in front. He could see the shape of the other Phantom lined up for takeoff at the far end of the airfield and, as the engines wound up to full power, a huge plume of dirty fumes enveloped the aircraft kicking up a heat haze. The fug cleared seconds later as the afterburners cut in. He ran up his own engines to max mil responding as he did so to the final challenge and response checks from his navigator, his eyes glued to the other jet as it started its take off roll. The familiar profile grew as the Phantom powered down the strip towards him. Please don't abort now he prayed as the nosewheel of the jet lifted from the surface. In slow motion, the oleos of the main undercarriage decompressed as the aircraft lifted into the air, afterburner plumes bouncing from the surface of the concrete. The shape changed from profile to planform as the nose pointed skywards, gear already travelling and it immediately cranked on 90 of bank, 2,000 feet ahead still only feet above the runway surface. The striking shape of the Phantom was momentarily etched in his mind, silhouetted against the horizon as the jet slewed across in front of him holding a tight, maximum performance turn, afterburners cooking. As soon as the runway was clear, he rocked the throttles outboard engaging reheat, acknowledging his take off clearance from Air Traffic and began to roll. The form of the F4 was still etched in his mind's eye, the green Suu-23 gun pod fixed to the centreline station. If only it had been carrying the familiar white air-to-air missiles on its launchers he would have been happier.

"Speed's on, 100 knots," he heard from the back seat. Holding the stick fully aft, he waited for the nose to respond cross checking the engines and the telelight panel. All was still well.

"120."

The nosewheel had risen and the airframe took on the feel of an aircraft rather than a huge unwieldy tricycle. In his peripheral vision, he could see the 19 Squadron jet downwind already pulling ahead of him.

"140 go!" from the back. He was committed to the take off, too late now to stop even in the direst emergency. The jet flew off and he checked the nose at 10 degrees of climb simultaneously bringing the gear up.

"180."

"77's airborne, 77, 57, stud 15, stud 15, go!"

"200 knots." The throttles still fully forward, he waited for 250 knots when he would raise the flaps.

"57."

"77 you're loud and clear, Crabtree 77 and 57 on frequency, climbing out of Wildenrath for join with Ascot 9612."

"300 knots," the back seater reminded him. The burners remained in, striving to rejoin his wingman almost a mile ahead. The Phantom accelerated swiftly.

"77, this is Crabtree you are loud and clear. Vector 100 degrees and cleared max rate climb to Flight Level 190. Tanker bears 100 range 60, presently heading east away from you. Shortly turning onto west for the join."

"350 knots, burners, called Tom."

"Thanks mate, they're staying in," he replied "57, jink port."

Ahead, his wingman, now climbing slowly and matching his own rate of climb, turned hard through 90 degrees towards them. The familiar planform was again evident as the Phantom crossed their nose, their flight paths now at right angles to each other.

" Reverse," called Burner bringing the wingman back into precise battle formation on the opposite side of the formation. The manoeuvre had recovered the tactical integrity of the formation at a stroke.

"Burner, burner, go!" he punched out over the R/T, prompting his wingman to re-engage his reheat. He straight away raised his own nose to 30 degrees, knowing that his wingman, initially, would lag behind but with the power of two reheated Rolls Royce Speys, he would quickly recover. The tanker was only 60 miles to the east, so it was vital to get to height as soon as possible despite the extra fuel burn. With an airborne fuel bowser with 109,000 lbs of fuel to giveaway it was not a detail that worried him. What was 2,000 lbs of gas between friends?

"Crabtree, 77, clear to turn the tanker," prompted Tom, "77 and 57 are passing Flight Level 90 for 190 in the climb and ready for immediate join."

Only seconds had passed and already they were half way to their cleared height. The join would come overhead the congested airspace above Dusseldorf.

"77, roger. Break, 9612 this is Crabtree, did you copy, cleared port about."

"Affirmative, 77 and 57 this is Ascot 9612 on frequency, hayraking 55 and commencing a port turn onto west for the join. Call me levelling Flight Level 190. This will be for an RV Delta."

"77 willco."

Already the jets were through 15,000 feet and still the reheats powered them higher. Burner pulled the throttles back anticipating his level-off height and, as he passed 18,000 feet, he rolled to the inverted, dragged the nose back down through the horizon and returned the aircraft upright, perfectly level at 19,000 feet. On his wing, 57 had mirrored his manoeuvre and began to close on 77 for the tanker join.

"9612 is rolling out on west."

"77 Judy," called Tom as he broke out the response on his radar, the large tanker still 45 miles away as it completed its long lumbering left hand turn. He began the mental gymnastics of setting up the radar intercept. The nominated RV procedure required him to set up a displaced 180 degree attack with the two formations approaching each other head-on at combined closing speeds of 800 miles per hour. At 15 miles, he would turn the tanker through 180 degrees across their nose, back onto an easterly heading, ideally adjusting his own heading to roll out 2 miles behind and only 1,000 feet below the refueller's height. This complex choreography would take them towards their holding CAP, a brief aerial ballet which demanded precision. Just a 5 second error in anticipating the turn would be the difference between success and failure. Too soon and they would roll out way behind the tanker and waste precious time and fuel closing in; too late and the geometry would be so tight that there would be insufficient performance available at this height to match the turn. Either way would be embarrassing and, with so much at stake, crucial.

"He's at 30 miles, displaced left by 6 miles. Jink starboard 30 degrees to increase the displacement."

He was looking for 8 miles lateral separation to give him vital turning room; this small geometry adjustment should do it.

"Range 25."

His front seater was uncharacteristically quiet, perhaps anticipating events to come. No matter, Tom had a job to do and being out of practice at assisted tanker joins, he already had his job cut out.

"Range 20, come back port onto the attack heading; turning the tanker shortly."

"Roger that."

"9612 start your turn now, showing 18 miles," he ordered.

"Call me every 30 degrees."

He needed to know exactly how the tanker's turn was progressing if he was to finesse the roll out. Some tanker captains, used to gentle turns with receivers plugged in, had been known to take so long to turn that the attack geometry was totally destroyed. Tom had no intention of being caught out on this occasion. The blip on the radar scope began to drift in towards the nose and he anticipated the first call.

"Passing 240 degrees," he heard, breathing a sigh of relief. It was checking out. The azimuth of the target on his radar display was exactly where he had expected it to be.

"30 left range 12," he called to his pilot knowing that his eyes would already be on stalks attempting to gain an early visual contact.

"20 left range 8."

"9612, passing south."

The profile was working out fine but he made a small correction to keep it sweet.

"9612, tighten your turn," he coaxed, making sure that both aircraft would simultaneously roll out on east and that he didn't roll out too far behind.

"On the nose range 4. Steady up on that heading."

His command coincided with the tankers call passing 150 degrees. The intercept was a little over displaced, wider than he would have preferred but no problems. With the extra speed the Phantom formation had in hand, they would quickly close down the range and it would give him time to get the pre-refuelling checks out of the way. He dragged his flight reference cards from the pocket of his G-suit and thumbed through to the AAR checks. It had been a while and he hoped that neither he nor Burner had lost the knack. He wondered what was happening at low level below them where the Battle Flight pair had been vectored inbound.

"Range 2 miles ready for checks?"

"OK lets have 'em." his pilot replied, the same thoughts going through his own mind.

"OK the HF is off and the radar going to standby. IFF?"

"To standby."

"CW?"

"To standby"

They ran through the drills, setting switches and arranging the fuel system to prepare the jet for accepting fuel until they reached the final check in the long list by which time they were virtually alongside the tanker. He could see the profile of the Victor clearly, its graceful curved lines and the raised T-tail unmistakeable. Above and below the fuselage, the red navigation lights flashed rhythmically. The two hoses trailed from the refuelling pods under each wing, already deployed for their benefit, small propellers whirring frantically on the nose of each pod providing power for the electrical system.

"77, 57 joining on the port."

"77,57 clear to join, state your requirements. We hadn't expected to see you up here today."

"You and me both! Both aircraft wet to full."

A wet contact was where fuel was actually transferred whereas a dry contact was merely for practise. With the unpredictability of AAR, crews practised the art regularly and their lack of currency would put pressure on everyone in the formation.

"OK, Probe coming out."

As Burner flicked the switch on the fuel panel which extended the refuelling probe from its housing in the starboard cockpit wall, there was a great thump as the probe door opened into the fast moving airflow. Outside the air around the cockpit was travelling at nearly 300 miles per hour. The telescopic probe with its shiny tip shuddered initially but extended slowly forward into position, phallic in its action, locking in place.

"77, 57 clear continue on the lights, wet to full," advised the tanker Captain.

It was to be a no R/T procedure which meant that at least he was confident of their abilities. As Burner eased from his station on the tankers left wing into formation on the right hand hose, he hoped the confidence was well placed. To his left, the 19 Squadron crew slotted into position behind the left hand hose. I wonder how long it is since he tanked, thought Tom, feeling slightly vulnerable in the back seat, the other aircraft only feet away jockeying in position in the turbulent airflow. The fighter crews waited patiently until the tanker crew had prepared their own aircraft for the transfer. A series of lights flashed various combinations of red and amber on the small light panel at the rear of the pods as the hoses were primed with fuel to keep them stable during the refuelling and valves slotted into position to effect the transfer. The red light which glowed on the pod meant that it was unsafe to close as yet and Burner bided his time awaiting clearance. Eventually the light snapped off leaving only the amber lights illuminated.

"Red's are off Tom, we're clear to close. Talk to me blue eyes!"

"Just a reminder Burner, emergency breakaway is back and down." The comment was almost superfluous but Tom was reminded of an incident in the past where a breakaway manoeuvre had been badly executed. The receiver had broken upwards and taken the tail off the Victor which had crashed with loss of life.

"Good call," came the quiet acknowledgement. They were all out of practice. During the closing manoeuvre, it was Tom's job to direct his pilot, passing corrections to make sure that the probe slotted directly into the centre of the basket and connected. Burner's task was simple. Just slot a small proboscis into a writhing basket, each attached to separate aircraft flying in close proximity at 300 miles per hour in turbulent airflow. In the past it had been described by one wit as taking a running f*** at a rolling doughnut. The analogy was apt. The most important factor was to start the pass from a good waiting position, ideally about six feet behind the basket and up the line of the trailing hose. Burner edged the throttles forward and eased stick gently back as he slotted carefully into position. Contacts which started from elsewhere were invariably unsuccessful. Happy with his line up and after cross checking that the red light was still out, he added a couple of percent extra thrust.

"Closing," he said calmly.

"Bring it right two feet," advised Tom, craning his neck through the small quarter light panel between the two cockpits and trying to estimate the trajectory.

"Up a foot," he cajoled, "Good line, hold that."

The jet crept slowly forward with less than 5 knots overtake, the basket ahead oscillating gently in the turbulent airflow as the gyrating aircraft moved along at 300 miles per hour. The basket passed the radome, the airflow over the nose causing a huge fluctuation forcing the basket to rise and fall wildly.

"Keep it steady," said Tom. "Don't chase it."

Burner could sense the wild gyrations in his peripheral vision and had to force himself not to look at the receptacle. He had chosen his formation references on the underside of the Victor and continued using them, his closure steady. Any peeping at the final stages would result in equally violent oscillations from the probe as he over controlled, undoubtedly out of synchronisation with the basket.

"Hold that line," called Tom as the probe moved within 3 feet of the basket, hoping that the oscillations would damp down at the critical moment but it was not to be. As the basket fell, it struck the top of the probe and bounced ineffectively away from the fuselage returning and striking the airframe with a resounding thump. Tom recognised the situation instantly; a busted flush.

"Back off; missed at 12 o'clock. There was no chance Burner, it was too lively. Not to worry mate, next time!"

"Rim, no damage," he transmitted to the refuelling operator whom he knew would be staring at him through the small periscope which protruded from the belly of the Victor. Any contact with the basket could damage the fragile material and his call would reassure the Victor crew that their refuelling equipment was still intact. Burner calmly eased the throttles back minutely allowing the Phantom to drop back smoothly to the waiting position, stabilised his velocity and readied himself for a further attempt.

"How's the 19 Squadron mate doing?" he asked casually.

"In first time," replied Tom.

"Tell me it's not true." He breathed.

The pressure was on. He reset his references, juggling the stick so that the basket was lined up with the E2B compass and once again started to close.

"Up a foot and right a foot," he heard from the back seat. Goddamn, he was low and left again. Not a good sign but the correction worked.

"In line, in line, hold that," came the calm commentary from the back. He held the stick rock steady, happy that his correction had been effective and locked onto his references to the exclusion of all else.

"In line."

Please go in, he pleaded with feeling.

"In line.......In line......"

His heart sank; time seemed to stand still.

"Down the middle," he heard as the reassuring thunk of a solid contact vibrated through the airframe. The green lights on the pod flashed on as fuel began to flow from the Victor's tanks into his own, replenishing his depleted stocks. A glance down at the fuel gauges confirmed the story; he was in contact. Glancing up, he surveyed the underbelly of the camouflaged, converted bomber a mere 20 feet above his head as his ragged breathing slowly settled. What a way to get current!

*

Yuri recovered to track, his map showing that he was still about 40 km short of the border when once more the radar warner lit up. Another SAM threat in the front right quadrant. He cross checked his jammer satisfied that it was already responding to the threat, intently listening to the audio tone in his headset unable to identify the system. It sounded similar to the Sa-6 tracker, the Straight Flush, but something was not quite right. There was another unfamiliar signal in there. The jammer responded, distorting the signal but despite its efforts, the missile guidance warning flashed on. Here we go again, he thought. With the threat in his front sector he knew that to break onto the beam would only take him into an adjacent missile engagement zone which was, as he had feared, now overlapping. It left him with only one solution. Snapping the stick hard over, he reversed his heading returning in the direction from which he had come. Craning his neck, he could see the missile smoke trail still in the distance. This was starting to become too familiar. He would wait for it to time out and self-destruct before resuming reversing his heading and try to give the site a wider berth to the south. It had worked before. So that was the surprise the Political Officer had been referring to last night. It was the Sa-11 he had heard about at the briefing a few weeks ago at Ramenskoye. It was an adaptation of the Sa-6 system which was just being deployed in the forward area. So that's what a Flap Lid looks like. A further warning flashed in his 12 o'clock, this time showing a Mig-23 air intercept radar. Goddamn, he thought, now they were vectoring fighters onto him and he had solved their problem by turning back towards them. So much for the Battery Commander's assurance that they only operated in separate areas. Here were fighters and missiles operating in concert and he was the target. Looking behind, he could still make out the threatening smoke plume and a further check of the jammer confirmed that it was still responding to the command guidance signal when suddenly it struck him. He flicked the jammer to standby realising that he was probably providing a beacon for the missile home-on-jam circuits. In trying to jam the missile tracking, the electronic box was probably making matters worse. He had another problem. His counter turn had sandwiched him between the two threats and, if he was to escape, he had to break the cordon. Firing up his radar, he scanned the sky above him for the fighter threat which he decided was the highest priority at that moment and immediately broke out a tight formation at quite short range. That they were tracking him this low was a minor miracle; or were they? Maybe they were just transmitting for effect. Maybe they were trying to bluff him into showing his hand. It was too late to reverse or he would offer his tail to the Mig-23s and would be a sitting target. Engagement was his only option. Suddenly, the solution came to him. Something good had actually come from the mind-numbing evaluation sortie at Ramenskoye! Flicking off the fly-by-wire circuit breakers, he snapped back on the stick, reefing the huge jet into the Cobra manoeuvre which he had practised so often before but never in anger. As the nose reared upwards, the rattle from the SAM abruptly stopped. The manoeuvre was considerably more precarious at low level and as he coaxed the nose back to level flight, aware of the close proximity of the ground, he switched his attention to the fighters. Designating the loose target on the outside of the formation, he locked it up. The indications settled and he flicked the missile selector on the throttle to R27, his radar guided missiles and squeezed. Two seconds later, a mighty whoosh and an enormous smoke plume erupted in front of him as the huge rocket boosted from its launcher under the fuselage and picked up its staccato guidance course towards its quarry. He peered through the HUD watching the gentle gyration of the target designator box marking the target as the Mig-23 grew rapidly in size.

Lt Trabinko in the 4th Mig-23 switched on his radar even though he knew that he should not; the leader decided when to use the sensors and Stargazer had been passing some good information. He gazed at the mass of garbled responses from the High Lark system knowing that even if there was a target in there he would never break it out.

"Thunder check gadgets," came the call from the leader. Damnation, he thought, that's me in the shit at the debrief. He's seen my emissions on his radar warner. As he moved his hand across to the transmit switch to acknowledge his error, he heard the rattle of the warning tone from his Sirena 3 RWR. Distracted, he glanced at the simple indicator which was giving a solid fighter threat from the front left hand quadrant. How could that be he questioned. The target is heading away from us. He eased his head left and right peering around the heavy gunsight glass which obstructed his forward vision looking for a sight of the aggressor to answer his muddled questions. He could just make out a dot in the distance.

Yuri watched the smoke trail from his missile snake crazily away from his aircraft, apparently well wide of its aim. Suddenly the missile re-entered his view from an impossible angle aiming directly at the hapless Mig-23.

Trabinko stared at the dot and was suddenly aware of smoke in his peripheral vision. He turned his head and froze as the blood curdling sight of the missile smoke plume fixed his gaze. The missile was tracking directly at him. It was his last thought as his aircraft disintegrated around him. He had no time to eject as the wreckage plunged towards the ground.

Yuri tried to remain detached as he watched the tumbling jet turn into a rapidly growing fireball. It was impossible not to feel something. If nothing else he felt regret at the demise of his fellow countryman as the doomed jet struck the ground. He hauled his aircraft back onto west.

*

In the Battle Flight jet, Flash could see the city skyline to the south as the pair of Phantoms accelerated eastwards, line abreast, with the speed passing Mach 1.2. He thought briefly of the havoc which the sonic boom, already travelling ahead of them, would cause but switched back to matters in hand. There was a vital mission to complete and, if they arrived too late, the prize would be lost.

"Loneship, Mike Lima 72 and 61 on frequency."

"72 and 61 loud and clear, multiple targets bearing 080 degrees, range 90, descending to low level, suspect hostile. Further target 075 degrees, range 72, last seen heading west but the contact has faded; now dark to me."

"72 roger, request instructions."

"72 and 61 intercept the singleton bearing 075□, identify and shadow, standby for further instructions."

"Roger Loneship, intercept and shadow, acknowledged."

"72 this is Loneship, pop-up contact on the singleton. He's returning east. Multiple contacts are strength 4 at high speed still heading west. All at low level."

The disappointment was almost palpable as both Razor and Flash assumed that their promised prize had aborted.

"72 this is Loneship, your targets are mixed up. I see a splash on one target! Confirm, splash on one target. The trailing formation is declared hostile, you are clear to engage if they enter the ADIZ. You are not, repeat not, cleared hot pursuit, acknowledge."

Flash acknowledged the instructions and concentrated on the scope.

"OK Razor, we know there are only three bogeys in there now, plus our boy. We're going to have to play it carefully or we may engage the wrong guy. Let's go for an offensive identification. We'll need to haul off if we get too close to the border. Let's hope our man makes it to this side."

This profile required the leading Phantom to accelerate ahead and carry out a close head-on intercept against the selected target. Depending on the identification, the jets would either, if the target proved friendly, allow it to proceed, or more likely, if it proved hostile, instruct the Number 2 to launch a Sparrow missile and destroy the target. At the merge, other members of the hostile formation would be taken on in an air combat engagement, hopefully by then with improved odds.

"Contact 080 degrees range 45" called Flash to his wingman. "Judy, Judy," he advised his controller, signifying that he had assumed control of the intercept.

"Accelerating. Eyeball - Shooter, 61 is Shooter." The clipped instructions punched out across the ether added to the growing tension. Glancing over, he ensured that the wingman had initiated the gentle weave which would drop him back into trail position about 5 miles astern while their own speed rapidly increased, generating the vital separation.

"Mix-up, 10 left at 43 miles, Razor, make your heading 075 degrees."

Flash knew that he could afford to lock on his radar to give him the critical tactical information. He needed that vital range and, in any event, it was preferable that the bogeys should be aware of their presence. It would complicate their air picture, concentrate their minds and maybe make them more predictable. If they turned and ran all the better.

"Check delta H", he prompted, asking for a reading from the instrument which indicated the target's height eliciting an instant response from his pilot that the targets were back at low level.

"OK we'll hold the height for now and descend when we hit 20 miles. I reckon they're heading west. On the nose for 30 miles."

"61 is in 5 miles trail," called the wingman in pursuit. The profile was working out.

"Bring it another 10 degrees port Razor, I don't want this intercept to go slack on me," said Flash. The intercept was entering its critical phase. If he failed to achieve a 180 opposition pass, he would give the opponent too much turning room and, if they proved to be Fishbeds that could be the end of their plans. Against a highly manoeuvrable adversary who could turn well inside a Phantom, the outcome of the air combat would be predictable; they would be totally overwhelmed. He intended to fight the engagement on their terms using the strengths not the weaknesses of the Phantom weapons system.

"Slightly right range 20, take out the height."

The lead Phantom began its descent, Flash and Razor cross checking their altimeters as they approached the ground. The intention was to pass at co-altitude with the target and, on this occasion, the normal peacetime rules of separation were void; they would blow past supersonic if necessary, passing within yards at the merge.

"I'm getting a J Band signal on the RWR Razor, it sounds like a Flogger to me."

The audio from the High Lark radar was distinctive and unmistakable and both crew recognised the almost musical tone in their headsets. This snippet of information refined their tactical plan as a Flogger was less manoeuvrable than a Fishbed but, nevertheless, carried the AA-7 Apex.

Any lock from the threat would be significant and could herald the launch of a long range missile. They became instantly more cautious. Razor reduced the rate of descent as the Phantom passed 1,000 feet and pushed it up to fighting speed of 500 knots. Things were cooking. He needed the extra knots now because his first turn would cost him energy which would bring him immediately back to the best cornering velocity of 420. Listening intently to Flash's commentary from the back, he attempted to build his mental air picture of the position of the players at the merge.

"I'm unlocking and looking for the rest of the formation," advised Flash. "Hit the stopwatch; we'll merge in 90 seconds." Up to now, Flash had concentrated on the lead aircraft but now switched the radar back into search mode to check on the remaining formation members. Razor hit the button on the stopwatch mounted on his cockpit coaming counting down to the merge.

"It looks like three bogeys. One hostile contact on the nose and a further pair out 10◻ left, already crossed ahead from right to left. There's a fourth contact separated from the rest at 45 degrees left."

Razor slowly absorbed the information. Flash hit the transmit button relaying the picture to his wingman receiving confirmation that they both had the same data.

"Formation's splitting. One jet still on the nose, the other's 20 left, estimate range 8."

Were the bogeys reacting to their presence? Razor cracked the throttles into min burner but selected a notch of airbrake to keep the speed down to 500 knots. He didn't want too much extra speed as it would increase his turning radius but neither did he want the heavy smoke trail from the engines which he knew would be pinpointing their arrival. Afterburner would kill the smoke. He looked ahead striving for the visual pick-up. Abruptly, to the left, he saw the planform of a Flogger as the aircraft entered a racking hard turn towards another jet. What the hell............?

The shape of his own target became more pronounced as he flicked his eyes back through the gunsight and saw the distinctive profile of another

Flogger.

"Lock him up Flash," he shouted, his enthusiasm overcoming his normal discipline.

"Hostile, hostile, hostile," he called to the wingman as Flash confirmed that the target was outside the minimum range for the Sparrow missile. A shot was still on.

"Fox 1 on the bogey bearing 075 degrees range 5," he called as simultaneously, he pulled the trigger and the Sparrow, after what seemed like an eternity, came off like an express train.

"Fox 1 on the contact 070 degrees range 9," responded his wingman immediately. They were entering the fight with two missiles in the air; a good start. Razor hoped silently that his wingman had identified his target carefully before shooting. He switched his attention back to his own missile as it snaked relentlessly towards the Flogger which had not yet reacted. The result was inevitable and the jet erupted and toppled violently before gouging a huge furrow in a small wood. The trees burst spontaneously into flames and a pall of smoke began to rise, the momentous event over in an instant.

"Loneship, 72 splash one bogey present position, engaged."

"I don't want to worry you mate but we've got a minor snag," called Flash from the back seat. "Right now, we're 4 miles inside East Germany. If we get this one wrong were going to have a very interesting bus ride home!"

Razor was totally unimpressed with the news. The wreckage would be indisputably on the wrong side of the border.

*

Tanks indicating full, Burner drew off the power and the hose stretched back, the coupling straining under the pressure as it attempted to retain contact but finally gave in. As yet he was completely unaware of the events unfolding just a short distance to the east. Connection broken, a fine spray of fuel issued from the receptacle as the non-return valve snapped shut sealing the Victor's tanks and the basket rose and fell violently as it settled in the disturbed wake. The stray fuel splashed the canopy causing a temporary reduction in visibility as it spread backwards across the perspex in the high speed airflow. They rapidly finished their checks bringing all the systems back on line ready for action.

"77,57 this is Crabtree, contact Loneship now on TAD 074. If no joy, back to me on this frequency."

"77."

Burner called the formation across to their new operating frequency and checked in with the controller. They had a task!

"Roger Sir," the fighter controller replied. "I show mix-up bearing 095 degrees range 65 miles at low level. Callsigns 72 and 61 are engaged with 4. I show a further friendly contact, detached from the engagement, bearing 090 degrees range 60, running out on west. Vector 095 to assist."

"Steady on 095," he responded making the instant heading change.

"Targets show low level," prompted the controller.

"Let's take it down to 5,000 feet," said Tom as they made preparations for the intercept. "Altimeters are set on the regional pressure setting, I'll check you through 19,000 feet."

The aircraft began to descend. In both cockpits, the navigators massaged the radars looking for the earliest radar contact on the "fur ball," even though 60 miles at the limit of their radar coverage. It had been fortuitous that the West German remote radar units had once again been deployed allowing GCI to pass an accurate air picture. Normal low level coverage in this area of the border was notoriously poor.

"77 you are reallocated. Snap vector 060 degrees."

The call came out of the blue.

"060 for 77 and 57, keep talking Loneship."

Disconcerted, the crews had mentally prepared for an engagement against 4 low level fighters already being engaged by friendly fighters. To be hauled off onto an unknown target without warning took them completely off guard. The controller was agonizingly quiet.

"What the hell is he playing at?" muttered Tom. "The boys need help down there. Four against two is not good odds."

"77, 57, your new target bears 065 degrees range 80, heading south. Singleton on barrier at Flight Level 300."

Barrier he had said. They were being vectored onto the AWACS aircraft!

"Bloody hell, it's above us," said Burner as he pushed the throttles back open and brought the airbrakes in. They had just passed 10,000 feet in the descent and were now faced with regaining their lost height and this time fuel was a factor.

"77 climbing," he prompted his wingman as they began the steady trudge back to 30,000 feet. They couldn't risk using the burners yet as they may need the fuel later.

"Loneship 77 request instructions."

"Roger 77, you are to intercept, identify and report back."

"Understand my contact bears 065 range 60," said Tom reporting the blip which had just appeared on his radar scope.

"Affirmative." There was a brief pause.

"Burner, am I missing something or does that put this guy over the border?"

"Yep, I reckon he's about 20 miles the other side," he replied.

"Loneship 77, are we cleared hot pursuit?" called Tom, underlining the point to the fighter controller. They had been ordered to identify the target which would mean closing in to visual ranges. That would be difficult from 20 miles away!

"77 standby, checking." came the response.

"Good to see they're on the ball," he muttered.

"Put them down a hole behind a scope and they forget that there's a real world out here!"

"Tell me about it."

"OK, I'm contact on this one, 065 for 60. Centre him up."

The pilot adjusted the heading bringing the contact onto the centreline.

"We're not going over the border without positive clearance. Reception committees from mad East Germans I don't need," he muttered.

"I'm with you!"

"77 Judy," called Tom taking control of the intercept. "Loneship do you have that clearance yet?"

"77 negative, err affirmative, you are not clear hot pursuit."

The bland statement temporarily threw Tom off balance as he had been prepared for a positive answer. The contact was 20 miles inside hostile airspace and visual contact was out of the question at long range. He desperately considered the problem.

"Look, if this is the barrier aircraft, I assume they want to give him something to keep him temporarily occupied," he thought aloud. "I'm going to lock him up and we'll give him a blast of CW to make him think we've targeted him. Let's see how he reacts. It may give the guys some thinking time. Right now he's range 50, we'll lock at 30.

"Understood."

"Hold that heading. He's heading south and we've got a 120 attack, target's crossing from left to right."

As they hit 30 miles, Tom positioned the acquisition markers over the response from the Mainstay and squeezed the trigger. Instantly, the combined energy from the main radar and the CW tracking signal highlighted the distant aircraft. They had 10 miles to run to the border.

*

Aboard the Mainstay panic ensued.

"Captain this is the EWO, hostile contact bearing 240 range 35, locked up..........Guidance signal! Emergency abort heading 090 degrees."

The Captain in the left hand seat of the AEW aircraft hauled the control yoke hard over to the left, not for an instant questioning the command, causing the aircraft to lurch uncomfortably. It was not designed for hard manoeuvre. He cursed. It had been a stupid move to push them so far forward despite the importance of the task. The border was only 30 Km away and the western forces were bound to want the Su-27 desperately. With the new Vega-M radar aboard the Soviet airborne early warning aircraft able to track targets out to 500 Km and, unlike the old Moss, with equally good radar performance overland, they could have done a good job from overhead Berlin. Here, right up against the border, they were completely vulnerable and it was he who would have to attempt to recover the situation.

"Have you got an identification on it?" he asked optimistically.

"Affirmative. It's a British F4 armed with AIM-7E Sparrow missiles. He's out of range at the moment but with supersonic performance, it will not take him long to run us down if he follows."

"Shit!" the pilot replied in frustration.

The Mainstay had only just been certified as airworthy and he hoped that the manoeuvre that he was about to carry out would not overstress the airframe, particularly the huge circular radome on top of the fuselage. Steady on his easterly heading, he pushed the yoke forward looking for zero G. As a former fighter pilot he knew that if he was to hit his best acceleration profile it would be in an unloaded condition at zero gravity. He also realised that the action would cause havoc down the back as loose items of equipment and coffee cups cannoned around the cabin and their very survival was at stake. He watched the airspeed indicator as it began its slow rise towards the never exceed speed, willing it to rise faster.

"Range of the F4 now?" he questioned urgently.

"Still range 30 Km."

It was a long tailchase and his turn had collapsed the engagement envelope of the Sparrow missile. As long as he kept running and unless the F4 pilot was either very brave or very stupid, he would get away with it. Unfortunately, the violent manoeuvre was more than the immature avionics suite could handle. With the flow of coolant to the massive transmitter temporarily disrupted by the lack of gravity, an immediate rise in temperature was inevitable. With the impending thermal overload, the system opted for self-preservation rather than self-destruction and closed down. Further advice to the Migs in Thunder formation from the onboard controllers ceased. Stargazer had been silenced.

*

"It worked Burner!" said Tom enthusiastically. "The bastard's turned and he's running out on east. Still range 15."

"Good effort!"

"77 and 57 Loneship, vector 360 to remain within the ADIZ. You are not, repeat not, cleared hot pursuit."

"Turning north, I see the bogey running on east."

For once, the Phantom crews had no difficulty in complying with GCI instructions. The line of the border, stark across the forest stretched north to south ahead of them and the reception on the other side would have been too hot to handle, particularly as 57, his wingman was barely armed with just the Suu-23 gun for company. They turned north maintaining their height, scanning the airspace to the east warily. Thankfully, the radar warning receiver remained silent.

*

Kalienko was stunned. Minutes before he had been completing a simple refuelling evaluation and yet here he was, his formation slowly being decimated around him. First the aircraft, which he now recognised as the prototype Su-27, a surprise in itself, had destroyed his number 4 and then, as he had wound up his turn entering the engagement, his Number 3 had been taken out by another threat. His radar warner was frustratingly silent so he had no clues who he was facing. Stargazer had gone suspiciously quiet and he was no longer receiving any control. His High Lark radar was worse than useless this low. Scanning the airspace rapidly, he tried to reacquire the Su-27 hoping that his wingman was following his turn. The Number 3 had been the only other sniper pilot in the formation; the remaining pilot was a rookie and would be of no use whatsoever. As he completed the turn, his Sirena 3 RWR flashed briefly indicating a fighter threat in the front quadrant. He could see the Su-27 across the circle and briefly questioned the contradictory information. There had to be another aircraft in the fight but what type? That sequence of lights had been briefed often enough during training but, surely, it couldn't be?

The pilot of Mike Lima 61 watched the Sparrow gyrate wildly before it screwed out of control and crashed into a farm outhouse.

"No kill, missile trashed," he called to his leader. Unbeknown to Kalienko, the fact that the brief warning on his RWR had ceased as the missile had aborted had signalled a short extension to his lifespan.

The Phantoms powered into the engagement and Yuri suppressed his natural urges to react, realising that his loyalties had changed. Dropping his nose, he tried to engineer a quiet exit from the engagement. He had no interest in prolonging the agony. His priorities lay elsewhere and an ejection at this stage would be the end of his mission in more ways than one. His jet was more than a match for any of the aircraft from either side wheeling around the skies around him but discretion was stronger.

The Su-27 straightened and descended, the pilot electing to disengage, his westerly heading telegraphing his intentions as clearly as words. He was making a dash for the border and Kalienko knew that his R23 missiles were useless at this height so close to the ground without a radar lock from the High Lark. He would have to rely on his R60 infra-red missiles. The Su-27 was ahead of him but still outside the range of his missiles. He would have to close so he eased lower attempting to keep sight of his quarry but, unfamiliar with the rigours of low level air combat, he was finding the pressures impossible. His training had been pitifully inadequate for this type of engagement and it was further complicated by the fact that his missiles were fixed to the boresight of the aircraft's weapons datum which was elevated by 2 degrees. Optimised for air combat, he realised that in order to bring the gunsight onto his target he would have to push his nose down, bringing his aircraft dangerously close to the trees below him. Maintaining his overtake on the Su-27, he began the delicate process.

The remaining pair of Floggers turned across Razor's nose but he realised that there were still three aircraft out there. Where was the other? He finally spotted it, leading the "daisy chain" which had developed ahead of him and he strained his eyes trying to make out the detail....... My God it really was a Flanker, the latest Soviet fighter. This was a prize worth taking home. He listened to Flash's ongoing commentary reassured that his tail was clear of threats, analyzing the disparate facts, building a mental picture of where his wingman was in relation to the other players. Confident, he switched his whole attention to the aircraft in front and matching the bogey's turn, flicked to Sidewinder on the weapons control panel realising that, as yet, the aircraft in front had not seen him.

"Good lock" called Flash, "In range. Your tail's clear."

Razor listened for the growl which was still faint but as he finessed his position, the Flogger in his gunsight reversed its turn, temporarily destroying his tracking solution. Further ahead, the lead Flogger had straightened out and was running down the Flanker.

"72 switching, this one's yours," he called to his wingman allowing the other Phantom to pull up and over his tail slotting directly onto the escaping Flogger. He turned his attention to his new target, the elusive leader.

"Keep the radar in search Flash. The last guy got a warning from his RWR. We'll take a Sidewinder shot."

The radar continued in scan as Flash kept up his running commentary.

Rolling off the bank and dragging the nose high, he pulled into a high yo-yo, a combat manoeuvre designed to reduce the high angle off the bogey's tail which had built up progressively. He momentarily lost contact with the bogey as it was obscured by the radome of the Phantom but, as the nose recommitted downwards and the wing dropped, it reappeared. The clock was ticking as the Flogger closed on the Flanker and Razor closed on the Flogger.

Kalienko pushed the nose down knowing that the range was good but nervous of the proximity of the ground. He watched it rush towards him, the altimeter unwinding rapidly and bottled out, the altimeter reading a mere 50 metres as he recovered. Climbing back up to a comfortable height with sweat breaking out on his brow, he had ceased to show any interest in his wingman and now concentrated solely on the aircraft ahead; he was fixated. He had to prevent this lunatic from defecting with the prototype and he repositioned for a further attempt at a missile shot. The Su-27 could eat him alive but it showed no sign of reacting to his aggressive moves. He fixed on the fleeing target. His missiles were primed.

Razor had him cold. The range was perfect and the target sat nicely at the base of his gunsight. A piece of cake; he had practised the manoeuvre a million times before in training. From Flash's commentary, he knew that his wingman was threatening the other Flogger so he pushed over and, registering the growl, simultaneously pulled the trigger. The missile leaped from the rails and writhed towards the Flogger trailing a smoke plume. It lurched sickeningly earthwards and, momentarily, he thought it would strike the ground harmlessly. As it completed its convolutions, it reared back upwards towards its quarry and struck the Flogger directly forward of the jetpipe. The tailplane detached causing the hapless jet to pitch nose down in a terminal somersault from which recovery was impossible.

Kalienko registered a brief note of disbelief as he died.

*

Inside the Mainstay, the Tactical Coordinator struggled with the errant radar system trying to reset the power and bring it back on line. The immediate threat from the F4 was past and, eventually, after a good deal of coaxing, the first signs of life burst onto the tactical display screens and he set about trying to re-establish the tactical air picture. Where were the Mig-23s and what had happened to the Su-27? More importantly, what were the F4s who had just tried to engage the Mainstay doing? He needed answers quickly. He could see the Brit F4s holding a northerly CAP pattern just the other side of the border and there were two more skirmishing just inside East German airspace. A separate contact ahead was the one he assumed was the Su-27. Goddamn, it looked as if the traitor would make his escape but where was the Mig formation? Why were they not stopping him? He hit the interrogator but there was no response from the Odd Rod system in the Migs, or from the Phantoms although that was to be expected. Assuming that the IFF system was still not back on line, he fine-tuned the radar picture trying to break out the primary radar responses from the missing fighters but could not. They seemed to have disappeared. Surely not; it was not possible!

*

The Soviet gunner twitched as his attention wandered. The officer had gone over the procedures for the live firing exercise in minute detail again and again and, with the best will in the world, he had heard the standard briefing a thousand times before. He struggled to pay attention. They had deployed forward of the main air defence elements as they would in a real land battle with his Sa-7 detail supporting the SA-8 battery. For the purposes of this exercise, a small exclusion zone had been established around the launch area to allow them to exercise free play. Unmanned drones would fly through the airspace and they would launch four Sa-7 Grail missiles in an attempt to take them out. The Sa-8 battery had fired most of its allowance the previous day but still had one missile to fire before it would be his sections turn. There were plenty of opportunities for live firing because the missiles had a finite life after which time they were supposedly useless. As they reached their expiry date they were offered up for just this type of exercise. The opportunity for his gunners to use real hardware was invaluable and had a positive effect on their morale; they all looked forward to these events. In his experience, the fact that they were life expired seemed to make no difference. They were so rugged, protected in their green canisters, that they seemed to work no matter how old they were. He trudged back down the farm track away from the disused farmhouse that had been set up as a temporary control post. Slipping the written orders, which reiterated the mind numbing briefing and his rules of engagement into his pocket he rounded the corner into the field and made his way towards his own tent. He could hear the whine of the auxiliary generator from the mobile Sa-8 unit as the crew ran the Land Roll radar system through its paces. The antenna nodded and gyrated as it ran through its inbuilt test programme and as the radar finished its check, the missiles began their own routine. The quadruple launchers turned slowly through 360 degrees before the missiles, in concert, elevated swiftly to the vertical position before slumping slowly to rest again. Very impressive he thought to himself but you couldn't beat the man-portable Sa-7 which he and his men operated. Small and lightweight, his own launcher could be carried by one man and could be made ready for firing in seconds. More to the point, NATO would kindly come down to low level which was the ideal environment for his little rocket. He had seen the mobile monsters bogged down in fields and stuck in self induced traffic jams and knew that without proper set-up routines, they were useless. Give me an Sa-7 any day he decided. As the troop gathered round, he began to run through the briefing feeling hypocritical having only moments before been criticising his officer for his verbose delivery. He pointed out the plinth which had been set up in the far corner of the field, its presence more a sop to military protocol than operational necessity. It was superfluous as his missiles could be fired from up a tree in a bird's nest. He ran over the salient points but returned to underline the key facts before finishing:

"OK, cutting through the bullshit, the most important point is that the drones will arrive from directly behind the firing butts and will fly away from us. That will give us a good infra-red response and a receding target is best suited for the missile. It prefers a bit of a crossing rate so bear that in mind. Go through your own arming procedures but I will exercise full control procedures. Fire only on my command. I'll be monitoring the command frequency net and I'll relay the engagement orders to you. Any questions? No? OK, start preparing the missiles."

The gunners returned to their tasks and the first nominated firer laid out his fire unit preparing it for the exercise. He laid out the launcher tube and clipped the stock into place half way along the base of the tube. Next, he withdrew the thermal battery and checked the fit in the housing before returning it to its carrying case. This would be his final action prior to firing as the battery provided the power for the acquisition circuits and the launch commands. Once fired up, the battery lasted only seconds and, without one, the missile was useless. For now, the missile would remain dormant. It had taken only seconds to assemble the one metre long launcher yet inside the missile, inert in the firing tube, was sufficient explosive to destroy a multi-million rouble aircraft. Tests complete they moved across to the firing point, morale running high.

*

"61 position" called Razor.

"5 seconds to kill," came the matter of fact response, followed by a smoke trail in the distance.

"Fox 2 on the Flogger turning left through east."

Concise, matter-of-factly delivered, a calculated termination. The full implications would only register later.

"Bugging out on west," called the wingman anxious to be back in safer territory.

"Acknowledged," called Razor, "RV in the Kassel Fritzlar gap," he instructed looking ahead trying desperately to gain sight of the Flanker which was still pressing on at high speed.

"Loneship, 72, 61, splash 4, going home, mission complete and in company!" he announced with excitement.

"Let's take this jet home." he said to his back seater.

Flash recalled the Station Commander's words about smoking holes in East Germany and felt slightly less ebullient. He glanced ahead around the ironwork and saw the incredible profile of the Flanker and suddenly felt slightly more bullish.

In his mirrors, Yuri could see the Phantom closing in his eight o'clock position but held the Su-27 on a rock steady heading nonetheless. In 10 km he would be safe but in the meantime there was safety in numbers. Just the last SAM and AAA belt to breach and he could look forward to a beer in the west.

*

A klaxon sounded and the gunner could see the missiles on the Sa-8 combat vehicle rotate and fix on a point in the distance as the radar scanner nodded gently, acquiring its target. The drones were fitted with both radar and infra-red enhancement devices to make them a more attractive target for these practice firings. The Sa-8 faltered momentarily as if making a choice, the missiles picking up one heading but settling back on the original vector. It gyrated furiously tracking its prey and, as a further klaxon sounded, he tensed in anticipation. There was a loud crack followed by a sharp hiss as the missile left its launcher shrouded in a cloud of smoke aiming towards its, as yet, invisible target. He listened to the chatter on the control frequency as the success of the shot was confirmed but the whole event had been completed without even gaining sight of the drone. No fun at all. Now it was over to his own team to show what they could do. The first gunner stepped onto the firing point and hoisted his launcher tube onto his shoulder while his team mate handed him the thermal battery. The battery was snapped smartly into place and the gunner raised a thumb in readiness. He rechecked the combat frequency and received confirmation that the drone was airborne and he was clear to fire. Anticipation heightened around the point.

"Wait for it!" A barked call across the firing point, his final gesture of control. Moving forward to a position adjacent to the plinth where he was more visible to the firer he raised both thumbs, his pre-arranged authorization for the launch, and received an answering nod from the gunner. Looking across the hedgerow he strained his eyes and ears for the approaching drone that he thought he could just make out in the distance. Unexpectedly, he was aware of movement in his peripheral vision as a pair of fast moving aircraft appeared from a heading 40 degrees off the threat axis. He reported the intrusion to his controller over the radio link expecting an immediate emergency termination but was astounded to hear the words:

"Engage fast movers, engage fast movers."

A moment of hesitation as he confirmed the instructions with increasing incredulity, before directing the gunners attention towards the screaming jets with his pointing stick. Without hesitation the gunner slewed his aim, flicked the battery into life and fired. There was a momentary delay followed by a dull pop and the noise of the missile leaving its canister and trailing skywards in pursuit of its receding quarry.

The Phantoms closed back into battle formation. They would remain at low level until they had safely re-entered western airspace, the crews knowing all too well the density of SAM and AAA deployments in this area of the border. As Flash glanced across the formation he was drawn to a puff of smoke from the ground as a missile plume tore upwards from the corner of a wood aiming directly at his wingman.

"61 Break port," he yelled as the Phantom instantaneously snapped on 90 degrees of bank away from him. The reaction had been unquestioning but there was little else could be done as, unlike most tactical aircraft, the Phantom was not fitted with flare dispensers. He watched with alarm as the missile guided unerringly towards the aircraft impacting beneath the jetpipe in a great shower of debris.

Its corkscrew motion had been true as it had guided inexorably towards the hapless aircraft which belatedly commenced a last ditch manoeuvre. Too late the gunner mused totally detached from events. Your only hope now is a flare. Suddenly, he found himself identifying with the luckless pilot who frantically countered the unexpected threat. The aircraft, which was now recognisable as an American-built Phantom, reefed hard into the missile attempting to outturn the projectile as the whole sequence appeared to run in slow motion. There were no flares and the missile struck the aircraft with a dull thump which was clearly audible from where he stood. It bucked visibly and lost height in its counter manoeuvre yet remained doggedly airborne. It steadied up on heading and flew on at a much lower level across the trees and disappeared from sight trailing smoke.

The airframe shuddered as the missile found its target embedding itself in the hot metal of the left afterburner. The response through the controls was immediate as the aircraft slewed wildly, reacting to the sudden loss of thrust on one engine further emphasised by the damage to the stabilator.

"Shit, we're hit. What's our position," yelled the pilot urgently.

"Still 5 miles inside East Germany," responded the navigator with equal imperative.

"I can't pull for height. It's going to take us up into the heart of the missile envelope. We couldn't take another hit. The left engine's wound down and we've lost utilities pressure. I'm doing the bold face drills, give me the rest of the checks from the flight reference cards when you can. I'm keeping it low."

"Best hold on the radio call until we're back inside our own airspace," prompted the navigator. "They could triangulate on us and work out our position. Is it still flyable?"

"Yes, stick with it, we'll make it!"

Both crew were working at the limits of their capacity trying to second guess the problems the missile strike would cause but if they were to recover successfully they would have to rely on automatic reactions instilled by years of training. They were each willing the border to appear. RAF Gutersloh was not far beyond. A border visit was mandatory for Germany-based aircrew and the lasting impression which every individual took away with him was of the impregnability of the border defences. What was crystal clear to both of them at this moment was that if they ejected here, there would be no chance of walking to freedom. The Phantom limped westwards. The missile had damaged key flight control systems and the handling of the aircraft was tenuous. Even under normal circumstances it would have been difficult to recover the aircraft and pilots lacking in experience had been known to lose control. Their predicament heightened the pressure. The watchtowers which dotted the border appeared, standing proud of the surrounding pine forest. The pilot deliberately aimed his aircraft between adjacent towers. To fly directly overhead when the guards' brief was to prevent anything, under any circumstances, passing from east to west, was courting disaster. A small arms bullet through the remaining hydraulic system would make life distinctly uncomfortable for them and would mean certain ejection.

In the other Phantom, Razor knew what the crew were going through in the crippled jet as the pilot struggled to keep it airborne and, with the aid of his navigator, attempted to diagnose the sudden emergency. Razor and Flash both stared at the stricken machine looking for signs of fire which would precede an inevitable ejection; the Phantom lacked a fire extinguishing system. It was a nightmare in hostile territory.

"61 sitrep," he queried not wishing to pressurise the hard worked crew but knowing that quick reaction would be their only chance of survival.

"Err Roger, we have a single engine failure and double utilities, Standby," came the shaken response from the other jet. This meant that as well as having lost an engine and its associated power control system which powered the flying control surfaces, the utilities system which operated other essential services such as the landing gear was also disabled. The aircraft was barely flying. Razor, hanging slightly back from the crippled jet tensed.

"Sorry mate but you're on your own. Gutersloh bears 320 range 60, continuing as tasked."

"61."

The radio call was abrupt but the sentiment accepted. Despite rule number one of airmanship which was that full assistance was always offered to other aircraft in distress, Razor felt that this mission must override his natural instincts. Nevertheless, he didn't have to feel good about it.

"See you on the ground 61, the beer's on me and best of luck!"

*

Back at Wildenrath the circuit was hot.

"Mike Lima 76 clearing the zone to tactical."

It had not been a good start to the sortie. Slats and JB, leading a four-ship 2v2 air combat training sortie had walked to their aircraft on time but, as they had checked in, the Number 4 had aborted with a failure of the electrical system. His efforts to change into the spare aircraft had been rewarded with a further hydraulics failure. Slats and JB had now left their Number 2 in the overhead at Wildenrath with a BLC failure. BLC or boundary layer control was a system which blew air over the leading edge flaps smoothing the airflow when the flaps were down, giving improved handling characteristics at slow speed. The air was fed directly from a tapping in the core of the jet engine but passed over the aircraft surfaces at extremely high temperatures. With a BLC failure, valves which channelled the air had failed in the open position when the flaps were raised, allowing air to bleed into the wing area around the aircraft fuel tanks. Hot air and fuel were an explosive combination and action was needed quickly to vent the bleed air to atmosphere. Once the flaps were lowered the air once again vented safely but a Phantom with a full fuel load and a speed limit of 250 knots with gear and flaps down was relegated to a particularly boring continuation sortie in the instrument pattern or the circuit until it could burn down to landing weight. As he monitored his wingman in the circuit, Slats had pondered on the poor serviceability record which the Phantom had shown in the recent past that had just decimated his four-ship. Something had to give soon he thought, conscious of his own mortality held in place by the slender thread of the technology around him. Having left the wingman to his own devices, Slats and JB decided to press into the low flying area as a pair with the single remaining Phantom and to carry out a mutual 1v1 exercise before setting up a fighter trawl through the area to catch some targets of opportunity. As they bored through the low level airspace, their heads rotating on gimbals, they were constantly aware of the risk of interception by other marauding NATO fighters whose pilots were always keen to send gunsight film of an unwary Phantom crew through the post to the embarrassed recipient. They were keen not to be caught at their own game.

"Entering the low flying area, clear down to 250 feet," called JB.

Slats eased the Phantom lower and as they passed the Wüpperfurth Lakes, they both relaxed slightly knowing that they were safely clear of the congested civil airspace around Köln/Bonn and Düsseldorf. It would definitely raise comment, not to mention invitations to survey Senior Officers' carpets, if a high speed Phantom was to transit a civil runway at low level. JB stared at the scope hoping for a random target to practise his skills.

"It's looking a bit quiet at the moment," he murmured to Slats as they pressed on eastward, both the radar and the RWR stubbornly inactive. All he could see was the occasional paint from the GCI site at Loneship.

"Let's aim up to the Hawk site on the hill near Warburg and check out Area 3. If there's nothing there we can switch to Area 2 and CAP at Reken to catch anyone recovering to Brüggen and Laarbruch."

"Sounds like a plan to me," responded Slats "but we'll just throw in a quick air combat 1v1 for matey boy before we press. We're in the sheets for ACT so it would be a waste not to give it a whirl."

"Suits me!"

JB held the Phantom down at 250 feet as they cleared the small village.

"Outwards turn for combat go."

The rules demanded that all air combat should take place above 5,000 feet. For realism, they would run in at low level but limit the first pass to defensive manoeuvring then pull up through the light aircraft zone to complete the combat in the block between 5,000 and 10,000 feet. The jets turned outwards through 45 degrees and began to diverge but inside the cockpits four sets of eyes were on gimbals, turning almost simultaneously to keep track of the opposing aircraft. The basic rule of air combat was "he who sees wins." Put another way by many an expert, "It's the one that you don't see that gets you." At this point in time, not one of the aircrew intended to be the one who lost sight.

"Padlocked," called JB squinting against the low sun, unable to drop his dark visor in case he lost the vital visual contact.

"Keep talking."

The navigator had a better view into the six o'clock particularly as, without the need to keep hold of the stick, he could screw his body around much further in the seat.

"Left 8 o'clock, 2 miles opening. He's on the deck."

"Still tally, our speed's 450."

The jets continued to the limit of visual contact, everyone tense, anticipating the call when they would be allowed off the leash. The turn back call was leader's benefit.

"Inwards turn go. Fight's on!"

Simultaneously, both jets cranked on 90 degrees of bank and pulled hard back towards each other, the navigators immediately trying to lock the radars to the simulated threat.

"Fox 1," over the ether. For one aircraft, had the engagement been for real, a missile would be in the air pre-empting a victory. In the other, the navigator's failure to lock would have presaged the cold realisation that the mistake had been fatal. For any crew, the preferred method of entry into a fight was at the end of a "smoking telegraph pole; the Sparrow missile.

"Red 1 tally."

"Red 2 tally."

"Continue"

The safety call was vital. With the jets closing at breakneck speed covering the scant miles between them in seconds, it was vital that the at least one crew member could see the other aircraft if a collision was to be avoided. Many a crew had listened, in dread, to the "continue" call having lost sight, knowing that the next call would be "Fox 2" from the gloating opponent. Inside the aircraft, the crews talked incessantly preparing themselves for the ensuing engagement.

"Bogey, 11 o'clock, 2 miles."

"Roger, missile's timed out. Good kill, continue."

"Putting him down the left hand side, stand by for the pass. We'll go straight into the vertical."

"Speed's good at 420 knots."

"Standby..... Bogeys now, pulling up!" The jets merged 1,000 feet apart.

"Tally Ho!"

The pilot watched the other Phantom flash down the left hand side and, as they passed, pulled the stick back hard into his stomach having already led with the afterburner. Pulling into the vertical, he dropped the left wing to keep the twisting jet in sight realising that as it drifted into his six o'clock where he would lose him. With relief he listened to the commentary from the back seat meaning that his navigator could still see the bogey.

"Bogey went left at the merge. He kept it flat. Got him, left 8 o'clock 1 mile."

Slats considered the implication as the jet climbed rapidly through 5,000 feet in a left hand oblique loop. Below, the other aircraft still held the low level turn trying to unsight him. Hanging above, inverted, he pushed to hold the height above the new hard deck of 5,000 feet trying to avoid having to recommit nose low until his opponent made his move. The move had to come soon but he was running out of options. If he returned upright, it would put the bogey below him and out of sight leading to a quick and embarrassing finale. Commit, commit, he breathed, sighing with relief as the other aircraft finally dragged its nose up and began to follow. He rolled off the bank listening to JB's commentary as he set himself up for the follow on.

"He's committing nose on at 7 o'clock, range 1 mile. Roll right, roll right. Stop. Pull!"

JB had watched the bogey closing in and had not liked what he saw. Slats had momentarily taken his eyes off his opponent and allowed him to move into a threatening position and JB had immediately called the counter-manoeuvre to negate the threat and keep the angle off high. His new problem was the revised "hard-deck". The hypothetical ground level was only just below them now. One bad call and he could command his pilot to pull into the "ground." Spatial awareness was vital and a base height violation was as terminal as a simulated missile shot against them.

"Keep pulling, 8 o'clock range 1 mile nose on."

As long as he was the only one sighted, he would continue to call the shots.

"We're making on him, 9 o'clock still nose on."

"God, why can't I see him," muttered Slats. "Roger, got him, Tally."

*

Thirty miles to the east, Mike Lima 61 wallowed westwards slowly, trailing smoke. Ahead was a most unusual mixed formation. The crew had finished their emergency drills and the situation was stable. They had avoided an ejection so far and the range to Gutersloh was winding down. They could make it back safe.

*

Slats had regained the initiative and could see the other Phantom and take over once again. Gratefully, he realised that JB had made some angles on the bogey and he was in better shape than when he had lost sight. Whilst still threatening, the opponent had made the mistake of keeping his nose on and, due to the hard counter turn, had built up an impossibly high angle off the tail losing energy in the process. His Sidewinder could not cope with the high aspect and, realising his mistake, the aggressor had rolled his wings level. Extending through the flight path, he had brought the nose up in a classic high yo-yo basic fighter manoeuvre. Had Slats not reacted, he could have recommitted, bringing his nose back on into a perfect position for a missile shot but air combat was not so predictable. Seeing the counter move, Slats had rolled off the bank matching his opponents move and pulled hard back towards him drawing him into a vertical, rolling scissors manoeuvre. The two aircraft carried on climbing, pulling haphazardly towards each other, apparently on collision course but as they rolled drunkenly, Slats began to dominate. As the flight paths crossed, despite the outward appearance, each move followed a precisely calculated pattern. Extracting the maximum performance from the weaving jet, Slats moved progressively behind his opponent's wing line. A shot beckoned.

"Check fuel," he heard from the back.

Bad timing but a vital check. Each aircraft hung on its afterburners, fuel being burned at the alarming rate of 2000 lbs per minute. This was the other factor which could win or lose an engagement; he who ran out of fuel ran out of ideas. There were two possible outcomes to this particular scissors. The offensive aircraft could make a mistake allowing the defender sufficient room to screw back, generate a defensive pitch back and escape. More likely, one aircraft could win the battle of wills and give too much separation easing outside the minimum range of the Sidewinder missile and leaving his tail open to the shot. Minimum range was important for two reasons. Firstly, the arming circuits would not have sufficient time to activate at extremely close range. Secondly, there would be a debris hemisphere around the target aircraft which would cause grief to any pilot fool enough to venture too close to his handiwork. Debris and jet engines were not happy bedfellows. Slats had, by now, made considerable ground on his less experienced opponent and as the bulk of the Phantom flashed though the gunsight a mere 300 yards ahead, his hand dropped to the weapons selector and flicked to guns.

"Good lock," he heard from the back as if by ESP his navigator locked the radar providing a tracking solution for the lead computing gunsight. The reticule glowed red in the sight glass as the Phantom slewed back through the centreline and he squeezed the trigger simulating a high angles gun pass.

"Snapshot, continue."

He was not yet satisfied. Some of the bullets from the high speed Suu-23 Gatling gun would have struck home but at such a high rate of fire, in excess of 6,000 rounds per minute, the majority would have whistled harmlessly past. This would have been exacerbated by the high rate of travel through the gunsight. He had insufficient performance left to keep the gunsight on the target. Nevertheless, hits from one or two HEI or high explosive incendiary rounds would be sufficient to cause mortal damage to a modern airframe. The explosive bullets would rip through hydraulic lines and cause devastation. Unhappy with the snapshot, he continued the engagement looking for a more conclusive opportunity. The range slowly increased as the crazy weave continued, afterburners still eating the precious Avtur, and as he approached missile parameters, his hand once again dropped to the weapons selector bringing up the Sidewinder indications. The missile growled quietly, registering the ambient infra-red emissions but as the heat of the target's engines in full reheat registered in the field of view, the tone changed to the familiar strident growl as it acquired the target. He squeezed the trigger.

"Fox 2, knock it off, roll out on north." he called to his chastened wingman underlining his victory. He could not suppress his growing feeling of satisfaction despite the fact that on this occasion his opponent had been a squadron mate. The second rule of air combat was "Fight to Win" and he had just satisfied rule 2. There was no feeling in the world quite like it. The Sport of Kings.

*

The lead Battle Flight aircraft, Mike Lima 72, had already pulled ahead to join the Flanker and was becoming, even now, a dot in the distance. Neither of the crew of Mike Lima 61 resented the decision to leave them because, with so much at stake, the collective gain was greater than the individual pain. The acceptance did not make the feeling of isolation any easier.

"I'm making all turns away from the failed wing," explained the pilot. With one of the major hydraulic systems dead and only the flying surfaces on one wing operating, he had little choice.

"Once we're over the border, I'll jettison the tanks and missiles to make us lighter and more controllable. When we're sure we're back in the ADIZ, I'll push out a PAN call."

"OK mate, I reckon just a couple more miles should see us. Can you see the towers, right 2 o'clock range 2 miles?"

"Got them..............that's a relief!"

"Gutersloh is 320 degrees range 60."

"Coming onto 320."

*

"Were back in the ADIZ," called Flash. "At least if they have to jump out now it will be a western helicopter that comes to pick them up."

Razor turned his attention back to the Flanker, knowing that really he should be shepherding his wingman home rather than following the foreign "guest."

"Can you see this guy Flash?" he inquired, "I just lost him."

"Yeah, he's in your one o'clock range two miles just starting to pull up from low level. Bring it starboard 20 degrees."

"Tally Ho" came the response as the pilot reacquired the Soviet aircraft. The Flanker was clearly visible now as it pulled up clear of the terrain. Razor checked his fuel yet again, aware that he had paid scant attention to the precious resource during the engagement. It was low but enough to get back to Wildenrath, although he would have to be a little wary about using any more afterburner. He eased the throttles forward and edged ever closer.

"Aircraft in the ADIZ, this is Mike Lima 72 come up 364.2 and identify yourself," he instructed. The frequency he had given was the NATO common intercept frequency which he knew would be carried by everyone in the vicinity. A pregnant pause.

"Mike Lima 72 this is Ramrod on 364.2 how do you read?"

"Loud and clear Ramrod and welcome aboard!" Razor eased alongside and rocked his wings, the universal signal that the aircraft in formation been intercepted and should comply with his instructions. He received a thumbs up from the Russian who slotted into a perfect formation position on the Phantom. They stared dumbstruck at the elegant lines of the Soviet aircraft which hung dramatically on the wing, the air of unreality pervasive. Before now, the sight had been confined to a few grainy intelligence photographs and poor satellite shots but this one was for real. Razor tapped his visor in an exaggerated movement signifying that the Russian should follow and initiated a gentle turn towards Wildenrath starting a slow climb to a more fuel efficient cruising level. Over friendly airspace and pushing down a friendly squawk, they could afford to be more relaxed.

*

The scar of the border slipped astern as the crippled Phantom eased back into West German airspace much to the relief of both crew. Their troubles were not over yet but black thoughts of incarceration in an East German gaol were receding into history allowing them to switch their attention back to handling the emergency. The drills had gone smoothly and proved the worth of the countless hours spent in the simulator. The emergency call to Air Traffic had started a flurry of activity and despite the wallowing response of the sluggish jet, both crew began to feel more optimistic over the outcome. The nervous gnawing in the pit of the stomach had not disappeared but the certainty of a "Martin Baker letdown" had faded.

"OK let's get rid of these tanks," he said to his navigator. Moving his hand down to the fuel control panel on the left hand console, he lifted the red guard on the outboard stores jettison switch.

"Check the jettison safety switch is to ready," he queried.

"Affirmative."

He cross checked the speed to ensure that he was within the safe limits and punched the switch. The navigator, watching over his shoulder, heard a loud thump as the ejector cartridges in the tank pylons fired and the tanks tumbled away from beneath the wings of the stricken aircraft. The jet became marginally lighter and easier to handle without the drag of the large external fuel tanks. More importantly, without the encumbrance, there was a greater margin for error with the limited thrust available from his remaining engine. The pilot had stressed his needs to the air traffic controller; all turns would have to be to the right and he would need the approach end arrestor cable for his landing. In this condition, if he once allowed the left hand wing to drop, he would not have the control to regain a level attitude and a crash would be inevitable. Being south of Gutersloh with the westerly runway in use, Air Traffic would have to set up a full orbit of the airfield to avoid that fatal left hand turn. Furthermore, he would need a long final approach heading of at least 15 miles to prepare him for the landing because his lack of control meant that he would have to avoid gross corrections of heading, height and speed. He chatted casually through the problems with the back seater reviewing the advice in the flight reference cards. Now that they were back on friendly territory, the incident had taken on a much more familiar air and training was taking over. As they finally turned downwind through the Gutersloh overhead, they felt ready. The airfield below was a welcome sight, a sanctuary from their difficulties but to reach that sanctuary the next ten minutes would be critical. The pilot settled the jet onto the downwind heading and adjusted his height. Let's get this thing in the groove, he subconsciously bantered to himself. If he followed the procedures it would run on rails but if he allowed himself into uncharted territory, the outcome was equally predictable or should that be unpredictable?

"15 miles downwind, come right onto 180," pattered the air traffic controller. "Come further right onto 240, closing heading, you are 14 miles from touchdown." The thought encouraged him.

"OK final approach checks," he prompted.

"Let's get the RAT out."

"RAT's extended."

"Speed below 350 knots...check. Keep an eye on that right hand PC pressure. OK we're ready for the gear and flaps." The simple error was to set a train of thought in motion which would prove nearly fatal.

"Turn right onto 272 degrees, final approach heading, said the Zone Controller as he brought the aircraft back westerly towards the airfield.

"PAN 61 contact Talkdown on 327.6"

"To Talkdown on 327.6, PAN 61."

The navigator dialled up the new frequency

"327.6 is set."

"Talkdown, PAN 61."

"PAN 61, Gutersloh Talkdown you are loud and clear, read back QFE set."

"61, 1016 set."

Both crew double checked their altimeters the critical pressure setting selected, their altimeters now showing height above the runway threshold and safety.

"Roger, slightly right of the centreline, come left onto 270 and maintain 1500 feet. Range 11 miles from touchdown."

"OK undercarriage coming down," he finally managed to inform his navigator through the chatter from the controller. He should really have blown it down earlier he realised. With a double utilities failure, the normal gear lowering system was inoperative and he would be relying on two pneumatic bottles to literally blow the gear down. Once in place, gravity would take over and lock the undercarriage legs in place. It was not unknown for the gear to lower asymmetrically and his worry now was that with reduced control he was rather close to the ground should the aircraft roll unexpectedly as he cycled the undercarriage.

"Gear going down," he called tensely. His left hand dropped to the gear handle on the front instrument panel. Normally he would move it downward to lower the wheels but on this occasion he gave it a sharp pull towards him to activate the emergency system, edgy as he did so. His eyes stayed glued to the indicators, three small "dolls eyes" adjacent to the gear handle. They briefly cross hatched as the air coursed through the pipes displacing the hydraulic fluid and jolting the gear selectors into life.

Left Main - the wheel symbol appeared.

Nosewheel - the wheel symbol appeared.

Right Main.......... after what seemed like a lifetime, finally the indicator rolled into place. Three positive indications.

"Gear is down and locked," he sighed, relieved. "Stand by for the hook."

He changed hands on the control column and the aircraft rolled drunkenly for a moment as his firm grip on the controls relaxed. His right hand moved over to the hook shaped lever on the right hand side of the instrument panel and hovered over it. Correcting the errors to the approach which he had just induced, he hit the transmit switch but was blocked by the incoming transmission.

"PAN 61 drifting left of the centreline, come right 2 degrees back onto 272. Commencing descent in one mile."

Distracted, he adjusted the heading as instructed and moved the hook handle firmly down. Once lowered, with a double utilities failure he knew that he could not retract it. The hook handle flashed briefly and came on steady; the hook was down.

"Gutersloh, PAN 61 is finals, 3 wheels, hook down, to land for an approach end cable engagement," he called eventually getting his message through.

"Roger PAN 61, clear to land into the cable. Start your descent now for a 2½ degree glidepath, range 6 miles."

The commands were coming thick and fast.

"OK, trim the ball to the centre, let's give it some," the back seater called trying to lift the atmosphere in the tense cockpit. Time was critical and the overworked pilot was at his limit. He eased the nose down to return to the ideal approach path watching the altimeter start to unwind slowly. The flaps when they lowered would change the trim of the aircraft and he had to get them down soon. He had left things late.

"Flaps coming to half," he muttered as his hand moved over to the emergency flap selector on the left hand cockpit wall. No hesitation this time. His hands were rapidly becoming a blur. The flaps lowered and because they were affected by the same problems as the gear, he was once again concerned at the risk of an uncontrollable roll. They began to move and he felt the jet respond. Jesus H Christ, the left wing was dropping! He struggled, moving the stick firmly but hard over to the right. The left wing continued to drop!

"It's a flapless approach with a double utilities," screamed the navigator. Get those flaps back up!" The mistake dawned on the overloaded pilot, his previous error unchallenged in the heat of events.

"The left wing's going down, I can't hold it. Stand by to eject!"

In the back, the navigator tensed and, locking his harness, his hands dropped to the seat pan firing handle.

"No...No, it's recovering, stay with it," he shouted. "I've got it." The left wing slowly came back up. "It's OK."

The unspoken accusation from the back seat was palpable if not entirely just. The debrief would come later. He recovered his composure realising that he had, unnecessarily, nearly lost the aircraft.

"If we miss the cable, we'll stay down and go for the overrun cable," he said attempting to reassert his authority and regain his confidence. If the hook jumped over the approach end cable it was vital that they both knew what they would do and he had already decided that with the aircraft in such a sorry state and his nerves already frayed, an overshoot for a further pattern was not a good idea. "If we go off the side of the runway, we eject. You go first but call me before you pull the handle."

In the back, the navigator was beginning to get the impression that there was only one route out of this aircraft.

"Passing four miles, below the glidepath, adjust your rate of descent," intoned the controller oblivious to the drama which had just occurred. The pilot looked ahead and could see the outline of the runway ahead, an enticing haven, immediately deciding to complete the approach visually, his desire to be back on the ground overpowering. The approach was sweet, nicely on the centreline and his height coming back under control. So close.

"Talkdown, confirm my hook's down?"

"PAN 61, from the runway caravan, your hook is down and your gear appears good." He had final visual confirmation and a weight lifted from his mind.

"Roger PAN 61 is visual going to Tower."

"Roger, contact Tower on 347.6, good luck."

Before he switched frequency, he heard the controller pass the final coordination call.

"PAN 61 is 2 miles finals cleared to land for an approach end arrest."

This call would alert all the aircraft on the Gutersloh frequencies of his presence. They would be waiting the outcome with a morbid fascination as they had all been monitoring his progress on the emergency Guard frequency as events had unfolded. Although the incident sounded routine, little could they guess that the real reason for his plight was a missile fired from a Soviet SAM battery. He glanced ahead, his hands making constant corrections to his attitude and rate of descent. As he approached the runway threshold the tension lifted but a few final obstacles remained. Across the end of the runway was a barrier system designed to stop a jet from overrunning the runway at the end of its landing run. His own hook now dangled 20 feet below his position in the cockpit so that if he misjudged his approach and landed short, he would rip the barrier from its mountings. It was designed to stop a jet at near walking pace not a 180 knot Phantom which was still airborne. His own landing point was the aircraft carrier style cable some 1500 feet beyond the runway threshold and he juggled to finesse his touchdown listening to the reassuring calls of speed from the back as the concrete rushed up towards him.

"On plus 5," he heard. Perfect. On speed was the ideal touchdown speed and 5 knots in hand was just what he needed.

"My straps are tight and locked," prompted the back seater as he dropped his own hand to check his seat locking handle. It moved forward to the locked position. Had he ejected, he would have been relying on the inertia reel system. Even now, the arrest when it came would be dramatic and he had no desire to inspect the instrument panel at close quarters. Another mistake. The hook scraped firmly on the concrete as it struck the runway surface. The main wheels followed with a thump as the jet returned to earth in a semi controlled state.

"Watching for the cable," called the back seater as the aircraft powered over the steel hawser at 160 knots. "Good arrest! We're in the cable."

The aircraft slowed dramatically as the hydraulic dampers played out, the cable slowly bringing the jet to a controlled stop in mere hundreds of feet. The tension drilled from both crew as they screamed in exultation. On Guard frequency he heard:

"Aircraft in the ADIZ, this is Mike Lima 72 come up 364.2 and identify yourself." The mission was continuing without them.

*

As they completed their air combat split over Warburg, Slats and JB in Mike Lima 76 heard the call on Guard frequency.

"Aircraft in the ADIZ, this is Mike Lima 72 come up 364.2 and identify yourself."

All aircraft in West Germany monitored Guard religiously as unauthorized intrusions into the ADIZ were not tolerated by either NATO or the Warsaw Pact.

"That's Razor and Flash," said JB.

"They're on Battle Flight today and they must have got a scramble after we crewed in, Lucky sods."

"How's about we loiter in Area 3 and pick them up on their way home?"

"Go for it!"

Slats waggled the wings to attract his wingman's attention and then eased the stick back bringing the nose above the horizon and at 1,000 feet, he pulled hard right using both hands on the stick screwing the aircraft around in a tight wingover. Selecting a small valley he dragged the nose back down through the horizon and aimed into the valley dropping the jet back to low level. He was hoping to use terrain screening to prevent the returning Battle Flight aircraft from detecting them on radar as they lurked awaiting their prey.

"Mike Lima 72 coming left," he heard on Guard. They were not too far away and as he followed the contours of the valley, he increased the separation from their intended target giving JB a good split range to set up his intercept. Seeing a village ahead, he eased the jet round giving it a wide berth. No point in upsetting the locals unduly. He was not to know the stakes were higher today. As the jet popped from the valley, having checked to see that his wingman had slotted into fighting wing formation, Slats pulled around onto east and climbed to 1500 feet in an oblique loop prompting an immediate response from the rear cockpit.

"Bring it further left Slats, I've got a contact bearing 070 degrees."

JB stroked the thumbwheel pointing his radar scanner directly at the distant aircraft, refining the still elusive contact. Flicking through into pulse mode the contact suddenly glowed brightly at 30 miles.

"Good contact, range 30, looks like he's at 10,000 feet."

The pilot adjusted his own heading, holding it rock steady knowing that his navigator was now trying to establish the heading of the target. Any inaccuracies on his part would suggest target evasion and would give a false assessment. Unless they each played their part the intercept would fail.

"I've got him heading 250 degrees. We'll go for a vertical profile, ease it back down to low level. He planned to attack from below, on a tight intercept limiting his lateral displacement and turning entirely in the vertical using a half loop manoeuvre. Hopefully, if he avoided locking on, the first the target would know of their presence was when they arrived one mile astern inside weapons parameters. Slats descended slowly eyes flicking to the radio altimeter, watching the trees that flashed past a mere 300 feet below. He listened closely to his back seater's commentary already in tune with his thoughts knowing that, in sacrificing the head on Sparrow shot, no RWR warning would be given to their opponent. With such a large amount of height displacement, they would fly a radar-to-visual attack and his job was to make visual contact as soon as possible. With such enormous height changes it would be impossible for the navigator to follow the target accurately on radar as they closed and without an early "Tally" they risked missing the intercept. The tactics were straight from Baron Von Richthofen's Air Combat Tactics Manual; the speeds and weapons from World War Three.

"Target's range 20 miles, happy with that heading. We'll start the climb at 5 miles."

Neither knew that an attack on the Battle Flight aircraft today was ill advised. JB would increase his commentary rate as the intercept reached its finale aiming to lock his pilot's "Mark One Eyeballs" onto the target in lieu of the radar contact.

"Range 15, target maintaining 10,000 feet, it will be a left to right pass at the merge. Ease it starboard 10 degrees. I'm starting to break out two targets in there. Looks like there's another in close formation. Keep a good look out as we commit." The words proved to be prophetic and timely.

"Holy shit!"

"What is it?" he responded alarm evident in his tone.

"Sorry.... no it's OK.... stay with it but we just missed a light aircraft! As you called, I looked out right and the little bastard was behind the canopy arch! If I hadn't moved we would have hit him!"

"What the hell was he doing down here with us, he's supposed to be in the light aircraft band?" exclaimed JB.

Light aircraft were supposed to operate above 1,500 feet. Careless illegal low flying had almost cost the aircraft and crew.

"He wants his head testing."

"Check range," the prompt from the pilot subtle. At this stage, further prevarication would cost the intercept.

"Start your pull now. Target's on the nose range 6 miles, 30 degrees high."

"Pulling"

"Still heading 250. We need to be vertical passing 5,000 feet."

Slats pulled firmly back on the stick and the aircraft rotated. As he passed 2,000 feet he cracked the afterburners to maintain his speed; he did not want to finish the manoeuvre slow.

"On the nose for 4 miles, 20 degrees high."

"No joy"

"Slightly left, 3 miles 20 high and holding. Through 5,000 feet. Keep that pull on."

"No joy."

The commentary became more urgent.

"On the nose for 2, losing contact."

"Looking..........Tally Ho," he breathed with a sigh of relief as the RWR erupted with a strident tone!"

"Disregard." shouted JB, "It's the Hawk battery. Press!"

As they had popped up from low level, the Hawk SAM Engagement Controller had decided to use them for a little extra tracking practise of his own, despite their friendly IFF response. Having analyzed the signal on his radar warner, JB relaxed. Settling into the familiar groove, Slats pulled the gunsight onto the familiar planform of a Phantom which was now rapidly growing in size. As he reached 10,000 feet, the aircraft still inverted and the ground now above his head, he rolled the aircraft through 180 degrees and returned the world to its rightful position. The whole manoeuvre had lasted only 30 seconds and he now sat one mile astern the target. The wingman, despite the hard manoeuvring, had held his position nicely.

"You're right JB, there are two in there," he said. The Phantom's in the lead. The other aircraft is a fighter but I can't quite make it out.....................Holy Cow!"

"What the hell now," called his, by now, twitchy navigator.

"This is more fun than I can handle!"

"You're not going to believe this but the second jet is no Phantom!"

"Nice intercept Boys. Come up Squadron Chat Frequency," came a voice over the ether. He had forgotten that it was a 92 Squadron crew they were intercepting. They had been spotted after all. Pulling alongside the pair, the wingman having moved over to the far side of the formation, Slats and JB marvelled at the sight of the grey Phantom with the light blue camouflaged Flanker tucked in tight on the wing. The picture was truly impressive and certainly one for the Squadron Scrap Book.

"76 this is 72."

"Loud and clear, Go!"

"We've been hunting! Can't talk now but suggest you CAP looking east for ten minutes. Things have been hot. If you get any contacts call Loneship and bug out pronto. See you on the ground. Don't take any chances boys, they're playing it for real today."

"Roger that, best of luck. Back to pre-brief."

Slats took one final look at the Flanker and plugged in the reheat hauling his aircraft away from the formation and back onto east. In the back, JB set up the radar to scan the airspace suddenly feeling more alert.

"Loneship Mike Lima 76 on frequency. Steady east and looking for trade."

"Mike Lima 76 Loneship you're loud and clear, say weapons state and stand by for instructions."

Razor and Flash had heard calls from Mike Lima 61 as he joined short finals at Gutersloh and they both breathed a sigh of relief that he had recovered safely.

"Wildenrath Tower, 72 for visual join with two."

"Roger 72, clear join runway 27, wind 260 at 12 knots, circuit is clear and confirm in company with 61?"

"Tower 72, err, negative. It's a long story but 61 has diverted to Gutersloh with a problem. I'll speak to you on the ground but brace yourself! 72 switching to operators for one."

Flash switched the radio quickly to the Squadron Operations frequency to speak with the Duty Authorizer on the Squadron Operations Desk.

"Cobra, Mike Lima 72."

"Go."

"72 on recovery, on the ground in 5. Confirm you've got another jet on Battle Flight."

"72, Cobra, that's affirmative, what's the story?" Razor recognised Killer's voice.

"Tell you inside but it's going to be a long debrief. You'll need another HAS open with a see-in crew and quick. We have another guest who needs sheltering; like yesterday!"

"72, he's for HAS 61. We'll get 60 opened for you."

"Roger 72 back to Tower," he responded as Flash reselected the tower frequency.

"72 flight, on the break to land."

He glanced over at the Flanker tucked in close formation on his right wing and waved him off. Simultaneously, he broke hard left into the downwind pattern for landing. The speed bled rapidly and, as he approached 250 knots, he lowered the landing gear watching intently for the indications which would confirm that it was down and locked. He parroted the remaining pre landing checks as the speed reduced further. 210 knots and he lowered the flaps as he began his finals turn looking ahead for the visual approach slope indicators, the VASIs, which would show him how accurate his height control had been. Looking at the runway threshold, he selected the precise position on the runway numbers where his jet would land and set his approach attitude. Carefully juggling the throttles he waited for the thump of the main wheels impacting the concrete which signified the end of another sortie, although on this occasion somewhat more eventful than average. The Phantom smashed onto the runway and he reached down for the chute handle and pulled.

"Chute's good" called Flash from the back as the brake parachute streamed into the airflow slowing their passage down the runway. As the aircraft decelerated to a walking pace, the crew looked up into the circuit at the uncanny sight of a Soviet Flanker downwind to land at their home base. This was the stuff of dreams or nightmares but on this occasion, NATO stood to gain a great deal from the experience.

The Phantom taxied onto the Operational Readiness Platform at the end of the runway and dropped its chute turning slightly to watch the incoming Flanker. It flared gracefully at the far end of the strip and the main wheels touched with only the merest hint of smoke as the wheels kissed. The pilot held the nose off the concrete carrying out aerodynamic braking using the planform of the wings to create drag and slow the aircraft. The Phantom had appeared ungainly and workmanlike in comparison. As the Flanker approached, Razor flashed his taxylight and immediately turned towards Delta Dispersal. Entering the loop he followed taxyway around acknowledged the marshaller and turned into the neck of their allotted HAS. Killer had done a sterling job and already there was frantic activity as the additional HAS was readied and groundcrew moved determinedly about their preparations. As Razor manoeuvred his jet in the tight confines of the revetment he watched the graceful fighter enter the adjacent HAS neck. Still bemused by the sight he wondered whether it would fit into a standard NATO HAS. Well they were about to find out and the trial was underway. Immediately his aircraft rocked to a halt, Razor threw off his ejection seat harness, the metal buckles clattering against the cockpit sides. He struggled free of the remaining straps and clambered quickly onto the ladder which had appeared over the engine intake and let himself down. He struck out towards the adjacent HAS which framed the precious newcomer closely followed by his back seater. As he neared, Razor could see the groundcrew clustered around the nosewheel of the unfamiliar aircraft with the Senior Engineering Officer in amongst them directing the operation, marshalling his troops, conscious of the need to shelter the jet from prying eyes as swiftly as possible. Eventually, towing arm in place and with a thumbs up from the Russian pilot, the aircraft began to slide into the HAS under tractor power. The flight line mechanic on each wingtip watched closely to make sure there was enough clearance from the wingtips as it eased slowly backwards under the concrete canopy.

Razor watched the activity around the massive futuristic looking Soviet fighter as it eased to a stop. A detachment of American F-15s had visited Wildenrath just a few months earlier from the US base at Bitburg and he could see a distinct resemblance. He hoped he'd be able to sit in the cockpit of this one as he had with the Eagle. It all seemed just too surreal and little had he thought he'd be looking at this sight when he'd taken over his jet on Battle Flight that morning.

Yuri watched the frantic activity around the front of his aircraft and, with a moment for contemplation, he wondered whether he had done the right thing. Only time would tell. The shadow cast by the concrete structure fell over his cockpit and the aircraft moved slowly back onto the chocks. Since he had been intercepted by the Phantom events had passed remarkably quickly and, so far, efficiently. He closed down the engines, watching the Phantom pilot coming towards him across the concrete apron and, as he entered the HAS, the tractor reversed away allowing the clamshell doors to close cutting the daylight from the scene. A dull fluorescent hue descended and he sat perfectly still, bracing himself. Finally, mentally prepared, he stood up and made his seat safe before pulling off his safety equipment and helmet and climbing down the ladder towards the reception committee. The RAF aircrew grinned broadly and the taller of the two offered his hand.

"Welcome to Wildenrath, I'm Mark Keene, "Razor" and this is Jim Gordon,

"Flash", my navigator. It's about time we debriefed the last engagement. You speak English? Yuri smiled and pumped the offered hand grateful for the warmth of the welcome. It was true; aircrew the world over were all the same. As he shook Flash's hand, a large bottle of Grolsch which had mysteriously appeared was thrust at him and the aircrew toasted each other in the time honoured fashion.

"I'm first to get a look at your jet," volunteered Razor, "Flash you're next but you'll be hard pushed to find the back seat."

Pleasantries over, they began to mount the ladder followed by an apprehensive Yuri while beneath them, the groundcrew fumbled with missile safety pins anxious to make safe the new 92 Squadron aeroplane. The aircrew figured that very soon, this particular jet might be off limits to all but a select few. As he watched the British pilot mount the steps, Yuri realised the Su-27 no longer belonged to him. He took a deep draw on the beer in his hand and contemplated the future.

11 PLANS

Kamov shifted nervously in his seat in the large vaulted ante room awaiting his summons. His recall had come at short notice and his mind worked furiously as he tried to think it through. The KGB guard, seated at a large carved mahogany table, shielded the entrance to General Sokolovskiy's outer office. His air suggested bored indifference, although Kamov knew only too well that he was one of the elite, chosen for total ruthlessness and selflessness. Not a man to be trifled with. The large panelled door opened and an aide ushered a distinguished looking guest from the chamber. Kamov watched, warily, sensing the tense atmosphere but he suspected that he knew the reason why. The General himself appeared at the door and beckoned to Kamov who followed meekly. No aide; odd. Igor Sokolovskiy cut an imposing figure, exuding charisma and Kamov felt a little less than his usual relaxed self, surprisingly intimidated by the surroundings and the trappings of power. He suddenly appreciated the potency of political influence which shaped people's destiny in Soviet Russia. It was usually he who applied the psychological pressure to shape his aims and he did not relish being cast in the role of victim. Following Sokolovskiy into the room, he took the seat at the imposing desk which was offered.

"Kamov, I will waste no time on niceties. We have a problem which needs immediate action. Indeed, I don't think it would be over-dramatic to say that the security of the Motherland depends upon success. You will know that part of our 5 year plan has been to upgrade our air defence capabilities to match the new American fighter aircraft. We, undoubtedly, have superior numbers but have been losing the quality race. Recently, we have developed a series of new designs for tactical aircraft; the Mig-29, a point defence fighter; the Su-25, a close air support aircraft and, perhaps the most significant, the Su-27, an air superiority and escort fighter. In concert, the new aircraft will form a family of fighter types which will be the mainstay of our defence until the turn of the century and beyond. These new prototypes have been undergoing testing at our test centre at Ramenskoye. Each is a vital link in the chain but, since yesterday, the chain has been weakened. The pilot of one of the aircraft defected to the West taking not only his aircraft but a full load of the latest air-to-air weapons with him. He crossed the border near Fritzlar."

Kamov was astounded and struggled to absorb the enormity of the loss. How could it have happened? The development facilities at Ramenskoye where the secret prototypes were based, were amongst the most secure installations in Russia and, by definition therefore, in Europe. More to the point, the Inner German Border was the most heavily defended airspace in the world and breaches were dealt with in a most conspicuous fashion. He realised his mind had wandered and returned his attention to the General's words.

"I'm told that you have recently recruited subjects at key NATO installations."

He was well briefed.

"I believe you will need to make early use of them. We know that the Su-27 was intercepted by Phantoms from the Quick Reaction Alert facility from RAF Wildenrath on the Dutch border. One of the Phantom aircraft which intercepted the defector landed at Gutersloh and the other returned to base. Intercepts of the transmissions between the aircraft, which incidentally destroyed a formation of Mig-23s sent to recover the Su-27, suggest that the aircraft which landed at Gutersloh was damaged and we would, therefore, guess that the Su-27 returned to Wildenrath. From the transcripts, it seems the Su-27 escaped unharmed. A number of missiles were fired and it seems we inflicted some damage on one of the Phantoms but not our main target. Your task is very straight forward Kamov, I want you to recover the Su-27 and, due to the sensitivity of the weapons system and its missiles, I want you to do it quickly before the Western intelligence experts have time to exploit their advantage."

Kamov hesitated knowing that what he said over the next minutes would be critical. Wary that his reply should not be misinterpreted, he chose his words carefully.

"General, I naturally appreciate the importance of the mission and, as you rightly say, I have contacts that will be able to provide information. I must warn, however, that the outcome is by no means assured. What if recovery is impossible? The NATO bases are heavily guarded and very secure. If the prototype is there, it's by no means certain whether they have had time to begin exploitation. Even so, recovery will not be easy"

"As I have already implied, the prime importance is to negate the value to Western intelligence given their unfortunate windfall and, consequently, speed is of the essence. If you have to destroy the aircraft so be it. If you can put it back to flying condition I'd like it back. If we lose it the programme will be set back months, if not years. I really would like it back," he said fixing Kamov with an unsettling stare. "My aide will clear your path through the normal bureaucracy. You will have all you require, when you require it."

Kamov paused.

"General, what of the defector?"

"Of secondary importance Kamov. It is clearly preferable if he is unable to give away too much but I leave his ultimate fate to you. Your instructions, should you be unable to recover the aircraft intact are equally concise. Listen carefully......"

Sokolovskiy watched the door close behind Kamov and picked up the phone.

"Director. General Sokolovskiy, how are you?

He listened politely, anxious to conclude the conversation quickly. His tone was carefully measured and he knew that the Director of Ramenskoye Test Centre would be unsettled by his conciliatory manner, expecting his wrath not his support in the wake of the defection.

"You will be contacted shortly by one of my men Kamov. Please offer him every assistance. When he asks for a pilot for his operation, I suggest Kazenko may be the most suitable."

He listened briefly, nodding.

"Good good, I'm glad he's your favoured choice. A good man. I'll be in touch again."

Replacing the receiver, the General smiled.

*

Kamov walked down the dingy corridor deep in the bowels of the Defence Ministry. He was dog tired and seemed to have spent his life in the back of aeroplanes, flitting back and forth between Düsseldorf and Moscow since this had all blown up. Despite his cover it was not good to be so overt in his movements. He pushed through the doorway to a small office and addressed the KGB major who sat at the large desk in the corner.

"I need a satellite pass and I need it quickly; in fact it may already be too late. I hear that you are the man who may help me."

"And you are?" the major responded with a casual arrogance.

"Kamov," he replied flashing his KGB identity card briefly, enjoying the flash of recognition. The Major visibly relaxed as he recognised the insignia and dragged himself from his seat offering his hand.

"Forgive me Comrade but I get so many idiots in here who think that I can magic up a satellite pass for this or a covert insertion for that as if it's as easy as diverting a staff car. The trouble with these guys is once they get a couple of stars on their shoulders, they think they can control the Western Theatre. But for you, Comrade, I could launch a special mission if you need it. Tell me what you want and I'll have it done inside the hour. What do you require?"

The transformation had been remarkable. Kamov lowered himself into the seat which had been offered.

"The exact details of the operation are irrelevant but I suspect you may already have something in orbit which covers the area that I am interested in; Wildenrath in West Germany, just on the Dutch border."

"Hmm, the Cosmos recon satellite which had been covering that area was recovered only yesterday. Perhaps I am going to have to be true to my words and divert the next launch for you."

Kamov was becoming increasingly impressed. This major was making all the right noises.

"Good man, this is what I'm looking for. The airfield is a standard NATO layout with an east/west main runway. The domestic site is on the north side with three hardened dispersals to the south. Check your data from yesterday just before recovery. A formation landed and I'm most interested in its composition. Somewhere in there, is an aircraft which landed yesterday afternoon with a British Phantom from 92 Squadron which is based there. I suspect it's sheltered in the south-westerly HAS site. That's an active site whereas the middle dispersal is only used for reinforcement exercises and is normally empty. I suspect that if they are intending to store the aircraft for any length of time, they will probably move it into the uninhabited HAS site."

"What are you particularly interested in?"

"Any shots of the aircraft in the open would be invaluable to me, mainly to confirm that the aircraft is actually at the base. I'm working on word-of-mouth at the moment and, hopefully, these other sources will provide confirmation but a picture would be indisputable. If the pass coincided with any movement of the aircraft that would be ideal as it would give me a precise location but I guess that's too much to hope for."

"What type of aircraft are you looking for. Are the Brits trying out some new type in the forward area? Perhaps my photographic interpreters will get some juicy snippets. The new Tornado maybe?"

"I can't tell you exactly what type of aircraft it is at this stage but I guarantee that if you find it, you'll be quite surprised!"

Kamov's voice took on a conspiratorial tone.

"I take it that it's not a Phantom in that case?"

"You're absolutely right. Maybe the General will give you the details?"

"Hmm, you really have whetted my appetite. I was going to set up a couple of passes on a routine orbit but if it's as interesting as you say, then I think I'll reprogram the next Cosmos launch and put it into geostationary orbit in that area. I can justify it by saying that I'm going to keep an eye on the build up of the AWACS deployment to Geilenkirchen. Yes, now I'm really hooked."

"And I'm in your debt. Perhaps I can help you out in some way? Do you smoke? I brought back some Marlboros from my last trip to the West."

"Comrade, for a couple of packets of Marlboros, I would consider taking up smoking."

Kamov tossed a couple of the precious packets onto the major's desk as his uniformed counterpart picked up the phone and dialled.

"Baikonur, Moscow Central on secure net. I want you to divert the next SS-6 launch and replace the Ferret ELINT bird with another Cosmos payload. A high priority surveillance mission has just come in and I need to get it airborne as soon as possible. The tasking paperwork is on its way but I need a geostationary orbit over the 2ATAF area." He listened. "Yes, I know that's unusual but we need to get some pictures as a matter of urgency. Yes, the precise targeting data will be in the signal."

"When can they get it in the air?" Kamov whispered interrupting his flow. The Major nodded.

"What's your expected launch time?............Seven hours! That's good even for you guys. The tasking message is on the wires right now."

it was still a magnificent sight. Razor walked slowly around the jet taking in the detail of the design. The aerodynamics were stunning but he was more aware of the roughness of the finish in places which he had not noticed on his first airborne encounter. Some panels appeared as though they had been fixed in place with a jack hammer. Nonetheless, he couldn't fail to be impressed. The leading edge root extensions blended gracefully into a complex wing design which was maximised for performance. Looking along the main axis of the airframe he took in the unusual configuration of the side by side mounted engines split by a deeply recessed tunnel which ordinarily contained the semi-active missiles. Without the missiles in place, the airframe seemed to lack substance. Although the engines were massive and, in the Russian way, built to provide immense power without undue concern over engine life, the airframe seemed almost frail in comparison. Around the HAS the analysts went about their task with a purpose. Panels had been pulled off and boxes sat alongside the jet carefully marked with labels suggesting they may not be there for long. Razor reflected that for the military, the Soviet system was the ultimate throwaway society and, where their equipment was concerned, no expense was spared. Pausing between the afterburner nozzles, he inspected the tail sting which housed the rear transmit antennae for the electronic warfare suite. The technicians had been busy inspecting this important system which, up to now had been a mystery. Small dielectric panels hung loose exposing the antennas for the jammers. It was a sober contrast to the woeful lack of any form of self protection systems on his Phantom. As good as the radar was, there had been no investment in this vital element of modern warfare and when he entered a fight he lacked even the basic chaff and flare system to counter the missiles that would, inevitably, come his way. In contrast, a Flanker pilot, he would be pushing out complex electronic jamming against the radar before he even hit the merge. They might feel like "King of the Heap" in Low Fly 2 but Day One of World War 3 might be a totally different experience. As he moved back towards the front pausing at the starkly functional missile pylons hanging below the wings he noticed that Flash had been drawn to the radome which housed the airborne intercept radar. At that moment the technicians popped the lock and drew the massive structure open. At last he had found an area where the Soviets weren't ten feet tall. Just on visual inspection it was obvious that the past the guardroom, he took it much more carefully. Luckily, he had not had to sign out or he may have shown too much distress to the RAF Police corporal on duty. Not once had he considered calling the agent's bluff.

*

The aircrew walked down the short path to HAS 61 from the personnel briefing facility and opened the wicket door in the right hand clamshell door. The hive of activity which greeted them inside would have done justice to any fighter squadron but, in this case, it had been caused by just one particular officer whose arrival they had assisted. Walking into the HS cabin where the 2ATAF Intelligence officer who had originally briefed them was writing on a chinagraph planning board they offered their identification cards.

"Sir, you said that we could take another look at the Flanker when things had died down a little," said Razor.

"I guess you do have a fairly high priority as you were the ones who delivered it to us," he replied waving away the identity cards. "Give me a minute."

He picked up the telephone and dialled and, after a brief conversation, directed the aircrew to a HAS in the centre of the dispersal.

It was apparent that the HAS had been carefully selected as it was impossible to overlook the main doors from any aspect around the airfield perimeter. It was almost a perfect choice for security which had been further enhanced by an armed guard patrolling the revetment above; although at the cost of advertising that something unusual was afoot. Flash rapped on the steel "wicket" door to the HAS which swung open to allow access. Inside, another armed guard stood discretely in the corner covering the entrance, although as soon he recognised the aircrew he relaxed lowering his rifle. The sight of the Soviet aeroplane which greeted them as they entered the HAS was without a doubt still exciting. The Flanker was bathed by banks of arc lights illuminating the holes in the airframe where panels had been removed by technicians who crawled over the surface of the jet giving it an almost Lilliputian appearance. Despite the disfiguration, of "The East" and "The West" which were displayed on the wall in front of him. He repeated the scenario in his mind which the defector had outlined at the hot debrief, staring at the map on which he had marked the key points. He would use the figures to reassess the intelligence estimates of the performance of the Flanker which the latest information had questioned. He would have to update the aircrew on the squadrons as soon as possible as they had also gleaned a good deal of data about the performance of the Flogger and, more importantly, some of the weaknesses which it had demonstrated. The encounter with the Phantoms had underlined the current superiority of the F4's weapons system and, at the same time, validated the tactics. Despite that, he knew the Soviet pilot had not tried too hard against the NATO jets. He had clinically dispatched a Soviet Flogger without too much effort. He had also penetrated the SAM belt which taxed the best minds at the bases at Brüggen and Laarbruch just up the road. It had taken years of effort to train the crews and it was reassuring to know that the pain had not been in vain. The first encounter had proved to be very one sided but it would not always be so. The Flanker was a visible sign that times were changing. It was almost the end of his shift. He hated the graveyard shift but, at least it was only a short drive to his room in the Officers' Mess. Others who lived off base had a longer drive. As he rose, the phone rang. Placing it to his ear he heard the enthusiastic tones of a cultured English voice which he did not immediately recognise.

"Keith old chap, it's John...John Kitching. I'm sorry to phone you at work but I'm in the area again. How about we meet? Can you make it? Same place; in an hour."

Keith recoiled, recognising the voice of the KGB agent.

"How could you possibly..." he spluttered cut short by the calm voice reassuring him. It would be a flying visit said his "friend" and he should be sure to make the rendezvous. The handset went dead. Looking at his watch he realised he was already pushed for time and that he could not make the rendezvous still dressed in uniform. He locked his documents in the safe and rushed outside to his car, started the engine and drove off at speed, quickly realising that, if he was to avoid attracting attention, he would have to observe the speed limits. As he left the base down the long straight road

"Outstanding," said Kamov excitedly. Can they really do a payload change in seven hours?"

"I'd bet my Marlboros on it!"

This major knew his stuff.

"This, Comrade, might cost you a bit more than two packets of Marlboros," the major continued. "You realise the effort involved in changing mission tasking at the last minute."

"For you, I'll put together the best package of goodies that you have ever seen and I'll personally deliver. In the meantime, keep the request deliberately vague. I don't want any undue speculation in case the photographic interpreters don't turn anything up."

"If it's there to be seen, my boys will find it, rest assured."

Kamov gripped his hand and they exchanged a conspiratorial look.

*

The Combined Operations Centre at Wildenrath, nestled in the pine trees adjacent to the main hard standing, its roof bristling with antennae. As with all hardened facilities there were no windows on the outside world; glass and bombs did not mix. The COC was the nerve centre of the station and housed all the major elements of the command structure. Within, in addition to the operational control desk which managed the station's aircraft, were other cells to control essential functions such as ground defence, explosive ordnance repair and engineering support. It also housed control desks for the Bloodhound and Rapier missile batteries. Entering the building, scrutinised by the ever present security cameras, it was easy to lose track of reality. Once through the entrance airlocks and inside the filtered and sealed cocoon, the babble of raised voices, all attempting to impart their own vital information to the various cells on the base, assailed the ears. In the main operations area, backlit display boards tracked the minute to minute progress of daily life on the busy station, regularly updated by harassed clerks dressed in "cabbage kit". Keith James sat at his desk in the COC and stared at his map of the tactical dispositions between the forces engineering of the device was old fashioned proving that at least "The Bear" was behind in some areas. Mind you, from what he'd seen in the air, it was not too shabby in combat. The pilot Andrenev had dispatched that first Flogger without too much effort.

The main reason he had wanted another look was to get into the cockpit and he climbed up the ladder. Out of habit, he checked the ejection seat pins finding that the system on the Soviet seat was similar to his own. Unlike the floppy black and yellow handle with which he was so familiar, he could see a solid red fixed handle with two large red loops in a similar place between the legs. There would be no missing that contraption if it was needed. Standing on the seat, he eased his feet either side of the control column which appeared like a cowled snake, festooned with weapons selectors, trim switches and transmit buttons. The putrid duck egg blue colour of the cockpit assailed his senses. Until now he had only seen pictures in the intelligence journals and had found it difficult to believe. How the Soviet pilots coped with such a gaudy colour he could not imagine; give me the dirty black of the Phantom any day, he decided. An electronic tactical display fitted snugly under the right hand cockpit coaming and he already knew from intelligence briefings that the radar information was fed into the head up display just like he'd seen on the F-15. Just as their own fit in the back of the Phantom, the radar sat just above the radar warning receiver indicator but buried on the right hand side. Why do designers stuff such an important instrument so low in the cockpit? The weapons management was obviously through the HOTAS or hands on throttle and stick controls and, despite peering at the unintelligible Cyrillic script annotating the switches along the front panel he was unable to decipher any of the functions. The basic flight instruments looked remarkably familiar and were almost a direct copy of western designs although they read in metres and kph rather than the more traditional feet and knots. The consoles either side held the traditional array of gauges and switches which controlled the aircraft systems. Looking forward, the view was dominated by the head up display and its chin level control panel. The view forward was barely impeded by the ironwork and he would have died for that view. The huge bubble which housed the infra-red search and track system protruded upwards into his sightline but the minor loss of view was worth it for the capability it provided. Above all, he was impressed by the spectacular view from the cockpit, although the Soviet designers had stopped short of fitting a true bubble canopy and had installed a slightly intrusive bulkhead to the rear of the canopy which reduced the view so vital in combat. Turning around in the seat he could see the wings and tailplane easily from his vantage point. He knew that it still had a little way to go to match the American F-15 where the pilot sat head and shoulders above the nearest ironwork and was the master of all he surveyed but it was certainly better than his old Phantom. Overall the cockpit had a more modern appearance than his own but seemed to be a slightly upgraded Phantom cockpit rather than a quantum leap forward in cockpit ergonomics that he'd assumed. The proof would be how the engineers had integrated the radar, the IRSTS and the missiles. He had no doubt that this thing could turn. Making way for Flash, he hefted himself onto the spine of the jet and gazed back at the planform which had so confused him as they had entered that initial merge. The enormous red stars on the wings, so apparent from where he stood, had been almost invisible in the heat of the moment. Red stars he thought, suddenly overawed by his experience. Surreal.

*

Yuri was feeling much more relaxed after a shower and a change into a formal dinner suit provided by the Station Commander. He walked slightly ahead of his host as he was ushered into the large dining room. The candlelit formal tables suggested opulence, the flickering light reflecting back from the high ceilings onto the long highly polished mahogany surfaces of the tables. The top table, intersected along one of its sides by three shorter legs was laid out with ornate place settings at regular intervals along its length. Interspersed among the silver candelabra were pieces of silver belonging to the Officers' Mess which spanned the history of both the station and the flying units and reflected the traditions of the fighting service with whom he now dined. In this less opulent era, the present day officers would struggle to make such a generous gesture but the heritage was not lost on him. A silver Phantom, the aircraft which presently equipped the squadrons sat alongside a large silver Spitfire, a memento of the war years and, quite close by, a biplane from World War One. Three quite separate eras captured in microcosm. The Warrant Officer escorted him to his seat to the right of the Station Commander as he watched the other officers take their places, smoothly as if rehearsed. Following their lead, he remained standing behind his chair as a short prayer, unfamiliar to him in modern day Russia, preceded a great scraping of chairs and the assembled company took their seats in preparation for the meal. He glanced around taking in the faces and the atmosphere. Dressed in their waistcoat-style formal uniforms in the distinctive Air Force blue, each officer chatted animatedly to his neighbour, relaxed and at ease. Yuri could make out the flying brevets of the aircrew worn on the left hand lapel of their uniform, ornate golden badges which made them stand out from their earthbound colleagues. He felt an immediate affinity despite being many miles from home. The single wing of the navigator and the famous double wing brevet of the RAF pilots which he recognised from the wartime shots of RAF aircrew who had fought in the Motherland during the Great Patriotic War. He tried to come to terms with the enormity of the change he had brought on himself as he struggled, torn between conflicting feelings. On the one hand, he had long regarded western aircrew as the enemy and a force to be opposed whereas he now sat among some of the most formidable fighter crews in NATO feeling a distinct camaraderie. It would take time.

A wall of stewards dressed in neat white uniform jackets appeared from behind a screened partition carrying bottles of wine which they began to serve. Listening closely to the Station Commander's gentle Scottish burr, Yuri forced himself to relax, soaking up the atmosphere. As the meal was served the conversation buzzed around him and he strained to pick up the rapid fire English. Discussions seemed to range from the quality of the food which Yuri was enjoying immensely, through aspects of local interest, to the virtues of the German wine which flowed freely. Not once did the conversation drift onto either Russia or the Su-27 for which he was extremely grateful. English would be his first language from now on and he would need to practice hard. The technical debrief which had begun earlier, a necessary evil, had already probed deeply and he was glad to be able to enjoy the evening for itself. The Station Commander was the perfect host as he asked gently about Yuri's experience living in and around Moscow. In front of him, he caught the occasional enquiring glance from the aircrew around the table. Yet another course appeared in front of him and he revelled in the pleasure of a fine fillet of beef served with a piquant German sauce. His attention flagged briefly as Wing Commander Admin, in charge of administration on the station sitting on his right, expounded the finer points of Mess management; administrators the world over were the same, he mused. Finally, the remnants of the meal cleared, a solitary empty glass remained in front of him which he was urged to charge from a decanter of Port which passed along the table. The Station Commander rose and prompted the youngest officer present, "Mr Vice", who sat at the end of the centre leg directly opposite them, to rise and drink the Loyal Toast. Every officer rose and in a hushed and solemn tone drank the health of Her Majesty the Queen, the significance of which was not lost on Yuri. Whilst in Russia, despite an undying love of the Motherland, loyalty was assured by the strictures of the Party. The unifying force here was not only a love of their Country but a deep and lasting loyalty to their figurehead; a much greater unifying force.

Toast over, the room erupted into mayhem, the solemnity of moments ago replaced by ordered chaos. Napkins rolled into balls, which had been carefully secreted, flew around and extra glasses and bottles of wine appeared from secret hiding places beneath the polished tables. Ashtrays, cigars and generous measures of liquors were placed on the table by the silent army of stewards and supplemented by after dinner coffee. Service complete, the stewards retired leaving the room to the officers. The Station Commander rose.

"Gentleman, and Lady," he smiled acknowledging the single WRAF officer in their midst. "Tonight is quite special. We pride ourselves on our readiness posture, in our ability to react to unforeseen circumstances and, when we do, to be able to carry out our professional task with the utmost efficiency. I believe we have a tangible example of that ability tonight. We have a special guest amongst us. The details of his arrival need not concern the majority of you but I am sure that you will have noticed there has been some unusual activity around the airfield of late. Should you be asked, you have no recollection of any strange goings on from this moment on. The reason for my suggestion of apparent amnesia will become clear. May I introduce to you all, Colonel Yuri Andrenev of the Soviet Air Force."

He paused for effect in the hushed room. Yuri rose and bowed formally to a sudden rapturous banging on the heavy tables. He felt something of a celebrity as the noise gradually faded but some around the room looked either surprised or dubious.

"Sadly, he will only be with us for a very short time as he will depart for Rheindahlen tomorrow and his onward movements are clearly none of our concern. Had the 2ATAF staff had their way, he would already have left but I'm afraid that, whilst I am Station Commander, there is no way that he could be allowed to leave without our offering him some hospitality!"

More banging of tables.

"I'm sure you will make him welcome this evening," he smiled "but I would ask you to spare him the ordeal of a debrief on the intricacies of flying aeroplanes. He will be debriefing non-stop over the next few days and, rest assured, you will be the first to know the outcome. Anyway, I have said too much and I will trust you all to be discreet." He let the implied threat hang in the air for just a few moments. "In the meantime let's move on to our other theme of the evening. We are dining-out a number of officers.........."

Yuri scanned the faces, some of whom still looked at him, feeling comfortable, albeit separated by a gulf in both political and cultural terms. He listened easily to the light-hearted stories of the antics of the departing officers gradually picking up the meaning of the unfamiliar words.

*

The SS-6 Sapwood rocket was already in place on the main launch pad at Baikonur Cosmodrome. A converted intercontinental ballistic missile, it was at the end of its service life and was becoming difficult to maintain. First put into service in 1957, it had been radical in its day with its four booster rockets housing the 20 main and 12 vernier motors in the first stage rather than the technically complex but larger booster motors. It had given the Soviet Union a head start in the satellite launching game but by now, there were very few remaining. A steady stream of condensed vapour issued from around the base as just a few drops of liquid propellant vented to atmosphere. Dusk had fallen and the projectile was illuminated by a series of high powered arc lamps positioned around the adjacent gantries. All movement around the rocket had ceased as the army of technicians, who only minutes before had swarmed over the gantries checking and cross checking couplings and panels, had retired to make final preparations for the hastily rearranged launch. At the tip of the rocket, the bulbous nosecone housed the hastily inserted Cosmos spy satellite. Unlike some of the other payloads, this was for orbital reconnaissance carrying high resolution cameras and a small orbital manoeuvring engine for precise positioning. Despite the enormous cost, the life of the spacecraft would be a mere 14 days before it would have to be replaced by a further example maintaining the constant watch on the opposition. In addition to the "recce" birds, the Soviet Army had a constant presence of Ferret electronic intelligence satellites to eavesdrop on the radio and radar emissions from western forces. The Ferret which had been planned for this mission had been hastily stowed in a nearby hangar pending reallocation. In the control room, the launch control team already busy at their consoles, made final preparations for the countdown. True to their word, only 6 hours had elapsed since the unexpected call from Moscow. Functions were systematically checked and cross checked and built in test equipment continually monitored the status of the key systems indicating that all was still "green" as the countdown entered its final 5 minutes. The tension in the room was visibly increasing as it always did just prior to a launch with technicians scuttling around. The senior coordinator flitted between the consoles making his final checks heightening the tension even more.

"T minus 20 seconds and counting," droned the voice over the public address system as the coordinator scuttled back to his console. He dropped into his seat and hit his transmit button.

"Propulsion status?"

"Go"

"Guidance status?"

"Go."

"T minus 15 seconds."

"Payload status?"

"Go."

"Systems, final status check."

"All systems are go."

"T minus 10 seconds."

"Launch commit," he announced and from that point on the outcome was irreversible.

"On my mark. T minus 5,4,3,2,1. Launch sequence initiate."

*

Yuri found himself pressed into the corner of the Main Bar as the final few officers drifted in from the dining room. Despite the Station Commander's warning, the small knot of aircrew which had formed around him slowly steered the conversation towards matters flying. As he responded, increasingly enthusiastically, to questions about the Su-27, he found himself asking equally frank questions about the Phantom. He had always held a grudging respect for this aging but capable war machine. Despite their differences, one thing clearly bound them all; the love of flying. Another beer was thrust into his hand.

*

Lt Gregori Porov had been called to the operations desk on the Spetznaz Special Forces Support Squadron at Mahlwinkel in East Germany to take a telephone call from Moscow. He had been unprepared for the unexpected challenge which he had just been set and it had begun a series of panic preparations. Poring over the charts which he had quickly drawn from the map store, he felt uneasy. There was massive scope for a screw up. His call from the KGB officer had been short and to the point. It would be a covert mission involving, at most, two helicopters. His planning should assume that he would carry at least 6 passengers and that it would be a night insertion which forced him to use at least one Hind Alpha, the original transport version of the attack helicopter. Unlike the Delta model, which would otherwise have been his favoured platform, the Alpha had no air-to-air weaponry and lacked the rotating chin-mounted cannon. Its only weapons were a fixed low calibre machine gun in the forward cabin and air-to-ground rocket pods on the stubby wings which protruded from the armoured fuselage. They would be of little value on this mission. He could however call on sets of the latest Ochki Nochnogo Videnya; night vision goggles, enhancement devices which clipped onto his flying helmet turning night into day. At least he would be able to ingress at ultra low level which would give him improved odds. Unfortunately, on this occasion, his target was deep in West German airspace; the RAF base at Wildenrath. His alternative target which had been suggested as a possibility had been another RAF base at Gutersloh which would have been relatively straight forward being only 130km over the border and he could have achieved that unrefueled. Wildenrath, however, was an entirely different matter and even with a final refuelling stop at a forward base, he would be forced to refuel on the other side of the border. As he considered the options, a plan began to crystallise in his mind. He would take a Hind Alpha to carry the passengers and a Hind Delta to provide fire support. He already knew that the fuel requirements would dictate that he completed the final stages of the mission alone, as the Delta had even less fuel than the Alpha. He could fit extra tanks but the Delta had space only for a small auxiliary tank and two refuelling stops would be out of the question. The prospect did not entirely appeal to him. Drawing a raft of charts from the planning table he began to make detailed preparations. He located the airfield at Wildenrath marking it with a target symbol giving the forward base at Schlotheim similar embellishment. Next he needed some significant navigational features which would provide suitable waypoints for his night mission. It would be vital to select areas away from major conurbations where the bright city lights would destroy the effectiveness of his night vision goggles. In any event, it was preferable to avoid such areas; heavy attack helicopters were the last thing the local population expected to hear or see, particularly at night. The West Germans were becoming radically "Green" and the military struggled to hold any sort of sway over the population. He would need to be careful how he planned this. As he began to link up his selected navigation points, the complexity of the fuel plan began to dawn on him and he realised that it would hinge on the extra tanks. A few doodles on a sketch pad and a short calculation later, he had the essence of a plan. Time was short and, as he strode across the room to the phone, he knew he would have to make some fairly swift arrangements. He dialled a number for the modification cell in the Special Operations Headquarters tapping his pencil anxiously as he waited for the reply.

*

On the launch pad, the arc lights suddenly dimmed as the massive surge of raw power from the four boosters lit the darkening sky with gouts of flame pouring from the containment pit at the base of the launch pad. Still restrained by the arms which extended from the gantries, the pressure of the thrust from the motors building, the rocket vibrated into life as light and steam erupted around the base. With an enormous clanking, totally drowned by the crescendo of noise, the gantries swung back and the rocket began its slow rise on a pillar of flame rapidly clearing the top of the towers, its vertical path pinpointed in the darkened sky by the shaft of light from the boosters. The launch personnel, some miles distant from the pad watched the launch with a detached fascination which never lessened despite having watched the spectacle on numerous previous occasions. The rocket thrust off into the night, its path clearly visible as it climbed rapidly through the atmosphere trailing flame and a massive exhaust plume.

*

In the control room of the North American Air Defence Command thousands of miles away in Colorado, a warning claxon sounded. The Duty Officer called up a display as he watched the huge wall mounted screen with a warning symbol directly over Baikonur Cosmodrome. Unusual he thought, this launch had not been pre-notified. The infra-red sensor which stared from the satellite 24 hours a day had detected the heat of the rocket plume and immediately triggered a warning. The complex software had already calculated a trajectory for the launch vehicle and, on first glance, it seemed consistent with an orbital insertion but he could take no chances. He picked up the phone and dialled the number for his supervisor.

At a point 64 Km down range, the first stage booster detached, allowing the second stage to cut in, maintaining the craft's acceleration towards escape velocity at which time it would shrug off the pull of earth's gravity. Its path had been carefully programmed to follow the direction of the earth's rotation and the precise orbit had been selected. At the point at which the satellite finally emerged from the protective cocoon in the nose of the rocket, it was directly overhead Wildenrath airfield, position 51 degrees north, 6 degrees east. Of more relevance, its orbit was precisely synchronised with the earth's rotation so that it would hold its station overhead the target of interest, Charlie and Delta Dispersals at RAF Wildenrath. As the lips of the spacecraft peeled back, the satellite emerged into dark space and small thrusters fired, moving it slowly away from the remnants of the rocket which joined the mass of accumulated space junk in orbit. The low orbit would not be sustained for long, however, and the debris would precede the satellite in its return earthwards by only a few days. The main body rolled gently as, with thrusters hissing, the camera ports were carefully aligned with the planet's surface. After only a few moments, inside the satellite camera systems came on line on command from launch control and began snapping slowly and rhythmically, the complex series of lenses and mirrors directing the images onto infra-red film, negating the effect of darkness. The images were then recorded on video and beamed back to earth for analysis where, in mere hours, the analysts on the ground would have sharp images of the NATO airbase for analysis. The Cosmos satellite followed its pre-planned course its cameras ignoring the magnificent panorama of the Earth's horizon which spread out into the distance as far as the eye could see. On the horizon, the first signs of light produced a halo effect as the snooper began its vigil.

*

The doors of HAS 61 opened with a clang as the heavy steel structure hit the restraining buffer allowing a small amount of subdued light to escape from the gap. A tractor moved in through the doors pushing a towing arm ahead and came to a stop in front of the Soviet aircraft which was picked out in the glow of the HAS lights. The NCO in charge of the team climbed down from the cab and gestured furiously at the young "liney" who struggled with the fittings around the nosewheel. Task complete, the airman climbed cautiously into the cockpit to act as "brakeman" for the short journey to Charlie Dispersal, although never in his wildest dreams had he ever expected to ride in the cockpit of a Soviet Flanker. He looked around his temporary refuge in awe before being brought rapidly back to reality by the jerk of the tractor as it began to move. His feet moved to the brakes and he gave a tentative push. The jet emerged slowly from the HAS proceeded by the straining tractor, revving strongly and turned down the taxiway before disappearing into the gloom of the airfield. Within moments the only visible signs were the small torches held by the wing walkers who walked alongside watching the wingtip clearances. Around the quiet dispersal, the gloom descended, emphasised by the lack of security lighting which had been temporarily but deliberately dimmed.

Overhead, the Cosmos satellite clicked away, recording every detail.

*

The barrier clanked as it struck the limit of its travel and the staff car moved off down the long access road. In the back seat Yuri relaxed. He still wore the formal dinner jacket which, remarkably, had proved to be a passable fit. His flying suit had been thrown into a bag in the boot along with another holdall containing some replacement clothes which, amazingly, seemed to fit. He could not help but notice the quality. Such clothes were available in Moscow only on production of hard western currency and then only if you had the right contacts or access to the correct Government shops. Even as a senior test pilot, his salary had been barely adequate to afford such luxuries particularly considering the enormous outlay on medical fees which he had accepted for so many years. Relying on the system to provide care was no way to succeed, he reflected as his thoughts drifted back to his wife. He knew her life could be counted in weeks rather than months but he hoped that they would allow her the dignity of dying in her own bed. She had not been involved in his decision to defect, it had been his alone and she deserved a break. The guilt, nevertheless, was not easy to live with.

*

The photographic interpreter pored over his stereoscope, the binocular type device which he used to add depth to the flat recorded images from the satellite. The subject was routine; yet further pictures of the NATO base at Wildenrath. Analysis of NATO installations kept him busy most of his working week and he was intimately familiar with every paving stone on every base from Nörvenich to Jever. He failed to see why he had been dragged in at this unearthly hour to study yet more pictures of the same old facilities. Look for something out of the ordinary, the major had said but nothing out of the ordinary had happened at Wildenrath since the Wild Weasel F4 squadron had come in from the States on their reinforcement exercise. The Phantom going off the side of the runway on arrival had been out of the ordinary. In this instance his request for guidance on the precise area to investigate had been met with an evasive response. So here he was, poring over the same old dull pictures of the same old dull installations. Something must have prompted the renewed interest, he thought. What was it? Collecting a further series of shots from the growing stack which was being fed by an NCO as the imagery arrived from processing, he laid them out on the illuminated inspection table. Once arranged, they made up a 2 metre long composite of the whole of Wildenrath airfield in uncanny detail. It was almost as if they had been taken from an aircraft flying overhead rather than from a satellite in orbit around the earth. He began at the Bloodhound site on the north easterly dispersal and inspected the missile launchers and the Bloodhound missiles for any unexpected modifications including a brief look at the tracking radars. The Fitter pilots at Cochstedt would be interested in these systems as they were currently tasked to take out Wildenrath when the Great War finally came. Nothing apparent there, he thought. Moving on to the main apron, he discounted the VC10 transport aircraft as he had seen the routine shuttle en route to the NATO installation at Decimomannu in Sardinia every week for the last year. He switched his interest to 60 Squadron and the Army Air Corps hangars but both were firmly closed with no apparent activity. All tucked up in bed, as I should be, he thought resignedly. Inspection of the Air Traffic Control Tower, the Aircraft Servicing Flight, the Airfield Damage Repair Facility and the Combined Operations Centre proved equally fruitless. With growing annoyance he turned his attention to the operations complexes on the south side and a glance at his watch emphasised his increasing impatience. What a rolling screw up this was proving to be. The small heater in the corner struggled manfully in its attempts to raise the temperature above freezing and he rubbed his hands together attempting to keep warm, the warmth of his breath white in the chilly air. A cursory inspection of Battle Flight revealed nothing untoward and knowing that the centre dispersal was empty, he moved on to the south western dispersal occupied by the other operational squadron. He immediately froze. Adjusting the focus on the stereoscope, he centred on the most westerly group of HASs on the airfield and zeroed in on the snout of an aircraft emerging from one of the shelters. His immediate assessment that he was looking at an American F-15 was quickly discounted as the colour scheme was all wrong. He checked the time stamp and it had been taken in the early hours of the morning; odd in itself. In the next shot, the jet emerged from the HAS and he had a better look. It looked like some sort of splinter pattern unlike the grey/green camouflage or the air defence grey scheme normally sported by the Wildenrath Phantoms. It was not unlike the latest Soviet style and he had seen the pattern on an intelligence picture recently. Now where was it? He opened a folder selecting large scale shots of the latest designs from Ramenskoye, the Mig-29 and the Sukhoi Su-27. He stopped, eyes widening, realisation slowly dawning on him. Surely not? Quickly selecting a further series of the photographs and brushing the previous set aside, he set the new batch in place. He could see the detail clearly with the jet easily visible as it was towed from the HAS and there could be no confusion. He was looking at a Soviet Su-27 air superiority fighter, the Frontovoi Istrebityel and what's more it was sitting on a British airfield in West Germany. How the hell it got there he could not begin to imagine but he set about tracking its progress across the airfield. Stunned by the incontrovertible facts, he scribbled a few notes and collected some good shots of the aircraft and set off down the corridor towards the secure communications centre.

*

Kamov scanned the document and photographs which had been delivered to him at the airport and smiled. It would cost him a great deal of his precious contraband but the results were worth it. The KGB major had come up trumps and he would remember him for future assignments; a contact well worth cultivating. He relaxed in his seat as the airliner sped westwards delivering him back to Düsseldorf and his next rendezvous.

*

Yuri enjoyed the occasional sight of the brightly lit West German villages as the car travelled through the darkened German countryside towards the Headquarters of the Second Allied Tactical Air Force, 2ATAF, at Rheindahlen. Again the contrast between these affluent hamlets and the austere villages which he had seen briefly during his overnight stop at Allstedt struck him. It reinforced his decision to have made the break. The two societies were poles apart. Contrasts in every way of life confirmed his view of the corrupt influence of the system he had left behind. East of the "Iron Curtain" people existed rather than lived, contained by a ring of wire and mines. Here he saw freedom on every street corner. The car rolled through an open check point past a large sign which welcomed visitors to HQ 2ATAF. Remarkable that life need not revolve around endless security checks even on a busy military base. Despite this, it was clear that the base had been constructed with security in mind, particularly in terms of attack from the air. All the buildings with the exception of the huge headquarters complex were single storey and he had little doubt that the functions normally exercised in the office accommodation in peacetime were able to be transferred to a hardened bunker somewhere within the vast complex in war. He also had little doubt that the base could be sealed as tight as a drum if required. What he saw was a willingness to relax military procedures to allow the inhabitants to enjoy a good standard of living; the military co-existing with the civilians in harmony. The car eased under the canopy in front of the Officers' Mess and he was ushered quickly but politely into the Reception area.

*

It was late as Keith James pushed his way into the restaurant, no longer the pleasurable experience it had been when he had first arrived at Wildenrath. He scanned the faces in the booths around him noticing that it was significantly busier than the last time he had visited. Perhaps less time had been available for preparation this time and he thought he knew why. Kamov sat at the same table but looked decidedly agitated unlike the last time only days before when he had appeared frighteningly calm. Sliding into his seat, Keith noticed that a glass of beer had been placed on top of a familiar looking envelope.

"Thank you for coming Keith, I should have been most disappointed had you decided not to join me."

"I don't think I have the stomach for another of your cheap porno productions," he snarled pushing away the envelope.

"No please, take another look my friend, it's of a different topic on this occasion."

As he withdrew the photograph, he instinctively knew that it would only be bad news which would greet him; and it was. The first shot showed him talking calmly to Kamov clutching a generous wad of cash but the second shot plumbed the depths of depravity. His wife lay on her back being pleasured by a very attractive man who was making every show for the camera.

"Perhaps my friend would be forced to pay another visit to your pretty wife. I'm sure she would be as pleased to see him as she knows so few people. He took so much care to make her acquaintance in England before she joined you."

Keith's immediate reaction was to grab Kamov by the throat but as he drew to his feet, the scraping of his chair causing a number of diners to stare at him, Kamov growled ominously.

"Unless you wish to end your career and mine at this very moment, I suggest you should sit down and listen carefully."

His entrapment was complete and total and any thought of resistance crumbled. As he slumped back into his chair, Keith waited for what he knew was coming and the wait proved shorter than expected.

"You have a Soviet fighter at Wildenrath," whispered Kamov fiercely "and I want to know precisely where it is, how it's guarded and what is it's state of readiness. I would also like to know the details of the airbase defences....now!" Kamov had watched Keith closely as he had posed the question and the resigned acknowledgement in his eyes confirmed the satellite data. The Su-27 was indeed somewhere on the adjacent airbase. He listened closely as, almost without hesitation, Keith listlessly launched into a precise description of the secrets of RAF Wildenrath. As they spoke, a man at the corner table shifted his position to give a better view of Kamov.

"The Bloodhound SAM LOMEZ covers the lower level airspace well to the east of the airfield," said Keith "and is only activated during exercises or at higher alert states. Within 20 miles of the airbase, the Rapier SHORAD, the short range air defence system is on alert during daylight hours but, without a radar tracking system, can only engage targets visually. The guns you see on the airfield are old Bofors guns and have not been operational for years; they are for decoy purposes only. The outer perimeter wire is monitored by RAF Police Dog Patrols and each of the dispersals, including the Bloodhounds, has its own inner security wire. Battle Flight has its own dedicated guards who patrol 24 hours a day."

He went on in a staccato monotone detailing the most favourable access points and the weakest areas in the perimeter. Sadly, he had learned all too quickly during his brief time at Wildenrath. Throughout the monologue Kamov smiled and nodded thoughtfully, making encouraging noises and gestures as the interrogation progressed. At the end of the inquisition, Keith felt drained and cheapened and his self esteem had sunk to an all time low as he attempted to fathom a way out of his predicament but with no success. As he watched Kamov leave, he realised that there was no easy way out and that any leak of his involvement was the end of his career and, goodness knows, with what he had just given away could even lead to a prison sentence.

Across the restaurant, the man eyed Keith suspiciously.

12 INBOUND

Following an orderly down a maze of corridors, Yuri was shown to a room tucked away in the centre of the Officers' Mess. The windows overlooked a small enclosed courtyard which still showed the last vestiges of what would have been a spectacular show of colourful flowers during the summer months. It was discretely secure. As the door closed, he found himself alone for the first time since he had climbed from the Su-27 and he had time to reflect. It had been a momentous decision but he had no regrets. His surroundings were pleasant but understated. The small sitting room contained a flowered pattern sofa and chair and the wall cabinet which was stacked with western books also contained a decanter of spirits and lead crystal glasses. Next door, a double bed faced a wardrobe containing another change of clothes and the small holdall which held the items he would need for his journey. At this time of night they were superfluous but he had already been briefed that he would be moving on tomorrow, although at this stage his destination was a mystery. Grateful for the solitude, he returned to the sitting room, poured a stiff shot of what he now realised was scotch whisky, and relaxed on the sofa. Yes he had been right!

*

Porov assembled the aircrew for briefing. The lights of the briefing room had been dimmed and the crews relaxed in the comfortable chairs. Around them, maps of the western Soviet districts and East Germany lined the walls but the map which he now projected onto the screen instantly caught their attention. West Germany! In front of him, suddenly attuned to his every word, were the pilot and weapons officer of the Hind Delta gunship and a second pilot for the Hind Alpha.

"Comrades, tonight we will conduct a covert insertion into an airbase. Due to the sensitivity of the mission, you will discuss what you are about to hear with no one, but no one! Any disclosure could have tragic implications. Shortly, the mission specialists will arrive. We have no need to concern ourselves with the detail of their assignment but what we must do is to put them down accurately on a pre-surveyed landing site just to the south of RAF Wildenrath in West Germany."

He paused, knowing that the concerned looks reflected his own reaction when Kamov had briefed him. The mood was transient, their professionalism swiftly reasserted.

"The plan in outline," he began, "is that we deploy forward to Schlotheim airfield near Erfurt where we will refuel. At 2330 local time we launch as a pair and route across the border north of Fritzlar airfield. From Fritzlar we will make use of terrain screening in the Harz Mountains to shield us from ground radar sites. There are a number of Hawk batteries on the hills to the east of Paderborn and we cannot discount random siting of the mobile West German Local Air Defence Radar units. They have pulse Doppler radars and are very difficult to avoid. After running down the Sorpe reservoir we'll aim for the refuelling site near Winterberg. The Alpha has been modified with additional fuel tanks in the cabin but unfortunately time has not permitted us to plumb them in. We'll have to land unsupported in a field site and transfer the fuel into the main tanks before we press on. This phase of the mission will be critical because we will come within the low level coverage of the Loneship air defence radar site which sits on a hilltop near Erndtebrück. If we are detected at this stage our mission will fail. The Delta will be range limited by then but we could still use it if we have serviceability problems; we will select which helicopter continues to the target but ideally it will be the Alpha. I have selected the overall route for a number of reasons but mainly because the area is well used by a number of helicopter types, particularly the West German CH53s, and I think we will cause enough distraction to achieve our aims. Both helicopters sound fairly similar. The final leg of the route takes us past the Wüpperfurth Lakes where our task becomes much more difficult as it's impossible to avoid the conurbations which straddle the River Rhein. Once in the Dormagen gap, south of Düsseldorf, we are completely exposed for our final run in to the landing site just on the southern perimeter of Wildenrath airfield. I estimate this phase will take about 15 minutes during which time we are in radar coverage of the civil airfields at Cologne/Bonn and Düsseldorf as well as our target airfield. Thankfully, most military airfields will have closed by then and it is only the alert aircraft at the Battle Flight facility which keeps Wildenrath open. If we're detected we should expect that Battle Flight will be scrambled. We've been fitted with a NATO IFF transponder which might confuse things enough to delay a reaction but it's not guaranteed. All being well, by then you should be safely homeward bound," he said looking at the pilot of the Hind gunship. Looking around he could see that he still had their undivided attention so he pressed on with his briefing.

"The alternative plan will be for the Delta to continue alone with just 2 passengers. It would refuel from the tanks in the Alpha to ensure it could reach its goal. Of prime importance, Comrades, we must not leave any hardware on the ground. Both helicopters are wired with self destruction charges and must be totally destroyed if they cannot be flown out. If we face this situation we already have a diplomatic incident on our hands but in any case, we must limit the potential damage."

He continued to outline callsigns, tactical data, electronic warfare procedures, formation and radio procedures down to the last precise detail. Each fact, as he moved systematically through the briefing, was no less important than the last and failure to comply with even the smallest detail could place the whole mission at risk. His request for questions but was met with a contemplative silence. His plan was either comprehensive or his team were naive; he hoped he was right in his assessment.

"OK, we wait for the covert team. Let's rendezvous back here at 17.00 for a final briefing. See you then."

13 SNATCH

The black Opel saloon cruised to a halt in the quiet leafy suburb of Wegberg, a small village about 10 Km from the main Headquarters at Rheindahlen. Largely a dormitory for the huge industrial towns nearby, it was surrounded by a ring road which diverted all but essential traffic away from the residential suburbs. It was an unlikely setting for the drama which was about to unfold.

Two men sat in the front seats, immobile and silent. They had followed the black RAF Granada staff car from Wildenrath the previous evening past the drop-off point at Rheindahlen, and all the way to the local hotel at Wegberg where its occupants had spent the night. The fact that the two individuals had avoided using on-base military accommodation and also that they had not returned their vehicle to the Service motor transport section at the Headquarters was significant. These particular operatives were not run-of-the-mill Service personnel. The men in the Opel, one small and thick set and the other large and brawny exchanged a few inconsequential words as they sensed their vigil coming to a close. They spoke in their native language and it was not English. Around them, were the first signs of the village coming to life as the heavy wooden shutters on the windows of the house opposite rattled open, the owner glancing briefly but innocently at the parked car. Meanwhile, the occupants of the Opel watched each and every car which passed the end of the quiet street. Ten minutes later, as they had anticipated, they spotted the black Granada as it passed the end of the small road, retracing its route of only hours earlier. The driver of the Opel, recognising the occupants immediately, started the engine and moved his car swiftly to the junction. A Volkswagen Golf flashed past and despite the streets being deserted, tailgated the Granada, briefly distracting the occupants. The Opel joined the light traffic flow slipping unnoticed into pursuit using the Golf as a buffer between the two vehicles. As the houses of Wegberg began to thin out, replaced by the inevitable pine forest, the Granada picked up speed. As it reached the Ring Road, it turned right towards Rheindahlen quickly resuming its progress while the Golf sped off in the opposite direction leaving the Opel unprotected and exposed. The driver hung back to avoid making his presence too obvious. He knew the stretch of road intimately having spent many hours studying local maps. As he had expected, traffic was light at this time of the morning but it was some distance to the spot where they had planned to make their move and there were no other suitable areas in between. They would rely on one particular narrow bend in the road. For the plan to succeed, they would need 5 uninterrupted minutes, sharp timing and some luck. If they made their move too soon, they would be in full view of the scattered houses which dotted the road; too late and their quarry would reach the busy access road to the Headquarters and be unassailable. The driver recognised one of his reference points. About 2 Km to go and he eased a little closer to the black staff car. As the gap narrowed, the passenger in the Granada turned, apparently assessing the Opel. A few words were exchanged and the car accelerated slightly. Matching the move, the Opel remained at its measured distance, the driver hoping that the adjustment had been coincidental. It quickly became apparent that the passenger was skittish and a further increase in speed confirmed their concerns. They had been spotted. With nothing more to lose, the driver accelerated hard and moved onto the Granada's tail. With still 1 Km to go to the bend, the speedometer slewed crazily to 120 Km per hour. It was too fast; it would attract attention which was the last thing they wanted. The passenger in the Opel was nervous his body language visible even from this far back. This phase of the mission should have been simple. They had covertly marked the target and predicted its movements correctly for the last few hours but poor tradecraft and over enthusiasm by the idiot driver of the VW had prematurely alerted their subjects to their presence. They would have to act, and act decisively, if the plan was to succeed.

"Move it. Take him now!" he said in Russian and the driver immediately gunned the engine of the powerful saloon and closed up tight on the Granada.

"For goodness sake, don't damage the staff car, we need it!"

Anxious to redeem himself, the driver watched the road ahead, anticipating the point where it would bend left then right through the narrow, blind double curve. Nearly all his options had evaporated but he had one left. Still 50 metres short, he began his move accelerating hard and pulled alongside the Granada which shimmied on the still slippery surface. Fixing the driver with an intimidating stare, the driver hammered the powerful engine which screamed in protest. He edged the vehicle closer, doors only centimetres apart. Thirty metres to the bend; please let there be no oncoming traffic he thought to himself. He repeated the threatening move yet again, sandwiching the staff car tightly against the roadside verge and causing the British driver to falter and dab the brakes in an effort to spit him out in front. This was unexpected as he had assumed that the other driver was a trained professional not a regular driver from the RAF pool. Thankful for the error he screwed his car at right angles across the road, brakes and tyres screaming in protest in a cloud of blue smoke. The Granada, its exit suddenly and finally sealed, matched the manoeuvre, grinding to a halt only metres from the now stationary Opel. Realising their fate, the two men from the Granada jumped clear, one making the instantly fatal mistake of making a dash for the tree line. The larger Russian took aim, felling him with a single shot from his heavy calibre handgun. Meanwhile the other man, seeing the fate of his partner, began to crawl on hands and knees retracing the route the car had taken only seconds before, keeping the stationary vehicles as cover between himself and his attackers. He could not prevent an involuntary flinch as a shot ricocheted off the road next to him, spitting up small shards of concrete into his face. Despite his frantic twisting and turning, he had failed to spot the marksman who had tucked into the cover of the undergrowth. The abrupt threat doubled his exertions. The innocent German motorist who rounded the bend just at that moment was unprepared for the sight which greeted him and the apparent mayhem left him little in the way of choice. His brain, still dulled at such an early hour, was slow to respond to the random chaos. His reactions were even slower to respond. The two vehicles which had slewed across the road gave the initial impression of a tragic motor accident and as he quickly scanned the immediate surroundings for a possible escape route he settled on a small gap between the trees. It was then that he registered the prone figure crawling along the road and his momentous decision of only seconds before became an attack of terminal indecision as his brain fought with the sudden conflict. He attempted, unsuccessfully, to establish the priority between avoiding a collision with the prone body of the defenceless man and the equally important desire for self-preservation. The conflict was never resolved as he froze, allowing the car to drift unchecked in a lazy left hand curve. The wheels bounced over the luckless man killing him instantly and the car careered into a tree, coming to rest with the trunk embedded in the bodywork. Steam issued quickly from the distorted metalwork around the crumpled bonnet. The two Russians wasted no time, patting down the two disfigured bodies removing all traces of identification and then dragged them over to the still steaming car. Hauling open the rear doors, the two corpses were manhandled into the rear seats and forced forward into distorted positions imitating the effect of the force of the impact. The charade would not stand close inspection but it would fool the casual observer. To assist with the subterfuge, a gently burning match introduced to the small amount of petrol leaking from the shattered engine compartment completed the impromptu task with a sickening whoosh. The engines of both the Opel and the Granada burst into life as the cars drew away from the growing inferno.

*

There was a gentle knock on the interconnecting door and the batman, a throwback to grander days in the Services, moved across towards the bed.

"Good Morning Sir. It's seven o'clock and it's a lovely bright morning. Would you like milk and sugar in your tea?"

Pleasantly surprised by the intrusion, Yuri grunted his assent.

"A message from Squadron Leader Silversmith, Sir. He'll meet you in the dining room for breakfast at 0745."

The door closed gently and Yuri sipped the welcome cup of tea.

*

The earth shattering events of the previous days still played on their minds as Razor and Flash strapped into their respective cockpits and donned their flying helmets. It was most unlikely that the Soviets would take it lying down; risk of retribution was high and it could manifest itself in so many ways.

The take off and climb out had been uneventful and as they reached their CAP height the radio burst into life.

"Mike Lima 67 this is Crabtree vector 070 degrees climb to flight level 250, I have incoming high level trade. You are clear to engage."

Outside the cockpit all was pitch black.

"Weapons checks Razor," called Flash "pick up your speed to Mach .9 as you climb."

"OK Mate," he acknowledged as he ran swiftly through his checks. CW on, interlocks out, Sparrow selected......."

"Crabtree 67, more help," prompted the back seater, hoping to increase the flow of information from his controller.

"67, Crabtree, your target shows high level, high speed, heading west, you have good cut-off."

The controller's initial vectors to a head on intercept point were putting the Phantom into a position where it could take over the intercept once it detected its target, a high level supersonic intruder, on radar. With such high closing speeds, the Phantom crew would need all their skill to complete the profile. Any delay in committing weapons or initiating the turn in behind the target would be crucial. Every ten seconds brought the target three miles closer and with their small weapons envelope, delay would mean the shot would be lost and the target penetrating their defensive screen would be able to generate mayhem.

"Target's on the nose already crossed ahead. The intercept is going slack," said Flash, interrupting the information he was receiving from the controller.

In the case of a supersonic target, any displacement in the attack geometry would drag the attack onto the beam away from the most effective aspect for the Sparrow missile. With only stern-aspect AIM-9G Sidewinders this profile would suck them around into the stern hemisphere which was not where they wanted to be against a high speed target. They may never roll out inside weapons parameters.

"Come port 40 degrees, let's tighten it up. The tropopause is at 36,000 feet, let's get up there; start a climb."

The tropopause was the area in the upper air where jet engines worked most efficiently. Above the tropopause, there was a marked drop off in performance and manoeuvring became tenuous; the jet was on a knife edge. Engaging high level targets, fighter crews would use the tropopause to give their aircraft the performance edge until the last moment at the point of committal.

"Contact 10 degrees right range 55 miles, target's showing 42,000 feet at Mach 1.6. Hold that heading."

"Steady 050, passing 25,000 for 36,000, I'll call you level."

"Crabtree, 67 is Judy, Judy."

Flash calculated the effect of his turn mentally and decided that his turn would sort out his attack geometry.

"Back onto 070 degrees, target range 50, accelerate to Mach 1.3. If we're not targeted, we'll take a double Sparrow shot and fly through," he briefed perfunctorily.

He had already appreciated that a re-attack on such a fast target was unlikely to be effective and decided to commit two Sparrows in the head sector to improve the kill probability before extending through.

"RWR's clean at range 30, your dot." He handed over the Sparrow steering dot to Razor. If the pilot flew the dot into the centre of the radar scope, it would give the missile a perfect collision course at the point of launch. With such a fast target the shot would come early so a swift handover was essential to give his pilot time to sweeten the shot.

"Locking up, stand by for the Sparrow shot."

Flash covered the target with the acquisition markers, squeezed the trigger on the radar hand controller and waited for the lock symbology. Nothing!

"No lock, stand by, trying again."

Unusual. The RWR squealed as the threat suddenly took an interest in the attacking Phantom. What now? They had yet to launch their own missile.

"Threat, 12 o'clock, counter port," Flash called excitedly, realising he had to honour the unexpected aggression. Without question, Razor hauled the stick over and brought the aircraft through 90 degrees. In the absence of visual references as it was pitch black outside the cockpit, he flew the manoeuvre entirely on instruments. The RWR fell silent again.

"67, this is Crabtree, pop-up contact 350 degrees range 10 miles, climbing through 25,000 feet," called GCI. Their turn onto North had brought this new threat to their nose. Jeez, a pincer attack! Whilst they had concentrated on the high speed intruder, another aircraft had outflanked them. A classic bracket!

"Thanks for the warning Crabtree," Razor replied realising that the new threat had sandwiched them and was well within the missile firing envelope at this height.

"Rackets, I band, 12 o'clock, break port," yelled Flash. "Missile guidance..... Oh shit, missile break, missile break," he added with even greater urgency, his voice almost hysterical.

Razor knew that this was a last-ditch situation and dragged the aircraft further round, by now retracing their flight path. Still the RWR audio assailed their ears. This threat was persistent! Suddenly, the whole airframe rocked and a loud thump accompanied the jolt. The warning panel erupted in a blaze of captions and the cockpits went dark.

"Double engine flame out!" called Razor. "Put out a Mayday, I'm carrying out the immediate actions. Throttles are both off, trying an immediate relight on the left."

Flash hit the stop watch as Razor jabbed the small relight button on the back of the left throttle and watched the RPM gauge, willing it to rise, hoping that the engine was restarting. The gauge stayed doggedly at zero.

"Put out the call Flash."

"Mayday, Mayday, Mayday, Mike Lima 67 on Guard, F4 with double engine flame out, 10 miles south of Gutersloh at Flight Level 300 descending, stand by," called the back seater.

"67, Clutch Radar on Guard, Mayday acknowledged, alerting SAR, standing by."

The crew were grateful. The tendency was for the air traffic agencies to initiate a stream of chatter in a misguided desire to assist. At this stage, all they needed were calm relaxed actions to sort out the emergency. Rule number one, fly the aeroplane; talk could come later.

"OK Flash, no joy on the left. Right throttle is off. Give me the cold relight drill; we're passing 27,000 feet."

"OK, wait until we pass 25,000 feet then right throttle to idle and hit the relight button. Put the RAT out."

The RAT was the Ram Air Turbine which would provide electrical power in the absence of the engines.

"Here we go. Let's see what we get."

Razor hit the relight button for the second engine but still nothing.

"Tighten your straps mate, we're passing 20,000 feet and still nothing."

"Clutch, Mayday 67 on Guard frequency. Still no joy, passing 20 thousand feet, we may have to eject."

"67 roger, Rescue 22 is airborne."

"One last chance Razor, we can try a GT start on the left once we're below 10,000 feet," said Flash shakily reading the drills from the cards. This used the normal starter motor which was designed to operate on the ground not in the lower atmosphere but if it provided any hope it was worth a try.

"Passing 10,000 feet, check speed is below 240 knots, Aux Air Doors emergency open,"

"Speed's good, Aux Air Doors Emergency Open, confirmed." replied the pilot. This would feed the engine with additional air.

"Hit the start switch and pray!" came the resigned call from the back. Razor watched the RPM...............Nothing.

"Straps tight buddy. Eject, Eject, Eject!"

"67 ejecting!"

Flash rocked back in his ejection seat locking the shoulder straps. He tugged the lap straps extra tight and flicked his visor down to protect his face. Straightening his back, he reached down for the seat pan handle, hands crossed and tugged. Involuntarily he closed his eyes tightly. The actions had taken seconds.

The canopy moved slowly at first, then faster. Flash anticipated the windrush........................ As the lights came on, the instructor's voice came over the intercom.

"OK guys, tidy up the switches in the cockpit and climb out. Looks like that Apex missile got you on that one. Good sortie, we'll debrief in five minutes. The Simulator session was over.

*

The Russian allowed the Opel to slow to a halt along the track and out of sight of the road. He turned off the engine and pulled the key throwing it out into the bushes alongside the road. The car had been stolen in Düsseldorf only hours before and carried false number plates. It would be some time before it would be traced and there was certainly nothing to connect it to the incident of a few minutes ago.

*

Yuri opened the door to the dining room and, recognising the RAF Squadron Leader who had escorted him from Wildenrath the previous evening, made his way over to the table.

"Please help yourself to breakfast Colonel. There's fruit juice and cereal on the table along with tea and coffee. If you would like an English breakfast, please just give your order to the steward."

"You are very kind," replied Yuri. He realised that he had been guarded closely from the moment he had arrived but the supervision had been discrete and he was grateful for that. If he was to be a prisoner, better a gilded cage.

"I would like a brief word this morning before you leave as I have a number of technical questions on the aircraft and your standard operating procedures which I would like to run through. You'll be collected this afternoon. The journey to the airport is relatively short; less than an hour and you have been booked on this evening's flight to London where your debriefing will continue. Naturally, I have arranged escorts for you throughout your journey."

"Which airline?" asked Yuri, more out of interest rather than necessity.

"Oh British Airways, old chap, naturally!" replied Silversmith. "I have a 32 Squadron HS125 on call but perhaps it's better to be discreet? But, please don't worry about any of the trivia. That will all be taken care of. I have a diplomatic passport for you and we've spoken to the airport security chaps. It's all in hand. Just relax and enjoy your breakfast and then we can have a little chat in the ante room."

*

It was mid morning as the black Granada rolled to a stop outside the main entrance to the Officers' Mess. The two men remained in the vehicle, impassive. The door opened and Yuri was led out by the Squadron Leader. The man in the passenger seat emerged, flashed an identity card discretely and opened the rear door. The two men shook hands and exchanged a few quiet words before Yuri climbed in, the whole affair brief, efficient and without fuss. The car pulled slowly away.

*

The two Hind helicopters crossed the airfield perimeter at Schlotheim and hover-taxied to the main dispersal. Short and squat, the Hind was a quintessential attack helicopter. The Alpha model, which was first to alight, had been the original design, developed to carry troops into battle in its armoured cabin. Although relatively lightly armed with only a machine gun protruding from the nose, the stubby wings which carried 6 rocket pods ensured that its arrival on the battlefield did not go unnoticed. The Delta model was even more fearsome. The flat, airliner-type cockpit windows of the Alpha had been replaced with two bubble fighter-style canopies for the pilot and a dedicated weapons officer. The light calibre machine gun was replaced with a rapid fire Gatling gun which protruded from a bulbous fairing around the base of the nose alongside another sensor housing. Above the cockpit, the two Isotov turboshaft engines which powered the five-bladed rotor were protected by infra-red suppressors which reduced the heat signature of the engine protecting the helicopter from IR guided surface-to-air missiles. Like the Alpha, the Delta also sprouted stub wings which, as well as carrying the 57mm rocket pods, could mount AT-6 Spiral anti-tank or R60 infra-red air-to-air missiles. Despite the enhancements, it could still carry a few fully armed troops in its smaller cabin. In all, the Hind was a helicopter to be respected and its functional appearance emphasised the fact. The pilot of the Delta who, unusually, occupied the rear cockpit, opened the door which was built into the bubble canopy and let himself gingerly to the floor. He began to direct the mechanics who had emerged from behind a power set which had protected them from the wash of debris which the helicopters had thrown up during their arrival. The turn round servicing was quickly underway as each individual slotted into a practised routine. Soon, a bowser pulled up in front of the lead helicopter and the fuel coupling was connected, pumping fuel into the newly installed auxiliary tanks. The crews who had drifted across the apron and now reclined on the grass, exchanged a few brief words before the noise of the bowser drowned out their efforts. They each relaxed, waiting for the mechanics to complete their task.

*

There was little conversation between the two men in the front of the car and Yuri felt no urge to disturb the silence. The signposts were unfamiliar to him but he noticed the increasing regularity of the international airport symbol as they neared Düsseldorf. Much had already happened over the recent days but he began to allow himself a feeling of optimism for the future, even though the next few days would be difficult as he was pumped for information. He had defected but he didn't feel like a traitor and it would be a fine dividing line between passing on the technical details of his aircraft and giving away information which would be truly harmful to the Motherland. He hoped that his years as a test pilot would have blunted his tactical knowledge and that he could legitimately steer the debriefing towards the Su-27 which he was happy to discuss. He hoped he could do this but realised that it would be difficult to maintain a sharp delineation. He doubted anyone back home would sympathise with his sentiments. The car drew up outside the Departure Hall breaking his reverie.

"Come in my dear chap, do take a seat. Can I get you a coffee?"

"Thank you Sir Richard, that would be most kind. It was good of you to see me at such short notice."

The grey haired, patrician gestured towards the leather armchair as he returned to his own seat.

"You said on the phone that you wished to discuss the defection of the Soviet pilot," he began gently. "I thought things had been going well on that front but you sounded somewhat disturbed?"

Sir Richard Courtney had been taking a keen interest in the operation since Martin Williams of MI6 had alerted him to the facts only 36 hours previously. Although aware of the military significance of the acquisition of the fighter, his interest lay in the political dimension. His Department within the Foreign Office was charged with maintaining the delicate balance in relationships with the Soviet Union and events such as these were often seen as irritants by his staff. It was a task which demanded a great deal of his considerable political acumen because the Soviets were notoriously unpredictable in their reaction to world events, even more so when matters of National Sovereignty were in question. Of overriding importance to them, bordering on the paranoia, was the desire to protect their borders from incursion. This was despite their own cavalier attitude to their neighbours.

"It was, Sir Richard, until this morning. How much are you aware of the facts surrounding the case?" Williams continued.

"I think it may be useful for you to recap, Old Chap. Best from the horse's mouth I should think."

Sir Richard had been extensively briefed by his desk officers but his vast experience told him that these one-on-one sessions often produced a more frank exchange of views and a greater level of detail. The "keep the master happy" syndrome amongst his staff could be counter-productive at times and he was more than aware of how delicate the situation was becoming.

"As you know Sir," the agent pressed on, "initial contact was made by the Soviet pilot himself...."

He began to outline the key facts.

"Things were going rather well until early this morning when we attempted to move him from Rheindahlen; that's the Headquarters near Mönchen Gladbach, to our safe house in Ascot. The escorts were ambushed as they made their way to the base for the pickup and, regrettably, the pilot was snatched back. I'm afraid they paid the price for their moment of inattention," he said quietly. "We found them stuffed into the back of a stolen car near the base. Very dead, I'm afraid. The KGB agents - and we can only assume it was KGB - stole their identity cards and the staff car and then made a really quite bold collection from the RAF Intelligence staff at Rheindahlen. A very smooth operation."

Sir Richard raised his eyebrows at the mention of violence. No matter how often his diplomatic path crossed that of the intelligence services, the more sordid aspects of undercover operations did not sit comfortably with his view of political relationships, Cold War or no.

"We assume they will try to get him out either by road or through a local airport," continued Williams.

"We have alerted all likely exits through the Bundesgrenzschutz and we have circulated photographs. The sad fact is that they are not constrained in any way. We're hoping they will assume that we're not yet on to them and go for the nearest border or airport. We closed the local crossings at Elmpt and Wassenberg to the west and its sealed tighter than a drum. We have extra staff on duty at Düsseldorf and Köln/Bonn. If they are foolish enough to try those places we should have them but unfortunately they could slip out anywhere."

The diplomat frowned as he listened.

"Our main concern and the reason I came to see you, is the political dimension. The aircraft's arrival has already caused some diplomatic ripples as I'm sure you're aware. The Sovs were not at all happy that the Phantoms involved in the incident strayed into their airspace. They also complained bitterly that their new AWACS, the Beriev A-50 command and control platform was targeted by another Phantom - as it went about its lawful business on a trial flight, yada yada. Unless we return the Su-27 quickly and turn a blind eye to their antics, I suspect we may find them becoming rather intransigent."

Sir Richard had listened carefully so far, silently weighing up the facts but at this point he interrupted.

"The key factor here, dear boy, is how important is this new toy to their future plans. Could it change the balance of power? Please consider your answer carefully."

His mind raced ahead.

"You must realise that I'm not an expert on these matters but I have been briefed by the Air Staff in MOD. I think I can say without a shadow of doubt that in pure quality terms, this aircraft redresses the deficiencies which we have always relied on for success. The MOD shares that view. Our effectiveness in responding to a pre-emptive attack has always been based on the technical superiority of our equipment. We have never been able to match the output of their war machine in pure numbers but we have assumed that we would beat them due to the calibre of our people and equipment. If they deploy the Flanker in any numbers to escort their bomber formations, it is doubtful if our air defences could counter that threat. It becomes a whole different equation. Unescorted bombers are relatively easy targets because they have to hit a target on the ground. They try to avoid the fighters even if they are intercepted. In short, they run away. With embedded fighters it's different. Their whole role in life is to mix it with the opposition. A spoiling tactic which leaves the bombers clear to sidestep the mêlée and run for their targets with obviously disastrous consequences. The Su-27 is the first aircraft which has given them the range and capability to carry out this task over our airspace. It's important all right."

"And, presumably, the information which this pilot could supply is of value?"

"Vital!"

"Then we must get him back, Dear Boy. Now you must tell me precisely how you intend to do that and leave me to tackle the Soviet Embassy. Perhaps it's time to call in a few favours if this is so important." His smile was enigmatic.

Martin Williams was surprised at the firmness of the response from the diplomat. It was unusual and, despite his apparent nonchalance, he had been carefully and comprehensively briefed already.

"Well Sir, we have already spoken to GSG7. If they try to use Köln/Bonn we intend to................" He outlined his contingency plans in detail. Sir Richard Courtney listened carefully, nodding occasionally.

"Very well, let's go with that plan shall we? Please let me know as soon as you receive any sighting reports. I must keep in close contact with my contacts in Bonn. After all, it's happening on their soil is it not? I think the nature of the incident outside Rheindahlen should give me some leverage with which to negotiate. We can't have these people indulging in their "James Bond" fantasies; those days are long gone. Even if we do agree to return their aeroplane, which I am sure we will have to do in due course, they must learn to act rather more responsibly. There are channels to achieve this sort of thing. It's not as if we stole the aeroplane in the first place is it?" He was clearly not at ease but his demeanour masked his anger in true diplomatic fashion.

"Thank you, Sir Richard, I'm most grateful," said Williams as he rose to leave. A brief handshake and the short engagement was at an end.

Sir Richard picked up the phone.

"Marjorie, could you get General Sokolovskiy in Moscow on the line for me? Thank you. He waited as a series of clicks heralded the connection. "General, it's been too long. How are you finding the Moscow weather? It must be a little cooler than you were used to in London."

"Sir Richard, it's so good to hear from you. It's been quite a change for me. I have to say, I enjoyed my time at the Russian Embassy. Dare I say that things can be a little austere over here at times. How are you keeping?"

"General Sokolovskiy, Igor, we seem to have a bit of difficulty in West Germany that I think we need to discuss over a few glasses of port. It seems there's been an incident on the border which has all the potential to excite the wrong people. Could we meet? I could be in Bonn tomorrow evening if it's at all possible?"

14 INSERTION

The shadowy figures moved in his peripheral vision, climbing into the helicopter cabin and Porov heard the thump as the heavy door closed behind him. The crewman tapped him on the shoulder giving him a thumbs-up signifying that all was loaded and they were ready to go. He looked across to the other Hind which glowed green in the reflected glare of the dimmed airfield lights, vaguely aware of the rotors chopping the air. The goggles attached to the front of his flying helmet were heavy and made the muscles on the back of his neck stand proud with the strain. The mission was impossible without them. He flashed his torch twice, the signal for lift off as he rotated the collective lever with his other hand increasing the straining power of the Isotovs above him. As he held firmly onto the cyclic, the heavy helicopter lifted slowly into the air. Alongside, the other Hind lifted effortlessly, its dimmed bulk slotting swiftly into formation. The extra fuel on board made his craft sluggish and he was conscious of the proximity of the other helicopter as he eased the nose down starting a slow walk forward at minimum height across the darkened airfield. Better this way, he mused. At least with its more powerful engines the Delta had plenty of performance in hand to avoid him. Air Traffic Control had been carefully briefed that the remainder of the mission would be completed in radio silence and he was relieved as the green light winked from the Control Tower giving them clearance to cross the main runway. Any radio calls this close to the border could alert the NATO listening posts which dotted the area. Staying undetected would be his primary concern and he had no wish to give them advanced warning with a careless call. His eyes adjusted to the green glow from the magnified light in the goggles and he unconsciously compensated for the rushing of the trees in his peripheral field of view as he left the confines of the airfield and set off across country.

Porov needed to practise the disciplines of nap-of-the-earth flying whilst he was still in his own airspace. Once over the border, he would have additional worries and the flying must be second nature. A wood drifted past on his right as the speed built up to 240 kph. He could no longer see the Hind Delta which had picked up its tactical formation position tucked in his seven o'clock where it would remain unless threats dictated otherwise. In the aft cabin, the insertion team who had joined them just prior to take off had carefully stowed their gear and strapped into the canvas seats along the cabin wall. They looked ready for all eventualities and he was glad he was not to be the subject of their attentions. Turning his eyes away from the lights of Mühlhausen which would flood the sensitive night vision goggles and make his progress hazardous, he concentrated on the terrain ahead. The flaring from the bright lights subsided and he became aware that the ground was rising gently so he eased the helicopter right a few degrees and selected a course along a wood-lined ridge. In the distance, he could see the steep rise of the ground as the flat plains made way for the Harz Mountains. At the point where the plain and the mountains blended together, the topography rose sharply to nearly 1,000 metres. Somewhere in there was the valley of the Werra river which would lead him across the border. He strained his eyes to pick it out. He could not avoid the villages of Wanfried and Eschwege but he knew that the border guards at the checkpoints in the area had been warned to turn a blind eye to any unusual activity; a significant concession in itself. The valley sides on either side of him were etched in relief, their covering of dense pine trees standing out in the glow of the goggles. As he pulled the helicopter around a spur he briefly noticed a reflection of stray light from the Hind following in close trail and was suddenly reminded of its proximity. Glancing down, he turned his Soviet identification system to standby; from now on he was covert. He would use the NATO IFF box which had been rapidly installed if he felt it would help the deception. To the left and right, he could see the ribbon of the Inner German Border stretching out as far as the eye could see cutting a swathe through the countryside. The watch towers stood out in sharp contrast against the surrounding pine trees, their guardrooms beacons of light amplified by his goggles. Normally, this would be the most complex piece of land in the world to cross, being protected as it was by dogs, anti personnel mines, barbed wire and armed guards. Tonight his passage was effortless, smoothed by covert commands in the correct ears. The teams with the Sa-7 Grail missiles had been stood down temporarily. Almost insignificantly, the brightly lit strip receded in his mirrors. As his thumb traced the meandering route along the river valley it reached the spot on the map where the mountains would give way to a narrow plain north of Fritzlar. He tensed in anticipation, realising that this was the first vulnerable part of the route. He was in NATO airspace and life had taken a rather sinister and unexpected turn.

*

The public address system announced the departure of yet another flight to a far-off destination as Yuri finished his coffee in the Düsseldorf Air Terminal. The ease of travel in the West was not lost on him. He was bracketed by his minders who had barely spoken other than to offer him the rudimentary refreshments. He was beginning to notice a marked dissimilarity in the treatment he had received at Rheindahlen and a surly air was beginning to emanate from his current companions.

"Aeroflot announce the departure of Flight Number 274 to Moscow. Would all passengers please make their way to gate number A27."

"How about we make our way along to the gate," said the larger of his two escorts, unexpectedly. "We don't want to delay anything, eh?"

Yuri glanced at his watch.

"We have about an hour before boarding, do we not?"

"Yes, but the flight we intend boarding departs somewhat earlier, Comrade!"

Yuri hesitated.

"We have a little something to help you sleep on your journey," the other man said as Yuri felt a sharp jab in his left thigh. Realisation dawned as he began to link events and a look of concern creased his features. A sudden feeling of intense fatigue struck him and he fought to control the desire to sleep, the confines of his world beginning to narrow as his peripheral vision collapsed. Feeling himself being bundled to his feet, he finally succumbed; his last thought one of abject failure as he drifted into the darkness. Flight Number 274 to Moscow! It had been so close.

*

In the Approach Room at Fritzlar airfield, the duty controller glanced at the radar display. Two contacts had appeared 7 miles to the north and were tracking directly west. He ran his trackball over them and attempted to interrogate the responses to establish their identity but could elicit no response. He hit the button on his mini comms suite connecting him to the duty controller at Erndtebrück; Loneship Control And Reporting Centre.

"Fritzlar here. Probably nothing but I'm tracking two slow moving contacts now 5 miles north of me heading west. I can't get a squawk from either of them. It could be a flock of birds but the speeds showing about 150 knots .... Affirmative."

*

The well dressed visitor pushed his way through the glass doors which fronted onto the street of the exclusive Gentleman's Club in the Embassy District of the West German Capital Bonn. His flight had landed just an hour ago. The maitre d' ushered him across to a leather studded chair in the elegant foyer and his host rose to greet him.

"Igor, so good to see you and thank you for coming at such short notice. I know how difficult it can be to make such arrangements. It's been too long," said Sir Richard Courtney as he shook hands. "I'm so glad you could make it. I have a table booked and we can discuss our little problem. I'm sure there's an amicable solution."

"You're looking well Richard. As you say, too long. Let's talk."

Drinks in hand, they were shown to a discreet table in a dimly lit corner of the dining room. There was little preamble as they took their seats.

"You'll be aware that there was a small incident along the Inner German Border yesterday. It would appear that one of your chaps decided to make a dash for freedom and bring his aeroplane along with him. I'm afraid that in the mêlée one of our crews from our air defence base on the Dutch border may have strayed over the border into East Germany and become a little over enthusiastic with his missiles. I'm sorry but it seems you may have lost one of your own aircraft in the fracas."

"Indeed Richard. I've been on the phone all day trying to calm a few hotheads. It seems that the General who is in charge of that sector of our air defences is rather unimpressed. Not only did it happen on his watch, which will do his career no good at all, but it's left a rather messy situation on the ground. It seems the Mig crashed on the outskirts of a village narrowly missing a community centre."

"Look I've been asked to offer our sincere apologies and we wouldn't want this to sour relationships. I know you will want to keep the details quiet given the sensitivities. I'm sure that we could make sure the press in London don't make too much of a fuss."

"There is the matter of the prototype Su-27 which, as you know, is the aircraft that the defector was flying and of course the fate of the officer himself."

"Please rest assured that he will be well treated Igor. I can't guarantee that he will be returned immediately but I'm sure we can agree a suitable exchange at some time in the very near future. We both know how these things work do we not?"

"I really must insist that the Su-27 is returned as soon as possible and that it will not be tampered with in any way. I'm already having trouble with some of our people who are demanding all manner of retribution; some of it quite radical. I may not be able to restrain them."

"My dear Chap, of course. I'll speak to my people as soon as I get back to Whitehall and find out what's going on. I'm not sure if it can be flown out but maybe we could ask our American cousins to get a C-5 Galaxy over to Wildenrath? We'll have it flown back to Ramenskoye as soon as we can make arrangements."

"Let me take that back and see if I can sell the idea. It seems like a satisfactory compromise. Where is Andrenev?"

Sir Richard smiled avoiding the question.

"Good, good. Now, I can recommend the Chateaubriand. It really is excellent and I took the liberty of ordering the wine. The Bordeaux here is supposed to be very drinkable."

The reality was that things were escalating rapidly. With the extent of the duplicity neither could know how their carefully crafted plans were being warped by the turn of events.

*

The 19 Squadron crew were settling down in the hard beds in Battle Flight. The pilot rolled over trying to find a position which suited him but, dressed as they both were in flying suit, boots and G-suits, comfort was almost impossible. The telebrief ticked monotonously from the repeater box on the table, the incessant irritant. Suddenly, the wail of the alert hooter rent the air snapping both crew instantly into action. Rushing from the bedroom towards their waiting aircraft, the HAS doors automatically opened ahead of them. On the floor of the HAS their lifejackets had been carefully arranged for precisely this contingency; the ability to launch night or day in a matter of minutes. The navigator, rudely awakened by the adrenaline shot checked in with Wing Ops as the pilot was already firing up the engines. Neither of them was particularly cheered to receive the scramble message with a vector towards the border. Neither of them could remember such a busy period of activity on Battle Flight. How many scrambles was this over the last few days? Outside the night was dark and it was very late.

*

None of the officers of the Bundesgrenzschutz paid particular attention to the group of three men who made their way through the departure lounge.

One had clearly enjoyed the hospitality in the Business Lounge and lolled drunkenly against another. But, they were disturbing no one, although the airline staff may have had other thoughts. Certainly no one at the Aeroflot departure gate found the "drunk" at all difficult. They had been carefully briefed and it was not the first occasion on which such an incident had occurred. Without fuss, the group were ushered discretely onto the waiting IL-62 airliner bypassing the assembled passengers.

*

Porov followed the contours down the Sorpe valley seeing the glint of the water below him, the whole world green from the effect of the goggles. The steep profile of the valley sides prompted memories of the British bomber crews during the Patriotic War who had flown their Lancaster Bombers on similar routes to bomb the dams. In those days they had not had the benefit of night vision goggles and he felt a grudging respect. Tonight, however, the descendants of those same crews may not be so glad to see him if they should meet. The radar warning receiver flickered briefly and the SAM light illuminated. He knew that he was passing close to a Hawk battery and paid closer attention to the instrument bringing it more into his scan hoping that he was not targeted. Thankfully the warning was transitory and the warner fell silent again. He had another 10 Km to go to the planned refuelling site. His fuel gauge showed approximately 2/3 full and he knew that once the additional fuel was transferred to the main tanks he could complete the mission. Leaving the reservoir valley, the wooded plain stretched out in front rising sharply at the far end blending into the hills. This area was popular with skiers during the winter months but he hoped that the resorts in the foothills were not yet occupied; the first snows of the winter still some months away. The selected site was southwest of Medebach at a spot where rescue helicopters put down to recover injured skiers. Intelligence had suggested that the site should comfortably accommodate the two Hinds and would be empty at this time of night. The medevac helicopters never flew at night. Clicking the transmit button in warning, he slowed his speed to 150 Kph in preparation for the approach. Behind, the Hind Delta slowed to match him, its pilot carefully adjusting his loose formation position. They had pre-briefed the approach speeds.

Above, the Battle Flight Phantom had been receiving vectors from Loneship. The controller had been tracking the small helicopters intermittently since Fritzlar had reported the contacts, attempting all the while to determine their identity. They seemed to be picking up an intermittent friendly squawk on Mode 3 but it was fleeting. The jet had descended to its safety altitude and could go no lower. This was the lowest safe height below which the aircraft risked striking the high ground and, unlike their target, the Phantom crew did not have the benefit of night vision goggles. Over the flat plains they may have been persuaded to drop lower given some moonlight but in the hilly terrain to the east it was out of the question. They listened intently to the commentary from the controller.

"Mike Lima 55, Loneship, your target is on the nose for 20 miles at low level. Target speed 150 knots. Any contact?"

"Negative," called the back seater who had stared fruitlessly at his radar scope since take off seeing nothing. Helicopters were notoriously difficult to detect and track with the Phantom radar and in the terrain around the Harz Mountains which screened their progress, almost impossible. The fact they had pulled their speed back to 150 kph meant the Hinds were even harder to track and looked not much different to a fast car on the autobahn.

Porov could make out the landing strip, picking out the small rescue hut alongside. He adjusted the controls, bringing the helicopter to a slow walking pace as he gingerly approached the confined site aware of the lack of depth perception when wearing the goggles. Aware of the proximity of the adjacent pine trees and the risk of downdraught from the steep slopes which rose in front, he continued his gentle descent touching down perfectly on the left hand side of the white "H" marker emblazoned on the grass. As he alighted, he killed the power and gestured furiously to the crewman to tie the helicopter down ready for the approach of the Delta. Quickly killing the switches and unstrapping simultaneously, he made his way to the cabin door to assist. They could afford no lost time during the refuelling operation and he was very conscious of the need to limit the time on the ground. There were challenging glances from his assembled passengers who were used to a more active role but, nonetheless, remained seated. Until he delivered them, he was in charge. As he dropped from the helicopter, the whine of a fast jet passing at relatively low altitude above him audible despite the noise from the approaching Delta, caught his attention and made him look up. He could just make out the flashing red of the aircraft's navigation lights as it entered a left hand turn before disappearing behind the mountain. He frowned. The moon had appeared from behind the clouds and would make the next part of the mission even more challenging as the glow from the moon reduced the advantage of his night vision goggles and made visual detection all the more possible. The last thing he needed was the unwelcome attentions of a fighter.

*

His mind was swimming as he regained consciousness. Coming out of a deep sleep, the high seat back of the airline seat in front of him confused him. Looking left and right, he recognised the faces of the escorts who had delivered him to the airport, Why was he overcome by a growing feeling of unease which, as yet, he couldn't place?

"Attention, Ladies and Gentlemen. Welcome aboard this Illyushin IL-62 flight to Moscow. If you would relax, the Captain has a further announcement in just one moment."

The dread took over. KGB! It was all flooding back. The needle in the leg. The fracas in the Departure Hall before boarding the flight to London! He cursed himself. He should have recognised the signs during the car journey but now it was too late; packaged and ready to return to Moscow. Slumping back in his seat, he began to think of what might have been. All the effort and his successful break through the border defences but it had all gone to waste. Thrown away but by whom? He should not only blame the British, he should have seen it himself.

"Relax Comrade, you are safely on board and in a couple of minutes the engines will start and we will deliver you safely to Moscow."

The voice cut him like a knife.

"There are a number of questions that important people will wish to ask you and they are particularly interested in how much you have had to say. I should begin to prepare yourself for the interview," the man said with implied menace in his tone.

Yuri ignored the threat, apparently oblivious to the implications of his "kidnap."

"Ladies and Gentlemen, the Captain."

Yuri found it strange after his brief interlude in the West to be listening once again to his native tongue.

"We have a short delay, I am afraid. The authorities have just advised me that there is a report of a suspect package in the hold. Please remain seated for the time being. I would like to stress that there is nothing to worry about at present and there is no immediate danger. This is almost certainly a hoax but we must take the threat seriously. We have a genuine concern for your well being. In the meantime, just sit tight. I shall arrange for an inspection of the hold before we take any further action. Once again, I apologise for the delay."

Yuri could not suppress a wry grin. The Captain could have no idea of the irony in his words. This was not the Aeroflot that he knew. Was this for his benefit?. The KGB minders exchanged nervous glances at the unscripted incident and Yuri, for his part, fidgeted, nervously, as the minutes passed.

"Ladies and Gentlemen, the Captain again. I am afraid that we have indeed found a package which should not be on board and it will be necessary to evacuate the aircraft as a precaution. I am sorry for the inconvenience but I think that it is only prudent to take precautions. Please do not panic as we have no reason to believe that there is any immediate danger and please follow the instructions of the cabin staff implicitly. We will direct you back to the departure gate until we have dealt with the problem."

The minder to his right placed a restraining arm over Yuri's chest.

"Let the rush die down before we make a move Comrade. It wouldn't do to get separated would it?"

Once again the implied menace. The minder gestured to the nearest stewardess and whispered some brief instructions prompting a brisk response as she immediately made her way, against the flow of passengers, towards the rear exit.

"But what if this package proves to be a bomb," questioned Yuri. "For me it's largely irrelevant but I have no desire to take you with me."

He could see that he had struck a chord but the KGB man knew that his own fate would be worse than a bomb blast if he failed to deliver his charge to Moscow. Yuri pressed his advantage trying desperately to prompt the man into an unplanned, ill conceived action. The bomb hoax was a blessing in disguise and he hoped fervently that it had been planned by the British. By now he should have been taxying towards the main runway. Being diverted back to the departure gate gave him one last chance of freedom. What he must avoid at all costs was another dose with the hypodermic needle and he hoped that it had been a one-off shot. The minders watched the other passengers as they filed past towards the forward exit, remarkably calmly under the circumstances. Despite his hopeless situation, he could not make a move until the way out was completely clear. Suddenly, Yuri felt the cold blast as the rear door of the Illyushin was dragged open by the cabin crew. He was hurriedly bundled to his feet and almost frogmarched towards the rear exit in the opposite direction to the remainder of the passengers. His mind raced. He was being split from the rest and his only hope had been to use them as a screen, and amid the confusion, he could make his break. His options were rapidly evaporating and he was drifting back into helplessness. Would he be able to make a break across the open manoeuvring area? It was unlikely and he presumed that the minders were armed and would give him little opportunity. Still, what else could he do? Unless he made an attempt of some sort, Moscow spelt certain and, probably painful, death. As he approached the door, flanked by the two burly agents, he tried to evaluate the situation. A glance around the surrounding area crystallised his thoughts. A large black limousine with an Aeroflot logo sat within 50 metres of the base of the steps and it was obvious that it had been positioned to move him back to the terminal. While he remained in the control of the airline he was lost but if he could make a break on the apron he would attract attention and become the responsibility of the local security force. Various items of ground equipment dotted the area. A replenishment and a catering vehicle, which had presumably serviced the airliner, had been pushed into a marked area alongside the fuselage and small servicing trolleys clustered around the steps. Despite the clutter, he would be hard pressed to find any sanctuary before a bullet found its mark. The sharp push in the back started him down the stairs with a jolt but, as he descended, he continued to glance, furtively, for a refuge.

"Don't even think about it Comrade," the coarse voice whispered in his ear. "I have a Makarov 9mm pistol in my pocket. It's not a terribly heavy calibre weapon but it will stop you dead in your tracks if needs be; literally! Let's just take it nice and easy and take a seat in this car that we have arranged for you. It will only be for a short time and then we can be on our way again. Slowly now."

His fears were confirmed. He trudged down the steps, his heart heavy. As they reached the base, a Bundesgrenzschutz vehicle squealed to a halt ahead of the limousine blocking its exit and a plain clothes officer climbed out.

"Gentlemen," he called out in a strident voice. "Could I please ask you to accompany me to the terminal for a few moments. You appear to have a short delay so I am sure it will not inconvenience you too much. I have a few questions to ask your colleague."

Yuri felt the grip on his arm tighten.

"We are Soviet citizens on Soviet sovereign territory Sir, I think not."

"No, I'm sorry but Soviet territory finishes at the doors of the airliner and you are now on West German soil and I must repeat my request for you to accompany me to answer a few questions."

The KGB men had moved protectively to Yuri's side effectively cutting off his one escape route. Despite the interruption, he still had no safe exit.

"Then I think we shall return to the airliner," said the minder who had been doing all the talking. "I am sure that the incident will be over in a few minutes."

"I am afraid I cannot allow that Gentlemen. It would be unsafe with a bomb on board. How could we explain our negligence to your Embassy if we allowed you to reboard?"

Yuri's heart leapt; it must be part of the set up!

"Please, you are under my jurisdiction and you are, I repeat, on West German soil. I insist that you come with me."

As if to emphasise his words as he spoke he unclipped the flap of a holster which had been concealed by his jacket. Both of the minders were still torn with indecision. Yuri tensed expecting the Makarov to be drawn at any moment. Suddenly the talkative one pushed Yuri into the arms of the other.

"Get him back inside," he shouted and pulled the pistol from his pocket raising it in the direction of the Security Officer. Yuri took what he thought would be his last chance, drew both his hands upwards breaking the grip of the massive Russian and chopped fiercely down into the nape of his neck. The Russian winced, temporarily off guard as Yuri ran for the cover of the nearest service truck. The Customs Officer was way ahead of the Russian and had already levelled his own pistol as the Makarov came to bear and loosed off two shots followed fractionally later by a third. The Russian only managed to fire one shot as he fell forwards, his aim spoiled, his shot ricocheting harmlessly off the concrete. Yuri dodged left and right spoiling the aim of the KGB man behind who was at that very moment aiming at him. The crash of the pistol shots had frightened him badly but so far he was unharmed as he crawled towards the back of the van and safety. Hearing the further crack of high velocity rifle shots from the direction of the terminal he doubled his efforts. Behind, the large Russian aimed his pistol at the fleeing figure.

"Bloody traitor!" he screamed as he drew a bead. At that moment two rifle bullets struck him in the chest causing him to sink to one knee. With a superhuman final effort, he raised the pistol and squeezed off two rounds before toppling forward, dead. Yuri reached the van and steadied his headlong flight with a raised hand. A bullet thumped into the metal of the van causing him to flinch involuntarily but the second bullet caught him in the shoulder spinning him violently and pitching him onto the tarmac where he lay still.

*

"Mike Lima 55, Loneship has lost contact with the previous track, anchor port in your present position," instructed the GCI controller ordering the Phantom into a holding orbit whilst he played furiously with the radar display attempting to eradicate the mass of ground returns in the area of the contacts. Furious, he banged the console as he realised that he really had lost them. He would have to keep the Phantom on station and hope that he could make some sense of the jumbled mess.

*

Porov struggled with the refuelling hose which protruded from the pillow tanks and dragged it across to the refuelling port on the side of the helicopter. Assisting the crewman to connect the heavy coupling, he moved across to the electric pumps and seeing a thumbs up, hit the switch starting the fuel flowing. He had already decided that the Alpha would continue the mission and, once it had covered their departure, the Delta could return to base. However, if the fast jet overhead proved troublesome, perhaps he would have another use for the Delta after all. He mulled over the options.

*

In the Phantom cockpit the crew stared at the radar beginning to convince themselves that the reported contact must have been spurious. Looking out they noticed that the moon had appeared, bathing the area in a bright reflected glow. The terrain stood out in sharp relief and they could pick up the features almost as if it had been daylight.

"How do you feel about going below safety height if we have to?" asked the pilot.

"It looks like daylight down there," responded his navigator. "I'd be happy but I'm not sure we should press it too far. I don't fancy wiping ourselves out on the one hill that we don't see. Is this really that important? I can't see us welcoming another defector so soon after the last one!"

The pilot commenced his third orbit banking the aircraft gently keeping a very close eye on the fuel. At this height the fuel consumption was considerably higher than normal and would reduce their time on task. As if by telepathy, his navigator prompted giving him a range and bearing back to base and his estimate of the fuel they would need to recover. Still plenty of time on task but GCI had been quiet for some time so he hit the transmit button.

"Loneship, 55, sitrep."

"55 the target faded in the Winterberg area. Maintain your present orbit and stand by."

"Good old GCI," he fumed looking at his watch and realising that it was well past midnight. "Well I guess we'd have nothing else to do but sleep."

*

Porov ducked in behind the tail as the Hind Delta dropped gently onto the adjacent hard standing. The dust swirled around as the helicopter settled, its rotors rapidly slowing as the pilot closed down, plunging the site into silence. Again the fast jet drifted ominously overhead maintaining a holding orbit and he realised that it could not be a routine flight. One pass had been coincidental; two passes meant that the jet had been vectored into the area for a reason. His mind raced as he made his way over towards his wingman. He beckoned to the pilot who climbed down from the bubble canopy of the gunship, dragging his helmet from his head as he did so. They conversed briefly and Porov gestured towards the sky and pointed back down across the plain from the direction from which they had just come. There was a moment of brief conversation and a nod of acceptance from the other pilot.

In the cabin of the Alpha, Kamov watched the two pilots. He realised that at this stage he was entirely in their hands. He had no expertise in helicopter tactics and any constraints he laid on the lead pilot could only confuse the issue. He lay back mulling over the detail of his part of the plan. Knowing that the run in to the field landing site was risky, he analyzed the risks. Although the majority of the area radars would be closed down for the night, Wildenrath would still be operating for Battle Flight. Additionally, there was a Nike missile battery just off the motorway near Erklenz which would also probably have its radar operating. Although the low level helicopter would be way below the engagement envelope of the high level missiles, detection would still be a real possibility. He was hoping that the western defences were a little more circumspect in their reaction to a possible intruder than the Soviet defences would be, otherwise his mission was doomed. In such circumstances back home, unidentified intruders would be engaged without question, possible recriminations would come later.

They would be dropped into a field to the south of Heinsberg before making their way to the southern perimeter fence of Wildenrath airfield. The intelligence officer had briefed him precisely on the nature of the perimeter defences and he knew that apart from an irregular perimeter patrol and further dedicated patrols around Battle Flight, the area should be relatively quiet. He intended to give Battle Flight a wide berth but what he could not predict was how much extra security would have been laid on in Charlie Dispersal after the arrival of the Su-27. Despite the heavy pressure, his victim had been unable to offer guidance on this score. As he looked around the cabin he was suddenly cognizant of the limitations of his small force. Kazenko, the pilot who had been selected to fly the Flanker looked petrified at the prospect of his task ahead. The four man Spetznaz team looked considerably more confident and, to a man, reclined casually on the rudimentary seats, their equipment stowed purposefully around them. The final man whom Kamov had felt it necessary to bring along was a flight line engineer. His discussions with James had suggested that the Su-27 could have been stripped down in some way and it would be this man's task to restore the aircraft to flight-worthy condition should it prove necessary. A heavy roll of speed tape might be the only way to make temporary repairs if panels were removed. As long as it will fly. He rehearsed the plan in his mind yet again aware of the noise of a fast jet overhead. That was not the first pass tonight, he thought. They are flying late tonight.

*

As he came to, the thought crossed Yuri's mind that this habit was becoming a little too regular. The bodies of the erstwhile minders were already being discretely removed, although keeping a firearms incident quiet at a busy airport would be impossible. As he shifted his weight, the pain from the shoulder wound was suddenly intense causing him to catch his breath. He decided to lie still on the tarmac as the medical orderly arrived, pleased to find a survivor. The Customs Officer who had confronted the KGB men was sitting on the bonnet of an adjacent vehicle in deep discussion with another man clearly shaken by his experience. As Yuri breathed deeply, an English voice caused him to open his eyes but he was unable to distinguish the features against the bright lights.

"Just lie still Colonel. We'll have that wound looked at quickly and there will be an RAF HS125 here within the hour to take you back to England. I think we've had more than enough drama for one day, don't you? No more risks eh?"

Yuri sighed. The events of the last few hours had certainly not been part of any script that he had run through in his mind but perhaps the outcome would be as he had planned after all. He groaned as he was eased onto a stretcher and loaded into a waiting ambulance.

15 ADMISSIONS

Yuri's eyes opened and he felt a jolt as the wheelchair bumped over a small ruck in the carpet. He had been drifting in and out of consciousness as he was moved through a discrete side gate in the Departure Hall just a short time since the slug had ripped into the muscle around his shoulder. The bullet wound was not too serious; in fact little more than a deep graze to the skin but he had been lucky to avoid damage to his shoulder. Even so it had bled profusely. After being dressed by a hastily arranged first aid worker she had protested that she should be allowed to transfer him to a local hospital for better treatment to his injuries. Quiet words had been spoken and her patient was swiftly escorted away. Still groggy, Yuri was helped down the flight of stairs from the jetway towards the waiting RAF executive jet, feeling dizzy from the loss of blood. He allowed himself to be helped up the steps towards the round cabin door where a concerned RAF steward waited for him. The pilot, standing discretely in the background moved back into the cockpit readying the jet for a swift departure. He began to feel that, perhaps, he really would finally see the famous green and pleasant land. The change in his fortunes had been a roller coaster ride and he was looking forward to taking the seat which beckoned him from the dimmed cabin. He took one last look over his shoulder at the Illyushin IL62 which still sat on the apron security guards swarming around the airframe. It had been close but the RAF roundel on the front fuselage gave the reassurance that the trip to London was now guaranteed.

*

The telephone rang and Group Captain Lennox lifted the handset from its cradle. It was the second time he had been woken tonight, the last time to notify him that Battle Flight was airborne. On that occasion, however, he had needed no warning as he had heard clearly the roar of the afterburners which had cut the night sky as the aircraft had launched.

"Station Commander."

"Sir, this is Flight Lieutenant Green, OC RAF Police. I have Squadron Leader Gails from the Provost Branch from Rheindahlen with me and I think we have a problem which we need to fix very quickly. May we come round to see you?"

"If you must, but I assume it won't wait until morning?"

"No Sir, I don't think it will."

Five minutes passed and he heard the Land Rover pull up outside. Group Captain Lennox opened the door to his residence and ushered the two officers through into his study. Still wrapped in his dressing gown, he motioned for them to take a seat.

"I do hope this is important gentlemen," he growled ominously.

If he had any concerns over the importance of the ensuing discussion it was quickly quashed as the Squadron Leader launched into his story.

"Flight Lieutenant James has only been with you for a couple of weeks but we have good reason to believe that he has been compromised by the Soviets."

The Station Commander looked astonished.

"These are very serious allegations you're making. You realise that if this is proven, this would be the end of this man's career."

"Sir we never make accusations such as these lightly but he has been seen and photographed in the company of a known KGB agent, one Viktor

Kamov, who operates the Düsseldorf area. Kamov is a specialist in agent recruitment and has a long track record as a field agent. We've known about him for years but he's a slippery character and hard to track down."

"Hold on, before you go any further I think we had better have a word with this young man. Let me speak with the Station Duty Officer," he said picking up the phone.

"Station Commander here. I want you to get hold of Flight Lieutenant James immediately and I want him round at my Quarters as soon as possible. Send a car to collect him straight away. Yes he had better bring his hat!"

"Hat On" was the normal indication that the interview was to be a formal affair.

"Go on Squadron Leader Gails."

Keith James knocked nervously at the door of the Station Commander's house. It was the first occasion that he had been "invited" and he thought that the circumstances might have been somewhat more pleasant. It could not be good news at this late hour. The defection had caused a lot of late nights recently but somehow this felt bad. The fact the RAF Corporal policeman was standing just behind him resting his hand on his white holstered pistol did little to make him relax.

The Station Commander opened the door and looked straight into his eyes.

"Into my study," he said quietly. "It would appear you have some explaining to do young man."

James was ushered inside and the policeman took up station at the door. As he entered, the presence of the Squadron Leader unmistakable in his uniform and wearing the red shoulder tabs of a Provost Marshall didn't look good.

"Perhaps you would care to outline the allegations you have just made?"

The Provost Officer repeated the tale as the young intelligence officer began to wring his hands; a strong feeling of despair taking hold. Conflicting thoughts passed through his mind as he considered his options. Should he lie? Should he invent a cover story? Should he divert attention to other players? No he decided, it had gone far enough. The only course now was to accept his guilt and take the consequences as the implications on his short and, hitherto, unblemished career flashed through his mind. Story complete and with James offering no resistance, in a move that was becoming predictable, he poured out in precise detail the whole sequence starting with his visit to the whorehouse.

Group Captain Lennox had listened closely and deliberated before responding. He stared at the crestfallen Keith James increasing his discomfort.

"You are a very stupid young man. Did you not stop to think that this agent is a professional and would never let you off the hook once he had compromised you. This was a carefully arranged operation. You were unlucky enough to be the target but, as an intelligence officer you should have known better. It could have gone on for years and cost the Country dear. You should have contacted OC Police Flight as soon as Kamov made his initial approach. There are procedures to prevent such incidents. I'm afraid there will be recriminations but maybe we can limit the damage which has been done and maybe even turn it to our advantage. Squadron Leader Gails, this is what I want you to do and, from what I've just heard, I want you to do it immediately. James fidgeted uncomfortably as he listened.

*

Entering a left turn shortly after takeoff, the engines of the HS125 throttled back to comply with the local noise abatement procedures. Glancing down, Yuri could see the lights of the suburbs to the east of Düsseldorf, cut by the ribbons of the numerous autobahns which encircled the airport. Outside, the light had faded and Yuri settled back into his seat to enjoy his escape to freedom as the PA system crackled into life.

"Gentlemen, the Captain. If you would care to look out of the left hand windows, it would appear that we have been given a special escort to the Dutch border."

Yuri glanced out, focusing his eyes on the horizon, seeing nothing of any interest but, as he watched, the now familiar sight of a fully armed Phantom emerged from beneath the wing and moved into close formation on the left hand side of the executive jet. The anti collision lights flashing red, cast an almost eerie glow across the wing of the HS125, reflecting against the bulk of the warplane. The lights went steady as it slipped closer into formation. He could see the faces of the crew wearing their white bonedomes looking directly at the aircraft tracking every movement as the two aircraft climbed slowly into the upper air. The Sidewinder missiles under the wing stood out white against the dark sky, as the Phantom pilot jockeyed slightly to maintain formation. Behind the jet the cloud formation broke, allowing the moonlight to spill through, framing the jet in a kaleidoscope of reflections. The effect was both reassuring and impressive and Yuri wondered if he would ever have the chance to fly one of these magnificent machines ever again. As he watched, the aircraft eased out from its close formation position and dropped back slightly, a brief salute in acknowledgement from the navigator. With a mighty roar, which was clearly audible even from inside the small jet, the pilot engaged the afterburners lighting up the night sky and, with a surge, the Phantom began to accelerate. As it passed just ahead of them, it cranked on 90 degrees of bank, momentarily presenting its aggressive planform complete with missiles and gun pod, before breaking away, rolling inverted and disappearing below the climbing aircraft. It reappeared many thousands of feet below and Yuri watched as the reheat blinked out as the jet popped back down into the clouds and vanished. Perhaps the opportunity to fly some of the latest western technology would be one of his bargaining chips, he thought. In the meantime, he had a lot of talking to do. His shoulder burned.

16 FEINT

Porov strapped himself back into the armoured seat of the Hind helicopter and rechecked the fuel gauge which now showed full. He turned his torch towards the Hind Delta, immobile on the hard standing beside him and flashed twice. Hearing the whine of his wingman's turbines, he simultaneously hit his own start switch and watched the engine RPM begin to rise. Turning back, he watched the gunship rise to a height of 10 metres and rotate slowly in place before moving off down the valley retracing its flight path and quickly disappearing into the night.

In the Phantom overhead, the crew stared at the radar without success.

"55, pop-up contact east range 5 miles, heading east at 100 knots," called the Loneship controller catching their attention. Any joy?"

The navigator knew that he had absolutely no chance of detecting a slow moving contact on radar when it was travelling in the same direction. At this speed they would rapidly overhaul it. Despite the fact that they were at safety altitude, they were still far above their target and to go any lower, would put the aircraft at risk. Their discussion had been inconclusive. They would hold their height for the time being. Both aircrew looked out at the eerie glow from the moonlit plain hoping in vain for a visual pick-up.

Porov watched as the Phantom passed overhead and then lifted off following the narrowing confines of the valley which stretched away from the landing site and rose into the foothills ahead. The still cold engines strained as he demanded an increased rate of climb to follow the rising terrain towards the 1000 metre summit near the village of Winterberg. He hoped desperately that the Phantom would follow the gunship as he headed off in the opposite direction.

"How brave are you feeling?" queried the Phantom pilot again.

"Go for it, this is a Battle Flight mission" came the response and, without further discussion, the pilot retarded the throttles, popped the airbrakes and began a tentative descent into the shadows. He listened intently to the commentary from the back as his navigator thumbed methodically down the map calling out the position of the high ground and passing regular height checks from the altimeter. The jet crested the peak to the south of Winterberg and began letting down slowly over the darkened plain.

"On your nose for 3 miles," called the controller as they strained their eyes, aware of the terrain flattening around them.

"Clear of the high ground, level off at 1,500 feet," called the navigator breathing a sigh of relief. This was their minimum height at night if they were to stay legal. They were over the plateau for at least 10 miles and had to make the intercept quickly or the chance would be lost. He looked out, eyes adjusting to the moonlight and turned the cockpit lights even lower to protect his night vision. Up front, his pilot stared intently through the front windscreen listening to the target information which was being passed by GCI and predicting where he thought the helicopter would appear.

The gunship pilot aimed directly at the neck of the valley about 15 Km on his nose. He could hear the RWR clicking intermittently, the audio giving indication of a scanning emitter in his rear right quadrant. A brief "AI" warning lamp flashed; a Phantom! He concentrated on maintaining his height knowing that if he could reach the safety of the valley neck, the fast jet would be unable to follow him. He eased up slightly as the bulk of a wood loomed large in front. Keep it steady.

"Tally Ho, 1 o'clock range one mile called the back seater excitedly. It's a helicopter, low level heading east. Lost it again!" He switched his attention rapidly to the radar now knowing precisely where to look for the target, finally breaking out the slow moving helicopter from the mass of ground returns. Locking up, he tried to decide on a course of action. It was pointless setting up a normal visual identification profile which would take them in to 200 yards from the victim. Against such a slow target flying so low it was suicide. The radar could break lock at any minute with all this clutter. Despite the moonlight, now that they were down at low level it was very dark outside. The best he could do was try to keep his pilot's eyes on the target. Avoiding the urge to put the contact onto the nose knowing that in the poor light he would lose it behind the glass of his gunsight, the pilot held an offset and closed rapidly on his quarry waiting for guidance from the back seat. It was a procedure they had never practised before. They were making it up as they went along.

"Set speed 250 knots, minimum manoeuvring speed and jink 5 degrees starboard," the navigator pattered, setting his pilot up for the closest pass he could engineer.

"Slightly right, range one mile, slow speed. We've got 100 knots overtake."

The pilot stared at the spot where he expected the contact to reappear as he gently played the throttles and dropped half flap to give better control of his sluggish machine.

"10 right, 1500 yards, 10 degrees down," he heard from the back, "He's right on the deck at about 100 feet. Keep a good watch on that height."

"Roger, the radio altimeter is bugged at 250 feet," responded the pilot realising that the only references he had to fly from were those bathed in moonlight. He was virtually relying on instruments in mountainous terrain. The tension gnawed at him. Listening to the gentle cadence of the commentary, he strained to identify the dark unlit shape which slowly emerged from the gloom.

The gunship pilot picked out the entrance to the valley which he knew would provide sanctuary and flew directly at it. In his mirrors he could see the flashing navigation lights of the Phantom as it bore down on him.

A frantic command.

"Pull up, pull up, pull up!"

The Phantom pilot selected full afterburner and yanked the stick back without hesitation. Checking forward at 30 degrees of pitch, he glanced out of the cockpit. He had been so intent on making the identification he had forgotten to fly the aeroplane. Ahead, the moonlit bulk of the 2,000 foot mountain filled the windscreen. His still heavy and sluggish aircraft responded slowly, climbing at 250 knots, supported only by the sheer thrust of the afterburners. The bright glow from the straining reheat lit the countryside. Below, the Hind slipped into the valley weaving around its contours.

In the Hind Alpha, Porov crested the ridge watching the lights of the town of Winterberg to his right and began the slow descent back down the mountain towards the town of Schmallenberg. In the other Hind the pilot was settling down. It hadn't been good to try to wipe out the Phantom crew on the mountain ridge but escape was paramount. There were no prizes for coming second.

17 DECEPTION

Porov looked across the flat calm surface of the Wüpperfurth lakes, the moonlight reflected from the glassy surface, the absence of wind giving a mirror-like and slightly ethereal look. His passage through the hills had been uneventful, the diversionary tactic using the Hind Delta to draw off the Phantom totally effective. Soon, the small but steep valleys would give way to the flat expanse of Nordrhein Westphalia and with it total exposure. The lights of Cologne to the south and Düsseldorf to the north shimmered in the distance and above, sharp flashes of light pinpointed airliners making their approaches into the civil airfield at Cologne/Bonn. The terrain flattened and he gradually became aware of a more woolly feel to the reflected light. He was uneasy as he realised that around him the features were becoming slowly more indistinct. It struck him in a flash; he had ignored the major limitation of night vision goggles - Fog! The calm conditions were perfect for its formation and as he had progressed along his track, pockets of fog had formed in the valleys and the shallow bank now obscured everything around him. He had lost all the references which were essential to maintain his low level penetration. Yanking back on the cyclic, he brought the helicopter clear of the invasive mist, popping instantly clear of the top of the fog bank realising just how much his view had become obscured. Ahead, a sea of unreal green mist stretched away, broken only by masts and power stations protruding through the blanket. In pulling up, however, the features on which he had been relying for navigation had disappeared, his Soviet radio navigation equipment totally useless so far from home, working as it did on entirely different frequencies. He had no choice but to revert to mental dead reckoning techniques which he had not practised for many years. Marking his pull up point on the map he laid off a precise heading for his next waypoint. At least fog meant that there was a lack of wind which would mean that there was little drift. He could see the glow of the reflected lights from the cities, just visible through the fog blanket, orientating him. He positioned his map, content that his heading should take him safely through the Dormagen Gap as planned. Another problem. He was now registering on every radar screen in the area and needed a cover - and quickly. Switching across to the Initial Contact Frequency for the local area radar station he transmitted.

"Clutch Radar this is Zack 11," attempting his best American accent. He hoped that the distortion caused by the beat of the rotor blades would cover the thickness of his accent. Helicopter radio calls were renowned for sounding as if they originated in a food mixer.

"Zack 11 Clutch Radar, go ahead."

"Clutch, Zack 11 is a CH53 en route from Büchel to Geilenkirchen entering the Dormagen Gap at 1500 feet heading 270. Suspect my Parrot is sick," he lied.

He hoped that the controller would believe that his IFF equipment, the device which identified him electronically to the NATO Air Defence Ground Environment was unserviceable. It was a gamble which he hoped would pay off but it was tenuous; there were few helicopter movements at low level in the small hours.

"Zack 11, I see you on radar, check intentions?"

"Roger Sir, 11 will remain at 1500 feet routing direct to Geilenkirchen."

"Roger 11, I have you identified 17 miles south of Düsseldorf. Maintain 1500 feet and contact Wildenrath on 327.6, goodnight."

"To Wildenrath 327.6. Goodnight Sir and thanks for your help."

He deselected the frequency but had no intention of contacting Wildenrath.

It would appear that his ruse had paid off.

"Wildenrath Zone, Clutch here. I have Zack 11, a CH53 at 1500 feet in the Dormagen Gap. He's on handover to you inbound to Geilenkirchen but his IFF's unserviceable. I have him primary radar contact only."

"Roger Clutch, I have him radar contact, I'll put him straight to Geilenkirchen Tower. I have no other traffic. Thanks Clutch."

Julie Kingston in the darkened radar room watched the contact passing through the narrow gap between the two civil air traffic zones and waited for it to turn southerly towards the NATO base. Strange she thought, it seems to be continuing on a westerly heading and should have turned inbound for Geilenkirchen by now. So that's why Geilenkirchen stayed open tonight, she thought. The Americans must have a night exercise running. Maybe he went straight to the Geilenkirchen frequency?

"Zone, Mike Lima 55 on recovery. We're overhead Kola at 5000 feet on the regional pressure setting, requesting radar vectors to the ILS, understand Runway 27 in use." The Battle Flight Phantom checking in. Suddenly her attention was diverted back to her own Phantoms.

"Roger 55, I have you identified overhead Kola, commence your descent to 3,000 feet on the Wildenrath QNH of 1015 and come right heading 300."

Distracted, she paid no further attention to the radar blip which tracked relentlessly towards Erklenz to the south of Wildenrath airfield.

Porov could see the edge of the fog bank, a sharp delineation between the weather and the flat terrain beyond. His mental calculations had been perfect and the motorway which would feed him into his landing site curved to the right of his nose. Headlamps of the cars on the Autobahn flickered annoyingly through his field of view causing annoying flare-ups in his goggles which he had eased back into place in front of his eyes. The improvement in the weather conditions would allow him to get back down to low level and as the fog receded behind him, he dropped beginning his gentle descent.

"55, Zone you're on the centreline range 10 miles, continue descent to 1800 feet and contact talkdown on stud 6 for ILS monitor."

"To Talkdown, 55," the pilot responded as his navigator switched the radio box to the new frequency.

"Talkdown, 55 levelling 1800 feet."

"55, talkdown loud and clear, decision height is 240 feet, read back QFE set and confirm to land?"

"1015 set, 200 feet, ILS to land, 55"

The Phantom settled down onto the glidepath, its pilot carefully adjusting the controls to centre the two needles of the Instrument Landing System. Providing he kept them precisely in the middle of the small instrument it would guide him to a precise touchdown point on the main instrument runway at Wildenrath. He hoped for a smooth and uneventful approach; he had had enough surprises for one night.

*

Porov fixed his eyes on the landing zone and transitioned the Hind to the hover. He could see electricity pylons to the south and walked the helicopter slowly away from the confliction towards his touchdown point. Behind him, the cabin door slid open and he heard the crewman start to patter away providing a commentary for the touchdown point in the pitch black field.

"Clear below. Come forward 5 metres. Go down. 10 meters, 5 metres, 1 metre. Steady, steady. You're down."

Porov felt the reassuring thump as the craft settled onto its tricycle undercarriage. For better or worse he had fulfilled his part of the contract and delivered the insertion team to their target. Braking the rotors, he began his shutdown checks as the team behind began assembling their gear.

*

The ILS needles were rock solid and centralised.

"55 passing your decision height," advised the talkdown controller who had merely monitored the Phantom's progress during the ILS approach. He was more used to having to provide a precision approach radar letdown and had enjoyed the unexpected rest, particularly at this time of night.

Looking up from the ILS instrument which he had followed religiously to the final stages of the approach, the pilot could see the bright approach lights guiding him in.

"55 is visual to Tower," he called, anxious to complete his night's work. The navigator switched the radio to Tower frequency.

"55 short finals to land."

"55 clear to land, surface wind is calm," he heard raising his head slightly, seeing the solid red centre line and the five "T" bars of the approach lights feeding him in to the touchdown point. Around the actual threshold the ground was dark. He played with the stick and throttle adopting the nose up attitude which marked a Phantom approach. He positioned his jet to touchdown on the runway numbers, 1,500 feet in from the threshold where he could see the arc lights either side of the runway trained inwards to illuminate the aircraft to allow the crew to confirm that the brake parachute had deployed properly. A final check on the VASIs showed three reds and a white; he was slightly low and played with the throttle to ease the jet over the threshold, checking again that the VASI indications had reverted to two reds and two whites showing him back on the ideal approach. As the jet neared the runway he held everything still. A Phantom landing was inevitably a controlled crash but the sturdy landing gear, built to absorb the stresses of carrier operations, would take all that was thrown at it. The aircraft smashed onto the runway and he chopped the throttles reaching for the chute handle by his left thigh. As he pulled, his hand snagged a stray strap from the ejection seat and he fumbled, momentarily releasing the handle. He immediately realised his error as behind the aircraft, the chute still neatly packed in its canvas bag, dropped uselessly onto the concrete. The Phantom without a chute did not stop as the brakes were little better than useless. He realised his predicament without the prompt reminder.

"No chute," called the navigator excitedly. "140 knots, 6,000 feet to go."

"We're staying down," he responded, probably unwisely and compounding the problem. His proper action should have been to bolt and set up a further approach touching down, at the slowest speed possible, precisely at the threshold.

"120 knots, 5,000 feet. They had already used 30% of their useable runway."

"We're too fast, drop the hook," called the back seater realising that they had insufficient landing run remaining. They would need the assistance of the RHAG, the Rotary Hydraulic Arresting Gear; a cable arresting system which stretched across the runway 1,500 feet from the far end designed to stop aircraft in emergency. He was well behind the drag curve and should have predicted these problems. Tired and having to be led by the nose he reached forward, slammed the hook handle down and feet the reassuring clunk from behind as the hook struck the concrete.

"120 knots, 4,000 feet to go." Still too fast, he thought; too fast even to apply the brakes. It was a Catch 22 situation. Until the speed dropped off to 100 knots he could not hit the brakes.

"Tower, 55 confirm my hook's down." At last he was taking control of the situation. He could feel the metallic grating from the rear of the aircraft as the hook dragged along the rough surface and it came as no surprise as he heard the local controller's confirmation that all was well.

"100 knots, 2,000 feet to go." He applied the brakes lightly not wishing to overheat them. They were committed to taking the cable, he just hoped it would stop them.

Just ahead and to the sides of the runway, the illuminated marker boards glowed brightly, yellow circles on a black background, marking the position of the RHAG. The cable was just visible on the surface of the runway sitting proud on its rubber grommets waiting to collect the hook. If he missed, he knew that they were committed to an ejection. Although a further barrier, a net system, stretched across the far threshold, the risk of the top cable penetrating the canopy and causing injury was well known and real. Furthermore, once the net enveloped the canopy, the crew would be trapped until cut out by the fire crews, unable to escape in the event of a fire. If they missed the cable the barrier would be stopping an empty jet; they would be making independent landings courtesy of Martin Baker ejection seats.

"80 knots , approaching the cable. Hook is down," called the nav as he craned his neck watching for the telltale sign of the RHAG tapes running out which would signal a successful arrest. If they were forced to eject, there would no time to lose once they were over the cable. They waited, time standing still already committed.

"We've missed it," the navigator screamed from behind, "Ejecting!"

The pilot heard a loud crack as the canopy left the aircraft closely followed by an ear shattering bang and a roar as the rear ejection seat fired. The night was illuminated by the rocket gun as the seat rapidly cleared the cockpit and the pilot realised that he had already overstayed his time. He pulled the throttles back, reached up for the top handle, paused briefly, straightened his back and pulled. The face blind covered his face cutting out his view on the world and the last thing he registered was a sharp pain in his back as the rocket gun fired with a loud crack forcing the seat up the rails. His head dropped forward onto his chest as the seat rose forced down by the sheer weight of his helmet.

The local controller stared aghast and hit the crash alarm as he saw the Phantom miss the cable. He knew that it was travelling far too fast to stop and that disaster was inevitable. What should have been a simple procedure had gone badly wrong. The aircraft veered from its path, forced by the sheer energy of the seats leaving the aircraft and no longer guided by its pilot. The hook had bounced over the cable and now shimmied uselessly along the remaining concrete towards the overrun area with nothing to restrain its forward motion. Ahead, the barrier hung motionless ready to receive the charging hulk which ran out of control towards the threshold.

At the apex, the automatic sequence of the ejection seats functioned, deploying the drogue parachutes and separating the aircrew from their seats. The fact that the ejection had occurred at ground level meant that separation was immediate and, almost instantaneously, the crew were hanging beneath the silk of their parachutes floating gently earthwards, stunned by the ferocity of the experience. It was dark but below them the airframe was bathed in the reflected glare of the runway lights.

In the Fire Section, the crews had been relaxing since the earlier mayhem of the Battle Flight launch. They had been brought to readiness as the aircraft had commenced its recovery but this was routine procedure, an everyday occurrence. As the klaxon blared out, they reacted automatically but with a certain disbelief. It was the crash alarm. They sprinted for their fire trucks pulling on the heavy protective suits as they ran.

The Phantom powered towards the barrier, its nosewheel canted off centre driving it towards the stanchion. It struck heavily and askew and as the net dropped around the screaming aircraft, the metal supports collapsed inwards breaking apart and dropping onto the twisting fuselage. Eventually they restrained the forward motion of the heavy airframe slowly dragging the careering hulk to a halt. The engines whined away with no one in the cockpit to shut them down.

The pilot came round as he floated to earth. It had only been seconds since he had pulled the handle but those last moments were a total blur. The ground rushed towards him and he realised that he had not had the chance to complete any of the ejection drills for which he had trained endlessly. His hands fell to the quick release fasteners in the small of his back and he squeezed, releasing his personal survival pack which fell free but still attached by a lanyard to his life jacket. He was so close to the ground that he struck immediately with a thump and, being so dazed, he failed to adopt the parachute landing position hitting the ground like a sack and crumpled. Pain coursed through his body and he lay still. Across the runway, his navigator landed, rolled over and flopped onto the ground in a heap. He was clearly less shaken than his crewman, dusted himself off and began to walk towards the prone figure. In the background, the fire and ambulance vehicles, blue lights flashing urgently, sped towards the jet already alerted by the crash alarm. The local time was 0200 and, despite the early hour, guards around the airfield drifted towards the runway drawn by the unfolding mayhem. It was a morbid break from their stultifying routine. Had they known what was about to unfold they may have stayed closer to their posts.

*

The last of the insertion team disappeared into the trees as Porov watched through the armoured front windshield of the helicopter. He flicked off the power switch on the goggles plunging the landing site into total darkness. The change was staggering. Unstrapping from the armoured bucket seat he allowed the straps to clatter down the side and struggled to his feet. The team had a long task ahead of them and it was important to camouflage the helicopter in the meantime. Hopefully there wouldn't be too many tourists in this neck of the woods at this hour but he could not be too careful. Dropping from the cabin, he landed alongside the crewman who was already well into the turnround servicing. A simple mistake such as failing to top up the oils could be the difference between success and failure if left unchecked. He had not come this far to fail in such a fashion. A short inspection of the adjacent tree line confirmed his initial impression. It would be possible to get the Hind in closer into a more protected position but not without firing up the engines and the extra noise would not be worth the minor improvement. He returned to the machine and signalled to the crewman to start fitting the camouflage net which had been hauled from the cabin and lay ready for use. The task was strenuous and dragging the reticent net over the drooping rotors without the usual willing support team exercised both his muscles and his patience. As they made the finishing touches, the faint yap of a small dog came from the undergrowth. Porov scuttled back into the cabin past the protesting camouflage net and retrieved his goggles from his flying helmet. Returning to the cabin door, he held the small binoculars to his eyes and peered through a gap in the net seeing the small animal scrabbling in the bushes nearby. As he watched, the dog spotted the hulk of the helicopter and trotted slowly towards him. Its frantic owner could now be heard whistling and crashing through the undergrowth in pursuit. Porov cursed inwardly. What on earth was this idiot doing, walking a dog at this time in the morning? They had selected the landing site carefully to avoid the major villages and yet they had unwittingly uncovered a midnight tourist. The man faltered as he registered the presence of the helicopter. His initial hesitation quickly overcome, he returned his attention to the dog which now scampered aimlessly around the undercarriage leg. Porov considered whether to remain still and brazen it out or whether to confront the visitor. One thing was clear, he couldn't allow him to leave until they had made their pick-up because the risk of an unguarded comment blowing the whole operation was too great. He stepped out from under the netting and decided to continue his American deception theme.

"Excuse me Sir, but you can't come any closer. We have a US military helicopter here and we're on night exercise." He glanced around to try to spot his crewman who had temporarily disappeared, hoping that his accent had been convincing.

"Oh you're American," came the response in a broad Lancashire accent. That's OK mate, I'm from the base at Wildenrath. RAF. I used to work on these things when I was stationed at Odiham in England. Used to service Pumas; French jobs."

Confused by the thick accent Porov realised that he still had a problem. If this man knew anything about helicopters he was very quickly going to realise that the shape behind the net did not resemble anything which had emerged from a factory in the United States. The man moved closer cocking his head and starting to take a closer interest. Porov glanced around looking for his crewman but still could not see him. He had to act and act now. As he came within striking range, he continued with his bluff.

"OK, if you're familiar Sir, would you care to take a closer look? What do you know about the Iroquois?"

He raised the camouflage net and beckoned as the man moved underneath and his head began to rise, Porov saw the stark realisation in his eyes as the red star, emblazoned across the fuselage in front of him, produced a predictable reaction. Porov stuck down hard at the man's neck and he dropped like a stone to the floor. What a time for a bloody walk, thought Porov irreverently.

"Find that bloody dog and get it into the helicopter," he called to the crewman who had miraculously reappeared now that it was too late. "We'll dump this guy before we leave but first, I'd better tie him up. Come on let's move it."

18 INFILTRATION

As the undergrowth closed around him, Kamov tucked in tight behind the Spetznaz team leader. So far, so good. The helicopter pilot had delivered them safely to the landing zone and they were within 5 Km of their target. Behind him, were the pilot who, if all went to plan, would fly the Su-27 home and the engineer who would tackle the recovery task. At this stage, it was impossible to know to what extent the intelligence analysts had stripped the aircraft, although it was still only a matter of hours since the defector Andrenev had flown the aircraft into their hands and he hoped that there had been insufficient time to get into deep strip. He suspected, and hoped, that their primary interest during the early stages of their evaluation would be in the avionics system rather than the airframe or the systems. He hoped! Nevertheless, if they had gone too far, the team were carrying sufficient Semtex explosives to slow down further investigation. The pilot was keeping up well but Kamov was starting to have doubts about the engineer who was already labouring under the effort and sounded like a steam train on the Murmansk line. It was particularly significant as he would be the one who would have the most important task during the early stages of the operation; if they could gain entry to the hardened aircraft shelter. Two further Spetznaz members brought up the rear but he had no similar worries about them. They were the insurance policy if the team was disturbed. A final member of the team had disappeared as soon as they had disembarked from the helicopter and had moved ahead to check out the lie of the land. The point man. The group broke through the tree line and there, about 2 km ahead of them lay the airfield, a point of brightness in the otherwise darkened countryside. They had selected the approach carefully and the bright lights of Wassenberg village lay well out to the west. They had been keen to avoid any areas of civilian population as their mission was purely military and should not disturb the locals. He could make out the two floodlit dispersals which housed the resident Phantom squadrons and the third dispersal which, if intelligence reports were correct, was where the Brits had secured the Su-27. He realised that a few brief frames from a spy satellite was rather tenuous evidence of its whereabouts but it was all he had to go on. He had expected the dispersal to be dark at this hour but, although the 2 operational dispersals were quiet, he could see bright floodlights fixed to temporary gantries bathing the centre dispersal in harsh light. The normal security lights, huge rectangular sodium lamps, added to the problem. He doubted that this was routine security and their presence suggested something more than the normal precautions. The remaining hike to the perimeter was across open fields where they would be at the whim of the cloud cover which constantly moved back and forth to cover the moon. He wished for more of the shallow fog which they had encountered over the eastern banks of the Rhine but suspected that he would be out of luck. A slight breeze was enough to keep it at bay. Skirting the tree line, they picked up some cover from a low hedgerow and continued towards the airfield.

In the 92 Squadron Battle Flight crewroom the phone rang. Flash picked it up recognising the voice of the Duty Operations Controller over the airfield in Wing Ops. Neither he nor Razor had slept since being wakened by the frantic activity as the other aircraft had been scrambled. Once it was airborne they had been stood down from cockpit readiness and returned to the small ops room. The returning Phantom screamed over the threshold of the runway just a few hundred metres from the Battle Flight Shed and thumped onto the runway. The throttles were cut as it ran down the runway on its landing roll, Suddenly, there was a loud "bang, bang" which could be only one thing. An ejection!

"Stand by, I'll call you back," said the Operations Officer.

He replaced the receiver turning to Razor with a tense look on his face. No words were needed; the look said it all. The phone rang again.

"The crew of 55 have just ejected." A simple statement. "The jet's in the barrier but they're both OK. Battle Flight's mandatory."

It would be a hive of activity around the stricken jet and the runway would be littered with vehicles and people trying to sort out the chaos. If they were to launch at this moment, they would have to fly over the top of the recovery crews adding to the risks. It was too hazardous for the remaining Phantom to launch over the top unless it was absolutely vital until the runway had been cleared. For the time being they were going nowhere. The phone rang again and he heard the breathless voice of Julie Kingston.

"Flash, I just heard about the 19 Squadron jet. It's terrible. Look, I've just come off shift, can I come round to see you?"

"We've just been declared mandatory so we're not going anywhere any time soon. " he offered grateful for the diversion. "See you in five."

At the far end of the airfield, mayhem reigned. One of the firemen still in the cockpit had just pulled the throttles back through the gate silencing the Rolls Royce Speys at last. The Phantom, now silent was swathed by the barrier net, only the partially empty cockpit protruding through the gaps. Two large poles which had guided the ejection seats out of the jet stuck eerily into the air. The wreckage of the barrier stanchions was strewn around the aft end of the airframe and pieces of distorted ironwork had penetrated the rear fuselage. The aircraft resembled something from a scrap heap. The whole scene was lit by the flashing blue lights and a hastily erected arc lamp making it seem even more surreal. On the edge of the runway, a medical orderly knelt by the prone pilot attempting to make him comfortable. He would not be moved until a proper immobilisation stretcher was available; back injuries after ejection were extremely common and any hasty action could cripple the pilot for life. The navigator was being assisted into the small crash ambulance and would be shipped immediately to the local Air Force Hospital at Wegberg. The fireman slowly made the aircraft safe as they had practiced so many times in the past and began the slow process of extracting the crippled jet from its shroud.

"OC RAF Police here. Orders from the Station Commander, we're to call out the Station Reaction Force. He's had intelligence reports of terrorist activity in the local area. I want the guards on Charlie Dispersal doubled immediately. Make sure the CVR(T) is deployed for a perimeter search and I want the gun loaded."

The CVR(T), military jargon for Carrier Vehicular Reconnaissance (Tracked), or Scimitar in normal parlance, was as the title suggested, a tracked light armoured vehicle equipped with a 30mm Rarden cannon. It was extremely capable when faced with a threat to the Station perimeter. It had been common recently for the Station guards to be armed as the base had been the target for IRA terrorists but loading the gun on the armoured vehicle was a little out of the ordinary and the sergeant who had taken the call raised an eyebrow.

"Get additional dog patrols out there and start full vehicle searches of everything that comes onto and goes off the base.....Yes I know it's 2 o'clock in the morning but I suggest that by 2.30 we have everything up and running or the Station Master is going to want a few answers!"

The sergeant knew when to hold his tongue and now was a good time.

Kamov followed the Spetznaz team leader, the remaining men spread out around them guarding the flanks. Their brief hike across the fields had been uneventful, despite the full moon, but any hopes of reduced visibility to cover their movements had not materialised. He glanced across at the engineer who still looked winded. The brisk march towards the airfield had proved tiring for him and he was obviously more used to vodka than exercise. The Su-27 pilot, however, seemed relaxed and confident. Tapping him on the shoulder the raised thumb elicited a positive response and he slapped him gently on the back in encouragement. The Spetznaz team fanned out as they approached the perimeter wire looking for a suitable entry point. On the other side of the wire the perimeter road bent sharply from view to either side of their vantage point and a large earth bank around an aircraft shelter obscured their forward view of the airfield. The team leader silently indicated a point on the fence and, immediately, a shadowy form approached it with a large pair of bolt cutters and began to snip away at the wire netting. Suddenly the lights of a Land Rover appeared from around the bend and they dropped to the ground stationary. Kamov glanced briefly at the engineer from the corner of his eye relieved that he had gone to ground; the rest of the team were more than capable of looking after themselves. The headlamps played over their heads as it made its way slowly around the perimeter track towards the adjacent dispersal. As the noise faded he could make out the gap in the fence which had appeared. Luckily the man in the Land Rover had been too intent on the road to pay much attention to the fence. A brief signal and the remaining members of the team squeezed through, ran across the road and disappeared into the undergrowth near the revetment. It was their turn and Kamov tapped the engineer and they followed quickly. Once through the fence, the team leader sealed the gap temporarily with small strands of wire before he himself moved silently into the undergrowth and disappeared.

"Charlie Dispersal Guard Post."

"Cpl Finney, this is the Guard Commander. The Station Commander has called out the Station Reaction Force. There's been some word from Rheindahlen and they've increased the defence state. The word is the Station Commander has had some warning of terrorist activity. You'll be getting some extra guards for Charlie Dispersal. I want you to double up and work in pairs. I'm sending out extra dog patrols."

"Yes Sir. Any reason why?" he asked. "It was all quiet over here until the Battle Flight aircraft made that racket."

"The IRA has been active so we can't relax. The Old Man's jumpy and doesn't want to take any chances. It wouldn't do to fall down on the job with all this going on."

"OK Sir, I'll walk round the observation posts now and brief the team. While you're on Sir, that was a hell of a noise as the last aircraft landed. Was that the crash alarm? We couldn't hear the tannoy out here on the dispersal. What's going on?"

"I'll brief you later but there's been a problem. The crew ejected and the aircraft went off the end of the runway. It looks like they're OK but they've been shipped off to Wegberg for checks. The aircraft's a hell of a mess."

"It's not our night is it?"

"You could be right there Corporal Finney, you could be right!"

The Spetznaz Leader drew a night scope from his pack and scanned the dispersal. There were guard posts on top of some of the adjacent revetments the shallow dugouts in the top of the earth mound covered in camouflage netting. A door banged and a figure in camouflaged fatigues and a blue RAF beret walked from the hardened bunker towards the nearest observation post. Obviously this was the NCO making his rounds but, little did the NCO know, that he was about to pinpoint the exact position of each and every guard on the site. He stopped briefly at 3 separate camouflaged positions before climbing to the top of the revetment. The Russian made a mental note and refined his plan. Watching him return to the Control Post, he crawled slowly back his team and whispered a quiet command before turning to Kamov to refine the plan of attack.

The guard closest to the runway could see the blue flashing lights at the far end of the airfield. He had been fascinated since hearing the bangs unable to see anything through the darkness. After the crew ejected from the Phantom he had watched events unfold with a morbid curiosity, his attention diverted by the intense activity. He was still fascinated. Involuntarily, he let out a strangled cry as he felt a sudden constriction around his throat. Lifting his hands, he clawed at the thin metal garrotte which, slowly but surely, dug into his skin cutting off his air supply. His eyes bulged as the bright lights of the dispersal dimmed and he gasped for breath unable to clear the restriction. Without knowing a reason, he died. His attacker dragged the body down into the observation post and dumped it roughly in the corner. Collecting the airman's self loading rifle from the floor, he removed the magazine and slid it into his pouch throwing the rifle after the inert body. He flashed a torch twice in the direction from which he had just come and turned his attention to the floodlit HAS.

Unaware of events in the adjacent dispersal Razor and Flash lolled across the easy chairs in the Battle Flight crewroom. Normally they would be wearing their full kit after the earlier cockpit alert but with the mandatory state declared they had taken the chance to remove their "G-suits" feeling a little more relaxed than usual. The door opened and Julie Kingston walked in and as Flash drew himself to his feet she threw herself at him.

"Thank God it wasn't you," she whispered.

Razor muttering polite excuses disappeared to make the coffee. Not like me to be diplomatic, he thought. Crew cooperation's a wonderful thing.

"I was just coming off shift when I heard about the ejection," she said. "Any idea what the problem was?"

"It seems like finger trouble," he replied uncharitably. "There were no calls suggesting there was any problem with the jet. It seemed like a normal approach so I bet he lost his chute and blew it!"

"Is the airfield clear again yet?"

"No they're still working at the far end trying to get the jet out of the barrier. Once that's done, I doubt they'll have much success tidying that lot up tonight. Ops reckon they've pulled the barrier supports out of the ground. I should think they'll clear the main debris and reopen the runway for us."

Razor returned with the coffee handing one to each of them.

"I'm going to try to get some shuteye. Let me know when the airfield's open again." he said as he closed the door to the adjacent bedroom "On second thoughts, don't bother. Not much else we can do if the hooter goes again is there?" Over the other side of the taxiway he could hear the drone of a tractor as a replacement jet was pulled into the 19 Squadron Battle Flight HAS. Life went on.

The three Spetznaz team members returned, each man nodding to the team leader signifying that their tasks had been completed. They edged slowly towards their goal, the HAS which they hoped contained the Su-27. Unlike the other HASs it had a vehicle outside and various pieces of technical support equipment were littered across the front of the doors. It seemed unlikely that it was being used for a Phantom as the equipment blocked access. If they were right that would have to be dragged clear. It was obvious that with a guard inside, it would be impossible to gain access unless he was persuaded to open the door for them. The heavy steel doors were secured by mechanical locks on the inside and were designed to keep out a 1000 lb bomb. Crouching in the pine trees next to the main entrance, the team were hidden from the rest of the dispersal and, with the exception of the NCO who had just returned to the Control Post, they were alone. Nothing else moved. He whispered to Kamov who nodded and made his way slowly towards the wicket door set in the huge clamshell door of the HAS. Rapping sharply, the sudden noise caused him to flinch and hearing a muffled challenge from the guard inside he shouted.

"Brought you a cup of tea mate, thought you might need one."

Predictably, the heavy locks were drawn back and the small door swung outwards. Kamov pushed his way inside startling the guard and gripped him around the windpipe. He head-butted the hapless victim stunning him instantly. As the guard collapsed, Kamov dragged him bodily to the side of the HAS. Leaning down, he checked his pulse pleased that he was still alive. Unlike his special forces colleagues he was more selective about killing. Hoping it wasn't an indulgence, he watched as the team filed in through the door. Turning back, he took in the sleek lines of the Su-27 relieved that their choice of HAS was correct but the red stars, normally so familiar, looked totally out of context in this small hangar so far from home. The rest of the team had filed in quietly behind him. He gestured to the engineer, apparently recovered from his ordeal, who began his preparations around the aircraft. His task was difficult in the absence of any test equipment but he set about it methodically and efficiently.

The RAF engineering officer clipped the radio handset back onto the lapel of his combat jacket, the breath from his mouth condensing in the cold night air.

"OK lads, let's wrap this up for the night. The light's not good enough and we might miss something. Let's tow the jet across to Aircraft Servicing Flight and we'll do a quick FOD sweep of the runway. We'll start again at first light."

Behind him, the hulk of the once impressive war machine was hooked up to an aircraft tug looking forlorn in the harsh glow of the arc lights, the guide rails of the discharged ejection seats protruding from the empty cockpits emphasised the enormity of their task. From his first look, with the deep gouges in the rear fuselage he suspected that the jet was Cat 5; a write off. The flashing blue emergency lights snapped off and the vehicles made their way slowly back to their stations the headlights forming a procession along the taxiway. The tug revved and the damaged Phantom began its slow drive over to the servicing hangar on the north side of the airfield.

19 FIREFIGHT

Over Magdeburg, the Soviet command and control aircraft, a Mainstay, banked gently as it completed yet another holding orbit. The large dish antenna above the fuselage rotated slowly and, in its wake, the wispy contrails marked its path through the sky. Onboard, the Tactical Coordinator watched as the incident between the helicopters and the Phantom unfolded but, despite his God's eye view of events, he had been unable to influence the situation. The lead helicopter had made its move efficiently suckering the Phantom crew into following the decoy. As it moved deeper into West German airspace he selected a pre-briefed frequency ready for the all important codewords which would indicate the success or otherwise of the mission. As he waited, the feeling of apprehension grew or was it perhaps envy? Something niggled and he could not ward off the desire to intervene. His natural desire to help was tempered. An ill timed comment over the radio could compromise emission security and even the whole mission. He relaxed, comfortable in his padded armchair, and sipped his coffee.

*

Four Land Rovers preceded by a Scimitar armoured reconnaissance vehicle drove into the dispersal threading their way around a barbed wire chicane, hastily erected across the road to deter unwelcome visitors. The convoy of vehicles clattered to a halt, the tracks of the armoured vehicle grinding a pattern in the asphalt as the guards dismounted onto the empty taxiway waiting for instructions. The Scimitar, its commander stationed in the small turret, jerked back into life bypassing the assembled group and rattled back towards the neck of the dispersal taking up station. On direction from the officer, the additional guards fanned out swiftly towards the observation posts to reinforce the stations, heavy boots and clattering rifles ringing out across the previously quiet dispersal. The officer watched his men fan out as he made his way over to the Control Post.

"Good evening Corporal."

"Hello Sir. It's all quiet over here. I did the rounds about 15 minutes ago and there's nothing to report."

"This is all probably a lot of fuss over nothing," he replied "but the Station Commander must have had a good reason to go to these lengths at this time of the night. It's also a bit unusual for the aircraft still to be flying. Something must be going on."

The phone rang and he picked it up.

"OP 4 here Sir, I think you'd better come over here right away. We've got a problem."

"OP 4 right now," he snapped at the Corporal suddenly alert.

In the HAS, the Soviet engineer had been working furiously. The Su-27 had been stripped down already but luckily, the majority of the flight systems were intact. The radar had been pulled out and a number of components including the control panel in the cockpit had been removed as had the radar warning receiver and the panel which controlled the electronic countermeasures equipment. It was unlikely that he could do anything in the time available other than tidying up the wiring to make the jet safe for flight. As an airframe it was still functional and without being able to check the fly-by-wire flight controls, he was reasonably satisfied that it was flight worthy. The controls worried him. In order to prove the system he would have to fire up the engines and complete a full pre flight test sequence. In the small hours, on a quiet dispersal in a strange country, he knew that was not an option without even asking the brooding KGB officer who, even as he pondered the problem, was pacing restlessly around the aircraft. Attaching the final connector he returned the avionics box to its housing and closed the access panel snapping the quick release fasteners back into position flush with the airframe. He climbed back up the ladder and sat in the cockpit turning his attention to the fly-by-wire monitor panel on the console. Pushing the test switch he attempted to engage the 3 pitch channels. Without the assistance of the computer the aircraft would be sluggish and unstable. It would certainly be flyable but would add pressure to the pilot's already high workload trying to escape from this strange airfield. Despite his piercing gaze, the warning lights on the panel remained doggedly illuminated deepening his frown. Down below, the pilot had been assisting with the replacement of the access panels. Luckily the British engineers who had removed them had been methodical and the fasteners were all neatly stored alongside the panels. Nevertheless, he struggled with a particularly elusive screw thanking his lucky stars that he was a pilot not an engineer. As the final panel slotted back into place he moved over to the large rucksacks which the Spetznaz team had carried, opened the nearest and withdrew first his flying helmet followed by the other items of his flying kit which he hoped he would need imminently. Looking up at the cockpit he could see the engineer, head buried in the instruments looking concerned. It did nothing to calm his already frazzled nerves. Kamov peered through the windows of the HAS management cabin at the frantic activity inside. The engineer was still busy while the Spetznaz team huddled in the corner engaged in a deep discussion, arms gesturing and fingers prodding, apparently forming a new plan. He was pleased with the progress so far but knew only too well that the most critical phase of the mission was yet to come. Once he gave the signal for the HAS doors to open and the jet noise disturbed the site, their actions would have to be perfect. At this stage he had no idea of the activity outside and was still under the impression that their activities were, as yet, undetected.

The Guard Commander sprinted across to the OP, his breath white in the cold night air. As he approached, he could see the new guard leaning against the camouflaged entrance. Pushing past he ducked under the low roof and peered into the gloomy foxhole. The prone figure had not been dead for long but, already, the smell of death was permeating the confined space. He snapped out his orders conscious that he sounded callous and uncaring but there was little time for sentiment.

"Move down a hundred yards and cover the track between HAS 33 and 35. Make sure that anyone that moves is challenged and detained. No exceptions. I'll sort out a medic; there's nothing more that we can do in here."

The guard nodded mutely, thankful for the mundane task to take his mind off the grizzly scene. He moved automatically to take up his new position. Returning to the Control Post the Guard Commander picked up the phone and called the Station Commander to give him the latest bad news. As he listened, he was given his new rules of engagement with a great deal more leeway to cope with the rapidly changing situation. He set out to update his men realising that the stakes had been irrevocably raised. The speed of reaction from his Boss to what he had assumed would be earth-shattering news suggested there was more below the surface. He began to wonder how his masters could react with such decisiveness but hesitated having almost forgotten the most important aspect of all. He should brief the guard in HAS 37 who was looking after the Flanker. Picking up the phone he dialled the number for the HAS phone.

Back in the cockpit, having made further adjustments to the fly-by-wire control unit, the engineer again hit the test button but the light still glowed, aggravatingly. He realised there was nothing more he could try and, dismounting, he moved across to the floor of the hangar to join Kamov and the pilot in the cabin to brief them on the state of the aircraft. As he entered, the phone rang and Kamov stared before, hesitatingly, answering its ring. He grunted a response hoping that his luck would hold for just five more minutes but, as he replaced the phone, the look on his face betrayed his fears and he almost barked at the team leader.

"Get this show moving. Time's running out."

The pilot pulled on his flying gear and sprinted up the ladder. No time for a walkround.

In the Control Post the Guard Commander looked quizzical.

"He didn't sound right," he said to the NCO. "Let's get over there and take a look."

The pilot, a new urgency in his actions took a cursory glance at the gleaming top surfaces of the aircraft as he stepped over the cockpit sill. Settling himself into the seat he surveyed the HAS making sure that his team had moved into position to see him off. A final check that the fire extinguisher was in place and he flicked on the battery power watching the warning captions flash into life around the cockpit. Why look at the extinguisher? This bird would fly no matter what state it was in. He was momentarily glad that he would fly out but a brief concern crossed his mind for the fate of those left below. The lights would slowly extinguish as the individual systems came on line after start up, with the exception of the fly-by-wire which, from the engineer's briefing he knew he would, probably, have to live without. The mechanical controls would be sluggish but it would still fly. It was an irritation but he hoped that the western SAM defences did not give him a hard time as he ran for the border. If intelligence was to be believed, they would not be active anyhow at this time of the night; part time soldiers. A slight tweak of the cockpit lights reduced them to a more comfortable level. He would need his night vision as soon as he left the glare of the HAS lights and it was unlikely that the local air traffic controllers would provide him with airfield lights for takeoff. Methodically running through his well rehearsed pre-flight routine, waves of familiarity calming his nerves, he drew the ejection seat straps down from the head box and slotted them into the quick release box. All the while he was checking each individual system as he pulled the straps tight. As he finished his final check around, his eyes strayed over the cockpit sill and he caught Kamov's eye and received a reassuring thumbs up in response. Nodding, he returned to the task in hand; he was set for engine start.

"It's probably nothing Cpl Finney but get the Scimitar round from the neck of Charlie Dispersal. I also want the mobile team to come with us to check out HAS 37. Contact each OP. I want every guard alert. Let's move it!"

The NCO, attuned to the tension moved off with purpose.

"Go, go, go," shouted Kamov as the bolts on the HAS door were driven back with a clang. The locking bar shifted upwards and the massive iron doors slowly pushed open. As they reverberated against the stops, the noise of the jets winding up split the air. The Spetznaz soldiers steadied the doors before running forward to the neck of the revetment throwing themselves prone, covering both sides of the taxiway, weapons at the ready. The pilot had watched the start switch click off as the Lyulka turbines surged through 55%, growling into life, the RPM increasing in tune with the rising whine. As the engines passed 65%, he brought the generators on line. He hit the button to fast align the inertial navigation system. It would take 2 precious minutes but it provided information to many key systems including his attitude displays and he could not afford to take off without it. The ground troops would have to cover for him. He watched the flashing caption which would tell him when the system was ready, tapping his fingers nervously on the cockpit sill. Waiting, waiting; willing the tardy electronics to play along. Outside the HAS, the moon glowed brightly and the first signs of dawn were tingeing the eastern sky. Not a welcome sight. Dark was good.

The guard team flanked the taxiway as they moved methodically towards HAS 37 when, suddenly, the whine of the Flanker's jets split the night air and the area around the HAS exit became a blur of activity. Shadowy figures dropped to ground in front of him. Reacting swiftly, he called for his own men to form a defensive ring. As he dropped, he fumbled with his radio which was clipped to his belt rapping out his instructions.

"Hold your fire."

He left a long pause so that his order would sink in not wishing to exacerbate what was rapidly becoming untenable. He needed thinking time. This was way outside anything he'd seen on exercise.

"Return fire only on my command or when fired upon," he snapped clearly and unambiguously. Thinking rapidly, he chopped frequency to the Air Traffic Control network knowing that the Station Commander would be monitoring.

"Sunray this is Charlie Dispersal, over."

"Go!"

"Sunray, we have an engine start in HAS 37. Suspect intruders on site, request instructions. Over."

"Acknowledged, stand by," came the response. There was a brief hesitation as the Station Commander considered his position but his Scottish drawl was clear, even through the static, as he passed his instructions.

"Roger, use minimum force and return fire only if fired upon. Attempt to disable the aircraft if it leaves the HAS but do not, repeat do not, destroy. Acknowledge."

"Charlie understood, back to tactical frequency. Out."

He waved the team forward and began the slow crawl, closing on the prone figures guarding the approach.

The Team Leader watched the opposing guard force take their defensive positions as he hauled out his night sight to mark them. The guards on the taxiway stood out clearly and, more importantly, were entirely predictable so he turned his attention to the OPs. He realised, instantly, that they had been reinforced and could now offer a threat if he tried to cross the taxiway. His covert posture had been well and truly blown by the jet which howled in the concrete shelter behind him but, nevertheless, the narrow confines of the revetment surrounding the HAS exit were easy to defend and would provide perfect cover for the aircraft as long as it remained in place. His problems would start once it emerged from the shelter and exposed itself on the taxiway. One good shot could be sufficient to immobilise any one of the myriad of complex systems which operated within the airframe. More to the point, the tyres were the most obvious weak spot and one which he would target in that situation. Just one bullet could stop the whole show. He had no choice but to take the offensive while time was still on his side. The fact that the opposition had yet to commit meant that he could yet dictate the fight.

The align light glowed steady and the pilot engaged the system with a feeling of relief running quickly through his final checks so that when he arrived at the runway he would be ready for an immediate takeoff. Engaging the nose wheel steering, he once again glanced down at Kamov, snapped off a brisk salute and moved the throttles forward to accelerate the jet from the chocks. He felt a momentary pang of guilt knowing that the team's work was far from over but the workload in the cockpit soon prevented him from becoming sentimental and drew his attention back to the job in hand.

As he watched the jet trundle forward, Kamov sprinted forward hugging the revetment walls aiming towards the Team Leader. He slipped, momentarily losing his balance and fell heavily to the floor alongside the prone figure realising for the first time that they were no longer alone and that a sizeable force now opposed them. His heart sank but he remained calm waiting for the Team Leader's directions; for the next short time it was his show.

The Guard Commander relayed the Station Commander's new instructions to the team but struggled desperately for inspiration. What should have been a relatively forward guarding operation was rapidly spinning out of control. He had counted three intruders so far but it was difficult to be precise with only the moonlight to assist.

"Pick up one of the Land Rovers and get it over to me, quick," he barked over the radio to one of the guards.

To his flanks, his team edged slowly forward attempting to pin down the prone figures but there was no visible reaction. He could feel the tension rising and he was suddenly conscious of the limitations of his small team. The guard force was made up of technicians, misemployed as guards. This was more akin to "Dad's Army" than the SAS and who knew the quality of the troops he faced. They were most certainly professionals judging from the manner in which they had secured the revetment in the short time since the HAS doors had opened. But why did he have such a bad feeling? It was his airfield and he was familiar with the layout of the dispersal. It was not lost yet. The Land Rover pulled to a halt next to him temporarily blocking his view and dulling the jet noise. Dragging open the door he gestured to the driver, emphatically, who nodded and pulled away to carry out his instructions.

The Team Leader watched the camouflaged vehicle pull across the dispersal and slot into place blocking the exit from the HAS. He could hear the door spring open, although it was shielded from his view. The driver would already be crawling back to rejoin his mates. The mistake was obvious. The driver's door faced the HAS within easy reach of the prone figure alongside him. He beckoned to the nearest trooper, pointing to the stationary vehicle making a chopping motion across his throat. A nod in acknowledgement and the shadowy figure crabbed towards the vehicle, a blur as he hauled himself into the cab without even pausing to close the door. The vehicle started using the keys which the nervous airman had left in the ignition in his haste to be gone. It roared into life and skidded onto the adjacent grass; the trooper rolling clear. It had barely slowed the pace for a second. With the trooper clear, another motion to one of his men and, suddenly, a burst of automatic fire raked the truck causing an instantaneous explosion and flames leaped into the air flooding the dispersal with a flickering light. Alongside him, Kamov could feel the enormous heat from where he lay.

The Guard Commander cursed his subordinate for making such an elementary mistake but how could he expect more? These were not professional guards, they were squadron technicians drafted into the role to replace Army soldiers who would guard the airfield in wartime. The Land Rover burned fiercely at the edge of the taxiway partially blocking his view of the HAS neck as he signalled for his team to spread out in an attempt to work around the inferno. In the background the jet noise dominated the night air emphasising that time was precious.

The Spetznaz team moved forward using the blazing vehicle as cover, squat machine pistols ready. As the leading element of the guard force appeared from behind the burning vehicle each trooper selected a target and opened fire selectively. Some dropped to the ground, some darted back into cover, others fell lifeless.

"Return fire," shouted the Guard Commander stunned at the ferocity of the attack. Up to this point, despite the loss of the guards in the OPs, the incident could almost have been just another exercise. Now the gunfire jarred his nerves; it was all frighteningly real. He had men down and one of his vehicles already a total wreck. Not a good opening move. He spotted one of the intruders and squeezed off a single round from his sub machine gun but watched his target duck back unhurt. At that instant, the jet noise increased in pitch and the graceful form of the Soviet aircraft nosed out from the revetment past the burning hulk and turned in front of him onto the taxiway. Taken aback by the sight of the unfamiliar aircraft, he realised that his guards were sniping at the intruders, their conditioning preventing them from targeting the aircraft which was making its escape. The Flanker moved towards the dispersal neck unharmed.

"Tracker this is the Guard Commander," he called to the Scimitar driver, "close in. Block the southern taxiway at Charlie Dispersal. The aircraft taxying for takeoff is an unauthorized movement. Disable but not destroy; repeat disable but not destroy."

He heard the beating of helicopter rotors in the background.

Captain Kazenko opened the throttles and released the brakes. The Su-27 jumped forward from the chocks and he moved past the burning hulk. He felt both aloof yet vulnerable as he watched the skirmish around him. Aloof in his cocooned environment but vulnerable to a simple rifle bullet as he sat head and shoulders above the cockpit sill exposed to any snipers who paid attention. He could see the winking of intermittent muzzle flashes pricking the darkness of the dispersal. The exit to his left was blocked by bodies across the taxiway so he turned right down the taxiway away from the firefight. He had completed his checks and was all ready for takeoff, all he had to do was make the runway. Easily said, harder to do. His taxi light flooded the loop taxiway and he could make out that it was free from obstruction all the way to the dispersal exit. He hoped fervently that the guards remained distracted and confused for a little while longer even though a stray round through the airframe from a misguided shot would cause havoc. As he emerged from the trees which surrounded the dispersal with the sporadic fire disappearing behind, he began to feel a little more confident.

The Guard Commander levelled his gun and aimed at a point midway down the fuselage of the receding airframe and snapped off a round. Seeing little effect from his efforts he returned his attention to the intruders who presented a more immediate threat. He hoped that one of the other guards would have a little more success.

The Su-27 emerged from the pine ringed dispersal and turned left down the darkened taxiway towards the threshold of Runway 09. Kazenko wanted to make his departure towards the east no matter what the wind direction. His intelligence briefing had suggested that the missile sites at Wildenrath would be inactive at this time of night; the Bloodhounds only operated on exercise and the Rapiers, without the new Blindfire radar, could not engage in the dark. Even so, he wanted to present a receding target to the Bloodhound site which was located on the dispersal at the north eastern corner of the airfield. He trusted his briefing and felt confident that there would be no Rapiers deployed in their dispersed locations in a defensive ring around the airfield perimeter. Suddenly, to his amazement and consternation, the airfield lights snapped on and the taxiway was highlighted in sharp relief, edged with blue marker lights. He pushed the throttles up and increased his taxy speed as fast as he dared.

The driver of the Scimitar had just finished his perimeter check as the Storno radio crackled and he recognised the voice of the Guard Commander. Accelerating down the taxiway towards the dispersal he looked for signs of aircraft activity.

The Battle Flight hooter erupted, snapping both Razor and Flash from a deepening sleep. Instantly awake they both stumbled from bed, sheets and blankets strewn in their wake. Flash fumbled to find his flying boots which had been placed carefully at the foot of the bed, his concession to comfort. Slipping them on but having no time to tie them properly, he followed the disappearing form of his pilot with some difficulty, towards the still dormant Phantom. A rush of bodies greeted him as he hobbled into the HAS where the groundcrew were already busy. He could smell the heavy hint of smoke in the night air and hear the chatter of automatic weapons. Confused, he struggled frantically into his lifejacket at the base of the ladder, hauled himself towards the cockpit seeing the face of his flight line mechanic staring down at him as he climbed. Dropping over the cockpit sill he plugged in his personal equipment connector, aware of the straps being fed over his shoulders by the groundcrew. He checked in still breathless. This was becoming too much of a habit!

"Wing Ops, Mike Lima 75 cockpit ready."

"75, Wing Ops remain at cockpit readiness and stand by for further instructions."

Razor wound up the right hand engine as he clicked the seat straps into the quick release box of the Martin Baker seat. They both waited seeing the lights on the airfield snap on from their raised vantage point in the aircraft.

The Team Leader prompted the move with a wind up sign above his head and, individually, the team members began to extract themselves, sniping at the disorganised guard force as they withdrew. Their location in the well protected revetment had effectively shielded them from any covering fire from the OPs and the diversion with the Land Rover appeared to have tied the mobile force in knots. So far he was well pleased. One by one they moved around the outside of the now empty HAS and began making their way along the dispersal fence towards the airfield. Behind them the noise of three fragmentation grenades thudded out across the dispersal causing further distraction among the guards. The last man was following his brief perfectly. As they moved along the fence line, Kamov bringing up the rear, a head appeared above the parapet of the nearest OP but with a sharp report from a machine pistol, the head dropped back out of sight.

The Scimitar driver could make out the dark outline of an aircraft emerging from the dispersal as it turned down the taxiway towards him. He could make out the profile, twin fins clearly prominent but it was unlike any aircraft he recognised! Suddenly, blinded by the taxi light, he dragged the control lever in his left hand sharply back, skewing the small armoured vehicle across the taxiway causing the engine to die as it came to a halt He cursed his heavy-handedness. Up in the turret, the commander added to the cursing with some more choice expletives as the driver set about trying to restart the engine, not overly concerned, knowing that he had already effectively blocked the taxiway. The strange aircraft was not going anywhere unless it was capable of going in reverse.

To the south of the airfield, Porov gazed across the unfamiliar terrain which looked unreal in the green glow of the goggles. The chimneys of the Hückelhoven coal mine loomed large to his left as he tried to pick out the shape of the small wood on the airfield. His nominated pick up point was slightly west of the wood and it was vital that he hit the precise spot. Time would be short. He dropped the helicopter lower and transitioned to the hover waiting for the signal from the insertion team calling him in.

"Mike Lima 75, this is Wing Ops with a sitrep. We have an unplanned movement from Charlie Dispersal. I'm checking with Crabtree but expect a scramble instruction. Mike Lima 57, maintain cockpit readiness this is a singleton scramble for 75 only."

"75 roger."

"57 Roger."

Flash looked at his watch. It was 05.30 and the first signs of daylight tinged the sky. It was too early to go flying.

"Oh Christ," said Razor "You realise what an unplanned movement from Charlie Dispersal means don't you. It looks like we're going to get another sortie with the Flanker but this time I guess we're on opposite sides. And it's dark. He must still be on the ground. I've not heard him get airborne have you?"

The Spetznaz team reached the tree line, the sniping sporadic behind them. In their confusion, the guards were shooting at shadows as all six remaining members of the insertion team were already back together. Shuffling forward on his stomach alongside the team leader, Kamov looked around expecting to see the Flanker readying itself for takeoff but he could see nothing, although he could hear the whine of the jets. He hit the transmit button on the radio. The first time he had used it tonight.

"Sword this is Alpha. In place ready for pick up."

"Inbound," came the clipped but concise response accompanied by an instantaneous throbbing of helicopter rotor blades in the distance behind him. With a sinking feeling, he realised that the Su-27 was immobile on the taxiway, its progress blocked by a small armoured vehicle. There was little more the team could do having already called in the helicopter. Moving the stationary tank was out of the question and the narrowness of the taxiway prevented any movement of the jet. He had failed at the final hurdle! Over his head, the dark shape of the Hind, rotors clattering, slowed down.

Flight Lieutenant Paul Hunter drew his car into the shadowy car park on Alpha Dispersal which housed the Bloodhound surface-to-air missile battery. He could see that a couple of other cars had already arrived and that the lights were just starting to come on in the Operations Room. He looked across the airfield at the Bloodhound fire units backlit by the bright sodium lights along the runway. As yet they were inactive. In the distance he could hear noises and what sounded like gunshots. It sounded like a pitch battle was underway. The Bloodhound was a medium range surface-to-air missile, a large central missile body with two smaller ramjets alongside which provided the initial impetus but were subsequently jettisoned. After launch the missile climbed vertically to high altitude before attacking its target from above like the proverbial avenging angel. The missiles sat through all weathers on a dedicated launcher pointing skywards and ready for action. It was, however, an old system and to conserve life was only brought up to the highest readiness states during station exercises or real alerts. At all other times it stood dormant but ready to be fired at very short notice. The call-out had come out of the blue and Wing Commander Operations had stressed that it was to be discrete for the time being, using only personnel essential to the operational task. He had not been given a reason for the alert over the insecure telephone line; his first priority would be to find out what was going on. As he walked quickly towards the Ops Room, he met the Engineering Officer coming out of the building.

"What's going on Jeff?" he queried.

"Nothing yet but I'll leave you to speak to Air Ops. Eng Ops know nothing. I'm just going out to supervise the system checks on the fire units, see you shortly."

He walked inside and, without even pausing to take off his coat, snatched the telephone from its cradle and hit the selector for the direct line to the Force Commander.

Porov flicked up his goggles, his approach to the landing zone open. The wood was clearly visible in the moonlight and the airfield lights which had inexplicably lit as he crossed the boundary gave him perfect references. The goggles tended to reduce the depth of field but he felt more confident landing without their assistance now that the light conditions were so much better. He was happy that the ground on the airfield would be firm and concentrated on the commentary from his crewman talking him onto the spot.

Kazenko looked at the armoured vehicle in front of him. There was no way around it and its headlamps had dimmed suggesting that the driver had stopped. It was time to play his trump card. The Su-27 was fitted with intake covers which protected the engines from debris which might be ingested during rough field operations. The covers dropped over the intakes automatically at slow speed and would already be in place. In addition, the low pressure tyres were optimised for rough field operations and it was time to prove the concept. He hoped the airfield surface was firm and that none of the technicians had tampered with the tyre pressures. Moving the throttles forward, he kicked the rudder pedals away from the tank and the jet began to move. The controls felt suddenly strange, spongy yet notchy, unlike their normally crisp feel. His concern was short-lived as the jet left the taxiway.

The Hind settled lightly on the grass and the Team Leader signalled for his men to emplane. Kamov was momentarily taken aback as a trussed body was unceremoniously dumped from the cabin and he wondered what the story was behind that incident. It didn't divert the trooper accompanying the engineer who was first to make his move leading the pair who scurried across the taxiway weaving from side to side making themselves a less predictable target. Covering the final 50 metres to the helicopter in seconds, they clambered aboard without even a shot being fired from the dispersal behind. Two more troopers followed but their progress was instantly slowed. A shot rang out from an OP hidden in the trees where the guard had finally woken up. One of the troopers fell a mere 10 metres from the safety of the helicopter and lay still. Kamov glanced at the Team Leader seeing the concern in his eyes but realised that there was no time for sentiment. A brief thumbs up and they launched themselves towards the waiting machine. Unencumbered by the heavy packs which had by now been discarded, they split and approached the machine from different directions. Kamov could see the gaping hole in the side of the helicopter; the cabin entrance which represented safety. To his left, as he ran, he heard the noise of the Su-27's engines rise but had no time to question events, his thoughts entirely on his own safety. More shots rang out and the team leader, well to his right, weaved and ducked frantically avoiding the shots which thudded harmlessly into the grass. The Spetznaz officer, much fitter than he, ran ahead and scrambled aboard. Kamov neared his goal and as he made his final lunge for the cabin lip, he was struck by a searing pain between his shoulder blades and he stumbled. The helicopter suddenly seemed a long way away as he fell, pain racking his body unable to move any further. He reached for the crewman, stretching out his hand but knew that he could never make it. The helicopter slowly lifted off and the crewman's face grew smaller as it rose.

Kazenko eased the massive Su-27 onto the grass, careful to maintain momentum. If he allowed it to stop he may bog down and that would be the end of his escape. The jet had enormous excess thrust which could actually work against him unless he was wary but, as he felt the jarring of the uneven ground, he felt more confident with the handling of the aircraft. He decided to take the shortest route to the runway and pointed the nose playing the rudder bars carefully to avoid locking the brakes. In the mirrors he could see the armoured vehicle still immobile. He had been concerned that it would attempt to follow and, in these conditions, it was much more agile than the heavy aircraft. It showed no inclination to do so. 100 metres to go and he would be back on the concrete and ready to go. The distance-to-go marker boards, glowed brightly. He could see the large 4 which indicated 4,000 feet. A quick conversion to metres and he realised that he would need a little more runway. Normally, using full afterburner, the distance would have been more than sufficient but he had no intention of taking a risk. The fuel tanks were not completely full and he would need as much flexibility on the return journey as possible. Only 50 meters to go and the armoured vehicle still had not moved

The commander of the Scimitar shouted excitedly at the driver to restart the engine. Already, the aircraft had sidestepped the trap and was disappearing across the grass towards the runway. The engine struggled into life belching smoke but it was too late to catch the aircraft which had too great a head start and had reached the runway. He called the gunner to traverse the barrel, raising his head through the hatch instantly reassessing his priorities with the changing tactical situation.

"Gunner, take aim, helicopter target range 150 yards, fire at will."

The gunner brought the sight onto line and raised it slightly. His new target, the Hind still rising slowly, came steadily but surely into the sight and as he squeezed the trigger, the 30mm Rarden cannon began pumping out rounds. Each fifth round was a tracer bullet and he could see the line of shot as the shells sped towards the target. Walking the shells methodically towards the helicopter he waited for a strike. The Hind juddered slightly as it transitioned to forward flight which meant that there was an element of luck involved in his aim but he had rounds to spare.

Porov steadied the Hind at 30 metres and rotated starboard on the spot intending to leave the airfield to the east and retrace his track through the Dormagen Gap. He had enough fuel for a high speed dash. The element of surprise was well and truly gone and he would return at ultra low level at maximum speed. The compass shifted through 045 degrees and he became aware of flashes abeam the cockpit. Tracer rounds! He dipped the nose picking up forward velocity looking for the swiftest exit as the helicopter gathered momentum. The airframe vibrated as a shell struck but it was still flyable. Already at 100 kph he was underway. Another violent crash as another round struck home and suddenly the craft began to rotate uncontrollably. It must have damaged the tail rotor. He struggled with the controls trying to keep a semblance of equilibrium knowing that his only hope was an autorotation. It would be a firm landing but he could do it. The rotation slowed marginally as his efforts took effect but instantly there was more horrendous splintering as yet another round destroyed one of the rotor blades. Further efforts were wasted as the Hind flipped onto its back and spiralled into the wood bursting into flames.

Kamov raised his head, the effort almost more than he could manage as the pain knifed through his nervous system. Tracer had appeared from over his shoulder and its success was inevitable. He watched round after round strike the slow-moving, hapless craft which shuddered before spinning inverted earthwards. The massive explosion, as it impacted the wood reverberated across the airfield and lit the night sky. He could still hear the jet engines of the Su-27 screaming behind him, although fatally wounded, he was too weak to turn around. He lifted the handset, pressed the transmit button and whispered.

"Stargazer, this is Alpha. Operation aborted, repeat operation aborted."

"75, Wing Ops. Orders from Sunray, your target is on the airfield attempting to launch. Standby for engagement authority, scramble, scramble, scramble, acknowledge."

"75 scrambling," acknowledged Flash. "Razor, tell me this is not happening!"

*

In the Mainstay high over East Germany, the Tactical Coordinator had heard the call from the insertion team bringing the Hind back to the airfield for the pickup. That was only minutes ago yet now he was hearing an operational abort. What could have gone so wrong so quickly? No matter. His instructions were perfectly clear and he would have to raise General Sokolovskiy as soon as was humanly possible. He had a message to pass and he needed guidance, and quickly.

*

Razor watched the left engine RPM stabilise and brought the remaining systems on line. Waving the chocks away he looked to the marshaller who had moved in front of the aircraft. Expecting an immediate clearance to move forward, the marshaller's hands were crossed above his head signalling that he should keep the brakes on. He banged the side of the aircraft impatiently, anxious to be on his way; they had a scramble time to meet and the clock was ticking. From beneath the aircraft the other flight line mechanic struggled to remove the chocks. In his desire to be away, Razor had left too much power applied, jamming the chocks in place under the wheels and it had required superhuman effort to release them. Finally, the marshaller's hands began to signal him forward. He already had the all clear from Flash as he opened the throttles. The Phantom emerged from the shed and he chopped the power, the residual thrust sufficient to keep the aircraft moving. With such a short distance to the threshold of Runway 27 the crew were already completing the last of their checks and had not wasted the time offered by the short delay in the shelter.

"Station Commander."

"Sir, Paul Hunter 25 Squadron Ops. Can you fill me in on the background to the call-out."

"Paul, good effort, that was quick. It's a little hectic down here at the moment but get the missiles on full status as soon as you can. Bring them up "weapons tight" for the time being but expect a "weapons free" order! I'll call you back."

Christ Almighty, he thought as he put the phone down. It's bloody World War Three. A call out at 3 o'clock in the morning and he was about to be given clearance to engage! He grabbed the tannoy.

"Attention 25, this is not an exercise. All fire units to immediate readiness. Engineering Officer check in with Air Ops."

He realised that he was hyperventilating. Calm down boy, he thought to himself. This is what you've trained for; don't blow it now. He punched the direct line to the Air Ops clerk.

"25 Ops here, I'm moving into the control cabin. Squadron Ops will be unmanned for a short while until the Ops Clerk gets in. The Station Commander was going to ring me back. Can you let him know where I am...... Thanks."

He rushed out en route to the radar control cabin from where he could he could control the engagement.

Kazenko approached the edge of the runway. There would be a raised concrete lip to contend with and he dabbed the brakes gently to slow the aircraft. Despite the rough surface he had managed to keep quite a respectable speed across the grass but if he struck the lip too fast he would risk taking off the nosewheel. Nose legs had sheared off in similar situations when aircraft had left the runway. The nose wheels mounted the concrete with a shuddering thump and Kazenko winced but the oleo flexed and carried over onto the firm surface. Unfortunately, he had unconsciously over-compensated with his braking slowing the aircraft almost to a standstill and, as he pushed the rudder bar left to line the jet up on the runway, the right main wheel struck the lip coming to a jarring halt. If he was not careful now, the sheer power of the engines could dig the wheels into the soft earth so he gingerly raised the power on the right engine attempting to use asymmetric thrust to ease the wheel free. The airframe strained under the effort and he briefly thought that he was trapped when, suddenly, the jet broke free like a cork from a bottle and he was rolling down the smooth surface of the runway. Backtracking a short distance, he applied full rudder to bring the massive aircraft slewing around in its own length to line up. To either side, the runway lights glowed bright white, the perspective giving a false impression of the runway narrowing to a point in the distance. With the shortened take off distance of little over 1500 metres, the end looked remarkably close and, for a moment, his confidence faltered. He decided to use the extra fuel for a full afterburner take off. No prizes at this stage for leaving a burning hulk at the far end of the runway. Final checks complete, with all but the fly-by-wire system and the decimated weapons controls serviceable, he began to open the throttles. What he had failed to see was the hydraulic gauge for the primary flying controls which fluctuated intermittently. The oscillation was insufficient to bring on the warning on the central warning panel but his failure to spot the incipient fault would be significant before the night was through. The wheels shimmied and he released the brakes, allowing the jet to start its take off run.

As he sat in front of the large radar console, Paul Hunter could see that the lamp of the direct line to the Force Commander was already glowing. He punched the button dragging on his headset at the same time.

"Sir, Go ahead."

"Paul, sorry about the delay. Right we have a problem. You know that we had the Flanker moved to Charlie Dispersal for the technical investigation. There's been a fire fight in that area. We thought at first that it was terrorists but my guess now is that it's a covert insertion team. Looks like the reaction force just destroyed a helicopter next to the southern taxiway." The ops assistant eased into his own seat and began to fire up the radar display flicking the mass of switches. The large plan position indicator in front of him burst into life and the time base began its circular movement around the radar tube. "What I do know for certain," continued the Station Commander," is that the Flanker is no longer in its HAS. I'm not prepared to engage it if it just makes a run for it but I want to be ready for any eventuality. I want you to track it as soon as it gets airborne and keep me advised. A word of warning. I have launched Battle Flight so there are going to be two tracks in the vicinity. Make sure you identify the correct one. Have you got the Battle Flight IFF codes?"

"Yes Sir, I have and I'll make absolutely certain but just a reminder. Our minimum engagement range is only 7 miles. Anything inside that and we can't touch it. We're really geared up for targets coming towards us from the east."

"Do your best Paul but let's be 100% sure that it's the correct target you're tracking. Keep me advised." The line went dead.

Paul returned his attention to his displays. Of his eight fire units one showed unserviceable but the green "GO" status lights glowed reassuringly for the remainder. He ran quickly through his checks bringing the surveillance radar and guidance radars on line. All was ready and he began to scan the scope for contacts when he heard jet noise.

"Mike Lima 75 scrambling!" called Razor on Tower frequency.

"75 hold, one aircraft already on for departure," responded the Local Controller.

"What the hell!" snarled Flash but his question was immediately answered as the Flanker in full reheat, gear only just retracting into the housings, flashed across the nose of the taxying Phantom only yards away and scant feet above. It cranked into a low level right hand turn directly over their heads and they could hear and feel the deep thundering vibration of the reheats transmitted through the airframe despite the noise in their own cockpit.

"75 clear immediate take off, wind easterly at 10 knots," said the controller.

A slight tailwind; it would lengthen their take off roll.

Kazenko lifted his aircraft gently into the air feeling a distinct twitchiness through the controls. He snapped the gear up before the wheels cleared the concrete relying on the weight on wheels safety circuit to inhibit their travel. This would mean that as soon as he was airborne the undercarriage would retract keeping his take off roll to an absolute minimum and reducing the drag as quickly as possible. Suddenly to his right he was aware of the rhythmic flashing of red navigation lights from a taxying Phantom. They had scrambled an aircraft after him. Looking for his check speed of 350 kph he snapped the stick to the right. The roll rate was instant but as he increased the back pressure to wind up the turn, he was aware of the effect of the failed fly-by-wire circuits. The response of the aircraft was sluggish. He could see the plan view of the Phantom on the taxiway and flew directly over the top at little over 30 metres knowing that he had to react to this new threat. Flicking the master arm on he selected Guns on the HOTAS selector. With only one R73 onboard, the remaining missiles having been removed, he was relying on the gun which, luckily, was still full. He would make good use of these rounds. In any event it was the preferred weapon for the tactic he had in mind.

Razor lined up and, with the aircraft still rolling, plugged in the afterburners by rocking the throttles outboard through the gate. A short delay and the reheat kicked in, accelerating the aircraft down the runway. All seemed normal as he heard the usual commentary from the back seat but then the cadence was interrupted.

"Shit he's turned downwind. I reckon he's setting up for a strafing pass. Keep those burners cooking and stay low. Bogey's 8 o'clock nose on, tracking!"

Kazenko held the Flanker low. With his controls so badly affected by the malfunctioning computer coupled with the fact that it was dark, he elected for a low angle strafe attack. He positioned himself half way down the downwind leg and turned back at right angles to the active runway. He realised immediately that he had made an error. He should have extended downwind and returned along the line of the runway. His tracking would have been much more accurate as he could have lined himself up using the runway lights for reference. He had allowed his desire to react quickly to overrule his tactical skill. He was committed but he would have his target crossing at high angles to his line of flight, passing only momentarily through his gunsight. If he succeeded it would be a miracle. The gunsight glowed brightly in his head up display and he turned it down slightly to preserve his night vision. The Phantom stood out in sharp relief to his right, the glow of its afterburners spotlighting its position. Kazenko held the target in his 2 o'clock holding the collision. To achieve the correct tracking solution, the Phantom would have to stay on a constant bearing holding the same position in the windscreen. If he allowed it to drift in too far towards the nose, his bullets would all fall behind the aircraft. His pattern was smooth and the point approached where he had to commit nose down for the attack. Being an Air Defence pilot and unfamiliar with air to ground profiles he had forgotten a key fact, that his guns were aligned 2 degrees above the weapons datum, actually pointing slightly upwards and optimised for air-to-air combat. As he committed nose down placing the sight onto the Phantom, but lacking the normal perspective he would see in the daylight, he allowed the nose to drop too far. As he tracked, the Phantom drifted into the reticle and he squeezed the trigger, hearing the staccato rattle of the 30mm cannon in the right wing root. He was suddenly and heart-stoppingly aware of the ground rushing towards him as the height wound rapidly down in his HUD and he hauled the stick back wishing for a serviceable fly-by-wire computer. He counted. The ground loomed and he was conscious of trees off the right wing above his head. Holding the stick in both hands, fully back in the pit of his stomach, he realised the speed was only just increasing and that the aircraft was hanging on the afterburners. He felt the warning signs of incipient wing rock, the first indication of a departure from controlled flight and he willed himself to ease off slightly. The next stage would be an unpredictable flick in any direction and an almost guaranteed crash. He considered ejection but realised that slowly the jet was responding and coming clear of the ground.

Razor, was above "Go" speed and committed to the takeoff so he held the aircraft rock steady. The nosewheel lifted from the runway and as soon as the aircraft was flying he had the capacity to shift his attention away from the runway. He glanced to the left as he instinctively selected the gear up, registering the dark shape of the approaching Flanker in stark profile in the moonlight. He realised, almost casually, that the 90 degree approach which the pilot had set up was bizarre for a strafe pass. The Flanker pilot opened fire way too early but it was probably a mistake which saved the pilot's life. The early open fire range coupled with the elevated guns meant that the bullets passed harmlessly over the top of the Phantom as it struggled into the air. The Flanker's horrendous nose down attitude was unsustainable and it was apparent that the pilot had already appreciated his predicament and was desperately trying to correct the suicidal flight path. The Soviet fighter plunged earthwards, nose now slightly above the horizon but its vector still downwards. Razor whipped up the flaps and holding the jet down watched expectantly for the speed to build up to 420 knots, his best cornering velocity but the wait was interminable. The Flanker wallowed through his slipstream still clawing for height, exacerbating the troubles for the Russian who had only just succeeded in bringing the jet under control. The disturbed air destroyed the lift over the wing and the jet snaked crazily across the airfield inches above the ground. Razor snapped his jet into a max performance turn, burners still engaged and as the wing dropped, the dark shapes of the HASs on Delta Dispersal flashed past only feet below him. The attack had been unsettling but the familiar instructions from the back seat snapped him into action.

"Bogey, left 8 o'clock, range 1 mile, in a starboard turn. Keep your port turn coming, he's running out on east at low level."

"Tally Ho," called Razor "Go head in, see if you can get him on radar."

20 ESCAPE

The telephone rang and the aide listened intently, nodding involuntarily as he took in the facts. Replacing the handset with barely a word, the sweat glistening on his upper lip, he pondered his options. It was nearly dawn and with Moscow time some two hours in advance of the operating area, he worked out that it would be first light over there. This would have to be sorted out immediately and the decision making was way above him. He may just catch the General before he boarded the flight back from Bonn. He lifted the handset again and dialled the General's number.

"Sokolovskiy."

"Comrade General, this is the Duty Cipher Officer. I'm glad I caught you. We have had a call from the aircraft on barrier over the border," reported the nervous aide. "He has reported an operational abort. I'm afraid further details are a little sketchy at the moment."

He sensed Sokolovskiy's anger immediately and felt the urge to continue but felt it safer to pause.

"It appears that the plan has hit a problem." He was careful to avoid any suggestion of any involvement.

"Has all this information been authenticated," interrupted the General testily, more in hope than expectation. He was clutching at straws as the majority of operational traffic was self authenticating.

"Yes Comrade General. The Command Post has double checked and there can be no doubt as to its authenticity."

"Go on."

"It would seem that the operation had been progressing as planned and the Illyushin IL-76 on barrier had monitored all the anticipated calls. The insertion had been faultless and the aircraft had been extracted from the Hardened Aircraft Shelter, although the team had encountered some light resistance. It was at that point that the situation became unclear. Intercepts on the tactical communications frequency suggest that a fire fight broke out on the airfield and the next transmission was from Kamov calling an operational abort."

"What of the fate of the Su-27?"

"That again is unclear Comrade General but I fear we must expect the worst; that it has fallen into the hands of the British, yet again."

"But we are sure that the insertion team had managed to infiltrate the installation and get the pilot into the aircraft.?"

"Yes Comrade General, that at least we are certain of. We heard a brief transmission from the aircraft as it taxied towards the airfield but contact has since been lost."

"Did the SU-27 get airborne?"

"It is, theoretically, possible General but our agent on the ground would have been unlikely to call the abort if he had seen the aircraft take off. The fate of the insertion team was secondary to the aim of the mission and would not have justified the call. Furthermore, we would have expected confirmation from the A-50 barrier that airborne activity had been detected."

"But we are sure the pilot is in the aircraft?"

"Yes General, sure."

"What of the insertion team? Have they cleared the airfield and are we still in contact with them?

"Nothing has been heard from them for at least 15 minutes General. The A-50 is still trying to raise them."

"Very well," he sighed. "We cannot risk losing the aircraft again and it would appear that the insertion team are no longer able to place the destruction charges. Relay this message verbatim to the Airborne Command Post; my instructions are "Volcano", do you have that? "Volcano". He will know what to do."

"Of course General."

He replaced the phone and stroked his temples but then smiled suspiciously.

*

Kazenko steadied up on east looking over his shoulder at the Phantom its afterburners still glowing. He knew that his primary tactic should be to run away but with a missile remaining and a partial gun load he had a little flex. However, despite the normally superior performance of his aircraft over the F4, he was more than aware of the limitations placed on him by the lack of a fully functional flight control system. Furthermore, air combat was not a practised skill in the Soviet Air Force. Air combat in the dark was unique. The accumulated stress abruptly overtook him as, increasingly nervous, he held the height at 500 metres hoping that the moonlight would hold out yet still hoping in vain that the Phantom would lose him. East. Home.

Paul Hunter dragged the marker on his main display over the target which had just emerged from his dark area. Entering the track into his computer, a designator appeared on the screen and he punched the interrogator button seeking a response from the electronic interrogation equipment aboard the target. Nothing. This one was not wearing a friendly squawk but was it the Flanker or was it the Battle Flight Phantom who had merely forgotten to turn on his IFF?

"Contact tracking 090 degrees range 4 miles heading east," he reported.

"Designate Track 001."

He had heard the crackle of gunfire from outside, the distinct whine of an aircraft's rotary cannon; things were happening out there. The opening shot computed against Track 001, which was rapidly moving farther away from him, was not the best for a Bloodhound but he would take anything offered to him at this stage. Before he could risk committing a missile he had to find the second aircraft to positively identify the Battle Flight jet. He was under no illusions that it was airborne because the roar of the afterburners as it had sped down the runway had been unmistakeable. Where the hell was it?

"Contact 090 degrees range 4 miles," prompted the assistant. Relieved, he dragged the marker over the new contact.

"Designate Track 002," he replied again hitting the interrogator but this time receiving the reassuring flash of a friendly squawk on the display. The Flanker was opening, now 7 miles east and the Battle Flight Phantom was in hot pursuit. He finally had the picture. Hitting the direct line to the Force Commander, he reported.

"Air picture, 2 targets, hostile east range 8, friendly east range 6. Confirm hostile in the lead. Request instructions."

*

The radio in the Mainstay crackled into life.

"Stargazer this is Arrow, I have a message, over."

"Arrow go ahead," replied the Tactical Coordinator.

"Volcano, I repeat Volcano, acknowledge."

The Tactical Coordinator recognised one of the special self authenticating codewords which had been issued in the operational orders and, without further misgivings, reached over to his multi function display and flicked back a bright yellow guarded switch. He tapped in a pre-briefed sequence on the keyboard and rechecked his display.

*

Kazenko held the Flanker steady checking his mirrors again. The red flashing lights of the Phantom flashed insistently in his 5 o'clock. The controls still felt sluggish nothing like the Flanker that he knew and loved and there was also an annoying notchiness in pitch which he could not pin down. He had practised manual control drills in the past but the aircraft felt even worse than he remembered. He looked down to check the radar warning receiver but a blank hole met his gaze where the western engineers had been busy. He had no way of knowing what the Phantom was doing behind but as it was still a good two miles astern, hopefully, they could not see him. Maybe the moonlight was not such an advantage after all because had it been a dark night, he would have had a strong chance of escaping undetected. He realised he was becoming reactive. He was losing the initiative and it was time to turn the tables. He would call the shots.

"Contact 20 degrees right, range 2 miles," called Flash as he played with the gain control on his radar, refining the target which had just appeared from the mass of ground clutter.

"Come starboard 20 degrees, make your heading 100 and make 500 knots."

Razor pulled the engines back out of burner. He could hold 500 in cold power. Checking his height, 1,000 feet, he returned his attention to the gunsight, knowing that Flash would position the target directly in front needing the extra confidence which an early visual contact would give him.

"Crabtree, Mike Lima 75 on tactical. Tracking one bogey on the nose for two miles at 1000 feet, request instructions," he called alerting the controller to his presence on frequency.

"75, Crabtree, you are loud and clear, standby I'm checking," came back the non-committal response.

"For God's sake guys, hurry up," he fumed "I can't keep this up all night, what do you want me to do? Let's make a decision for once shall we?" Unprofessional but essential. He was following one of the most potent fighters in the world.

"Hold your heading," called Flash "range 1½. I reckon we've got about 50 knots overtake on him, target speed 450 knots."

"Crabtree 75 instructions," hectored Razor trying desperately to force the issue knowing that whilst he had the edge at the moment, the tactical advantage against an opponent such as the Flanker could reverse in seconds.

"75, standby, still checking," came back the equally frustrated controller obviously in the process of consulting a senior officer higher up the chain of command.

"OK, taking a lock called Flash, "It's on the nose range 1 mile."

Unaware of the dialogue between the Phantom crew and the Ground Controller and equally unaware of the accuracy of his timing, Kazenko reefed the Su-27 into a hard left turn. Careful to avoid over-controlling, he checked the stick at 80 degrees of bank and applied a firm back pressure to tighten the turn. The headings in the HUD began to spin rapidly and despite his lack of practise at manoeuvring so close to the ground, particularly in the dark, he stole a look over his shoulder seeing the lights of the pursuing aircraft still tucked in tightly. He flicked his navigation lights off.

"No lock," called Flash as the radar display erupted into a mass of unintelligible returns. The radar, in trying to lock-on had temporarily stopped its scan and was nutating around the point in space where the target had been. All the available energy was directed unerringly towards the target providing a tracking beam for the radar guided missile to follow. With no target in the beam to acquire, the radar was thrashing around ineffectually. After a few more seconds it reverted to scan and, as the radar settled, Flash realised that the target had disappeared.

"I lost him," he called becoming just as frustrated as his front-seater.

"Hold your heading. Last seen heading 100 degrees at 1000 feet at 450 knots. Bring your speed back to match him." The last thing Flash wanted was to be spat out in front of the hostile aircraft. Razor complied reluctantly.

On the bridge of the COC, the Station Commander considered his options. The Flanker had made good its escape and no matter what he did now there was no way he could force it down at a western airbase. It was still armed and could respond and he did not want to lose a Phantom or its crew unnecessarily. No peacetime intelligence gain was worth any more lives. He had the Bloodhound radars tracking it; he had the F4 a mere two miles astern in firing parameters, so at this very moment he could order its destruction and, what's more, he would be entirely justified after the unprovoked attacks. The aircraft had fired on the Battle Flight jet as it had lifted off so he could legally exercise the right of self defence but what would it prove? The aircraft would be destroyed and delay the Soviet programme by a couple of months but at the cost of yet another life even if it was of a potential enemy. The events of the last few hours had been way beyond peacetime norms. A diplomatic incident was inevitable but what was probably more relevant was that they would gain not an iota of additional intelligence. From what he'd heard from the HAS the avionics which were so important had been left behind. They might be more valuable than the airframe. He hit the direct line on the communications console.

"All units, this is the Force Commander, remain weapons tight, repeat weapons tight, acknowledge."

The grudging response from the SAM battery emphasised their perception of a lost opportunity for glory. He turned to the operations controller alongside him in the Ops room and said resignedly,

"Haul off Battle Flight. Bring him home."

What he could not know was that this crucial message would not get through. He slumped back in his chair, the stress relieved, his decision made, for better or worse.

Working hard in the pitch black conditions, slightly disorientated by the blinking lights of a village which flashed beneath him, Kazenko was elated to see the F4 continue its flight path. He only had one missile and he would have to make it count considering the negligible chance of achieving a night guns kill even with a full moon. Another furtive glance confirmed that the Phantom was still pressing eastward and in a blinding flash he realised that he now had another reference to work to. The other aircraft! Providing he stayed above it and used the winking lights to orientate himself he would be able to position for a shot and in the meantime stay safe. Suddenly he felt happier; he was on more familiar territory. As the Phantom tracked inwards towards his HUD reticle, he listened for the tell-tale tone which would mean that the R73 had acquired its target. He had no radar information but the missile circuits still seemed to be working. The darkness enveloped him, relentlessly pressurising, but he waited patiently for the faint but strengthening tone. As it stabilised he released the missile head into self track mode but was instantly diverted by the attention getters and the female voice of the audio warning system in his headset announcing further misfortune.

"Hydraulic failure, hydraulic failure" the system complained presaging a violent twitch on the control column which caused the aircraft to balloon through its intended flight path violently. What he failed to notice in the ensuing panic was that the missile had not acquired its intended target, transferring instead to the hot metal of a burn-off chimney in the midst of a chemical plant below. The seeker had certainly found a target which, to its circuits, had appeared identical to the hot jet pipe of a fast-jet aircraft. In fact the indications offered to Kazenko in his head up display also showed a solid lock but what he had failed to notice was the missile tracking cue which had firmly buried itself at the base of the gunsight showing that the missile head was looking a long way from the intended target. As he pulled the trigger in response to the increasingly strident tone, more of a knee-jerk reaction than a considered action, he was confused by the lack of response from the missile. It was his first firing for years, the last one having been in the calm and ordered environment of a practice range. In his enthusiasm, he had failed to allow for the system reaction time, the lag between trigger press and the missile leaving the aircraft. For the second time that night he was caught out as the missile finally ignited sounding like a steam engine. Night was suddenly turned into day as the rocket motor lit the cockpit area during its passage down the left hand side of the aircraft before it tracked violently across his nose, plunging harmlessly to earth. Not realising his own mistake, he cursed the missile manufacturer to hell and back before hauling off the attack and selecting his escape heading.

"Bogey left 8 o'clock, break port." yelled Flash. "He's on us, 8 o'clock one mile," he repeated, hoping that the front seater would waste no time in his reaction.

"Tally Ho, countering," responded Razor entering a maximum performance turn.

"Missile release, break, break, break," yelled the back seater knowing from the g force which assailed his body that the aircraft was already being flown to its limits. Razor had needed no prompting; he had seen the bright flash of the rocket motor at the moment of ignition and had rammed the throttles against the firewall knowing full well that there was nothing more to be done. His reaction under the circumstances was ill-advised, the correct response being to chop the throttles in a classic infra-red defensive manoeuvre. The reduced throttle setting would have cooled his jet pipes giving the missile a less attractive target and maybe even destroying its tracking solution. In the event, in his desire to increase his performance, he was offering a perfect target; the two massive beacons of his reheated Spey jet engines. In full burner, he pulled for dear life wishing for some infra-red flares unaware that the missile was already history.

Kazenko fought the bucking controls and started a gentle climb clear of the ground. His missile had failed and the Phantom pilot could yet take him but right now he had a bigger problem. The hydraulic pressure had fallen to zero, further limiting his controllability and he tried desperately to interpret the myriad of warning captions in a vain attempt to identify his problems. As he struggled, all he could surmise was that during the fire fight on the ground, he must have collected a stray round. Dragging out his flight reference cards and shining his torch on the vital instructions trying desperately to read them, he began to work his way through the emergency drill. A small jink 30 degrees right, an almost futile evasive turn, may be sufficient to throw the Phantom off his tail. Quick confirmation that his navigation lights were off so that he didn't give his pursuer any more assistance than necessary and he returned to the task in hand easing the crippled fighter into a steeper climb.

*

The later Aeroflot Flight, Flight Number 276 had lifted off from Cologne/Bonn International airport a few minutes before and set course across Nordrhein Westphalia towards the Berlin Corridor. The early morning flight would land in the Russian Capital in just over 3 hours most of the passengers were readying for their business meetings that morning.

*

Razor held the left turn relieved that the missile which had been fired had failed. He watched it fall harmlessly away realising what a lucky escape it had been.

"The threat's off us," called Flash as he watched the planform of the Flanker bathed in moonlight, continue its turn across the circle. It was obvious that it was not manoeuvring to its full potential because, if it had been, the Phantom would already have been threatened again within a single turn. Razor realising that he was making angles on the bogey and slowly gaining the advantage flicked his left hand deftly across to the missile control panel selecting Sidewinder, hearing the comforting tone from the missile in his headset. It was time to get his own back.

"Crabtree, 75 has been engaged. Returning fire."

A simple statement full of foreboding. He pulled the gunsight onto his quarry realising that it had straightened and was climbing gently away. He switched his attention to the Sidewinder steering dot on the radar display in front of him and coaxed it towards the centre of the aiming circle bringing the weapon into parameters. Suddenly, the dark shape ahead did not seem quite so threatening and he hesitated, considering whether to attempt to shepherd the aircraft back to Wildenrath. To hell he thought, the bastard just tried to dust me off!

"Contact on the nose range 2 miles, he's just out of range hold your fire," came the prompt from his back-seater.

"Wait until he's in weapons parameters Razor," the disembodied voice from behind cautioned. The sight moved restlessly onto the target and he was suddenly hesitant, unsure of the morality of such an easy kill against a target which was no longer fighting.

*

Kazenko gripped the stick tightly and the oscillations through the airframe slowly damped down as the height on the altimeter increased. He realised that his attack on the Phantom had been ill-conceived and, on reflection, there had been very little chance of success. The flight controls were a disaster area and he should have realised earlier that the notchiness which he had felt had been a sign of incipient problems. His ham-fisted efforts at engaging the British fighter had been the last straw and the power control actuators had finally failed, catastrophically, having been unable to maintain pressure on the ruptured system. On top of that it had cost him precious fuel which he could ill afford. He racked his brains for a way out of his predicament; he needed inspiration and he needed it quickly! Low level escape was no longer a player considering the state of his crippled airframe as the lack of controllability would make operating close to the ground suicidal. He had no IFF equipment to deceive the western control radars and felt a sudden surge of bitterness at the ease with which the traitor Andrenev would have made his journey in the opposite direction. But what other deception was available to him? In the distance, the high intensity strobe lights of an airliner on climb out from Düsseldorf winked languidly. Slowly the germ of an idea formed in his mind. Pushing up the throttles and just tapping the burners, he picked up an intercept course on the airliner. Cursing, he immediately drew the power back as he realised that he had just advertised his precise position to the trailing interceptor. The flash of light from the igniting fuel would act as a signpost in the sky, pinpointing his presence to his pursuer. Of more immediate interest, the trim changes as the reheat bit, caused the pitch oscillations to resume and the jet became uncontrollably unstable sending a sudden shot of adrenaline coursing through his veins again. He fought the violent bucking motion but only succeeded in introducing even more violent fluctuations and he could feel the impending departure from controlled flight evident through the controls. Suddenly he remembered his basic flight training and released the stick allowing the natural effects on the controls to damp the motion bringing the jet back under control. He resumed his grip on the controls.

Heart still racing, his thoughts returned to the airliner which flashed indifferently in the distance. It was difficult to gauge range in the absence of a radar but he figured it must be about 5 miles, quite slow as it climbed to its cruising level, crossing his flight path from right to left. Providing that he could make the intercept quickly and then maintain close formation in his battered aircraft, he could use the airliner for cover. As he closed, he could make out the markings on the fin, brightly lit by white floodlights mounted in the surface of the wing. The small cabin windows glowed with light behind which, the passengers would be enjoying the first gin and tonic on the flight. In the cockpit he strained to recognise the insignia hoping to second- guess its destination hoping for a West German domestic carrier which would mean that it could be bound for an airfield closer to the border and would suit him admirably. The high tailplane looked familiar and, as the markings began to stand out, he realised that his luck was still holding. Aeroflot the Soviet National airline. He had latched onto an Illyushin IL-62 and it was almost certainly bound for the Berlin corridor and maybe even Moscow.

"Mike Lima 75, Crabtree, your target bears 090 degrees range 3 miles passing Flight Level 70 in the climb. You have a stranger bearing 120 degrees range 5 miles also passing Flight Level 70 in the climb. Maintain Flight Level 60, I'll call you when the stranger is clear."

"75 is contact both," responded Flash.

"OK Razor, our guy is on the nose for 2, the other guy is 35 degrees right range 4, showing same level, any joy?" said Flash refining the coarse data which GCI had passed.

"Affirmative, padlocked on the stranger and intermittent contact on our man but he's turned his lights off, keep talking."

"More speed, give me 400 knots, hold Flight Level 60 and hold your heading. The stranger will cross ahead; he's already drifting in and should cross the nose at 2 miles."

The crossing angle between the flight paths of the two aircraft would mean that the airliner would pass safely clear and ahead of the Phantom, despite the fact that their heights were close.

"75, Crabtree, the stranger now bears 100 degrees range 3 miles any contact?"

Flash realised that his controller was pressing the normal air traffic avoidance criteria to the limits but, even so, he could not prevent his harsh response.

"Affirmative, Crabtree. Judy on the bogey and weapon contact on the stranger, he snapped.

"Continue," came the sharp response. He had pissed him off but their problems were greater than the Controller's at that precise moment.

"Hold your fire Razor, we can't risk a missile shot with the other contact in so close. Let's wait until they separate and we can take a clear shot."

"Goddamn but you're right, switches safe." He could take no chances.

*

Kazenko watched the airliner cross overhead and gingerly anticipated the turn positioning his aircraft directly beneath the brightly lit civil jet. He began easing up gently towards its massive bulk, the shape of the airframe slowly taking shape out of the gloom, red and green wingtip lights marking the limits of the airframe. He had deliberately selected his position underneath to keep out of sight of the cockpit. A worried Captain would do him no favours at this stage and as he eased gently into close formation under the belly, he hoped that both the Captain and Air Traffic Control had also been too busy to register his approach but doubted it. He was banking on the fact that being so close, the individual radar contacts would have merged into one and he should now effectively be invisible. Settling down in formation, he checked his heading - 045 degrees - a little off the mark. He would have been happier heading east bearing in mind that his fuel gauge was inexorably dropping and already read a little below half. The engagement had cost him all of his contingency fuel but he had just enough to complete his mission providing the airliner did not divert too far from the assumed track. A glance at his map and he could see that they were heading towards the centre leg of the Berlin Corridor and his spirits soared. About 100 Km to the border and he would be home and dry and unless the idiot in the Phantom pressed his luck it should be plain sailing. With 100 passengers sitting only 20 metres above his head the options available to the Brit crew had just evaporated because they could not dare to intervene putting civilian lives at risk. Diverting a civilian airliner going about its lawful business may be acceptable in the Soviet Union but it was a bad business in the West. A look in his mirrors and he could see his pursuer, navigation lights blinking rhythmically, hanging astern. The aircraft appeared to have maintained its original course despite his attaching himself to the airliner. Had they lost him? Above him, none of the passengers on the Aeroflot jet could be aware of the fact that below the belly of the airliner, the Soviet fighter had tucked in close, a mere shadow.

*

"75, Crabtree, contacts merged. I show them passing Flight Level 90."

He hit the transmit button.

"75 confirmed."

"Shit Razor, that must have been a close pass," said Flash as he frantically thumbed the elevation wheel of his radar scanner attempting to break out the Flanker from the airliner as the blips merged.

"The stranger is now 20 degrees left range 2 miles going away. I've lost the other guy for the moment. Hold your heading," he called frustratedly to his pilot, scanner still moving methodically attempting to re-establish radar contact.

"Come on Flash, do you choose your moments to foul up. Where the hell is he?"

"Hold your heading, I'm looking." the beleaguered navigator responded defensively. Not now please, he groaned inwardly.

"The stranger's out left and clear. Switches going live," muttered the equally frustrated pilot.

He watched the Phantom continue on heading. He had done it. Despite the odds, Kazenko had retrieved the prototype from a guarded HAS site on a foreign airfield at night. Even the lack of a weapons system and only half a hydraulic system, the rest of which was shot to hell had not stopped him. He was in close formation with his ticket home and was enjoying the sweet taste of success. His thoughts wandered briefly to the insertion team and he wondered how their own escape was going. Hell, he thought, they're big boys, they'll be half way home by now. In the mirrors, the Phantom continued its easterly course apparently oblivious to the deception. Let's bring this heading round onto east Captain he muttered, spirits rising by the minute.

"The stranger! He latched onto the stranger Razor. No wonder I can't see him, the bastards in our 9 o'clock going away! Reverse port onto north."

"Crabtree, 75, snap vector for the stranger!" he called resignedly.

"75, stranger bears 350 degrees range 6 miles heading 045. Suggest heading 350 degrees to close."

"75 steady north! Give me 500 knots Razor."

The burners cut in, accelerating the Phantom rapidly towards the receding civil airliner with the Flanker in tow. He had made 6 miles on them in the twinkling of an eye but the chase wasn't over yet. How far was it to the border?

*

Sokolovskiy relaxed in his seat aboard the Illyushin and allowed the feeling of self-satisfaction to wash over him. It had been a long struggle over the years but his promised revenge was sweet. His plan had hatched all those years ago on the temporary airfield on the outskirts of Berlin. When he landed he would call Kazenko at the Sanatorium in the dank suburb of Moscow where he had been incarcerated for the last few years. Sokolovskiy had meticulously arranged his stay. Heroes of the Soviet Union were normally cared for more generously by the State but his secret doctoring of Kazenko's wartime records had ensured that his lifestyle had been less than comfortable in the years since the end of the war. Sokolovskiy reflected on the years of careful planning which had been needed to bring him to his point of triumph. It had taken a good deal of influence to place Andrenev's wife at the research laboratory and her slow poisoning with the faulty radiotherapy equipment had cost him dearly. The technician's assistance had proved particularly expensive. He would have to arrange a suitable demise for that greedy young man, he reflected. The leukaemia had been slow to develop and the bribes had been necessary for longer than he had anticipated but time had not been a factor. The previous Director of the Test Centre had been easily despatched. The anonymous bribe for the mechanic to fix the car's brakes had been accepted without protest, even gratefully. He had, after all, been remarkably generous and such routine car accidents were never questioned; all part of the shoddy system. His sponsorship of the idiot scientist, and the painstaking arrangements to ensure that he was subsequently appointed Director at Ramenskoye had proved more difficult. It was hard to promote a donkey and it was only his own credibility as an ex-fighter pilot and war hero which had convinced the appointment committee to follow his advice. It had, however, been the perfect catalyst to push Andrenev sufficiently hard to guarantee his defection and thereby the success of his scheme. As Kazenko's son had been the only other Su-27 pilot capable of undertaking the recovery mission, his selection had been a foregone conclusion. There had been a number of opportunities to terminate Kazenko during the mission and Sokolovskiy was amazed that he had survived to the final stages. No matter, to die in an aircraft was the ultimate irony and gave him a perverse sense of justice which he would exploit to the full. His own part in the affair was carefully buried and, to the outside world, Kazenko Junior would be feted as a hero. Sokolovskiy's remaining desire was to hear the anguish in Kazenko's voice when he heard of the real reason for his son's demise. He would ensure that there was no doubt as to who had engineered his fate. Revenge for his brother's futile death all those years ago in Berlin had been his overriding passion for most of his career and even now the memories and the pain were still raw. Kazenko would finally pay. His only regret was the temporary setback to the Su-27 programme. The West may have gained intelligence about the aircraft but it was a good design which they would find hard to match in any case. The programme would recover. He would arrange a meeting as soon as he landed, savouring the moment. Revenge!

*

Aloft in the Mainstay, still orbiting gently, the Tactical Coordinator looked once again at his display, double checking his actions as he moved his finger to cover the guarded switch. He could not understand his orders as there were now a number of radar tracks in the Wildenrath area which he had just designated. Surely there must be some doubt? Perhaps he should report the tracks; they may be significant. "Volcano" he mused, feeling both confusion and a moments remorse, cognizant of the implications of his actions. He knew Sokolovskiy from way back and the wily old goat was well aware of his actions. Enough indecision. His instructions were perfectly clear; he hit the button.

*

In the bowels of the Flanker a red light blinked on as the short-dwell timing mechanism began its count-down.

As Sokolovskiy sipped his drink, there was a shuddering below his feet. The low rumble grew louder and, in seconds, the cabin erupted in a blinding flash. He died never appreciating the irony. "Volcano".

*

"On the nose range 4, closing rapidly. Still only see one target."

"Visual."

"Hold your fire, that's the airliner you see."

Razor cursed silently and flicked the Master Arm selector back to safe, concentrating on the strobe lights ahead. Flash locked the radar to the airliner now only 3 miles ahead. As he watched the display settle, suddenly and without warning, the cockpit of the Phantom lit up and night turned to day. The dim shape that was in reality an aircraft erupted in a dazzling ball of flame. The huge fireball grew as thousands of tons of aviation fuel ignited. He watched as the elevation markers on the radar begin to drop rapidly as the radar tracked the wreckage of the Illyushin as it began its long fall to Earth in its terminal dive.

"What the…………"

Flash broke lock bringing the elevation markers back to level searching for the Flanker. It must be somewhere close.

Nothing. The sky ahead was empty.

"Am I dreaming or did you just see that too?"

"Oh my God!"

As Razor dropped the wing to keep sight of the flaming fireball the red star on the fin of the Illyushin was illuminated briefly as another tank ruptured and more fuel ignited. It tumbled in the airflow.

It was suddenly deathly quiet in the cockpit.

GLOSSARY

AAA. Anti aircraft artillery.

ADIZ. Air Defence Interception Zone.

ADMISREP. Air Defence Mission Report.

AEW. Airborne Early Warning aircraft.

Anchor. Set up a holding pattern in your present position.

BFPO. British Forces Post Office.

Blip. Nickname for a radar contact on the display.

Bogey. A hostile aircraft.

Bug out. To leave a combat engagement and separate from the fight.

Cabbage Kit. Slang for disruptive camouflage uniform.

CAP. Combat Air Patrol.

COC. Combined Operations Centre.

Coolant. Gas cooling to lower the temperature and increase the sensitivity of the infra-red seeker in the sidewinder missile.

CRC. Control and Reporting Centre.

CVR(T). Carrier Vehicular Reconnaissance (Tracked) a light tank armed with a 30mm cannon.

CW. Continuous wave radar which acts as guidance for the semi-active Sparrow radar missiles.

Dark. A radar contact disappears from the radar scope probably because it has descended below coverage.

Delta H. The relative height of a target above or below a fighter. Delta H Plus Ten is 10,000 feet above.

DDR. Deutsche Demokratik Republik. The former East Germany.

ELINT. Electronic intelligence.

Endex. End of the exercise.

FOD. Foreign Object Damage or items of rubbish which could be drawn into a jet engine causing damage.

Form 700. Aircraft Log and Servicing Schedule.

Fox 1. A Sparrow missile firing.

Fox 2. A Sidewinder missile firing.

Fox 3. A gun shot.

GCI. Ground Controlled Interception.

Gadget. A codeword for the radar.

GRU. The Soviet Army Intelligence Agency.

Guard. The distress frequency.

HAS. Hardened Aircraft Shelter.

Hayrake. Transmitting on air-to-air TACAN. This gives a range between cooperating aircraft.

HF Radio. Radio operating in the high frequency radio band.

HIMEZ. A high level missile engagement zone.

IFF. Identification Friend or Foe. An electronic system which transmits a code to identify an aircraft as friendly.

IGB. The Inner German Border. The border between the former East and West Germany.

ILS. Instrument Landing System.

INAS. Inertial Navigation and Attack System.

Interlocks. Safety devices to prevent premature firing of missiles outside parameters.

IRSTS. Infra-red Search and Track System.

Judy. A codeword indicating the fighter crew has taken control of the intercept.

LCOSS. Lead Computing Optical Sighting System. Gunsight.

Liney. Slang for Flight Line Mechanic.

LOMEZ. A low level missile engagement zone.

Low Fly 2. Slang for low flying area 2.

Low Level North Departure. A visual departure procedure to exit the Military Air Traffic Zone.

Mandatory. A Battle Flight state where only essential operational scrambles can be flown due to a significant risk to the safety of the aircraft or crew.

Master Arm. A final safety interlock in the weapon selector circuit.

Mike Lima 66. The callsign. The two letter code (ML) signifies the home base in this case Wildenrath. Each aircraft carries a unique number.

Mix Up. A mêlée when jets come in close proximity during an engagement.

NAAFI. Navy, Army and Air Force Institute. The Forces shop.

NCO. Non commissioned officer.

Noddy Guide. Aircrew Information Folder containing mission data.

OP. Observation post.

Padlock. To see a target visually and to monitor its behaviour.

PAN. An emergency condition giving an aircraft precedence over other traffic. PAN is just one level below Mayday, the universal distress term.

Parrot. Codeword for IFF box.

PBF. Pilots Briefing Facility.

Pop up contact. A radar contact which appears on radar probably because it has climbed out from low level.

Port. Left.

QFE. A pressure setting for the altimeter which when set gives height above runway touchdown.

QNH. A pressure setting for the altimeter which when set gives height above sea level.

QWI. Qualified Weapons Instructor.

Radar CAP. An elliptical holding pattern (Combat Air Patrol) using radar to detect attacking formations.

RAT. Ram Air Turbine which provided electrical power in an emergency.

Readiness 5. An alert state. Aircraft should be airborne within 5 minutes of a scramble message.

RHAG. Rotary Hydraulic Arrestor Gear. A cable stretched across the runway which stops an aircraft by using the tail arrestor hook.

RWR. Radar Warning Receiver.

R23. The AA-7 Apex medium range semi-active missile.

R27. The AA-10 Alamo medium range semi-active missile.

R60. The AA-8 Aphid short range infra-red missile.

R73. The AA-11 Archer short range infra-red missile.

SAM. Surface-to-air missile.

SATCO. The Senior Air Traffic Control Officer.

Sirena. A Russian Radar Warning Receiver.

Sitrep. Situation Report.

Smokey Joe's. A famous navigation feature in West German airspace. A power station.

Snap vector. An instant heading towards a contact.

Splash. To claim a kill against a target.

Starboard. Right.

Station Wheels. Slang for Station Executives.

Stranger. An unidentified aircraft.

Stud. A pre-programmed radio frequency selection.

TAD. Tactical Air Direction frequency.

Tally Ho or Tally. A call meaning the crew member has visual sight of a hostile contact.

TD Box. Target designator box in the head up display.

Telebrief. Secure Telephone Briefing Facility.

Trade. Nickname for targets.

Walkround. External pre flight inspection.

Weapons tight. Missiles armed but clearance to engage not issued.

Weapons free. Missiles armed and cleared to engage.

Willco. Will cooperate.

WRAF. Women's Royal Air Force.

2ATAF. 2nd Allied Tactical Air Force. The Command Headquarters for allied aircraft in Northern Germany.

ABOUT THE AUTHOR

David Gledhill is an aviation enthusiast and aviator. Already holding a private pilot's licence at the age of 17, he was commissioned in the RAF in 1974, and after training as an air navigator, converted to the F4 Phantom in the Air Defence role. After tours in the UK and Germany, he went on to be a radar tactics instructor on the Operational Conversion Unit. After transferring to the new Tornado F2 as one of the first instructors, he eventually became the Executive Officer on the OCU. His flying career finished in the Falkland Islands where he commanded No 1435 Flight flying the Tornado F3. During his later career he served as a staff officer in the UK Ministry of Defence and the Air Warfare Centre. He also served on exchange duties at the Joint Command and Control Warfare Center and the US. Air Force Warfare Center in the United States of America and as the Senior Operations Officer at the Balkans Combined Air Operations Centre.

OTHER BOOKS BY THE AUTHOR

"The Phantom in Focus: A Navigator's Eye on Britain's Cold War Warrior" - ISBN 978-178155-048-9 (print) and 978-178155-204-9 (e-book) published by Fonthill Media.

"Fighters Over The Falklands – Defending the islanders Way of Life" - ISBN 978-178155-222-3 (print), also (e-book) published by Fonthill Media.

"Tornado F3 – A Navigator's Eye on Britain's Last Interceptor" - ISBN 978-178155-307-7 (print) published by Fonthill Media.

"Tornado In Pictures - The Multi Role Legend" (print) published by Fonthill Media.

"Maverick" and "Deception" will be released in 2015 on Amazon Kindle.

Made in the USA
Charleston, SC
20 January 2015